Smooth, good-looking, charming and
wealthy, these Italians have it all—except
the right women

Latin Lovers
ITALIAN PLAYBOYS

Three fabulous stories from reader
favourites Melanie Milburne, Kate Hardy
& India Grey

LATIN LOVERS COLLECTION

COLLECT ALL SIX!

Latin Lovers

ITALIAN PLAYBOYS

Melanie
MILBURNE

Kate
HARDY

India
GREY

MILLS
BOON

All the characters in this book have no existence outside the imagination
of the author, and have no relation whatsoever to anyone bearing the
same name or names. They are not even distantly inspired by any
individual known or unknown to the author, and all the incidents are
pure invention.

Mills & Boon, an imprint of Harlequin (UK) Limited, Eton House,
18-24 Paradise Road, Richmond, Surrey TW9 1SR

LATIN LOVERS: ITALIAN PLAYBOYS
© Harlequin Enterprises II B.V./S.à.r.l. 2011

Bought for the Marriage Bed © Melanie Milburne 2006
The Italian's GP Bride © Pamela Brooks 2007
The Italian's Defiant Mistress © India Grey 2007

ISBN: 978 0 263 88996 3

027-0911

Harlequin (UK) policy is to use papers that are natural, renewable
and recyclable products and made from wood grown in sustainable
forests. The logging and manufacturing processes conform to the
legal environmental regulations of the country of origin.

Printed and bound in Spain
by Blackprint CPI, Barcelona

BOUGHT FOR THE MARRIAGE BED

Melanie Milburne

Melanie Milburne says: "I am married to a surgeon, Steve, and have two gorgeous sons, Paul and Phil. I live in Hobart, Tasmania, where I enjoy an active life as a long-distance runner and a nationally ranked top ten Master's swimmer. I also have a Master's Degree in Education, but my children totally turned me off the idea of teaching! When not running or swimming I write, and when I'm not doing all of the above I'm reading. And if someone could invent a way for me to read during a four-kilometre swim I'd be even happier!"

CHAPTER ONE

NINA stared at her twin sister in shock. 'You surely don't mean to go through with it?'

Nadia gave her a defiant look from beneath lashes heavy with thick black mascara. 'I can't cope with a baby. Besides, I never really wanted her in the first place.'

'But Georgia is so young!' Nina protested. 'How can you possibly think of giving her away?'

'It's easy.' Nadia pouted. 'This is a once-in-a-lifetime opportunity. If I don't take it with both hands it might never come again.'

'But she's only four months old!' Nina cried. 'Surely you owe it to Andre's memory to raise her.'

'I owe him nothing!' Nadia spat. 'You seem to be forgetting that he refused to acknowledge her as his child. He wouldn't even agree to a paternity test, no doubt because he didn't want to upset that cow of a fiancée of his.' She paced the room angrily. 'I should've known he wasn't to be trusted. The Marcello males are known for their playboy lifestyle; you have only to look at yesterday's paper to realise that.'

Nina was well aware of the photograph of Marc Marcello, Andre's older brother, in the Sydney weekend broadsheet. It was rare for a week to go past without some reference to his billionaire fast-paced fast-women lifestyle. His dark good looks had been the first thing she'd noticed when she'd opened the paper.

'Does Marc Marcello know about your intention to give his niece up for adoption?' she asked her sister.

Nadia turned back to face her. 'I wrote to his father in Italy a few weeks ago but he flatly refused to acknowledge Georgia as his granddaughter. So this time I sent a photo of her. That should set the cat among the pigeons, when he sees how like Andre she is. I felt the need to twist the knife since it's his precious son's fault my life has been stuffed up.'

'But surely—'

Nadia gave her a bristling look. 'As far as I'm concerned, I want nothing more to do with the Marcello family. I gave them a chance to claim Georgia but they brushed me off. That's why I'm leaving now to get on with Plan B.'

'*Leaving?*' Nina stared at her in consternation. 'Leaving to go where?'

'America.'

'But what about Georgia?' she gasped, her heart tripping in alarm. 'You're surely not thinking of…' She couldn't even frame the rest of the words.

Nadia gave a dismissive shrug of one shoulder. 'You can look after her for a month or two—you do most of the time anyway. Besides, it's clear she loves you more than me, so I don't see why I shouldn't hand her over to you temporarily. You can take care of her until someone adopts her.'

Nina's stomach rolled over painfully. It was hard for her to imagine her sister having so little regard for the tiny infant who lay sleeping in the pram near the window. How could she be so unfeeling as to walk away from her own baby?

'Look—' she tried to reason with her '—I know you're upset; it's only been a few months since Andre…went.'

Nadia turned on her furiously. 'What's with the euphemism? Andre didn't *go* somewhere—he *died*.'

Nina swallowed. 'I—I know.'

'I'm just glad he took his stupid fiancée with him,' Nadia added in a surly tone.

'You surely don't mean that?'

Nadia's features twisted in bitterness. 'Of course I mean it. I hate the Marcello family and anyone connected to them.' She tossed her mane of blonde hair over one shoulder and looked back at her sister. 'I have a chance at a new life with Bryce Falkirk in America. He loves me and has promised me a part in one of his films. This will be my chance at the big screen. I'd be a fool to let it slip out of my hands. And if I play my cards right he might even ask me to marry him.'

'Have you told him about Georgia?'

Nadia rolled her eyes. 'Are you nuts? Of course I didn't tell him. He thinks Georgia is your child.'

Nina stared at her in alarm. 'How can you even consider the possibility of marrying the man without telling him of your past?'

Nadia gave her sister a cutting look. 'Bryce wouldn't have considered being involved with me at all if I'd told him anything like that. He thinks the sun shines from my "childlike innocent" eyes, and I'm going to make sure he keeps thinking that way, even if I have to lie through my teeth every day to ensure he does.'

'But surely if he really loves you—'

'Look, Nina, I don't want to have the sort of life our mother had, flitting from one bad man to another and shunting kids off into horrible foster homes whenever things got tough. I want to have money and stability and I can't have that with a kid hanging off my hip.'

'But surely you could—'

'No!' Nadia cut her off impatiently. 'You don't get it, do you? I don't want that child; I never did.' She dumped Georgia's changing bag next to the pram, the soft thump as it hit the floor striking a chord of disquiet in Nina's chest. 'You were the one who talked me out of getting rid of the pregnancy, so I think it's only fair you get to look after her now until I can find a private adoption candidate.'

'Private adoption?' Nina instantly stiffened.

Nadia gave her sister a streetwise look. 'There are people out there who will pay big money for a cute little baby. I want to make sure I get the best deal I can. With my connections with Bryce I might even be able to find a Hollywood actor who will want Georgia. Think of the money they would be prepared to pay.'

Nina's eyes flared in shock and her heart began to thump unevenly behind her ribcage. 'How can you do this to your own child?'

'It's none of your business what I do,' Nadia said. 'She's my child, not yours.'

'Let *me* adopt her,' Nina begged. 'I can do it. I'm a blood relative, which would make it so much easier, surely?'

Nadia shook her head. 'No. I'm going to use this opportunity to its fullest extent.' Her eyes glinted with unmistakable avarice. 'It's like a lucky windfall when you think about it. It's my chance to free myself of Andre's child and make a whole heap of money in the process.'

'You're so mercenary.'

'Not mercenary—realistic,' Nadia insisted. 'We might be identical twins but I'm not like you, Nina, and it's high time you accepted it. I want to travel and I want the comfort of wealth and privilege around me. You can keep your long hours in a boring old library—I want a life.'

Nina straightened her shoulders, her chin lifting in pride. 'I enjoy my work.'

'Yeah, well, I enjoy shopping and dining out and partying. And I'm going to do a hell of a lot of it when I get to Bryce's mansion in Los Angeles. I can't wait.'

'I can't believe you're simply going to walk away from your responsibilities. Georgia isn't some sort of toy you can push to one side. She's a baby, for God's sake. Doesn't that mean anything to you at all?'

'No.' Nadia's cold grey eyes clashed with hers. 'It means absolutely nothing to me. I told you—I don't want her.' She scooped up her bag and, rummaging in it, handed her sister a document folder. 'Here is her birth certificate and passport; keep them safe for when it's time to hand her over.' She hoisted her handbag back on to her shoulder and turned for the door.

'Nadia, wait!' Nina cried, glancing at the pram in desperation. 'Aren't you even going to say goodbye to her?'

Nadia opened the door and, with one last determined look, closed it firmly behind her.

Nina knew it would be hopeless running after her to implore her to come back. For most of her twenty-four years she'd been pleading with Nadia to stop and think about her actions, but to no avail. Her wayward and wilful twin had gone from one disaster to another, causing immeasurable hurt in the process and showing little remorse. But this was surely the worst so far.

There was a soft whimper from inside the pram and, moving across the small room, she reached inside to pick up the tiny pink bundle.

'Hey, precious,' she said as she cradled the infant close to her chest, marvelling yet again at the minute perfection of her features. 'Are you hungry, little one?'

The baby began to nuzzle against her and Nina felt a wave of overwhelming love wash through her. She couldn't bear the thought of her niece being handed over to someone else to rear. What if things didn't work out and Georgia's childhood ended up like hers and Nadia's? Nina remembered it all too well—the regular stints in foster care, some of the placements a whole lot less desirable than the neglect she and her twin had received at home. How could she stand by and watch the same thing happen to Georgia?

Nina knew how the legal adoption system worked but this private process made her feel very uneasy. What if someone totally unsuitable offered her sister a huge amount of money? What sort of screening process would the prospective parents go through, if any?

She became aware of the seeping wetness of Georgia's clothing and, carrying her through to her room, laid her on the bed and gently undressed her as she'd done countless times before. She got down to the last layer, a tiny yellowed vest that was frayed at the edges. She peeled it over the tiny child's head, cooing to her niece as she did so until the soft nonsense of her words dried up in her throat as she encountered what the vest had hidden from view. Her eyes widened in shock at the purple welt of bruises along Georgia's ribcage, bruises that exactly matched the length and width of her own fingers as if she'd done the damage herself.

'Oh, Nadia, how could you?' she gulped, fighting back tears for how she hadn't been able to prevent her niece from suffering what had been commonplace in her own childhood and that of her twin.

Nina determined then and there that she would do whatever she could to keep Georgia herself. Surely there was a way to convince Nadia to give the baby to her permanently.

She had to find one!

Other single mothers coped, so too would she—somehow.

She chewed the ragged edge of one nail as she considered her options. It wouldn't be easy for her—she could hardly afford childcare on her present salary at the library.

She looked down at the sleeping infant, her chest squeezing painfully at the thought of never seeing her tiny niece again.

No. She would simply not allow her sister to go through with it.

She would be Georgia's mother and if anyone thought differently, too bad.

No one was going to take her niece away from her.

No one.

Marc Marcello frowned as his secretary informed him via the office intercom that his father was on the phone from the Villa Marcello in Sorrento, Italy.

He picked up the receiver and, swivelling in his leather chair, looked out at the expansive view over Sydney Harbour as he pressed the talk button.

'Marc! You have to do something about that woman and do it immediately,' Vito Marcello burst out in rapid-fire Italian.

'I take it you mean Andre's little whore?' Marc answered smoothly.

'She might be a whore but she is also the mother of my only grandchild,' Vito growled.

Marc stiffened in his chair. 'What makes you so certain all of a sudden? Andre refused a paternity test; he said he had always used protection.'

'He might have used protection but I now have reason to believe it failed.'

Marc frowned and turned his chair back to his desk, the sudden thump of his heart in his chest surprising him into a temporary silence.

'I have a letter in front of me with a small photo of the child.' Vito's voice cracked slightly as he continued. 'She looks exactly like Andre at that age. It is Andre's child, I am sure of it.'

Marc pressed his lips together as he fought to get his own raw emotions under some semblance of control. The death of his younger brother had privately devastated him, but for the sake of his terminally ill father he'd carried on the family business without a single hiccup. The Sydney branch of the Marcello merchant bank was booming and he had every intention of maintaining the punishing hours he'd adopted to block out the pain of his brother's death.

'Papa.' His voice was deep and rough around the edges. 'This is all very hard to take in…'

'We have to get that child,' his father insisted. 'She is all we have left of Andre.'

A tremor of unease passed through Marc at the determined edge to his father's tone. 'How do you intend to accomplish this?'

'The usual way,' his father answered with undisguised cynicism. 'If you offer her enough money she will do whatever you ask.'

'How much money are you expecting me to spend on this mission of yours?' Marc asked.

Vito named a figure that sent Marc's broad shoulders to the back of his chair.

'That is a lot of money.'

'I know,' his father agreed. 'But I cannot take the chance that she might not accept your offer. After the response I sent to her previous letter she might avenge my assessment of her character and deny us access to the child.'

Marc inwardly cringed, recalling the content of that letter. His father had emailed him a copy and it had certainly not been complimentary. He could well imagine the Selbourne woman reacting to it out of revenge, particularly if what she said was true—Andre had indeed fathered her child.

He was well aware of Nadia Selbourne's reputation, even though he hadn't met her personally. He'd seen one or two photos, however, which had shown a beautiful woman with thick long blonde hair, eyes that were an unusual smoky grey and the sort of figure that not only turned heads but turned on other parts of the male anatomy at an astonishingly rapid rate as well. His brother had been completely besotted with her until her true character had come out. He could still recall Andre's scathing description of how she had responded when he'd informed her that their short but passionate affair was over. She had hounded him for months, following him and harassing him relentlessly.

But somehow the thought of his dead brother's blood flowing through the tiny veins of her child stirred him both unexpectedly and deeply.

'Marc.' His father's desperate voice cut across his reflections. 'You have to do this. It is a matter of family honour. Andre would have done the same for you if things had been the other way around.'

It was hard for Marc to imagine ever allowing himself to get into the sort of disasters his younger brother had for most of his life, but he didn't think it worthwhile pointing that out now. His father had already suffered enough; he'd lost his beloved son.

It had been no secret in the Marcello family that Andre had always been his father's favourite. His sunny nature and charming boisterous personality had won everyone over virtually from the day he'd been born, leaving Marc with his more serious disposition on the outside.

He frowned as he considered his father's plan. What would it take to convince this woman to hand over the child? Would she take the money and go, or would she insist on something more formal, such as…

His stomach tightened momentarily as he recalled how his brother had told him that Nadia Selbourne was relentless in her search for a rich husband.

But surely his father wouldn't expect him to go *that* far!

So far Marc had managed to ignore the pressure to marry, although he had come very close a few years ago. But it had ended rather badly and he'd actively avoided heavy emotional entanglements since then. Besides, Andre had always made it clear he was going to marry young and father all the Marcello heirs so the family dynasty would be secure. Marc had decided women were not to be trusted where money was involved. And in the Marcello family a *lot* of money was involved.

His heart contracted at the thought of a small dark-haired infant with black-brown eyes—eyes that would one day soon dance with mischief, as her father's had for his too short thirty years of life.

'So will you do it?' Vito pressed. 'Will you do this one thing for me and your late mother?'

Marc pinched the bridge of his Roman nose, his eyes squeezing shut. The mention of his mother always tore at him deeply, the sharp guilt cutting into him until he felt as if he was bleeding. He still remembered that last day, the way she had smiled and waved at him from the other side of the busy street in Rome. She hadn't seen the motor scooter until it had ripped the shopping bags out of her hands, spinning her into the pathway of an oncoming car.

He couldn't help believing that if he had been honest with her about why he was going to be late, maybe she would not have been killed. His father had begged him, and he had honoured him by doing as he'd asked, but the guilt even now was like a deep dark current that dragged at his feet, weighing him down relentlessly.

When his brother had been killed so soon after the death of his mother, Marc hadn't been able to rid himself of the feeling that his father would have grieved a whole lot less if it had been him instead of Andre in that mangled car.

He let out his breath and, releasing his fingers, answered resignedly. 'I will see what I can do…'

'Thank you.' The relief in his father's voice was unmistakable.

Marc knew his father's days were numbered. How much more precious would they be if he could hold his only grandchild in his arms?

'She might refuse to even see me, you know,' Marc warned, thinking again of that vituperative letter his father had sent. 'Have you considered that possibility?'

'Do whatever you have to do to make her see reason,' Vito instructed. 'And I mean anything. This is simply a business arrangement. Women like Nadia Selbourne expect nothing more and nothing less.'

A business arrangement.

What sort of woman was this, Marc thought, who would bargain with the life of a small child?

He put the phone down a few minutes later and turned once more to the sweeping view outside. His dark eyes narrowed against the angle of the sun as he considered what he'd just agreed to do.

He was going to visit the one person he hated more than any other in the world—the woman he believed responsible for his brother's untimely death.

CHAPTER TWO

NINA had not long fed and settled Georgia on Monday morning when the doorbell rang. Giving the small neat room a quick glance, she made her way across the threadbare carpet, wondering what it was that her elderly neighbour wanted now. Ellice Tippen had already borrowed a carton of milk and half a packet of plain biscuits and it wasn't even lunch time.

She opened the door as she plastered a welcoming smile on her face but it instantly faded as her gaze shifted a long way upwards to meet a pair of dark, almost black, eyes.

'Miss Selbourne?'

'I…yes,' she answered, unconsciously putting a hand up to her throat.

The tall figure standing before her was even more arresting in the flesh than the grainy newspaper photo had portrayed. He was taller than average, well over six feet, his shoulders broad and his overall stance nothing short of commanding. The hard angle of his lean clean-shaven jaw hinted at a streak of intractability in his personality, and his eyes held no trace of friendliness. His perfectly tailored business suit superbly highlighted his strong lean body, suggesting he was a man used to a great deal of punishing physical activity.

'I am assuming you know who I am.' His voice was deep and had a hard edge to it as if he wasn't the type to block his punches.

'I…er…yes.'

What else could she say? The weekend paper was still open at his photo on the coffee table behind her. Every time she'd walked past she'd told herself to screw it up and throw it out, but somehow she hadn't. She wasn't entirely sure why.

'I understand you have my brother's child,' he said into the stiff silence.

'I…yes, that's correct.' A vision of Georgia's dark bruises flashed into Nina's mind and her rising panic increased her heart rate to an almost intolerable level. She *had* to keep him away from her niece!

'I would like to see her.'

'I'm afraid she's sleeping just now, so…' She let the sentence trail away, hoping he'd take the hint.

He didn't.

He held her gaze for a lengthy moment and just when she began to close the door he put his foot out to block it.

'Perhaps you did not hear me, Miss Selbourne.' His tone hardened even further as his diamond-hard eyes lasered hers. 'I am here to see my brother's child and I will not be leaving until I do so.'

Nina knew he meant every hard-bitten word and, stepping back from the door, sent him a chilling glance. 'If you wake her I'll be extremely angry.' *Please stay asleep, Georgia,* she silently pleaded as he moved through the doorway, coming to stand right in front of her as the door clicked shut behind him.

He gave her a sweeping up and down look and when his eyes met hers they were full of contempt. 'Andre told me all about you.'

Nina frowned in confusion. She'd never once met her sister's lover. Nadia's affair with him had been brief but explosive, just like all her others.

Surely he didn't think…

'He told me you were trouble, but little did I realise how much,' he continued when she didn't respond.

She stared at him for a moment, wondering if she should disabuse him of his error in thinking she was her sister, but in the end decided to let him go on, to see what his intentions were with regard to Georgia. After all, what harm could it do? All she needed to do was pretend to be Nadia for a few minutes to tell him that she had changed her mind about the letter that had been sent to his father. Once she had convinced him she had no intention of giving up 'her' daughter, hopefully he would go away.

It wasn't as if she hadn't done this type of thing before. So many times in the past Nina had stepped into Nadia's place to take the brunt of whatever punishment their dysfunctional mother had dished out. Surely if she'd been able to hoodwink her own mother, Marc Marcello would be an absolute pushover.

'Your brother's criticism is ironic considering his own behaviour,' she put in crisply.

A menacing glare came into his dark-as-night eyes. 'You dare to malign my dead brother?'

She lifted her chin. 'He was a cheat. While he was fathering Georgia, he was committed elsewhere.'

'He was formally engaged to Daniela Verdacci,' he said bitterly. 'They had been together since they were teenagers. You set your sights on him, no doubt lured by the prospect of his money, but he only ever had eyes for Daniela. Did you really think he would stoop so low as to tie himself permanently to an unprincipled opportunistic little tramp who has slept her way around most of Sydney?'

Nina tensed in anger. She knew her sister had been a little promiscuous at times, but the way Marc Marcello phrased it made it sound as if she had been a call girl instead of the insecure and emotionally unstable person she really was.

'How absolutely typical!' she spat back. 'Why is it men such as yourself and your brother can sow several continents with wild oats but women must not? Get in the real world, Mr Marcello. Women own their sexuality these days and have the same right to express it as you.'

His dark unreadable eyes raked her from head to foot again. 'While we are speaking of rights, the little matter of Andre's child needs to be addressed. As much as I lament and abhor the fact that the child is a Marcello, the fact remains that she is entitled to see her paternal relatives.'

'Surely that decision is up to me?'

'No, I am afraid not, Miss Selbourne.' His voice lowered threateningly. 'Perhaps you do not realise quite who you are dealing with here. The Marcello family will not stand back and watch a street whore raise a blood relative. Unless you do as I say I will do everything in my power to remove her from you so you cannot taint her with your lack of morality.'

Nina's eyes widened in alarm. She was in no doubt of his ability to do as he threatened. There could be few people in Australia who weren't aware of the monumental wealth of the Marcello family. Their influence and control stretched far and wide across the world. With the best legal defence and with a total lack of scruples, she knew it wouldn't be long before Marc Marcello did exactly as he had promised.

Oh, what had Nadia done?

Nina did her best not to appear intimidated, but never had she been more terrified. If he were to find out that she wasn't actually the child's mother, he could remove Georgia right here and now and there would be nothing she could do to stop him.

But he was *not* going to find out. Not if she could help it.

Garnering what courage she could, she stood rigidly before him, her grey eyes issuing a challenge.

'I might appear to be a woman of few morals, but let me assure you I love that child and will not stand back while some overrated playboy sweeps her away. She's a baby and babies need their mothers.'

Marc's gaze swept over her rigid form, noting the tightened line of her full mouth and the stubborn set of her chin. Her startling eyes flashed with venom and, for the first time, he realised just how severely tempted his brother must have been. That pint-sized frame was incredibly alluring, so too the lustrous blonde hair that perfectly offset the creamy quality of her skin. Her figure had snapped back into place rather quickly, he thought, considering she'd not long been delivered of a child. Her air of innocence, however, he knew was the façade of a money-hungry whore who had already demonstrated her intentions by trying to trap his brother with the oldest trick in the book—pregnancy.

'Under normal circumstances I would agree with you,' he said in an even tone. 'Having had the benefit of a wonderful mother, I would be the last person to suggest a child should be raised by anyone else. However, your track record does not inspire the greatest confidence in me that you will be able to support and nurture Andre's child. After all, who was it that sent a missive to my family in Italy stating your intentions to have the child adopted?'

'I…It was a knee-jerk reaction. I was upset and not thinking straight,' she said quickly. 'I have no intention of giving her up. Georgia is mine and no one—and I mean *no one*—is going to remove her from my custody.'

Without warning he stepped towards her, his formidable height casting a dark shadow over her slim form. Nina fought with herself not to shrink away, but it took everything in her to hold herself steady under his threatening presence.

'How remiss of me,' he drawled as he reached inside his suit jacket pocket for his wallet. 'I should have known you would want to twist the screws a bit. How much?'

She looked at him blankly.

One dark aristocratic brow lifted. 'I assume this is what this holding pattern is all about?'

'I have no idea what you're talking about,' she said, her throat suddenly bone-dry.

His mouth twisted into a cynical smile as he fanned open his wallet, 'Come now, Nadia. I am a rich man; I think I can just about afford to pay you off. Name your price.'

Marc was surprised by how much he was enjoying playing with her, seeing her struggle to hold on to her temper, knowing that any minute now she'd cave in to the temptation he was dangling before her beautiful come-to-bed-eyes.

'My real name is Nina and I don't want your stupid money.'

This time both his eyebrows lifted. He paused strategically, wondering what game she was playing now.

'I thought your name was Nadia? I am sure Andre told me it was—or was that a lie too?'

Nina schooled her features into exactly the sort of expression her twin sister was famous for. 'Nina is my real name but I thought Nadia sounded a little more sophisticated. I've since changed my mind.' She inspected her hands in another imitation of her sister before raising her eyes back to his. 'How did you know where to find me?'

'There is only one Miss N Selbourne listed in the phone book in this suburb.'

Since Nadia had moved in with her after the birth of Georgia, her sister's erratic approach to paying bills meant that Nina had left the telephone in her name alone, which had obviously made it even easier for Marc to assume she was her twin.

She allowed one tiny inaudible breath of relief to escape the tight frame of her lips.

So far so good.

'Well, then…*Nina.*' He drew her name out suggestively. 'If you are not after money, what do you want?'

'Nothing.'

The cynical smile was back. 'It has been my experience that women like you are always after money even when they insist to the contrary.'

'Your experience must be terribly limited, for I can assure you I have no need of your money.'

'Not mine, perhaps, but you must be aware that my dead brother has left a considerable estate. You have given birth to his child, which means she has a legal right to claim some, if not all, of that estate when she comes of age.'

Nina swallowed. This was getting more and more complicated by the minute.

'I'm not interested in Andre's estate.'

'You expect me to believe that?' he growled. 'Behind those eyes of yours I can see the dollar signs already rolling in anticipation.' His dark gaze left hers to sweep the room before coming back to glare down at her. 'Look at this place! It reeks of poverty and neglect. Do you think I will allow my niece to live in such a hovel?'

Nina felt pride straighten her spine. 'It's all I can afford at present.'

He gave a harsh laugh. 'At present is right. No doubt you have already got some other poor unsuspecting man in your sights for your next free ride.' He gave her a look of undiluted disgust and continued. 'You must be offering something pretty special underneath that "butter would not melt in your mouth" pose for anyone to take you on with another man's baby in tow.'

Nina had never considered herself a volatile person; Nadia had been the firebrand, her unpredictable mood swings causing many an unpleasant scene. But somehow, hearing Marc's disdain, even though it was directed at her twin, bit her deeply and on her sister's behalf she fought back.

'Are you offering to take up where Andre left off?' she asked in a tone dripping with sultry provocation.

His dark eyes glittered with hatred so intense it secretly unnerved her.

'I can see how you want to play this,' he said after another nerve-tightening pause.

'On the contrary, I want nothing other than for you to leave my home immediately. You're not the least bit interested in my n...er...daughter.' She took a quick breath to disguise her vocal stumble. 'If you don't leave then I will have no other choice than to call the police and have you thrown out.'

Black eyes clashed with grey for endless seconds but finally Nina was the first to lower her gaze.

'Please leave, Mr Marcello. I have nothing else I wish to say to you.'

'I want to see my niece.' His adamant tone brought her eyes back to his. 'I want to see the child my brother fathered.'

Nina pressed her lips together as she saw the struggle he made to keep his emotions under control. She heard it in his voice and saw it in his rigid stance as he faced her, his dark eyes shining with sudden moisture.

She hadn't expected him to have such depth of human feeling and it shamed her to realise how seriously she'd misjudged him. After all, she reminded herself, he had not long buried his only sibling under tragic circumstances. Even with all Nadia's distressing foibles, she knew that in the same situation she would be little less than devastated.

'I'm sorry.' Her voice came out unevenly.

His mouth twisted. 'Are you?'

She didn't answer but moved past him to the pram under the single window. She was conscious of his tall frame just behind her as she peeled back the covers so he could see Georgia's face.

She felt him standing close beside her, his arm brushing hers as he looked down at his brother's child for a long time without speaking. The silence was so intense she could hear the sound of his breathing, his chest moving in and out with the effort of controlling his reaction to seeing his niece for the first time.

'Can I hold her?'

Nina felt as if her heart had done a complete somersault in her chest at his simple request. What if he held her the wrong way and she cried?

'Um…I don't think—'

'Please.' His raw tone brought her eyes back to his. 'I would like to hold my brother's child. She is all that I have left of him.'

Nina released an uneven breath and carefully lifted the sleeping baby from amongst the covers, cradling her gently before turning and handing her to him.

She watched as a thousand emotions flashed over his handsome features as he brought the tiny bundle close to his broad chest, his dark gaze thoughtful as he looked down at the perfection of Georgia's peaceful face.

'She is…beautiful.' His tone was distinctly husky.

Nina had trouble keeping the emotion out of her own voice. 'Yes, she is.'

His eyes met hers briefly. 'What did you call her?'

She lowered her gaze a fraction. 'Georgia.'

'Georgia,' he repeated as if tasting it. 'It suits her.'

She chanced a look at him and was surprised to see how at ease he was holding the infant, one of his large hands cradling her securely while the other explored her miniature features as if in wonder.

'Does she have a middle name?' he asked into the heavy silence.

'Grace,' she answered, wondering if she should tell him it was her own middle name, but at the last minute deciding against it. She'd been so touched when Nadia had told her of her choice of names, and for a while had hoped her sister was going to finally settle down and face her responsibilities. But within a few short weeks of Georgia's birth she had gone back to late-night partying and drinking, leaving the baby with Nina so often that Georgia had begun to cry whenever Nadia had made any approach at all, as if sensing her total inadequacy as a carer.

Nina was increasingly aware of the silence in the room as Marc Marcello held his niece, his dark gaze fixed on the child's face.

She said the first thing that came into her head. 'I think she looks like Andre, don't you?'

Marc swung his gaze to where she was standing, his hard

expression instantly clouding. She thought he was going to agree with her but instead he turned back to the child in his arms and asked, looking down at her, 'Did he ever see her?'

'No.'

She'd been furious when Nadia had told her that Andre hadn't wanted to see his baby, and couldn't help wondering if that was the reason her sister hadn't bonded with the child in the first place. The whole way through the pregnancy Nadia had had all her hopes pinned on Andre falling in love with his child once he saw her, thus ensuring a secure future for Nadia as his wife. When he had flatly refused to take a paternity test to establish whether or not the baby was his, Nadia had gone into a deep depression, closely followed by a spate of reckless partying.

'No,' she repeated, her tone holding a distinct note of bitterness. 'I expect he was too busy preparing for his wedding.'

Marc didn't answer but Nina could see the sudden tightening of his jaw as if her words had annoyed him.

She watched as he laid the baby down once more, his touch sure but gentle as he tucked the light bunny rug back into place.

When he turned to face her she found it difficult to hold his piercing gaze as she thought of how she was deceiving him. It suddenly occurred to her what a dangerous game she was playing. Wasn't there some sort of law against impersonating another person? Marc Marcello was nobody's fool and if he were to ever find out how he'd been duped there would be hell to pay, she was sure.

'Miss Selbourne.' His deep voice brought her troubled gaze back to his.

'Y-yes?' She moistened her lips, somehow sensing he was going to state his intentions, all her instincts telling her she wasn't going to like them one little bit.

'I want to see my niece on a regular basis and, while I understand your aversion to such an arrangement, I think you know I will pursue this legally if you refuse.'

'I'm her mother,' she bit out. 'No court in Australia would remove her from my custody.'

'You think not?' His lip curled. 'What if I told them about your little affair with a certain prominent politician just a few weeks after giving birth to my brother's child?'

What affair? Nina thought in panic. What politician? What the hell had Nadia been up to?

He must have seen the flicker of alarm cross her features as he added in a cool deliberate tone, 'You see, Miss Selbourne, I have all the dirt on you and I intend to use it in order to bring about what I want. I have heard how you tried to extort money from the poor fool when he called a halt to the relationship. You have been lucky that little affair did not get the press's attention, but one word from me and, well…' He paused for effect. 'You know the rest.'

She sucked in a ragged breath, even her fingertips growing icy cold with dread as it spread through her body like the flow of mercury in her veins.

'What exactly do you want?' Her words came out like hard pellets.

Marc waited for a few moments before he answered. Until he had seen Andre's child—and one look told him she was indeed his—he had not really thought much further than waving a truck-load of money under the mother's nose and walking away with the baby as his father had planned. But somehow seeing Nina with the baby, the way she looked at Georgia so lovingly and cra-dled her so gently, he wasn't convinced that he would be acting in the best interests of his niece by removing her from her mother, unless he was absolutely sure she was not up to the task of car-ing for her. If indeed he could, considering that ill-judged letter of his father's, and its vicious rejection of the baby. The woman had a powerful weapon there, if she chose to use it.

Which left him with only one other course of action.

His obsidian gaze held hers determinedly. 'I want to claim my brother's child as my own.'

'You can't do that! She doesn't belong to you! She belongs t-to...t-to me.'

'I can, you know.'

'How?'

She shouldn't have asked, Nina thought later. She just should never have asked.

His dark eyes locked with hers and a persistent tickling feather of fear began to tease its way up the entire length of her spine.

'I want that baby and I will do anything to have her, even if it means I have to tie myself to you to do so.'

She blinked at him, wondering if she'd misinterpreted his chilling statement. 'Tie yourself? What do you mean *tie* yourself?'

His mouth twisted into a smile that didn't quite reach his dark-as-sin eyes. 'My brother refused to marry you, but I have no such scruples. You will be my wife within a fortnight or I will make sure you never see your daughter again.' He kept his features still, knowing his bluff was convincing. But would it work?

It took Nina a moment or two to find her voice, her head pounding with a combination of shock and outrage.

'Do you seriously think I will be coerced in such a way?' she finally spat indignantly.

'I am more or less counting on it. Andre told me your main goal in life was to land a rich husband, so here I am, ready to step into the role.'

She opened her mouth to speak again but her throat closed over at the steely determination in his dark gaze as it clashed with hers.

She considered coming clean, telling him she was really Nadia's twin, hoping he would understand her need to protect her niece, but his air of icy hauteur changed her mind at the last minute. She'd be damned if she would give up her niece without a furious fight, even if it cost her everything she had, including her freedom.

She flashed him a look of pure loathing at the way he'd cleverly herded her into a corner from which she could increasingly see there might be little chance of escape. She saw the glint of anticipated victory in his dark gaze and her blood ebbed and flowed through her veins in a tide of anger and growing fear.

'I suppose it's to be expected a spoilt playboy like you would assume he can always get whatever he wants,' she said.

'I will, of course, pay you generously,' he said, his dark eyes watching her steadily. 'How much do you want?'

Nina was very conscious that in her place Nadia would have asked for some outrageous sum, but something stopped her from taking the charade that far. The ice she'd inadvertently skated on to was suddenly very thin in places, but taking money in what was little more than a bribe was surely going to lead to more trouble than she could cope with at present.

Besides, little Georgia was lying asleep less than a metre away from him, her tiny body badly bruised. She'd been lucky this time but if he took even one look beneath that vest…

Forcing her chin upwards, she tilted her head at him, her arms folded in front of her chest, and informed him with unintentional irony, 'If you think you can bribe me then you've got the wrong person.'

His eyes flicked to her where her breasts were pushed up by her folded arms, taking his time before returning to her face.

Nina stood silently fuming under his mocking appraisal, wondering how in the world her sister's behaviour had brought her to this. She knew her anger should be directed at Nadia and not the man before her, but everything about him goaded her beyond bearing.

'I told you before, I don't want your money. I'd feel tainted by taking anything from you.'

'Nice try, Miss Selbourne,' he drawled back. 'I can see what you are doing. You are pretending to be nothing like the avaricious young woman who seduced my brother, but I can see through your little act. Do not think that you can deceive me so easily; I have made up my mind, and you will do as I say, whether you accept payment from me or not.'

Nina did her best to hide how his statement affected her while her mind raced on, wondering how in the world she was going to get out of this farcical situation. God, she was going to kill Nadia for this! Surely she couldn't be forced to marry the man just to keep her niece? But what else was she to do? Nadia was an unfit mother and—like her—Marc apparently had enough evidence to prove it.

'I want some time to think about this.' She was a little unnerved by how like Nadia she sounded, but carried on regardless. 'I like to look at all the angles on things before I commit myself.'

'I am not here to negotiate, Miss Selbourne,' he said intractably. 'I am here to step into the role of Georgia's father and I want to do it as soon as possible.'

She looked up at him in growing alarm. There was an intransigent edge to his tone that suggested he was well used to getting his own way and would go to any lengths at his disposal to do so.

Tell him the truth, she mentally chanted. *Tell him who you really are.* But the words were stuck somewhere in the middle of her chest where her heart was already squeezing at the thought of never seeing Georgia again.

She tried to think rationally and clearly but it was hard with him standing there watching every tiny flicker of emotion on her face.

What if she went along with his demands for now? He'd said two weeks. Surely she'd be able to wriggle out of it by then. Hopefully Nadia would be in contact soon and she'd be able to sort something out. She *had* to sort something out. She couldn't possibly marry a perfect stranger!

Marc took her continued silence as acquiescence. 'I will have the necessary papers drawn up immediately.'

'But…' She stopped, her heart giving another funny skip in her chest. Oh, God! What had she done? Surely he wasn't serious?

She tried again. 'H-how soon do you want me to…' She found it hard to finish the sentence as his hard eyes cut to hers with a look of total disdain.

'Perhaps I should make something very clear at this point. I do not want *you*, Miss Selbourne. This will not be a proper marriage in the true sense of the word.'

'Not legal, do you mean?' She frowned, trying to make sense of his meaning.

'It will be legal, I would not settle for less, but it will be a paper marriage only.'

'A paper marriage?' Her finely arched brows met above her eyes.

'We will not be consummating the relationship,' he stated implacably.

Nina knew she should be feeling overwhelming relief at his curt statement but for some inexplicable reason she felt annoyed instead. She knew she wasn't looking as glamorous right now as Nadia customarily did, but her figure was good and her features classically appealing. It didn't sit that well with her to have him dismiss her desirability so readily, as if she held no physical appeal at all.

'You expect me to trust you on that?' she asked with just the right amount of cynicism in her tone.

He lifted a long-fingered tanned hand and made a sign of a cross over his chest as his eyes pinned hers.

'Cross my heart and hope to die.'

Something about his air of supreme confidence tempted Nina into giving him the sort of seductive look she'd seen her sister casting men's way for years. She placed her hand on her hip as she tilted her pelvis provocatively, the corners of her mouth tipping upwards in a taunting little salacious smile as she drawled breathily, 'Then I would say you're as good as a dead man, Mr Marcello.'

CHAPTER THREE

MARC gave an inward smile at her overblown confidence. She was just as Andre had described, all pouting little girl one minute, raging sex siren the next. It was a heady combination, he had to admit, but while Andre hadn't been able to contain his desire for her, temporary as it had been, Marc felt confident he was in no danger of being tested beyond his control. Nina Selbourne was the total opposite of what he most wanted in a partner.

He loathed shallow money-hungry women who had nothing better to do than preen themselves in the hope of attracting a rich husband. He'd been surrounded by them for most of his life, with the exception of his French-born mother, who had had both style and grace without affectation.

No, Miss Nina/Nadia Selbourne was fooling herself if she thought he would fall for her physical charms.

'I am not like my brother, Miss Selbourne,' he informed her coldly. 'My tastes are a little more upmarket.'

Nina wished she could slap that imperious smirk off his handsome face but knew there would probably be distasteful consequences if she did. She clenched her hands into fists and glared back at him.

'I could make you eat those words and we both know it. I saw the way you ran your eyes all over me the moment I opened the door.'

'I admit I was a little intrigued as to what made my brother act so incautiously.' His lazy look took in her heaving chest and feisty gaze. 'But I can assure you I have no appetite for vacuous women such as yourself.'

Nina schooled her features back under control with difficulty. 'I take it this marriage arrangement you're proposing leaves you free to liaise with whomever you want whenever you want?'

'I will do my best to be discreet if the need should arise.'

'What about me?' she asked. 'Am I allowed to indulge myself similarly?'

He didn't answer immediately but she could almost hear the cogs of his brain ticking over as he considered her question.

'Well?' she prodded with an arch look.

'No.'

'*No?*'

He shook his head in slow motion, 'Absolutely not.'

'You can't possibly be serious.' She snapped her brows together again.

'Deadly serious,' he said and folded his arms across the broad expanse of his chest.

'You surely don't expect me to agree to such a double standard?' she asked. 'What am I supposed to get out of this arrangement?'

'You get to keep your child, with a rich husband thrown in as a bonus.'

She let out her breath in a whoosh of feminist outrage. 'I thought men like you died along with the dinosaurs. Seems I was wrong. So, how are things on Planet Chauvinism these days?'

'I am not by nature a chauvinist but I am sure it will do you good to be celibate for a while to concentrate on your responsibilities as a mother.'

. Ironic laughter bubbled to her lips before she could stop it. Unlike her sister, who had lost her virginity at the age of fourteen, Nina was technically still a virgin. Technically because she firmly believed every modern woman had the right to explore her own body and find out how things worked, although she still wondered what all the fuss was about. The earth hadn't exactly moved and she'd more or less given up on herself, deciding she was one of those women with unusually low sex-drives. But on principle she wasn't going to let him have things all his way. He already thought her the biggest tart outside of the red-light district and a perverse little part of her was enjoying every dangerous minute of encouraging him to maintain that view.

'You find the prospect of being responsible amusing?' His tone dripped with contempt.

She coiled a strand of her long hair around one finger, hoping he wouldn't notice her chewed nail as she affected another seductive pose.

'You're a laugh a minute, Mr Marcello,' she said. 'All this talk of being celibate is hilarious. I haven't been celibate for ten years and I'm not about to start for you or anyone.'

Anger briefly flashed across his features as he looked down at her. Nina saw his hands tighten into fists as if he didn't trust himself not to reach out and touch her.

A flicker of sensation unexpectedly erupted between her thighs at the mere thought of any part of his tall hard body touching her. She began to imagine what that firm disapproving mouth would feel like crushed to hers, his tongue searching arrogantly to duel with hers. She felt her breasts start to tingle and, almost without realising she was doing it, her tongue came out just a fraction to sweep over the surface of her lips.

Marc felt the sharp tug of sudden errant desire hit him in the belly like a closed fist punch. He struggled to control it, annoyed with himself for being tempted when he'd been so assured that he would be able to resist her, but something about her struck at him deeply. She positively oozed with sexual confidence, the smoky grey of her eyes and full-lipped mouth making his skin lift in anticipation of feeling her touch.

He decided to strike a deal with her even though he had cause to wonder if he was shooting himself in the foot in the process.

'Since you seem unwilling to agree to my terms, I am willing to make a small compromise,' he announced. 'For the period of one month following our marriage we will both remain celibate; how about that?'

She pursed her lips as if considering it. 'One month? Hmm...I think I could just about manage that.'

His jaw tightened and she gave him another sexy smile. 'But no longer or I'll go out of my mind. But then, from what I hear of you—' she ran her eyes over him from head to foot as if undressing him thread by thread '—maybe you will too.'

'I think I will manage to contain myself,' he responded coolly.

'I take it you don't have a current mistress?' She sent him a lash-fluttering glance.

'I am not currently close to anyone.'

Nina couldn't help wondering how good he might be when he was *close*. He was the whole knee-trembling spine-loosening package, even though it irked her to admit it. He was handsome beyond belief, his dark mesmerizing eyes promising explosive passion from within their glittering depths. His mouth was currently stretched into a hardened line of derision but she was in no doubt of its power to persuade if he allowed himself a moment of weakness and brought his head down to hers.

The pram near the window suddenly gave a squeak of protest as Georgia shifted in her sleep.

Marc swung his gaze to the pram before turning back to face Nina, his voice low and deep with concern. 'Is she all right?'

Sending him a now-see-what-you've-done look, Nina went over to soothe her. The mewing cries stopped as soon as her hand stroked Georgia's tiny legs, the gentle rhythmic movements sending the infant back to sleep within a couple of minutes.

Nina was intensely aware of the watchful gaze of Marc Marcello a short distance away. She could almost sense his cool assessment of her, no doubt weighing up her skills as a mother.

Once she was sure the baby was soundly asleep she turned and faced him, her grey eyes meeting his with as much equanimity as she could.

'You said earlier you intended to marry within two weeks. Why the hurry?'

'My father is terminally ill. He wishes to see his only grandchild before he dies. There is not much time.'

'A fortnight isn't very long.' She gave her bottom lip a surreptitious nibble.

'I will see to all the details. You do not have to do anything but turn up at the registry office.'

Nina knew it was pathetic of her to be feeling disappointed, but if by some quirk of fate she had to go through with this, her lifelong dream of a beautiful white wedding in a city cathedral was going to have to be shelved indefinitely.

'But what about a dress?' she asked, trying not to think of Marc Marcello's motives for marrying her.

'I have no real interest in what sort of outfit you wear,' he said. 'However, I do think it would be highly inappropriate of you to wear white.' His eyes flicked to the pram and back again. 'Don't you?'

She held his gaze for as long as she dared. 'I happen to like wearing white. It suits my colouring.'

Marc was certain she'd still look stunning even if she was covered from head to foot in a nun's habit. Her come-to-bed eyes had tugged far too many men into their seductive orbit and he had to make sure he didn't join their number.

'Wear what you like; the ceremony will be over within minutes anyway. I will make an appointment with my lawyer to draw up the necessary paperwork.' He made a move towards the door, slanting a warning look her way. 'I should remind you at this point that if you wish to pull out of the deal I will have no choice but to activate proceedings to remove Georgia permanently from your custody. And do not think I cannot do it, for I assure you I can and will if I need to.'

Nina wished she could throw his threat back at him but the thought of losing her niece was just too wrenching. She knew he only had to see those fading but still present bruises on Georgia's tiny chest for the fight to be over right here and now.

She only hoped that maybe in time Marc would see how much she too loved the baby and wanted the best for her. But what would he do if or when he found out the truth?

'I won't pull out of the deal,' she said, wishing her voice hadn't sounded quite so hollow.

'No, I imagine not.' His eyes held hers with a caution reflected in their glittering depths 'I will, of course, be providing you with an allowance for the duration of our marriage.'

Nina instantly stiffened, but for some reason couldn't find her voice.

'What will you do with all that money to spend, I wonder?' he mused insultingly.

She gave him one of her sister's casual shrugs. 'Shop and shop and shop, probably.'

Marc's lip curled distastefully. 'You are a complete and utter sybarite. Have you ever done a decent day's work in your life?'

'Work?' She wrinkled her nose in repugnance. 'Why work when you can have fun instead?'

'I must be out of my mind,' he muttered under his breath. 'You sicken me. I can hardly believe you lured my brother away from Daniela. She postponed the wedding because of you. If you hadn't come along when you did, Andre—'

'How typical to blame the woman in the middle,' she shot back furiously on her sister's behalf. 'He didn't have to sleep with me; he could always have said no.'

'You hounded him for months,' he tossed back. 'He told me how determined you were, how it became impossible to keep you at arm's length.'

'I think I can safely say he enjoyed it while it lasted. And I bet you would too. I can guarantee it.'

'Sorry to disappoint you, but that will not be happening. You know the score and if you put one foot out of place I will use all the weapons at my disposal.'

Nina could well believe it. He quite possibly had cards up his sleeve that could prove to be a little too tactical for her liking. She had two weeks to think of a way out and she was going to do her best to find one, for it was becoming increasingly clear she was seriously outmatched in her opponent.

'Will any of your relatives be attending the ceremony?' she asked in an effort to hide her disquiet.

'No, my father is unable to travel and my mother is…' He hesitated slightly before continuing. 'She died a couple of years ago.'

Nina couldn't help feeling a wave of sympathy for his father, who had been dealt a double blow of grief in losing his son so close to the death of his wife. She imagined Marc was dealing with overwhelming grief too and it made her anger towards his treatment of her soften around the edges.

'It must be a very difficult time for you all,' she said gently.

Marc threw her a look of disgust. 'How dare you offer sympathy when if it had not been for you, my brother would still be alive?'

Nina stared at him in shock. This was getting even worse than a nightmare. What did he mean?

'That's a heavy accusation,' she managed to get out. 'Exactly what evidence do you have to substantiate it?'

'You were the last person to see Andre before he went to pick up Daniela from the airport.'

Nina hadn't known that little detail and wondered why her sister hadn't mentioned it.

'So?' She made her voice sound as unconcerned as possible even though her stomach was rolling in consternation.

'Daniela was understandably upset at what had gone on

whilst she had been in Milan visiting her family the first time,' he said. 'She was threatening to call off the wedding altogether but Andre was adamant that his involvement with you had ceased. She knew about the baby and it caused a great deal of trouble between them, as she was concerned about him having further contact with you. She lived long enough after the accident to tell me that Andre had been on edge when he arrived to pick her up, as you had visited him the night before making your usual outrageous demands. He had not slept well after you left and his concentration was all over the place. A truck ran a red light and he did not have the necessary reaction time to avoid the collision.'

'And you think that's my fault?' Nina asked tightly. 'I wasn't driving the truck!'

'You might as well have been, as far as I am concerned. Andre was deeply ashamed of himself for getting involved with you. It almost destroyed his relationship with Daniela.'

'He should have thought about the consequences before he gave me the come-on,' she threw back.

'Have you not got that the wrong way around?' he asked with a flash of black eyes. 'It was not Andre who was lying naked in the hotel bed that first night—it was you.'

Nina did her best to hide her shock at his statement. There was so much she didn't know and the further she became embroiled in this farce the harder it was to maintain her cover. Nadia had told her virtually nothing, which meant she now had to lie her way through this emotional minefield.

Lie after lie after lie.

She'd read somewhere that if a person were to tell one lie they then had to go on and tell thousands to keep that single one in place. Now she could well believe it.

'So?' She tried the casual tone again. 'He could have said no.'

'There are very few men who could say no when such temptation is dangled in front of them,' he said, raking his gaze over her once more.

Nina tilted her head at him provocatively. 'So you admit to being a little tempted yourself?'

His hand left the doorknob as he strode back across the room to stand in front of her, his expression so full of hatred she had to force herself not to step backwards to escape the heat of it coming off him in scorching waves.

His eyes burned down into hers forcefully, the inky depths glittering as if he was only just managing to keep his temper under control.

'You might have the body of a goddess and the face of an angel but I would not touch you even if you held the key to life itself,' he ground out heavily.

Injured feminine pride made Nina hitch up her chin another fraction, her eyes issuing him a challenge she knew deep inside she should not be issuing but she just couldn't help it. How dare he dismiss her so confidently?

'Want to lay a bet on that, big boy? Put your money where your mouth is—so to speak.'

The line of his mouth grew even tighter until his lips appeared almost white. Nina could tell she had taken things a little too far but it was too late to back out now.

'All right.' He finally released his breath. 'I will lay a bet on it. If I touch you other than in the most casual way during our marriage, you win the bet. I will double your allowance on the spot.'

She suddenly realised that Nadia would have asked how much he intended giving her by now but it simply hadn't occurred to Nina to do so.

'Um…how much are you intending to pay me?'

'Much more than you are worth, I can assure you.'

Her eyes burned with seething hatred at his denigration, everything inside her quaking with anger until she could barely stand still. She felt it rumbling in her stomach, flash-flooding her veins as it was carried to every single cell of her body.

'That remains to be seen,' she said in Nadia's confident

flirty tone even though her teeth were being ground to powder behind her seductive smile.

His midnight eyes gleamed with confidence as he looked down at her, the small smile that was playing on his lips a combination of both mockery and challenge.

'Go ahead, Miss Selbourne, go ahead and make me pay.'

She opened her mouth to respond but before she could get the words out the door opened under his hand and he stepped through and closed it behind him with an ominous click of the lock as it fell back into place.

She stared at the door for a moment or two, her stomach in tight knots of panic, her head throbbing with tension and her legs trembling at the thought of what she'd just done.

She turned and leaned heavily on the arm of the old sofa, her frazzled brain trying to find a satisfactory way out of her predicament.

If she told him who she really was he would have even more reason to claim Georgia, for she could hardly provide for her the way he obviously could and, with Nadia already abandoning her daughter, what hope would there be of fighting back?

But marrying him?

Her heart gave another heavy thump of panic at the thought of being formally tied to him in marriage, all the time having to keep her true identity a secret. But unless Nadia reappeared and claimed her daughter, Nina knew she was going to have to continue with the charade for as long as necessary. What other choice was there? Georgia needed her. She couldn't let her down.

Two weeks…that was all she had and it wasn't anywhere near long enough.

She gave a tiny shiver as she thought of him towering over her the way he had, his eyes aflame with dislike. He was ruthlessness and power personified; he was used to simply paying for any obstacles in his path to be removed and she would be the first to be crushed beneath his well-heeled foot.

She gave a little jump when the telephone rang on the small table beside her and, reaching out a still shaking hand, picked up the receiver and held it to her ear.

'Nina?' Nadia's voice rang out airily. 'I thought I'd call you en route. I'm in Singapore for a couple of hours while the plane refuels.'

'Do you have any idea of what you've done?' Nina choked, clutching at the receiver with both hands.

'I know you don't approve of me leaving Georgia,' Nadia said. 'But quite frankly I don't care. I want—'

'Will you shut up and listen to me?' Nina bit out. 'How could you do that to your own daughter? Not only did you abandon her but you hurt her!'

'Look.' Nadia's tone hardened. 'She was crying for ages while you were out. It drove me nuts.'

Nina's stomach churned at the thought of the abuse happening under her very own roof.

'She's a defenceless child. You were one once; don't you remember what it feels like to be so vulnerable?'

'I don't remember a thing, so drop it, OK?'

Nina sighed with frustration. Her twin was an expert at burying her head when things got tough. There was nothing she could say or do to change the habits of a lifetime. Her sister was damaged and all she could do now was accept it and do what she could to protect Georgia from repeating the pattern in her own life.

'Any news from Andre's people?' Nadia asked as casually as if asking what the afternoon's weather had been like in her absence.

'He came here,' Nina said through clenched teeth.

'Who?'

'You damn well know who!' She felt close to screaming. 'Marc in-your-face Marcello.'

'I thought he might.'

'How can you be so casual about this?' Nina cried. 'He thinks I'm *you,* for God's sake!'

Nadia hooted with laughter. 'Does he really? How amusing.'

'Well, guess what—I'm not laughing,' Nina ground out. 'And you'd better get back here as soon as you can and sort it out.'

'I'm not coming back,' Nadia said determinedly. 'Bryce is expecting me in LA tomorrow. Why don't you just tell him who you are and be done with it?'

Nina whooshed out a breath. 'Because he wants Georgia, that's why.'

'Does he now?' Nadia's sugar-sweet voice grated along Nina's shredded nerves. 'So the photograph did the trick then.'

'What do you mean?'

Nina heard the sound of her sister's long artificial nails tapping a nearby surface as if she was mentally planning something.

'He'll have to pay, of course, but it's where she belongs anyway. Think of how rich she'll be when she comes of age, an entire family of billionaire merchant bankers to call on for a loan or two.'

'I can't believe you can be so unfeeling about this,' Nina said reproachfully. 'Do you know what he means to do?'

'What?' Nadia's tone sounded bored.

'He's forcing me—I mean you—to marry him, which is really me because you've flown the coop and he doesn't realise it, and I'm up to my neck in lies and I don't know if I can face it because I have no idea how to handle men like Marc Marcello and I have work commitments and no childcare and—'

'Whoa!' Nadia interjected. 'Slow down; you lost me at the marriage bit. What do you mean he wants to marry you?'

'Not me—*you!*' Nina shrilled. 'He thinks he's forcing *you* into a paper marriage.'

'A paper marriage?'

'He wants to adopt Georgia and is prepared to marry me—I mean *you*—to do it.'

'And you agreed?' Nadia sounded surprised.

'He didn't really leave me with much choice,' Nina answered resentfully. 'He threatened to expose you as an incompetent mother and you gave him all the evidence he needed by hurting Georgia the way you did. It was just pure luck that he didn't notice—'

'What's he paying you?' Nadia asked.

Nina gritted her teeth at her sister's total lack of remorse. How could Nadia be more concerned about money than her own baby?

'Even if I have to starve I am not taking his money,' she bit out. 'He thinks he can buy me but no way is some overindulged playboy going to—'

'Tell him you've changed your mind,' Nadia said, interrupting her again. 'Tell him you want ten million.'

'*Ten million?*' Nina shrieked. 'I will do no such—'

'Then you're a fool,' Nadia said. 'He's a billionaire, Nina. You can name your price. He'll pay it.'

'No, absolutely not. This marriage thing is bad enough.' She let out a ragged breath and added, 'Besides, I feel sick at the thought of what he's going to do when he finds out he's got the wrong person.'

'Don't tell him.'

'What?' Nina squeaked. 'You expect me to go through with it?'

'You want Georgia, don't you?' Nadia said. 'Here's your chance to keep her with a whole trailer load of money thrown in. In fact, if you play your cards right we could both really scoop up big time on this.'

Nina didn't care too much for her twin's mercenary tone. 'What do you mean?'

Nadia gave a soft little chuckle that sent a river of unease up her spine. 'You are about to marry a billionaire. You will have access to cash, lots and lots of cash. I've been doing some checking up on Bryce and he's not quite in the same league as your Marc. But we can make up for that with some clever accounting on your part once you are married.'

Nina cleared the blockage in her tight throat. 'Nadia, I can't marry Marc Marcello! It wouldn't be legal!'

'Who's going to know?' Nadia asked airily. 'As far as I recall, I didn't tell Andre I had a twin, so his brother is unlikely to ever find out unless you tell him or he sees us together, which is hardly likely as I'm going to be on the other side of the globe. No, the more I think about this the better it sounds. We both stand to benefit. You get to keep Georgia and I get compensated by a regular income provided by your very rich husband.'

Nina felt her stomach drop in panic. 'Nadia, please don't do this to me. I can't marry a man who hates the very air I breathe!'

'He doesn't hate you, he hates me,' Nadia pointed out. 'Anyway, once he gets to know you he might even fancy you, or at least he might if you'd whack on a bit of make-up and something other than a shapeless tracksuit from time to time.'

'I can't afford the sort of scraps of fabric you usually pipe yourself into,' Nina said sourly.

'Come on, Nina. Think about it. This is a chance in a lifetime. You've always wanted to get married and have kids. What are you complaining about?'

'I would have liked to choose the groom for myself, that's what I'm complaining about!' Nina shot back. 'And I wanted a church wedding, not some hole and corner affair at the local registry office.'

'You're such a hopeless romantic. Do you think a marriage has any more hope of survival if it's performed in a church? Come on—get in the real world, Nina. Marrying a billionaire should more than make up for the absence of a dress and veil and the blessing of a priest.'

'Yeah, well, somehow it just doesn't,' she answered. 'I wanted more out of life than a rich husband.'

'You could spend your whole life looking for love like our mother did and, just like her, never find it,' Nadia said. 'If I were you I'd grasp at this with both hands and make the most of it.'

'But I'm not you, am I?' Nina reminded her coolly.

'No.' A hint of amusement entered Nadia's voice again. 'But Marc Marcello doesn't know that, does he?'

CHAPTER FOUR

NINA called in sick at the library the next day in order to sort out childcare arrangements but her efforts were not encouraging. As she didn't have a car, she was limited to using a private centre whose fees were extortionate. She had no choice but to make the booking, hoping that her niece would cope with the change without too much fuss.

The next two days passed without any further contact from Marc. At times Nina wondered if she'd imagined the whole thing, so unreal it seemed, but on the third day a letter arrived, the first page of the thick document informing her that the marriage ceremony would be on July the fifteenth.

She felt her spine buckle in trepidation. It seemed there was no way out. She would have to marry Marc in order to keep Georgia. She would have to continue to deceive him, even though in doing so she was going to be fuelling his hatred even more.

The thought of pretending to be her sister for months, maybe even years on end, terrified her but she couldn't see any alternative. It was incredible to think that a few simple words stood between her and her freedom. If she told him: 'I am not Georgia's mother', the marriage would be called off.

Five words and she would be free.

Five simple words that would grant her instant freedom, but take away her niece—permanently.

As she had more or less expected, there had been no further

contact from Nadia. Nina had tried her mobile repeatedly, but each time the message service informed her the phone was out of service, and the numerous text messages she'd sent went unanswered. As her sister hadn't given her a forwarding address it made it even more impossible for Nina to escape the tight net that was surrounding her minute by minute.

She tossed the letter from Marc aside to respond to Georgia's cries for attention, doing her best to keep her mind away from the thought of being married to a man who hated her so much.

As she came back out to the small sitting room with Georgia tucked close to her, the phone rang and she reached to answer it.

'Nina.' Marc's deep voice sounded in her ear. 'It's Marc.'

'Marc who?' She was back in Nadia's personality as if by simply hearing his smooth as melted chocolate voice an internal switch had flicked back on inside her.

She heard his indrawn breath and mentally congratulated herself for winning this small battle even though she knew he was more than likely to win the war in the end.

'I am quite sure with the reputation you have worked on so assiduously you have doubled up on some names by now,' he drawled insolently.

'Wouldn't you like to know,' she threw back.

'Did you get my letter?'

'Let me see…' She rustled the small collection of bills that had gathered on the table beside her just to irritate him. 'Ah, yes, here it is. It's a pre-nup, isn't it?'

'You surely did not think I would marry you without protecting myself?'

'That depends on what sort of protection you're talking about.'

'This is a business deal, Nina, nothing more and nothing less.'

'Fine by me,' she said. 'As long as you don't try and go back on your word. How do I know if I can trust you?'

There was a brief but tense pause.

Nina imagined him grinding his teeth on the other end in an effort to maintain some sort of politeness and her stomach gave another funny little quiver.

'You will get your allowance as soon as the marriage is conducted and not a second before,' he bit out at last.

'Don't you trust me, Mr Marcello?' She used her sister's tone with relish. 'Do you think I might try and dupe you?'

'I would very much like to see you try,' he challenged her darkly. 'I am sure I do not have to warn you of the consequences if there is any double-dealing on your part.'

Nina couldn't help an inward shiver at the irony of his coolly delivered statement. As far as double-dealing went, hadn't she already dug her own grave?

'By the way,' he said, 'since we are marrying in a matter of days it is hardly appropriate for you to continue to call me by my surname.'

'Marc.' She breathed his name seductively. 'Is that short for Marco?'

'No, it is short for Marc,' he said. 'It is French, like my mother.'

'Do you speak French as well as Italian?'

'Yes, along with several other languages.'

She was privately impressed but wasn't going to acknowledge it to him.

'What about you?' he asked when she didn't immediately respond.

'Me?' She gave a quick snort. 'All that foreign rubbish? No way! English is the universal language, why anyone would bother chattering away in anything else is completely beyond me.'

She was more or less fluent in both his mother's tongue and in Italian, but had decided to keep it to herself. She'd studied languages at both school and tertiary level and enjoyed a certain level of proficiency. But it suited her purpose to let him think her a complete airhead who had nothing better to do than primp and preen to fill the time.

'I have made an appointment with my lawyer to meet us at

my office for us to sign the pre-nuptial agreement. You will also need to bring along your birth certificate so I can arrange the marriage licence,' he said. 'Is ten a.m. tomorrow convenient?'

Nina's heart started to pound with misgivings. Pretending to be her sister had been manageable to begin with, but now she was going to be signing binding documents in the presence of a lawyer. What if she were sent to prison for fraud? What would happen to Georgia then? Just as well she'd told him her real name was Nina, and even more fortunate she was the older twin, for only her name appeared on the document, making no mention of her twin as was the practice at the time. But what if he ever looked at Georgia's birth certificate? Nadia's name was printed there, not hers. How would she be able to explain that?

'Nina?' His deep voice interrupted her quiet panic.

'Sorry.' She hitched her niece a little higher on her hip. 'Georgia was slipping.'

'You are holding her?'

Just then Georgia gave a happy little gurgle as if she were responding to the sound of her uncle's voice.

'Yes,' Nina said, smiling down at her niece. 'I was about to put her back down for a sleep when you called.'

'How is she?'

'She's fine.'

'Does she wake much at night?'

'Once or twice,' she told him. 'But she soon settles back down.'

'Tell me something, Nina.' An indefinable quality entered his voice. 'Do you enjoy being a mother?'

Nina didn't hesitate in responding, 'Of course I do.'

There was a strange little silence.

She wondered if she should have been quite so honest. Perhaps Nadia would have answered completely differently and he was temporarily thrown by the sudden change of character.

'You do not strike me as the maternal type.' His tone was laced with scorn.

'What do I strike you as, Marc?' she asked in her most seductive voice, determined to make amends for her previous lapse in character.

Sitting in his office, Marc sighed, ignoring her last remark. 'I'll pick you up at nine-fifteen tomorrow,' he told her.

'Do you have a baby seat in your car?' she asked.

Marc frowned. He hadn't even thought about those sorts of details.

'I will have one fitted this afternoon.'

'I can catch a bus,' she offered. 'Where is your office?'

'I insist on picking you up.'

'I won't be going with you if your car isn't adequately fitted for carrying a child. It's not safe.'

Marc released his tight breath. 'I will have the seat fitted if it is the last thing I do, all right?'

'Good,' she said. 'Can I trust you on that?'

Marc closed his eyes and counted to ten.

'Marc?'

His eyes sprang open at the sound of his name on her lips. She had such a breathy voice, like a feather stroking along the sensitive skin on the back of his neck.

'Yes…' He cleared his throat. 'You can trust me.'

'I'll see you tomorrow then,' she said into the small silence.

'Yes.' Marc released his suddenly choking tie. 'See you tomorrow.'

The doorbell rang at nine-fifteen the next morning, but Georgia was still crying, as she had done from the moment she'd woken at five a.m.

Nina was getting desperate. She was already aching with tiredness, and the beginning of what promised to be a monumental headache was marshalling at the back of her eyes.

She gently patted Georgia's back as she answered the door, her hair hanging limply around her shoulders and her eyes hollow from lack of sleep.

When she saw the tall imposing figure of Marc Marcello

standing there it was all she could do to stop herself from howling in a similar vein to the small child in her arms.

'Is she sick?' Marc asked, stepping inside.

Nina brushed a long strand of hair out of her face and gave him an agonised look as the door closed behind him. 'I don't know. She's been like this from the moment she woke up.'

Marc took the baby from her, resting his open palm over the baby's forehead to check for a temperature.

'She is warm but not overly so.' He lifted his eyes back to Nina's. 'Has she had a feed?'

Nina shook her head. 'She turned away from it. I've offered it three or four times but she keeps pushing it away.'

'Maybe she needs to see a doctor,' he suggested. 'Who do you usually see?'

Nina looked at him blankly. For the life of her she couldn't think of who Nadia had taken Georgia to for her monthly check-ups, if indeed she had at all.

'I...'

Marc gave her an accusing look. 'You have taken her to a doctor, haven't you?'

'Ah...'

He let out his breath on a hiss of fury. 'This is a small child,' he railed at her. 'She is supposed to have regular jabs and weigh-ins to make sure she is growing to schedule.'

'She's perfectly healthy,' Nina said, wincing as Georgia let out another howl of misery.

Marc raised an accusing brow as the baby continued to cry in his arms. 'You think so?'

Nina bit her lip. 'Maybe she's teething.'

'She is how old? Four months? Isn't that a little early?'

'I don't know! I've never—' She stopped herself from saying the rest. How close she had been to telling him she knew nothing about babies! What sort of mother would he think her?

Marc had turned back to the infant, his strong capable hands stroking along Georgia's back as he held her. After a moment or two the crying subsided to a few soft hiccups and after another minute or two the tiny eyelids fluttered closed.

Nina couldn't help admiring his technique. God knew she'd been up for hours trying to get the baby to settle to no avail. A part of her felt resentful that he'd achieved it instead of her. Another part of her secretly admired him.

'Go and get ready.' Marc spoke to her in a lowered voice so as not to disturb the child. 'We have a few minutes up our sleeves but the traffic at this time of day is always an unknown variable.'

Nina made her way to her room and softly closed the door behind her. She peered into the contents of her wardrobe with dismay. Most of her clothes were either too conservative or out of date. Her work as a librarian didn't require any degree of fashionable attire, and as she'd so often had to bail her sister out of debt she hadn't bought anything new for herself in ages. She had jeans in abundance, mostly cast-offs from Nadia, and a collection of tops, also from Nadia, most of which showed far more than they concealed.

In the end she chose one of Nadia's cast-offs. She was supposed to be her sister so she figured she might as well dress like her, even though she cringed at the thought of showing off so much of her body, especially to someone so discerning of female flesh as Marc Marcello.

Everything about him unsettled her. It wasn't just the fact that he thought her to be her sister, although that in itself was a major stumbling block, especially to her peace of mind, but his whole manner seemed threatening in an overtly male sort of way. Although she was aware that deep down he was acting out of similar motives to her own, she couldn't help feeling on edge around him. She knew some of it probably came from her lack of experience with men; she just didn't know how to manage a man who was so strong, so in control and so determined.

Marc Marcello wasn't exactly the type of man one could ignore. He was the sort of man who was used to being obeyed—insisted on it, in fact.

She sighed a little shakily as she straightened the close-fitting dress. She wished pretending to be her sister was as easy as putting on her twin's clothes: that way she wouldn't feel so nervous all the time in case he saw through her act. She snatched up a cashmere cardigan, slung it casually around her shoulders and made her way out to where Marc was waiting.

He was standing with the baby in his arms, the usually hard lines of his face soft as he gazed down at her sleeping form.

Nina drew in a painful breath at the sight before her. He clearly adored his brother's child and would do anything to protect her, even going so far as to marry a woman he loathed.

Marc turned to look at her and his expression instantly hardened. 'Are you ready?'

She nodded and, scooping up Georgia's changing bag, followed him out of the flat.

The trip to Marc's office was a silent one and Nina was immensely grateful for it. Georgia had finally accepted a bottle and fallen asleep not long after she'd been placed in the baby seat in the back of Marc's showroom-perfect car. Marc himself was concentrating on the thick morning traffic in front of him, his dark unreadable eyes looking straight ahead, his gaze never once veering her way.

Nina inspected her chewed nails for a moment as she considered what lay ahead. What had he told the lawyer about their sudden marriage? Was she supposed to pretend things were normal between them just like any other couple, or had Marc informed his lawyer of the particulars, Georgia of course being the primary one?

She curled her fingers into her palms and drew in a ragged breath.

Five words, she reminded herself. Five words and it could all end right here and now.

Sure, he'd have the power to remove Georgia from her custody, but maybe she'd be able to convince him to let her see her occasionally. Aunts had some sort of rights, didn't they? Not only that, she was also Georgia's godmother, although she'd never really understood why Nadia had bothered with the formality since the last time she had been in church was probably when she had been christened herself.

She sent him a covert glance but his head was turned towards the parking turnstile beneath the office tower he'd turned into, his hand reaching out of the driver's window to swipe his entry card.

The car surged forward as the boom rose and Nina turned back to face the front, not sure she wanted him to see the indecision and guilt written all over her face.

Once they were parked she got out of the car and began fitting the baby carrying pouch to her chest, her fingers almost shaking as she tried to fasten the buckle.

Marc handed Georgia to her, helpfully feeding the infant's legs through the appropriate holes. Nina felt the brush of his hand on her left breast and reared backwards as if he'd touched her with a heated brand.

His eyes met hers, the dark depths of his black gaze glittering with dislike.

'I would advise against any overt displays of distaste for my touch whilst we are in the presence of my lawyer,' he said. 'He believes this to be a normal marriage and I would prefer him to continue to do so in spite of what we both know privately to be true.'

Nina's eyes flashed as she adjusted the baby-carrier straps over her shoulders. 'It's not exactly normal to force someone to marry you.'

He activated the central locking and alarm system on his car before responding. 'You will be more than adequately compensated for your efforts.'

'Isn't the fact that I'm coming here to sign a pre-nuptial agreement going to make him suspicious?' she asked.

'Pre-nuptial agreements are commonplace these days.

Besides, I have shareholders and investors I need to protect, not to mention my father, who started the business from scratch. I will not stand by and watch a money-hungry little whore take half of all we have both worked so hard for if the marriage were to end.'

Although Nina knew everything he said was reasonable under the circumstances, she still felt hurt by his assessment of her motives. She wished he could see through her thin guise to the person she really was, not an opportunistic money-grabbing bed-hopping pleasure seeker, but a young woman who cared deeply for her tiny niece, so deeply, in fact, that she was prepared to marry a complete stranger.

She closed her mouth on her response and followed him into the lift he'd summoned. She stared fixedly at the numbers on the panel rather than look at him, but she was acutely aware of him standing beside her, his broad shoulder not quite touching hers, although she could feel the warmth of his body all the same.

The lift felt too small. Her chest felt too tight. Her legs felt like wet wool instead of toned muscle and bone. Her mind was a mess of disordered thoughts—thoughts of escape, thoughts of telling the truth, thoughts of what would happen if she went along with the lies she'd told, spending the rest of her life waiting for the axe to fall when the truth finally came out, as she knew it most certainly would.

So far she'd been lucky. He hadn't asked for Georgia's birth certificate, but it wouldn't be long before he did, particularly if he intended to formally adopt her. She knew he intended for his father to see his only grandchild, which would mean a trip to Italy. Would it even be legal for her to take Georgia out of the country? What if somebody asked to see the birth certificate and found out she wasn't in fact Georgia's mother? What then?

Suddenly conscious of Marc's probing gaze, she quickly covered her inner disquiet by plastering a vacant smile on her face.

'What are you smirking at?' Marc looked down at her derisively. 'How quickly you are going to work your way through your allowance?'

'That depends on how generous it is,' she tossed back.

Marc rolled his eyes and stabbed at the lift button once more as if to hurry its pace.

'We are not married yet so I would advise against counting your pennies until they have been dispatched,' he growled.

The lift doors sprang open and Nina followed the rigid line of his back as he made his way to his suite of offices.

It gave her a much needed sense of power to see how much she rattled him.

As far as she knew she had never got underneath anyone's skin before; that had always been Nadia's role, and yet the thought of Marc Marcello fighting an unwilling attraction to her was both strangely tantalizing and terrifying. She'd seen the way he'd looked at her when he'd thought she wasn't looking, his dark eyes lingering on her body as if he just couldn't help himself. It made her skin prickle all over in awareness to even think about him seeing her in such a light, let alone ever acting on it.

Her reaction to him totally confused her. She was supposed to hate him for what he was doing but somehow it wasn't quite working. Every time his eyes moved over her she felt as if he was transmitting heat from his body to hers. That brief accidental brush of his hand over her breast had felt like an electric shock, sending her pulse racing and her heart kicking in reaction.

She had to take better control, she mentally chided herself. To fall in love with Marc Marcello was asking for the sort of trouble she could well do without, considering the mess she was already in.

The reception area of Marc's banking empire could leave no one in any doubt of the company's considerable profits, Nina thought a short time later. From the sweeping computer console in the reception area fitted out in shining galaxy black marble, complete with a catwalk perfect receptionist, to the plush ankle-deep carpet on the floor, and the stunning views over the city from every window, it all left one with the impression that the Marcello merchant bank knew how to do business and do it extremely well.

Nina glanced towards a painting hung over the waiting room area, her eyes widening when she realized it wasn't a print but an actual Renoir.

'Mr Marcello,' the receptionist purred at her boss. 'Mr Highgate is waiting for you in the guest lounge adjoining your office.'

Nina's eyebrows rose. Even his lawyer thought the common waiting room beneath him, did he?

'Follow me,' Marc addressed Nina over one shoulder.

Something in her decided right there and then that she wasn't going to be ordered around in front of his staff, and in particular in front of his gorgeous receptionist, who had done nothing but stare at her the whole time she'd been there.

'Hello.' Nina held out her hand across the reception desk. 'I'm Nina, Marc's fiancée. And this is Georgia. She's Marc's niece, you know. Andre's child.'

The receptionist reared away from Nina's outstretched hand as if by touching it she might be fired on the spot.

'I…I thought your name was Nadia,' the young woman finally managed to get out. 'And don't you remember?' She eyeballed Nina accusingly. 'We've met before.'

Nina hadn't even considered the possibility that her sister might have called at the Marcello office tower at some stage in the past.

Her colour came and went as she tried to think of an excuse for not recognising the young woman but her brain felt as if someone had pulled the plug and she was left floundering.

'It was when Marc was in Italy last September,' the receptionist went on, her mouth tight with reproach. 'Andre was in a meeting but you insisted on seeing him.'

Nina was very aware of Marc listening to every word of this exchange and had to think on her feet to find a way out of it without blowing her cover.

Mentally counting back the months she realised Nadia must have come to see Andre well into the pregnancy, possibly as a last attempt to try to force his hand. She lowered her head in a gesture of contrition, her hand idly stroking the back of baby Georgia's head where she was snuggled up against her in the pouch.

'Yes…well, I wasn't really myself back then…hormones, you know…'

The receptionist peered over the console at the sleeping baby, her stern expression instantly softening. 'She's very like Andre, isn't she?'

Nina nodded, deciding it was probably wiser not to respond verbally even if she could have located her voice.

'Hold all my calls please, Katrina,' Marc's deep voice commanded, interrupting the tight little exchange. 'Come on, *cara*, we have some business to see to.'

Cara? Nina disguised her frown just in time. She wasn't sure she could handle him addressing her with Italian endearments. It made her feel as if their relationship was shifting to another level, a level she had no experience in dealing with.

She followed him down the spacious hall where even more priceless artworks were hung in stately array, each one reminding her of the amount of money Marc Marcello had at his fingertips if ever he decided to run her out of town—without Georgia.

'In here.' Marc held the door open for her. 'Take a seat and I will summon Robert Highgate to join us.'

Nina took one of the plush chairs facing the huge desk and, positioning Georgia into a more comfortable position against her, began to look around.

It was a huge office by anyone's standards. It was lined with bookshelves along two walls, the thick volumes rich with both a wealth of knowledge and variety of taste. Unless they were there simply for show, which somehow she seriously doubted, they indicated Marc was a man who read widely, for apart from the obvious financial and legal tomes she could see some recent bestsellers as well as some of the classics she'd read and loved herself.

It gave her a funny feeling to have read the same books as him. It gave her a connection with him she wasn't all that sure she wanted to have.

The door opened behind her and she turned in her seat to see a man of about fifty-five or so enter the room carrying a document folder under one arm. Marc was close behind with one of his impossible-to-read looks on his handsome face.

'*Cara*, this is Robert Highgate. Robert, this is my fiancée, Nina Selbourne.'

Nina began to rise but Robert hurriedly gestured for her to stay where she was on account of the baby nestled against her.

He shook her hand instead and looked down at the sleeping infant, his warm light brown eyes visibly softening.

'What a little treasure. I have two daughters of my own. They are both my life and my daily torture.' He grinned at her meaningfully.

Nina gave him a tentative smile. 'It's not easy being a parent.'

'No, but worth the struggle, I can assure you. My eldest is getting married in a few months; it seems only yesterday she was in ankle socks arguing with her mother over the length of her school uniform.'

Nina gave a somewhat forced little laugh. She had very clear memories of similar scenarios between Nadia and their mother but none of them were particularly amusing. She saw Marc stiffen at the sound of her chuckle, his dark eyes so piercing she had to look away in case he saw more than she wanted him to see.

'Now,' Robert said as he opened the folder on the desk and glanced across at Marc. 'I've drawn up the document the way you suggested but perhaps I should explain it to Nina first?'

'Explain away.' Marc's tone bordered on uninterested.

Nina felt herself shrinking in her seat in embarrassment. She had no real understanding of legal terms and wasn't sure if she'd be signing her life away. Surely the least Marc could do was go through it with her as well?

'As you wish.' Robert opened the file and laid it in front of her. 'Don't be put off by all the legalese, Nina, this is pretty straightforward. This simply states in the event of a divorce you agree to a reasonable settlement but not a division of Marc's total assets.'

Nina did her best to read through the wordy text but it made little if no sense to her. She kept searching the document for Georgia's name, hunting for some sort of clause Marc might have inserted to take the child away from her if the marriage was to fold, but as far as she could make out there was none.

'This bit here states that you will receive an allowance during your marriage.' Robert Highgate pointed to the relevant section.

Nina stared at the figure nominated there and swallowed. 'That seems a little…excessive.' She looked up and caught Marc looking at her strangely. She lowered her gaze to the documents once more, her heart pounding in her chest. She would have to be much more careful in future. Marc wasn't a fool. If he began to suspect he was being duped…

'If you could just sign here.' Robert Highgate indicated the dotted line for her. 'And over here.' He turned the page and she dutifully signed. 'There, that's all right and tight.' He closed the document and bundled it back in its folder as he turned to Marc, who was leaning against the filing cabinet behind his desk, his dark eyes still trained on her.

'May I offer you both my heartiest congratulations on a happy and fulfilling marriage?' Robert said. 'I know these are sad times but much joy can come about in spite of it.' He cleared his throat discreetly and added, 'How is your father, Marc?'

Marc pushed himself away from the filing cabinet. 'He's coping…just.'

Robert Highgate tut-tutted sympathetically, 'A terrible blow, and so soon after your mother.'

'Yes.'

Nina privately thought Marc's one word response spoke volumes. While he showed little emotion on his face, something in his voice suggested to her he was a man who felt deeply for all that. It made her see him in a new light. Not so much a hard-driven businessman who wanted to conquer the world, riding over people obstructing his way, but a man with a need to protect those he loved and felt responsible for.

He would make a wonderful father for Georgia.

The thought slipped into her mind and once in there took hold until she could think of nothing else. Visions of him with Georgia during her first Christmas, her first tooth, her first steps, her first day at school…her first boyfriend…

'What do you think, Nina?' Marc directed his gaze towards her.

Nina stared at him in blank confusion. 'Sorry?'

'Robert suggested we draw up a separate trust file on Georgia. Andre's estate now belongs to her, but until she comes of age—'

She got to her feet in sudden agitation, holding Georgia close to her chest to avoid disturbing her. 'I told you I'm not interested in Andre's estate.'

Marc sent her a quick warning glance but it was too late. Robert Highgate had seen the exchange and was at liberty to make his own conclusions.

'I'll have the necessary papers drawn up,' he informed Marc diplomatically as he reached for the door. 'Again, I wish you both well.'

'Thank you,' Marc said and, turning to Nina with an arch of one brow, prompted, 'Nina?'

She gave the lawyer a wan smile. 'Thank you, Mr Highgate, for explaining everything to me.'

'No problem.' Robert held out his hand and grasped hers firmly. 'You know you're nothing like I thought you'd be, if you don't mind me saying.'

'I—I'm not?' Nina's stomach rolled over. God, had Nadia met him too at some stage?

'No,' Robert said. 'But then you know what those gossip columns are like; they make that stuff up to sell the next magazine.'

Nina's heart instantly sank. She shifted uncomfortably from foot to foot as she tortured herself with images of her scantily clad sister cavorting at God knew which of Sydney's nightclubs in order to have her photo plastered over some seedy gossip page.

She lowered her gaze to the child in her arms and affected a demure pose. 'That's all behind me now. I'm a changed person.'

'I congratulate you for it,' Robert Highgate said. 'Bringing up a child is a very maturing experience. Do you have any family—parents and so on?'

She shook her head, carefully avoiding his eyes. 'No, no family. My father died when I was a baby and my mother died three years ago.'

Marc frowned as he listened to the exchange between his lawyer and his soon-to-be wife. He suddenly realised how little he knew of Nina and her background. He knew she was known to be an unprincipled whore who had made it her life's goal to hunt down a rich husband to set her up for life, but he hadn't known she had grown up without a father and had so recently lost her mother. His own grief reminded him of how devastating losing a parent could be and something inside him shifted a little ground. Yes, she was undoubtedly an opportunist and she sure as hell had driven his brother to his untimely end…but she clearly loved Georgia, which still somehow surprised him.

The door closed behind the lawyer and Georgia began to

grizzle. Nina extracted her from the baby-carrier and, reaching for the nappy bag, looked across at Marc who was standing in a brooding silence behind his desk.

'I think she needs her nappy changed,' she said.

'Would you like me to do it?' he offered.

Nina stared at him in silent horror for a moment. How could she let him change Georgia's nappy with the faint smudge of bruises still on her tiny chest?

'No,' she said flatly.

Something came and went in his eyes and she knew she had offended him. He wanted to be a father to Georgia, a real and involved father who would feed and change a baby without rearing away in distaste as some men would do. But until those bruises were gone she had no choice but to keep him well away from Georgia without the shield of her clothes.

'There is a bathroom two doors down,' he said, moving from behind the desk. 'Do you have what you need with you?'

Nina gave him an imperious look as she held up the well-stocked nappy bag. 'I have done this before, you know.'

Marc didn't answer but he held the door open for her as she stalked past him with her head held high. He watched as she made her way down the corridor to where the bathroom was situated, Georgia snuggled on one of her slim hips, the baby's tiny hands buried in the length of her shiny blonde hair.

His own fingers itched to do the same, to see if it was really as silky as it looked, but with a silent curse he thrust his hands deep into his trouser pockets and let the office door click shut as he went back his desk.

He ignored his chair and instead turned to look out of the window as he had done thousands of times before, but this time he saw nothing of the harbour.

All he could see was a pair of smoky grey eyes.

CHAPTER FIVE

NINA took as long as she could in the bathroom seeing to Georgia's needs. She needed time to think. So much was happening and happening so fast she hadn't had time to get her head into gear.

She felt a fool for not anticipating people such as Marc's receptionist having met her sister previously. And no doubt there would be other people she'd have to pretend she knew. And that little slip about the allowance— Oh, God! Her stomach clenched with tight fingers of fear as she thought of her charade coming unstuck in such a way.

She daredn't even think about Marc's reaction.

He turned from the window when she returned to his office and, in spite of her determination to keep cool and calm under pressure, she couldn't help a tiny flip-flop in her belly at the sheer height and presence of him as he came towards her.

'It has occurred to me that there are quite probably things Georgia needs, such as new clothing or toys,' he said, taking the baby from her with gentle hands. 'I have some time available now, so we could go shopping if you like.'

Nina stared up at him, uncertain of how to answer.

Georgia was in desperate need of clothes as she was growing so fast, but shopping with Marc as if they were any normal couple...?

She lowered her gaze and pretended to be re-sorting the changing bag to avoid looking directly at him as she hunted her brain for some sort of excuse.

'Since your own clothes are designer labels, surely your child is entitled to the same?' A hard edge had crept into his voice.

Nina tensed as she pushed the lid back down on the baby wipes container. She'd picked up one of Nadia's cast-offs thinking it was one of the more conservative of the collection she'd left behind, never dreaming it was actually haute couture.

'This old thing?' she quipped with a disdainful glance down at the cashmere she was wearing.

Marc's mouth curled. 'I suppose you only wear an outfit once before it is thrown to the back of the wardrobe?'

Nina almost laughed at how close he was to describing her sister's attitude to clothes. She could have afforded designer wear herself if she'd been given a dollar for every time she'd picked some discarded article up off the floor after one of Nadia's wild nights out.

She tossed her long hair behind one shoulder and smiled up at him saucily. 'Is it my fault I get bored easily?'

'You know something, Nina Selbourne?' He gave her a cutting look. 'I am almost looking forward to being married to you so I can teach you how to behave. You are the shallowest young woman I have ever had the misfortune to meet. I think it will be a great pleasure to bring you to heel as someone should have done a very long time ago.'

Nina pretended to shudder in trepidation. 'Oh! I am *sooo* scared of you, Mr Marcello.'

His black eyes glittered with contempt. 'If I was not holding Georgia right at this minute I would be tempted to begin lesson one right here and now,' he bit out.

Nina's eyes flashed at him with false bravado. 'You lay one finger on me and you will be the poorer for it.'

'It would be worth it, I can assure you,' he shot back.

'You think?' She tilted her chin at him. 'Your brother certainly thought so.'

Nina knew the only thing that saved her at that point was the fact that Georgia was in his arms. Her tiny starfish hands were clutching at the stark whiteness of his business shirt, her little elfin face looking up at him as if in wonder, her brown-black eyes so like his own with their thick fringe of lashes.

Nina saw the struggle he had to control himself playing out on his features as he stood before her. The line of his mouth was grim, his jaw tight with suppressed anger and his eyes sparking at her as if he wanted to torch her to the ground right then and there.

The intercom on his desk broke the brittle silence.

'Mr Marcello?' Katrina's cheerful tone entered the room like a light being switched on in pitch blackness. 'Your father is on line two.'

Marc handed Georgia back to Nina without meeting her eyes. 'Excuse me.' He turned his back to attend to the call.

Nina reached with one hand for the baby pouch where she'd left it earlier when she heard the first few words of Marc's conversation with his father. Even though he spoke his native tongue rapidly she had studied the language long enough to pick up on the general gist of the exchange.

'Yes,' Marc said. 'I have found a solution. I am marrying her on the fifteenth.'

Nina couldn't hear what his father said in response but she could more or less piece together the rest on Marc's reply.

'No, she insists she does not want any money or anything to do with Andre's estate… I am not sure but I suspect she is trying to butter me up by pretending to be a changed person… Yes, I have arranged an allowance but it will not take her long to work her way through that, I am sure… Yes, I know she is everything that Andre said and more… I know, I know…she is an unprincipled whore…'

Nina had trouble keeping her reaction disguised. She silently fumed and vowed revenge on his insulting assessment of her as she eased Georgia back into the pouch.

'Yes…I know, I will watch my back, and yes…' Marc gave a distinctly male chuckle '…my front as well. *Ciao.*'

Nina smiled guilelessly as she turned back to face him. 'So, where are we going shopping?'

A short time later, as they began trawling the department stores as well as exclusive designer boutiques, Nina had cause to wonder if she had catapulted herself into some sort of shopaholic's dream. Marc's credit card was flashed so many times she thought she was going to go blind with the amount of currency going past her eyes as he bought item after item for his niece. Beautiful clothes, expensive toys, special feeder cups for when she came off her bottle—all were parcelled off to be delivered to his office.

When it was time for Georgia's next feed Marc suggested they go to a quiet café where she could feed the baby whilst they had a coffee and a sandwich.

Nina wished she wasn't starving so she could refuse, but she'd missed breakfast due to Georgia's crying bout and her stomach was letting her know in no uncertain terms it was well and truly time for a pit stop.

They were soon seated in a booth in a café overlooking the lively shopping mall below. The rushing lunchtime crowds and talented buskers performing below added to the high energy of the city.

Georgia's bottle was soon heated and brought back to the table by a young waitress. Once she'd gone, Nina was about to offer her niece the bottle when she caught Marc's dark gaze on her.

'Would you like to feed her?' she found herself asking him.

His dark eyes held hers for a brief moment of silent hesitation.

'Sure, why not?' he finally answered and, standing up, reached across the table to gather Georgia in his arms.

Once he was seated, Nina handed him the bottle and a soft cloth she used to catch any drips. She leaned back in her own seat and watched as he positioned the teat for Georgia's searching mouth.

Seeing the way he held the child set off a funny reaction deep inside Nina's belly, like the sudden unfurling of a tightly wound ball of string. She shifted in her seat and forced herself to look at the menu the waitress had left for their perusal but the words all seemed a blur to her as her thoughts shot off in all directions.

Marc was so at ease handling his niece and she wondered if he had ever wanted children of his own. If so, why was he tying himself to her in a loveless paper marriage?

She knew Italians had a deep sense of family, and the value of children in their lives was high. But surely marrying a stranger, even though she was supposedly the mother of his brother's child, was going a little too far in terms of familial duty?

It had occurred to her that he might annul the marriage at some point in the future and apply for full custody of Georgia. It was an uncomfortable scenario as she knew she wouldn't stand a chance once her true identity became known. She would be seen as a scheming, manipulating liar and no magistrate would hand her niece to her, even for access visits, let alone assign her full or partial custody.

Suddenly her earlier gnawing hunger faded and she pushed the menu away with a slump of her shoulders.

'Not hungry?' Marc's eyes met hers across the table.

'I'll just have coffee.' She shifted her gaze from his. 'Black.'

The waitress came over and took the order from Marc, lingering to hover over the baby who had by now finished her bottle.

'How old is she?' the young girl asked.

'Four months,' Nina answered.

The waitress smiled as she looked between the baby and Marc. 'She's like her daddy, isn't she?'

It was on the tip of Nina's tongue to say that Marc wasn't actually Georgia's father but something stopped her at the last minute.

'Yes,' she said instead, shocked that she hadn't seen it before now.

Georgia did have a look of Marc about her, seemingly more so as each day passed. Her olive colouring was one thing, so too the dark eyes and silky black hair. But she could also see evidence of herself and Nadia in the rosebud mouth and the slightly *retroussé* nose and wondered if he could too.

The waitress bustled off to get their coffee and Nina watched as Marc eased Georgia up against his shoulder, gently patting her tiny back as if he'd done it a hundred times before.

'Have you given any thought to having a child of your own some time in the future?' she asked before she could stop herself.

Marc's expression gave little away but Nina was sure she saw a flicker of regret pass through his dark-as-night eyes before he quickly disguised it.

'No.' He shifted Georgia to his other shoulder. 'I had not planned on marrying and doing the whole family-rearing thing.'

His answer intrigued her. She knew there were plenty of sworn-in life members of bachelordom about the place, but somehow Marc didn't seem the type.

'Was this your father's idea for us to marry?'

His eyes met hers, holding her questioning gaze intently. 'What makes you say that?'

'I…' She fiddled with the edge of the tablecloth, doing her best to avoid the full force of his all-seeing eyes. 'A hunch, I guess. I've heard Italians are pretty big on kids.'

'I suppose that is why you sent him that letter to twist the knife a bit,' he said, leaning forwards on the table so the other diners couldn't hear his harsh accusation. 'Did you ever consider how much you were hurting an elderly man who is already doing his best to cope with unbearable grief?'

Nina wished she could tell him the truth. It hurt so much to have him think so poorly of her when in fact it had been her sister who had acted so unthinkingly.

'No.' She let the edge of the tablecloth go and raised her eyes to his condemning ones. 'No, it was very insensitive of me. I'm sorry.'

Her answer seemed to surprise him. If it had come from Nadia, it would have surprised even her, Nina thought wryly. She couldn't recall a single time when her sister had apologised for anything; 'I'm sorry' just wasn't in her twin's vocabulary.

'Sometimes sorry is not enough,' he said, leaning back again, settling Georgia more comfortably against his shoulder. 'Once the damage is done there is no going back to undo it.'

Nina felt sick at the truth of his curt statement. How much damage had she already done with all the lies she'd been forced to tell on her sister's behalf?

'Yes, I know.' She stared at the salt and pepper shakers standing side by side like small china soldiers on the table in front of her. 'I guess I was so confused at the time… I hardly knew what I was doing.'

There was a small silence broken only by the soft gurgling of Georgia, who had found the breast pocket of Marc's business shirt, her tiny fingers clutching at the fabric in delight.

'You deliberately tried to trap my brother, did you not?' he upbraided her. 'By using the oldest trick in the book.'

She wished she could deny it on Nadia's behalf but knew that too would be yet another lie. Her sister had deliberately set about to snare Andre Marcello by fair means or foul. Nina had been appalled when Nadia had told her of her plan to trap him, casually revealing the way she'd sabotaged a whole box of condoms in order to bring about a pregnancy as if it was all a game, not real life with the potential for irreparable damage to occur. Nina still tortured herself with her own guilt at not being able to talk her sister out of it. Maybe if she'd spent more time with her, had counselled her to think a little further ahead than the next moment of pleasure…

'It was a stupidly impulsive thing to do…' she finally said, her voice low, her eyes downcast. 'I had no idea of how it would backfire on…me.'

Again her answer seemed to surprise him. She chanced a look at him and found his hard accusatory expression had softened slightly as he looked across at her, the child in his arms nestling against him preparatory to sleep.

'There are few of us who get through life without one or two regrets,' he offered.

Nina gave him a rueful smile. 'Don't tell me the great Marc Marcello admits to getting it wrong now and again?'

He held her gaze for a moment before looking down at the child in his arms. 'I have made one or two errors of judgement in the past but I have no intention of ever doing so again.'

Nina wondered if he bore the internal scars of a broken relationship which had made him wary of emotional commitment. The more she thought about it, the more likely it seemed. What better way to take himself out of the game than to marry for convenience, not love? He would be free to liaise with whomever he chose without the pressure of formal commitment due to the piece of paper that would soon be documenting her as his wife.

His wife…

She swallowed a lump of panic as she thought about all such a relationship would entail. Even though he'd stated implacably that the marriage would not be consummated, they would still be living in the same house which would force certain intimacies on them both regardless.

She imagined seeing him in less formal attire, perhaps in sports gear or after a shower with a towel around his waist, his long strong body exposed. Or seeing him unshaven in the morning, his chiselled jaw dark with stubbly growth, the sort of growth that tingled female skin if it brushed up against it…

Nina pulled back from her thoughts with a little jerk in her chair, her guilty glance meeting Marc's questioning one.

'Is something wrong?' he asked.

'No, of course not.'

'You do not seem yourself,' he observed.

'Oh, really?' She gave him one of Nadia's scathing looks. 'And you know me so well after, what is it—' She checked her watch for the date and looked back at him. 'Less than a week?'

'Suffice it to say I am familiar with your type,' he answered smoothly.

'So you think one size fits all?'

His smile was cynically lopsided. 'I have been around long enough to recognise danger when I see it.'

'Danger, eh?' She arranged her lips into a smirk. 'You see me as dangerous? What exactly are you threatened by? My sex appeal?'

His mouth tightened and she knew she'd scored another hit. It struck her as ironic that he was fighting an attraction to her when she was pretending to be someone else. What chance did she stand of him being attracted to her as Nina—the *real* Nina? The Nina without the reputation or the Nina without the baggage? Not to mention the Nina without the designer wardrobe. The Nina who was in very great danger of falling in love with a man who despised the very sight of her.

'Your ego no doubt has had considerable stroking over the years but I refuse to join your band of avid admirers,' he said. 'If you are looking for compliments I am afraid you will have to go elsewhere.'

Nina gave him an arch look. 'But you do find me attractive, don't you? Go on, admit it.'

'I admit nothing.'

She laughed. 'You'll get sand in your eyes if you bury your head too deeply.'

She saw his jaw tighten another notch. 'Women like you think they are irresistible but let me tell you, you are not. Do you think I am so easily swayed by full breasts and pouting lips and come-to-bed eyes?'

She pursed the said pouting lips and affected a super-confident pose. 'I can *feel* your interest from right over here,' she said in a breathy undertone. 'I bet if I slipped my hand under this table and examined the evidence for myself you'd have some serious back-pedalling to do.'

Black eyes met grey in a challenge that rocked Nina to her very core but she was determined not to back down. She held his look with a spirited defiance she hadn't thought herself capable of.

Although he tried to disguise it, she noticed he shifted backwards in his chair as if he didn't trust her not to do exactly as she'd said. Her mind began to wander of its own volition... What would he feel like fully aroused? Would he shudder at the touch of her fingers around his length or would he groan with deep out of control pleasure? And what would his reaction be if her mouth were to close over him, drawing from him a response that would spill his life force out of his body in an explosion of pleasure?

'It's time to leave.' His announcement was curt as he got stiffly to his feet.

Georgia gave a soft rumble of protest about the sudden movement but soon settled back against his chest, her tiny eyelids fluttering closed, her miniature fingers still grasping his breast pocket.

Nina rose with less speed, taking her time to gather up the baby's changing bag and her own handbag, shooting him a glance from across the width of the table.

'Do you think it's worth disturbing her to put her back in the pouch?' she asked.

Marc looked down at the tiny infant against his chest and shook his head. 'No.' He lifted his gaze back to hers. 'I will carry her.' He scooped up the bill the waitress had left and added, 'Is there anything else we need to buy?'

It was the 'we' that really got to her. Seeing him with Georgia cradled so tenderly in his arms, she couldn't help feeling a deep sense of regret over how circumstances had led them both to this. How different things might have been if they had met without the baggage of both of their wayward siblings. If the truth were known they probably had more in common than not. He was the solid dependable type, anyone could see that, and she...well, she was hardly the sleep-around town tart he thought her to be.

If only he knew!

'No.' She carefully avoided his eyes in case he saw the glitter of sudden moisture. 'I think we're more or less done.' She hoisted the changing bag over her shoulder and followed him out of the café with her head well down.

The city streets were so busy as to make conversation both difficult and unnecessary. Nina was glad of the reprieve. Guilt flooded her from every direction. Maybe she should have been firmer with Nadia, should have insisted she stay and face her responsibilities. But then, when had Nadia ever faced anything? Her policy had been to move from one disaster to the next with her twin picking up the pieces behind her. Nina had even done it for their mother in the past, becoming the parent instead of the child in an attempt to provide some level of security for them. Much good it had done in the end, she thought sadly. Her mother had still drunk and drugged herself into an early grave and there had been nothing Nina could do to stop it.

Marc pressed the pedestrian button and flicked a glance down at the silent figure beside him as they waited for the lights to change. 'You are very quiet all of a sudden.'

Nina shook herself out of her mental anguish and sent a vacant smile his way. 'I'm just tired.' She yawned widely. 'Georgia woke me early.' She patted her mouth and forced another smile. 'Kids; who in their right mind would have them?'

Marc was saved a reply by the lights changing. It was clear to him that money was Nina's primary motive and she had targeted the richest man she could and had got on with the business of falling pregnant to him. But it was still somewhat of a mystery to him why she hadn't asked for a whole heap of money when he'd offered her marriage. He'd been expecting her price to be in the millions and yet even the allowance he'd organised for her had seemingly surprised her. And, as for pretending she had no interest in Andre's estate, what possible reason could she have other than to try and fool him into thinking she had somehow changed from a money-hungry pleasure seeker to a woman of high morals?

But he knew Nina was trouble from the top of her shiny head to the soles of her dainty feet. She had a disturbing habit of switching from sultry siren to wide-eyed innocent as if she was deliberately trying to confuse him about who she really was. If Andre hadn't told him how manipulative she was he would sometimes be tempted to think he was dealing with someone else entirely.

He slanted a covert glance her way, instantly noting the line of her slightly anxious brow and the way her small white teeth nibbled at her bottom lip.

He gave a rough inward sigh. Marrying her was going to be the easy part; however, he was starting to think that if he wasn't very careful, keeping his hands off her was going to be something else indeed.

CHAPTER SIX

ONCE Nina was confident there was no trace of Georgia's bruises remaining she arranged to return to work. However, when she made to leave the childcare centre the following day, her tiny niece howled miserably, her little arms reaching out to her from the carer's hold.

'Don't worry, Miss Selbourne,' the childcare worker reassured her. 'She'll settle down once you leave. They all do.'

Nina bit her lip in an agony of indecision. Georgia's little face was bright red, her eyes spilling tears and her desperate wails increasing in volume.

'Maybe I should call work and tell them I can't make it.'

'Of course you shouldn't,' the woman said. 'She'll be fine. I'll take her to look at the toys while you leave. Feel free to phone as soon as you get to work but I am sure you've got nothing to worry about. Come on, Georgia,' she told the child with a smile. 'Let's go and look at the nice teddy bears over here.'

Nina could still hear Georgia's cries as she made her way outside the building, her heart squeezing painfully at the thought of her niece being so upset at the prospect of being abandoned. It made her realise anew how important it was to protect her, for it was obvious the baby considered her to be her primary carer. If Marc were to find out who she really was now, Georgia would be the one to suffer, for Nina felt sure he would evict her from the child's life as soon as he possibly could.

The library was a few blocks away and she walked there with dragging steps, wondering how mothers across the globe dealt with leaving their children in someone else's care.

She loved her job but she loved her niece more. If push came to shove she would have to quit work, swallow her pride and accept the allowance from Marc that his lawyer had arranged in the pre-nuptial agreement.

'Hi, Nina,' Elizabeth Loughton, one of the other librarians, greeted her as soon as she arrived at work. 'Hey, where have you been the last few days? Sheila said you called in sick. Are you OK now?'

Nina placed her bag in the staffroom locker in order to avoid her friend's probing look. 'I'm fine, just a bit tired. It's been one of those weeks.'

'Don't tell me your sister has been giving you trouble again,' Elizabeth said. 'I don't know why you don't tell her where to get off, really I don't. She takes advantage of you so much, no wonder you're not well.' She pursed her lips for a moment, then, moving over to close the staffroom door, turned back and handed Nina a recent edition of a popular gossip magazine. 'I suppose you've already seen this?'

Nina disguised a gulp as she looked down at the magazine article Elizabeth had shown her. There was a photograph of her twin outside one of Sydney's best known hotels, dressed in a revealing dress that left little to the imagination, her arms flung around the necks of two well known football personalities who both had dubious reputations with regard to their treatment of women. The caption hinted that, according to hotel staff sources, last Friday night Nadia and her male escorts had engaged in a drunken noisy threesome upstairs.

'Oh, God.' She shut the magazine and handed it back as they sat down together. 'This is just what I don't need right now.'

'Are you all right?' Elizabeth peered at her in concern.

Nina met her friend's hazel gaze. 'I have to tell you something but you have to promise not to tell anyone else.'

Elizabeth used a finger to zip her lips. 'Mum's the word.'

Nina's mouth twisted wryly. 'That's exactly right. Mum *is* the word you now have to use when referring to me.'

Elizabeth's eyes went out on stalks. 'Oh, my God! You're pregnant?'

Nina rolled her eyes. 'Of course not! No, but I am now acting as Georgia's mother.'

As Nina filled her in on previous events, Elizabeth's face fell in horror.

'Are you completely nuts?' Elizabeth had got to her feet in agitation. 'What the hell are you thinking? This Marc Marcello will eat you alive when he finds out! You could go to prison or something!'

'What else can I do?' Nina asked. 'Georgia needs me. Nadia was going to give her up for adoption but this way I can keep her and give her the love she deserves. It's a small price to pay.'

'A small price?' Elizabeth gaped at her. 'What do you know about this guy?'

Nina couldn't help a tiny smile. 'I know he adores Georgia and she adores him.'

'And what about you?' Elizabeth gave her another probing look. 'What does he feel about you? Does he adore you too?'

'No.' Nina lowered her gaze.

There was a short silence and Nina looked up to see her friend's contemplative gaze trained on her.

'I think I'm starting to get the picture,' Elizabeth said. 'You're in love with him, aren't you?'

'How could I possibly be in love with him?' Nina's eyes darted away once more. 'I hardly know him.'

'You must feel something for him because, knowing you as I do, you would never agree to marry someone if you didn't respect and admire them at the very least.'

Nina thought about it for a moment. Yes, she did respect Marc. In fact, if circumstances were different, he was exactly the sort of man she could come to love. He had qualities she couldn't help admiring. He was fiercely loyal and protective and his sense of family was strong.

'Come on, Nina,' Elizabeth continued. 'I can see it in your eyes. You're halfway there already.'

'You're imagining things.'

'Maybe I am, but I'd watch it if I were you,' Elizabeth cautioned. 'You're not the hard-nosed bitch your sister is. You are going to get yourself seriously hurt if you don't take care.'

'I know what I'm doing,' Nina said. 'Anyway, I don't have a choice. I love Georgia and would do anything to protect her.'

'Sounds like you and that future husband of yours have rather a lot in common, don't you think?' Elizabeth mused as she opened the staffroom door. 'You both want the same thing and are prepared to go to extraordinary lengths to get it.'

Nina didn't answer. She was starting to think it might have been a mistake to tell Elizabeth the truth about her situation. Her friend was seeing things Nina herself had pointedly refused to examine too closely.

She turned to the phone on the wall and quickly called the childcare centre to check on her niece, relieved to hear that Georgia had finally fallen asleep. She hung up the phone and made her way out to the front desk, glad she had something to do other than think about Marc Marcello and how she really felt about him.

Nina had not long returned home with Georgia later that day when the phone rang.

'Nina?' Her sister's voice sounded in her ear. 'Is that you?'

'Who else would it be?' Nina said tersely.

Nadia laughed. 'Well, for a minute there I thought you sounded just like me.'

Nina ground her teeth. 'That is *so* not funny. You do realise that all because of your stupid actions I will be marrying Andre's brother in a matter of days, don't you?'

'Lucky you,' Nadia said. 'I'm sure you'll be more than adequately compensated. A billionaire to call your own.'

'His money means nothing to me,' she bit out.

'Good,' Nadia said. 'Then you won't mind sending it to me.'

'What?' Nina stiffened.

'Come on, Nina. You'll be loaded. We talked about this the other day, remember? I expect you to share your good fortune with me. Besides, we're sisters, twin sisters.'

Nina drew in a breath. 'I am *not* taking his money.'

'Don't be stupid; he's giving it to you in exchange for marriage. You have to take it.'

'I have no intention of doing so.'

'Listen.' Nadia's voice hardened. 'If you don't take it I'll tell him who you really are.'

Nina swallowed, her hand on the receiver growing white-knuckled. 'You can't do that. He'll take Georgia off me.'

'Do you think I care?' Nadia said.

'How can you be so callous?' Nina cried. 'You're her mother, for God's sake!'

'If you don't take the money and give it to me I will tell him how you've deceived him. Somehow I don't think he'll take all that kindly to the news.'

Nina could well believe it, but this wasn't about her at all. It was about Georgia. She loved her niece and couldn't bear the thought of never seeing her again.

She considered going to Marc and telling him the truth before Nadia got the chance but knew in the end it would be pointless. He would simply remove Georgia from her custody, would no doubt be relieved that he didn't have to bind himself to her after all. He would have no regard for her feelings as the child's aunt even if she was to plead with him to allow her a place in Georgia's life.

'I haven't got any money yet,' Nina said. 'The marriage doesn't take place for another few days. Marc told me I won't get the allowance until the ink dries on the marriage certificate.'

'Well, when it does I want you to send me it. All of it. I'll give you my bank details.'

Nina put the phone down a few minutes later, the numbers on the piece of paper in her hand making her feel sick to her stomach.

Her sister had just sold her child.

CHAPTER SEVEN

NINA had not long settled Georgia for the night when the doorbell rang. She didn't have to check through the peephole; she knew it was Marc by the way her skin had started to tingle all over.

She opened the door and stepped aside to allow him to come in, her tone reproving as she said, 'You should have called to say you were going to visit. Georgia's just gone down. I don't want to unsettle her.'

'I am not here to see Georgia right now,' Marc said, closing the door behind him.

Nina tucked a strand of wayward hair behind one ear and did her best to hold his unwavering gaze. 'W-what did you want to see me about?'

'Where were you today?' he asked.

'Um…why do you ask?'

'I called you for hours but you didn't answer.'

'I am allowed to go out, aren't I?' She gave him a hardened look. 'Or is my being a prisoner part of your stipulations?'

'No, but I would prefer it if you would keep me informed of where you and Georgia will be in case I need to contact you. Do you have a mobile phone?'

'Yes, but I don't have it on a lot as it wakes Georgia,' she said half truthfully.

'I have something else I would like to discuss with you,' he added and, reaching into his coat pocket, took out the magazine Elizabeth had shown her that morning.

She took it from him with unsteady fingers and placed it on the coffee table without opening it to the damning page.

'I take it you have already seen it?' he said.

'Yes.'

'And?'

She met his diamond-hard gaze. 'That was more than a week ago. Besides, you know how these magazines like to blow things out of proportion.'

'Did you sleep with those men?'

Nina's stomach quivered at the steely edge to his tone but she forced herself to respond with a steadiness she was nowhere near feeling. 'No.'

'You lying little—' His mouth snapped shut as if he felt tainted by even uttering the rest of the vilifying sentence.

'I am not lying,' she stated quietly.

His jaw tightened and his hands went to fists at his sides. 'I am going to ask you again where you were today and I expect you to tell me the truth.'

'I went to the library.'

'The library?'

She lifted her chin and folded her arms across her chest. 'Yes, it's this really boring place full of books where you have to be quiet all the time. I thought I'd check it out, you know, to improve my mind a bit.'

'You went there all day?' He looked sceptical.

'For a big part of it,' she answered. 'That's why my phone was switched off. What did you do all day?'

'I was working.'

'Oh, really?' She gave him an equally sceptical look. 'Can you prove it?'

He frowned at her. 'I do not have to prove anything to you.'

She tilted her head at him. 'Nor do I to you.'

'If I find out you are lying to me, Nina, you will be very sorry.'

'I don't have to answer to you until we are married,' she said. 'And even then I will not tolerate you bossing me around as if I don't have a mind of my own. Now, if you have finished discussing what you came here to discuss, I think you should leave.'

'I will leave when I am good and ready.' He closed the small distance between them, one of his hands going to the wall at the side of her head, his eyes holding hers as his body pressed close.

Too close.

Nina felt the sharp nudge of desire his sudden closeness evoked, her legs weakening beneath her and her heart thumping erratically behind the wall of her chest. Her breasts seemed to swell as she pressed her back against the wall, the spicy fragrance of his aftershave teasing her nostrils as he leaned even closer.

'P-please go away.' Her voice came out choked.

She felt herself drowning in the fathomless depth of his dark eyes. The silence stretched and stretched until she could hear a faint ringing in her ears. She wondered if he was going to kiss her and her gaze instinctively flicked to his mouth, her heart doing another funny kick-start at the thought of those sensual lips pressed to hers.

Her eyes returned to his and instantly widened as she began to feel the metal of his belt buckle against her stomach and the potent strength of what she could feel was stirring just below. She could feel the energy of his body sending a charge of crackling electricity to hers, making her flesh prickle all over with sensory alertness.

She drew in a shaky breath, her breasts rising and falling against his chest as her heart began to race. His eyes dipped to her mouth, lingering there for endless pulsing seconds before he lifted his hand and traced the contour of her bottom lip with the blunt pad of his thumb, back and forth, slowly, tantalizingly.

Just when she thought she could stand it no longer, he dropped his hand from her mouth and stepped back from her, his expression closing over.

'I will see you tomorrow. What time would be convenient for me to call around?'

It took her several seconds to get her brain back into gear. 'Um…about this time is good. I'll be out all day.'

He gave her a wry look as he reached for the door. 'The library again?'

'Yes…I thought I might read some books to Georgia. It's supposed to be good for language development.'

He looked as if he was going to say something but apparently changed his mind at the last minute. Nina watched as he opened the door and stepped through, casting her one last inscrutable look as he shut it behind him.

She stared at the door while she waited for her heart rate to return to normal.

Elizabeth was right, she thought as she let out a little uneven breath. As far as falling for Marc Marcello went, she was more than halfway there already.

Georgia was even worse the next morning when Nina tried to leave the childcare centre. The pitiful cries shredded her nerves and, even though the assistant was just as reassuring and confident as the day before, Nina felt the full weight of her guilt drag her down as she made her way to the front door, her eyes stinging with the threat of tears.

She didn't see the tall figure leaning against his car near the front entrance until it was too late. She came to a stumbling halt as Marc's shadow blocked out the watery sunlight, her heart leaping towards her throat.

'M-Marc…what are you doing here?'

'I could ask you the very same thing but I already know the answer.' His dark gaze flicked to the childcare signage behind her. 'So this is where you relieve yourself of your responsibilities towards Georgia, no doubt so you can cavort all day with your lovers.'

'No…*no!* It's not like that at all.'

One dark brow rose in cynicism. 'Perhaps you would like to explain to me why you have placed my niece in the care of complete strangers.'

'They're not exactly strangers,' Nina said. 'They're highly competent childcare workers.'

His mouth tightened as he took her by the arm. 'Then we will go and see just how competent they are, shall we?'

Nina had no choice but to follow him for his hold, though loose, was under-wired with steely determination. She could feel the latent strength in his long fingers as they circled her wrist.

It wasn't hard for him to find where Georgia was being looked after. Her cries were echoing throughout the building. As they approached the babies' room Nina felt the tightening of Marc's hold as if his anger was travelling through his body to where it was joined to hers.

'There, there, Georgia,' the childcare assistant was cooing as she cuddled her. 'Mummy will be back later…now, now, don't cry…Oh, hello again, Miss Selbourne,' she said as she turned around. 'I'm afraid your little girl is not settling all that well this morning.'

Nina took Georgia from the woman's arms and the howling stopped immediately, to be replaced by tiny hiccups and sniffles as the baby clung to her.

'That's all right,' Nina said. 'I don't think I will leave her today, after all.'

'We can try again tomorrow, if you like,' the woman suggested. 'As I said the other day, lots of babies find separation from mum hard at first but they soon get used to it.'

'Miss Selbourne will not need your services any more,' Marc announced in clipped tones. 'We have made other arrangements.'

The woman's eyebrows rose slightly and Nina hastily inserted, 'This is my…fiancé, Marc Marcello.'

'Oh…well, then…' The woman gave a slightly flustered smile.

'Come on, *cara*.' Marc took Nina's arm and escorted her to the door.

Nina waited until they were outside before she turned on him crossly. 'You had no right to cancel my arrangements like that!'

He gave her a glowering look as he unlocked his car. 'Your arrangements were putting my niece at risk. Look at her. She has obviously been crying hysterically; she is feverish and over-tired.' He took the baby from her arms and cuddled her close, glaring over the top of her head at Nina. 'I cannot believe you would be so insensitive to leave a clearly distraught baby with total strangers.'

'Oh, for God's sake!' She let out a frustrated breath. 'Get into the real world, Marc. Mothers all over the world put their children into childcare. They need to in order to work.'

'But you do not work so it is not necessary for you to engage such services.' He turned away to secure Georgia in her baby seat in the car.

'How did you know I was here?' she asked after a moment of silence. 'Were you following me?'

He straightened from settling Georgia. 'In the light of that magazine article, I decided it was wise to keep some tabs on you.'

She gnawed at her bottom lip and then began uncertainly, 'Marc…' She tried not to be put off by his stern expression and continued, 'I haven't been completely truthful to you. I…I have a job.'

'What sort of job?'

'One that pays me money.'

'That certainly narrows it down a bit,' he commented dryly. 'What sort of work do you do?'

'I'm a librarian.'

She saw the flicker of surprise come and go in his dark gaze as it held hers. 'Andre did not mention it.'

'Andre didn't know. It's been a…recent thing. I wanted to improve myself…for Georgia's sake.'

'Doesn't one have to study at university in order to be a librarian?'

'Er…yes, I did that a few years ago…before I…you know…went off the rails a bit.'

Nina knew she was skating on ever thinning ice. She could see the suspicion growing in his eyes as he watched her.

'How important is this job to you?' he asked after a small pause.

She looked at the now sleeping baby in her baby seat in the back. 'Not as important as Georgia,' she answered softly.

Marc drew in a breath and opened the passenger door for her. 'Get in. We will talk about this later.'

Nina slipped into the seat and clipped on her belt, all the time wondering if she had blown it. She hoped not, for the thought of never seeing her niece again was unbearably painful.

She spent the rest of the silent journey wondering how she was going to maintain her charade. When she looked up she saw that they were not at her flat but in the driveway of an imposing looking mansion in the exclusive harbourside suburb of Mosman.

She turned in her seat to look at him. 'This is your house?'

He looked at her for so long without responding that she wondered if she had just made another slip. She'd always assumed that Nadia had met Andre in hotels but it suddenly occurred to her that perhaps she had visited him at home—this home.

'Do you not remember coming here?' he asked.

She disguised a nervous swallow. 'It looks vaguely familiar,' she hedged.

The line of his mouth thinned in anger. 'You appear to have

a very convenient memory pattern, Nina. You simply delete the things you find distasteful to recall.' He got out of the car and came around to open her door, his expression still tight with fury. 'Let me remind you, then. You came here the night before Andre was killed, banging on the door and making a general nuisance of yourself. God knows where you had left Georgia. My brother had no choice but to let you in and once inside you tried to seduce him.' His dark eyes glittered dangerously. 'Remember now?'

She opened and closed her mouth, not sure how to answer.

'I could go into more detail if you would like,' he added. 'Or are you starting to remember all by yourself?'

'I don't need you to tell me how dreadfully I behaved,' she said, lowering her gaze. 'I was…upset and lonely, and I didn't know which way to turn.'

Marc watched her in silence, wondering if he was being too harsh. There was so much about her that was confusing. Just when he thought he had her all figured out she would go and do something that would contradict his assessment of her. Lately he had even started to question all his brother had told him, wondering if Andre had deliberately painted a worse picture in order to exonerate himself from any wrongdoing on his part.

Having a baby without the support of the father was undoubtedly a stressful, worrying experience and, although her behaviour had been outrageous, a part of him wanted to find an excuse so that he didn't have to hate her quite so strenuously. It had only been just over four months since she'd given birth; she might even be suffering from some sort of hormonal imbalance and the last thing she needed was the heavy hand of judgement. It intrigued him that she could be so shallow one minute and yet so devoted to her daughter the next. Unless it was all an act for his benefit, he knew he would have a fight on his hands convincing any magistrate she wasn't a fit mother. The truth was, as far as he could tell so far, she was a wonderful mother. The very fact that she had tried to juggle work and childcare in order to provide for her daughter without a handout from him, even though he'd offered it, surely demonstrated that she was keen to turn her bad reputation around.

'It is pointless discussing it now,' he said. 'What is done is done and cannot be undone.'

As they approached the large front door of his house a woman in her late fifties and of Italian descent appeared in its frame. She greeted her employer with deference but the look she cast Nina's way would have curdled milk.

Marc spoke to her in Italian but, to Nina's surprise, he didn't say anything remotely derogatory about her. He simply informed the housekeeper of his plan to marry within the next few days and that Nina and Georgia were to be made as comfortable as possible.

The woman muttered something Nina didn't quite catch and Marc admonished her. 'Yes, Lucia, I do know what I am doing and why I am doing it. You will treat both Nina and Georgia with respect at all times.'

The housekeeper grunted something in reply and sidled away as Marc turned to Nina. 'Just as well you do not understand my language,' he said. 'You have not made a good impression, it seems.'

'No, I imagine not.'

She followed him inside and tried not to look too much in awe of her surroundings, but it was impossible at times not to openly gasp at the priceless works of art which hung from every wall and the plush furnishings that spoke of unlimited wealth.

'I will have Lucia bring us coffee shortly,' Marc informed her as he opened the double doors leading to a formal sitting room. 'But first I would like to speak to you about the arrangements I have made for our marriage.'

Nina followed him into the room, watching as he repositioned Georgia, who was still fast asleep in his arms. He indicated for her to be seated and once she had sunk to the sofa he too sat down, his long legs stretching out in front of him as he tucked Georgia close to his chest.

'I have to go to Hong Kong on business,' he said. 'I will be away until the day before our wedding.'

'I see.'

'I would like you to move in here while I am away to settle Georgia into her new home. Lucia can help you with Georgia so you can continue to work, if that is what you would like to do, although you will need to take some leave of absence, as the day after the wedding we will be leaving for a short trip to Sorrento in Italy to visit my father.'

Nina had to stop herself from springing off the sofa in agitation. She stared at him in shock and consternation. She couldn't leave the country with a child that wasn't hers! And, even if she dared to do so and wasn't stopped, how would she cope with a long-haul flight after what had happened the last time she'd flown? Her flight home from a friend's wedding in Auckland had hit severe turbulence during a storm. It had been the most frightening experience of her life and she had not flown since. The mere thought of boarding a plane made her break out in a sweat, but boarding it with a small child in tow could only be a hundred times worse.

'I—I can't go,' she said. 'I don't like flying.'

'Oh, really?' He gave her one of his cynical looks. 'Is this a recent thing?'

'Yes. I had a bad experience three years ago.'

'But I assume not bad enough to prevent you from flying to Paris last year to hound Andre,' he observed.

Nina had forgotten all about Nadia's trip to Paris.

'I… It comes and goes. The fear, I mean. Sometimes I'm fine, other times I get all panicky.'

'Well, perhaps flying in my private jet with my staff to wait on you will alleviate some of your fears,' he said coolly. 'I will need your and Georgia's passports to make the travel arrangements.'

'I would really prefer not to go.' She got to her feet and began to pace back and forth. 'I have to work.'

'I think in the interests of Georgia you might consider taking leave from work. Most new mothers take a few months off. I am providing you with a generous allowance, so unless you are in particular need of any mental stimulation your job provides, I would suggest taking a break.'

Nina wished she could tell him what to do with his money but unless she went along with Nadia's plan everything she had fought so hard for would be lost.

'What am I supposed to do with my time?' she asked after a moment or two of silence.

'Look after your child,' he answered. 'I do not expect you to do so all on your own, of course. I will help whenever I can and so too will Lucia. She is an experienced mother and grandmother and will do an exemplary job of minding Georgia whenever the need arises.'

'I don't want to live here until absolutely necessary.'

'You have no choice, Nina. I have already contacted your landlord and informed him you will be terminating your lease as of tomorrow.'

'You had no right to do that!'

'I have every right. I will be your husband in a matter of days. I would be failing in my duty to protect both you and Georgia if I did not ensure you were safely housed in my home as we begin our life together.'

'You're only doing it because you don't trust me, so don't insult me by pretending anything else,' she spat.

'You are correct. I do not trust you. As soon as my back is turned, no doubt you will be off with one of your men friends, but this way I get to keep Georgia safe.'

'You make it sound as if I mean to do her harm.'

He held her fiery gaze with equanimity. 'You may not intentionally mean to do so but your erratic, irresponsible behaviour of the past indicates you do not always act in her best interests.'

'It seems I have little choice in all of this. You have organised it all without consulting me.'

'All I have arranged was what we agreed on. We will live as man and wife and jointly raise Georgia until such time as we both feel the marriage is no longer viable.'

'It's not viable now! We hate the sight of each other; what sort of marriage is that going to be?'

There was a knock at the door and the housekeeper came in bearing a tray of coffee and biscotti. Marc exchanged a few words with her and she left with a black look cast in Nina's direction.

'Do not take any notice,' Marc said once the housekeeper had left. 'She had rather a soft spot for my brother.'

'So, like you, she blames me for his death?'

Marc gave her a studied look before responding. 'It is hard sometimes for those who are still grieving to see the other side of the story.' He glanced down at the sleeping infant in his arms and added, 'It cannot have been easy for you, left alone with a child to raise without her father's support.' He lifted his eyes to hers and asked, 'Did you ever consider an abortion?'

'I—I was talked out of it.'

'By whom?'

Nina looked at her hands in her lap. 'By someone who has done her best to support me through my difficult years.'

'A close friend?'

'More than a close friend,' she said. 'More like…a sister.'

There was a small silence.

'I am glad you did not get rid of her, Nina,' he said. 'Georgia is my last link with my brother. Thank you for having her. I know it cannot have been easy, but I cannot tell you how much it will mean to my father to hold Andre's child in his arms.'

Nina gave him a weak smile as she reached for her cup, her stomach fluttering nervously at the thought of how complicated her life had become. Within days she would be married to

Marc Marcello, living with him and jointly raising Georgia as their child.

For now her secret was safe—but how long was it going to be before he realised he had married the wrong woman?

CHAPTER EIGHT

NINA was glad Marc was absent when she and Georgia moved into his house. It was bad enough dealing with the surly housekeeper, who seemed intent on making Nina as unwelcome as possible. Her treatment of Georgia, however, was an entirely different story. Lucia cooed and smiled at the infant with great affection and looked for opportunities to spend time with her alone.

Nina resisted her attempts at first but after a while realised the older woman genuinely cared for Andre's child so she allowed her to watch her once or twice while she attended to unpacking their things into the bedroom and nursery Marc had assigned.

She had handed in her temporary leave notice at work the day after Marc had left and was surprised how much better she felt knowing Georgia would not have to suffer the fear of separation any longer. The baby seemed happier already and, while she kept telling herself she was probably imagining it, Nina couldn't help wondering if Georgia was intuitively aware that she was living in her loving uncle's house and under his protection. Having grown up without a father, Nina knew Georgia would be blessed indeed to have someone as strong and dependable as Marc to nurture her throughout her childhood. It made the sacrifice she was making a little more palatable; her tiny niece would never know the aching sadness of not having a reliable parent to lean on.

* * *

On an impulse she wasn't entirely sure she understood herself, the day before the ceremony Nina withdrew the last of her savings and bought herself a wedding gown and veil. Without a mother or father to help her prepare for the wedding she had dreamt about for most of her life, she decided that no one was going to stop her being a proper bride, even if the marriage itself was just a sham.

She stood twirling in front of the full-length mirror in the boutique's fitting room, the soft organza floating around her like a fluffy cloud while Georgia chortled delightedly in the pushchair beside her.

'So what do you think, Georgia?' she asked as she lowered the veil over her face. 'Do I look like a real bride?'

Georgia began to suck on one of her tiny fists, her black-as-raisins eyes bright with alertness as she peered at her aunt through the cloud of fabric.

'Peek-a-boo!' Nina crouched down and popped back the veil to expose her face to her niece, who began to chuckle again.

She felt a rush of love fill her at the happy sound and, leaning forward, pressed a soft kiss to the baby's downy head, her eyes misting over with sudden emotion.

'One day I hope you will marry a man for all the right reasons, Georgia, a man who will love you to the ends of the earth and back. The way every woman deserves to be loved.'

She straightened and, spreading her voluminous skirts around her, turned to face her reflection in the mirror. The magnolia creamy white of the gown made her eyes a bottomless grey and the tone of her skin like velvet smooth cream. She knew it was quite possibly as close to stunning as she was ever going to get.

Too bad it wouldn't be appreciated, she thought with a little sigh.

* * *

Nina was still settling Georgia for the night when she heard the sound of Marc's car returning, the low growl of the powerful engine as it pulled into the sweeping driveway making her stomach turn over in reaction.

In less than twenty-four hours she would be his wife. She would share his name and his life but not his bed.

She heard him enter the house and the sound of his tread on the marble staircase as he approached the nursery where she stood watching Georgia drift off to sleep.

Marc met her eyes in the soft light. 'Hello.'

'Hi.'

She stepped away from the cot so he could check on his niece but in the small space she felt the brush of his body against hers and her pulse instantly quickened. She stood to one side and watched as he gazed down at Georgia, his features softening as he listened to the snuffling sound of her breathing.

He looked tired, Nina thought. His eyes were slightly blood-shot as if he hadn't slept well for days and his jaw looked as if it hadn't been near a razor for over twenty-four hours. She longed to run her fingers over his face to feel the rough raspy growth through the soft sensitive pads of her fingertips. She wanted to press her lips to the line of his mouth, to make it soften in desire. She wanted to feel him reach for her and...

She jerked away from her wayward thoughts as he turned his head to look at her, his dark gaze tethering hers.

'Is something wrong?'

'No.'

'You look...flustered.'

'I'm not.'

'Have you settled in?'

'Yes.'

'I would like to talk to you about our trip to Italy,' he said, moving across to hold the door of the nursery open for her. 'I will meet you in my study in twenty minutes. I would like to shower and shave first.'

Nina moved past him and made her way downstairs, taking the portable baby monitor with her. Lucia had left for the day so she set a tray with coffee and some cake the housekeeper had baked and carried it through to Marc's study to wait for him.

He came in a short time later, his black hair glistening with dampness, his face cleanly shaven and his casual jeans and long-sleeved close-fitting black T-shirt making Nina's pulse start to race.

'How was your trip?' she asked, disguising her reaction to him by concentrating on the coffee tray.

He took the cup she had handed him, his eyes meeting hers. 'Am I to presume you are rehearsing your role as my wife by serving me coffee and asking me such solicitous questions?'

She turned away from the cynicism she could see in his eyes. 'You can presume what you like. I don't care how your stupid trip went. I was just being polite.'

'Do not exert yourself trying to be polite to me, Nina. It does not suit you.' He took a sip of his coffee but when he met her slightly wounded expression he instantly regretted his terse words. He put the cup down and came across to where she was standing and, taking one of her hands, slowly lifted it to his mouth and pressed a barely there kiss to her fingertips.

She stood transfixed, her heart thudding behind her breast as she held his mesmerizing gaze.

'Why did you do that?' she asked.

'I am not sure,' he answered somewhat gravely. 'To tell you the truth, Nina, I sometimes feel when I am with you that I am dealing with two different people.' He paused for a moment, his dark eyes boring into hers before he added musingly, 'I wonder which one I will be marrying tomorrow.'

Nina pulled her hand out of his and put some distance between them as she tried to stem her rising panic.

'I can't imagine what you mean by that. You make it sound as if I have some sort of multiple personality disorder.'

'My brother told me many things about you but I am at a loss for I do not see any evidence of those things that disturbed him the most.'

'Perhaps I've changed,' she said, deliberately avoiding his eyes. 'People do, you know. Having a child is a very life-changing event.'

'Undoubtedly, but I cannot help thinking there must be more to it than that.'

'W-what do you mean?' She gave him a wary glance, her hands twisting in knots in front of her.

Marc watched the play of emotions on her face, the shadow of worry in her eyes and the way her smooth forehead adopted that slightly anxious look that he found so incredibly engaging. He had spent the whole time he was away thinking about her, wondering what it would be like to sleep with her, to have her long blonde hair splayed over his chest, her slim limbs entwined with his, her body satiated by his. It was as if, knowing she was forbidden to him, his body had decided to crave her relentlessly. He could feel it now, the steady throb of desire pounding through his veins, making him hard just looking at her.

He wanted to hate her, needed to hate her in order to keep her at a distance, but in spite of all his efforts his hatred was slipping away to be replaced by something much more dangerous.

'I sometimes feel as if my brother was talking about someone else entirely. It just does not add up.'

Nina was at a loss to know what to say in response. She thought of chipping back with a Nadia-type retort but couldn't bring herself to do it.

'Have you nothing to say, Nina?' he asked after another long silence.

She lifted her gaze to his, deciding the only way out of this was a complete change of subject. 'You said you wanted to discuss our journey to Italy. When do we leave?'

'We will leave the day after the ceremony. I will get Lucia to pack for you. She will accompany us to help with Georgia.' He reached for his discarded cup and refilled it from the pot before turning back to her. 'I should warn you that my father will not welcome you with open arms. He is an ill man who is still grieving. I will try to protect you from any unnecessary unpleasantness but I cannot guarantee things will be easy.'

'I understand.'

'The ceremony will be conducted at ten a.m. tomorrow,' he said. 'It will be a low-key affair as befits the circumstances.'

Marc watched as she made a movement towards the door as if she couldn't wait to be rid of him. He considered calling her back but thought better of it. It was asking for trouble to spend too much time alone with her. He was already treading a very fine line and it wasn't going to take too much to push him over.

As the door closed softly behind her, he wondered if he was more than halfway there already.

CHAPTER NINE

Marc stood at the foot of the stairs the next morning and watched as Nina came down dressed in full bridal regalia. She gave him a defiant look from beneath her veil as she traversed the last steps.

'You look very nice,' he said, giving her a wry look. 'Going somewhere special?'

She twitched her train out of his way as she moved past him. 'Nowhere special, I just felt like dressing up.'

She was certainly dressed up, Marc thought with an inward frown. She looked absolutely stunning, just as a real bride should look. Why had she done it?

Nina stood silently beside Marc half an hour later as the brief ceremony was performed.

'You may kiss the bride.'

Her eyes widened in alarm at the celebrant's words, her palms sticky with sudden nerves as Marc turned towards her, his hands reaching out to lift the gossamer of her veil from her face.

'I don't think—' Her hastily whispered protest was cut off by the descent of his firm mouth towards hers.

She closed her eyes and did her best not to respond to the feel of his lips moving over hers, but it was hard, if not impossible, to ignore the warmth of his mouth heating her in places she didn't want to be heated. She felt every nuance of his mouth, his firmness against her softness, the way his skin rasped hers as he moved to gain better access.

She could feel her mouth swelling beneath the insistent pressure of his, her tongue moving forward inside her mouth as if seeking the probing warmth of his.

She felt something begin to unfurl deep and low in her belly but before she could identify what it was he lifted his head to look down at her, his dark gaze inscrutable.

She swallowed and turned back to the celebrant, who was smiling at them with indulgent approval.

For better or worse she was now married to Marc Marcello.

The reception was little more than a brief lunch with some of Marc's colleagues at a private function centre and as soon as it was over Nina changed into one of her sister's outfits, a silky sheath of a dress which clung to her rather too lovingly. She stood in front of the mirror in the powder room and tried to adjust the fabric so it didn't reveal too much of her cleavage, all the while doing her best to ignore the nervous flicker of unease in her eyes.

She ran her tongue over her lips experimentally. Her mouth looked the same but it somehow felt different. Her lips felt highly sensitive now, as if the brush of Marc's mouth on hers had triggered something under her skin, making her want more of his touch. Recalling the way his kiss had felt, his warm sensual mouth and the looming threat of his tongue about to slip between her lips, still made her stomach tilt alarmingly. Even now she could imagine how it would feel to have the rough maleness of his tongue searching for hers to mate with, arrogantly, demandingly—devastatingly.

She remonstrated with herself for craving something she could never have. What was wrong with her? What quirk in her personality made her ache for his desire, his approval, for a smile of affection or even a kind word?

She had no right to desire such things, certainly since it had been her own deception that had brought about their marriage. What would he do if he ever found out?

Once she made her way back out to the last of the lingering guests Nina found herself being escorted to where Marc's car was waiting, Georgia already settled in her baby seat in the back.

He drove to his house in Mosman, seemingly content not to engage in conversation during any part of the journey.

Nina used the time to get her head around the fact she was now his wife. His legal wife, she reminded herself with another deep lurch of her stomach. In name only, though. The mental reassurance restored some order to her insides, but then she thought about his kiss and her belly did another somersault.

'I have given Lucia the rest of the day off,' Marc said as he pulled into his driveway. 'There is a meal already prepared for later.'

Nina had never felt less like eating in her life. The thought of being alone with him in the big house with only her tiny niece as chaperon unsettled her terribly.

'I think Georgia needs feeding and changing,' she said once they were at the front door.

Marc held the door open and she slipped past him, holding Georgia like a shield.

'I have a couple of calls to make,' he said. 'Let me know if you need a hand with anything. I will be in my study.'

She was halfway through feeding her niece a little while later when Marc came into the kitchen. She looked up to see he had changed out of his suit and was now dressed in casual trousers and a long-sleeved dark T-shirt which hugged his broad chest, highlighting his superb physical fitness.

Nina tore her eyes away to concentrate on Georgia.

'Would you like me to take over so you can change before dinner?' he asked.

'No, I'm almost done,' she said. 'She doesn't seem all that interested in this anyway.' She put the spoon down and got to her feet, reaching for a cloth to wipe up a spill.

'She looks tired,' Marc observed as Georgia began to rub at her eyes.

'Yes.' Nina twisted the cloth in her hands, lowering her gaze to avoid his studied look.

'Nina…'

She turned away and scrubbed at the bench once more. 'I think I'll give dinner a miss, if you don't mind.' She tossed the cloth in the sink and turned back to reach for Georgia in her baby chair.

Before she could unbuckle the clasp Marc's hand closed over hers and she had no choice but to meet his eyes.

She edged her hand out from under his and straightened to her full height but he still towered over her, his body far too close for her to breathe with any comfort.

'Even if you do not choose to eat I have things I wish to discuss with you,' he said.

'W-what sort of things?'

'Ground rules, that sort of thing. I do not want you under any misapprehensions as to our arrangement.'

'I can't imagine what you mean by that.'

'Can you not?'

'No.'

'Living in the same house will mean we will, by necessity, be sharing a certain level of intimacy. I would not want you to get the wrong idea.'

She elevated her chin and injected her tone with sarcasm. 'Who exactly are you reminding of the terms of our agreement—you or me?'

His eyes hardened a fraction and a tiny nerve began to leap at the side of his mouth as if he was fighting with himself to remain civil.

'From what my brother told me, it appears you do not always play by the rules. It would do you good to remind yourself of them just in case you are tempted to act outside the boundaries I have laid down.'

'While we're speaking of breaking the rules, I thought your kiss was a little inappropriate at the ceremony,' she put in crisply.

His dark eyes hardened as they held hers. 'There will be times when we will be required to keep up appearances.'

'What do you mean?'

'We will have functions to attend occasionally and as my wife you will be expected to act in a certain way towards me.'

'You mean fawn over you?' She gave him a disgusted look.

'I would not have put it quite like that.'

'How would you put it?'

'All I am asking is for you to show some level of maturity when we are in the company of others. Apart from my house-keeper and of course my father, everyone else assumes this is a normal marriage.'

'I'll do my best but I'm not making any promises,' she said.

'Good. As long as we both know where we stand.'

He turned away and left the room, the door swinging shut behind him.

Nina looked down at her niece, who was staring up at her with dark eyes bright and round with interest.

'Men,' she said, scooping her up into her arms. 'Who can work them out?'

Georgia gave her a wide toothless smile.

'Maybe I should try that,' she mused as she cuddled Georgia close. 'It seems to work for you. You only have to look at him and he melts.'

She buried her face in the soft down of the baby's dark hair and sighed.

Once Georgia was asleep later that evening Nina had a shower and changed into one of her comfortable tracksuits. Her damp hair was scraped back in a high ponytail, her face free of make-up and her feet bare.

She was on her way down the stairs when the door of the large lounge opened and Marc stood in its frame, his eyes taking in her casual appearance in a sweeping glance.

'Dressing down for the evening?' he commented wryly.

'One gets so tired of haute couture.' She fabricated a bored yawn, 'Besides, lugging all that expensive material around sapped my energy.'

'You look about fifteen years old.'

'Would you like me to change?' she asked, giving him a direct look.

'No.' He stepped aside to let her in the room. 'You look fine. Great, in fact.'

'Thank you,' she said simply, clutching the small compliment to her gratefully, hoping he wouldn't see how much he had affected her.

'Would you like a drink?' he asked.

'Something soft,' she answered.

'No alcohol?'

'I don't drink.'

He gave her an assessing glance as he handed her a glass of sparkling mineral water. 'A reformed drinker?' he observed. 'How very commendable of you.'

Nina wished she had the courage to toss the contents of her glass into his arrogant face. However, given her sister's behaviour over the last few months, she knew that his opinion, although distasteful, was probably warranted. Nadia had come in far too many times in a state of heavy inebriation for her to be under any illusions about the truth of his comment.

'There are a lot of things I have changed in my life lately,' she said instead.

He took a leisurely sip of his drink before responding. 'Dare I hope Andre's death has made some sort of impact on you to bring about these changes?'

If only he knew how it had impacted on her!

'It would be an insensitive person indeed who wasn't in some way affected by the untimely death of another,' she answered.

'Do you miss him?'

Nina stared into the contents of her glass, wondering how Nadia would respond.

'I try not to think about it,' she said.

'No, of course not,' he said. 'If you thought about it you would have to take some responsibility for it, would you not?'

She kept her eyes down, unwilling to face the venom in his. 'I did not have anything to do with the death of your brother.'

She heard the sharp chink of his glass as he set it back down and stepped backwards instinctively as he came towards her, his eyes narrowed into dark slits of wrath.

'Do you think by saying that enough times it will change what you did?' he asked.

Nina wished she could tell him the truth. The words hovered on her tongue but every time she opened her mouth she thought of Georgia and swiftly closed it again.

'You have guilt written all over you,' he said. 'I can barely look at you without thinking of my brother's final agonising minutes trapped in that car while he bled to death.'

Nina felt sick.

Marc swung away to refill his glass and she took the chance to draw in a ragged breath, her hands twisting in front of her in anguish.

She knew he was still grieving and was entitled to feel the whole spectrum of human emotions, including anger, but it didn't help to have it directed solely at her. She didn't have the hardened exterior of her twin to deal with such heavy criticism. Each time he berated her she felt as if another part of her was dying.

She turned to leave the room.

'Where do you think you are going?' he demanded as he put his own drink aside.

She bit her lip and gestured to the door. 'I think it might be wise to leave you to brood on your own.'

He closed the distance between them in two strides, grasping her upper arms in his strong fingers, his eyes glittering with fury as they clashed with hers.

'You think you can get off that easily? I will not let you escape unscathed. I am going to do everything in my power to make you pay for the destruction you have brought to my family,' he snarled down at her, his fingers tightening cruelly.

Nina did her best to appear unfazed by his anger but beneath the fabric of her tracksuit pants she could already feel the betraying wobble of her legs.

'I hardly see how marriage to me is going to help your cause. Not unless you're going to lock me up in some tower and feed me nothing but bread and water,' she said with a flippancy she was far from feeling.

She felt the bruising strength of his hold as his eyes bored down into hers and, unable to withstand the hatred burning there, she dipped her gaze to the harsh line of his mouth, her tongue snaking out to nervously anoint her lips.

'Damn you!' he growled and hauled her roughly against him, his mouth crashing down on hers for the second time that day.

Nina's gasp of shock and surprise was silenced by the assault. She tried to use her hands to push against the hard wall of his chest but it was impossible to remove that punishing mouth from hers. She was imprisoned by his hold, his body rammed up to hers, imprinting its maleness on the soft feminine curves of her frame.

His kiss became arrogantly intimate, the full thrust of his tongue through the seam of her lips taking all the fight out of her. She felt her legs begin to buckle beneath her and the hands that had pushed him away began curling into the fabric of his T-shirt to keep her upright.

His tongue roved the interior of her mouth in a search and destroy mission that left her floundering in an unfamiliar sea of sensation. She felt the feathering of need run down her spine to render her legs useless, the solid press of his muscled thighs against hers reminding her of his indomitable strength and power.

Her breasts felt heavy and full where they were crushed

against him, her lower body on fire where his hard length probed her blatantly, unashamedly.

He deepened the kiss even further, the pressure of his mouth eliciting a response from her she had not intended giving. She reprimanded herself even as she brushed her tongue along the stabbing length of his: he was the enemy, he was danger—but it did no good. Her body was on automatic pilot and acting independently of her common sense.

Suddenly it was over. He stepped back from her so abruptly that she almost stumbled, her body not quite up to the task of standing without his solid support.

His dark eyes glittered dangerously as he wiped the back of his hand over his mouth in an action that intended to inflict shame and embarrassment.

Nina refused to give him the satisfaction of seeing how close to the mark he'd come. Instead, she schooled her features into contempt and, reaching for a tissue from her sleeve, lifted it to dab at the swollen tenderness of her bottom lip where her tongue had tasted blood.

She saw his eyes follow the movement of her hand and was surprised to see a dull flush slowly ride up over his cheeks.

'Forgive me,' he said heavily. 'I did not intend to go so far as to hurt you.'

She sent him a scathing look as she tucked the tissue away once more. 'How far did you intend to go, enough to double my allowance?'

His mouth hardened. 'I have no intention of handing you anything more than the sum we agreed on. I told you before—our marriage will not be consummated.'

'Fine by me,' she snapped. 'But I suggest you run that past your body for clearance first.' She gave his pelvis a pointed look before returning her eyes to his. 'Somehow I don't think it's quite got the message.'

His eyes locked on to hers, the air between them crackling with palpable tension.

'I would advise you, Nina, not to push me too far. You might not like the consequences.'

She lifted her chin defiantly. 'You'll have to try a little harder if you want to frighten me. Don't forget I'm well used to dealing with ruthless men.'

'I could ruin you,' he reminded her. 'One exclusive from me and even a city as large as this will not be big enough to hide your shame.'

Nina felt the pinpricks of fear at his chilling threat. If only she knew what her sister had been up to she might have been able to call his bluff. But she daredn't risk it, not with Georgia's welfare to consider.

'I hardly see what benefit it will be to you to assassinate the character of the woman you have just married,' she pointed out.

'I will not act on my threat unless your behaviour falls short of the mark.'

'How very gracious of you,' she taunted. 'But what about your behaviour? Does that, too, come under scrutiny?' She touched her fingertip to her bottom lip and gave an exaggerated wince.

'You have my word it will not happen again,' he said, dragging his eyes away from her full mouth. 'Not unless you ask me for it, of course.'

Nina's eyes widened in defiance. 'How absolutely typical! You can't control your impulses so you blame me for inciting them!'

'You were being extremely provocative.'

'Oh, yeah? Well, you were being a complete and utter barbarian!' she threw back. 'It's no wonder your brother had all the ladies after him. Unlike you, he at least had a certain level of finesse.'

She stalked past him towards the door, but before she could open it his hand came from over her shoulder and slammed against the door to keep it shut.

She could feel him behind her, the heat of his body seeping

into hers as surely as if he were touching her again. She kept her gaze fixed on the woodwork in front of her, unwilling for him to see the bright glitter of unshed angry tears in her eyes.

'Let me go, Marc. I want to check on Georgia.' To her dismay her voice sounded defeated, nothing like her usual defiant tone.

His hand left the door to touch her on the shoulder, the gentle but firm pressure turning her to face him.

He was so close she wasn't game enough to draw in a deep breath in case the expansion of her lungs brought her breasts into contact with his chest once more. She raised her eyes to his, doing her level best to control the tremble of her chin as she fought to bring her wayward emotions under control.

'Don't make me hate you any more than I already do,' she said, her voice not much more than a thin whisper of sound.

He held her gaze for so long that Nina felt as if he were seeing right through her flesh to who she was underneath.

To whom she *really* was.

To what she *really* felt.

Just as her composure was threatening to crack he dropped his hand from her shoulder and stepped away from her. She watched in silence as he turned to his discarded drink and, tipping back his head, downed the contents in one deep swallow.

Nina took an unsteady breath and eased herself off the flat plane of the door.

'Marc?'

He turned to look at her, his eyes unreadable as he removed a piece of paper from the pocket of his jeans and silently handed it to her.

She took it with nerveless fingers, unfolding the paper to find it was a bank receipt documenting that several thousand dollars had been deposited in her account that day.

Her allowance.

She stared at it for a long time without speaking, not even noticing when Marc left the room, shutting the door with a soft click behind him.

CHAPTER TEN

NINA had not long returned to her bedroom when she heard her mobile buzzing from inside her bag on the floor. She lifted it out and stiffened when she saw her sister's name flashing on the screen. Lowering her voice to a whisper, she cupped her mouth around the phone and answered it warily. 'Is that you?'

'Of course it's me,' Nadia trilled. 'How soon can you send me the money? I'm in a bit of bother with some bills.'

Nina clenched her teeth. 'What about your boyfriend? Isn't he turning out to be the dream ticket you thought he'd be?'

'Cut it with the sarcasm, Nina. We had an agreement, remember? If you don't follow through I will come and collect Georgia and begin the adoption process and you will never see her again. It's your choice. You can phone bank the money to me right now or you know what will happen. Don't forget, I only have to make one little phone call to that new husband of yours and your secret will be out.'

Nina knew she was caught in an impossible situation. It was too late for explanations to Marc about who she really was. How would he deal with the news of her deception so soon after tying himself to her in order to give Georgia her father's name?

'How did the wedding go, by the way?' Nadia asked with a hint of mockery. 'Was it everything you dreamed of?'

'You know it wasn't,' Nina bit out. 'I felt like a complete fraud the whole time.'

Nadia laughed. 'But not for wearing white, darling. You're one of the few brides entitled to wear virginal white. What a pity your husband doesn't fancy you. I bet I could get him into my bed if the tables were turned.'

Something in her sister's tone irked Nina enough to respond. 'Actually, he does fancy me.'

Nadia's mocking chuckle grated on Nina's nerves. 'Only because he thinks you're me. If you were acting in your own personality he wouldn't take a second look. You're too boring.'

Nina held on to her temper with an effort. 'I don't think it's such a good idea for you to call me. If someone other than me picks up my phone—'

'I'm going to keep calling you until the money is in my account,' Nadia threatened. 'And if I don't get you on this phone I'll try the land line.'

Nina let out a sigh of resignation. 'All right, I'll do it. I will transfer the money.'

'Atta girl,' Nadia cooed. 'I knew you'd see sense in the end. *Ciao!*'

Nina waited until her fingers had stopped shaking before pressing in the necessary digits to process the transaction. Once it was done she did her best to settle for the night but she found it impossible to relax enough to get to sleep. But, strangely enough, it wasn't the money and what she had just done with it that was keeping her awake. No matter how hard she tried, she couldn't get the feel of Marc's mouth out of her mind, the way his tongue had darted with male urgency into the soft recesses of her mouth, making a mockery of every single kiss she'd ever had bestowed upon her in the past.

Marc didn't kiss tentatively or even in an exploratory manner. He kissed with ferocious intent, setting her blood instantly alight. She could still feel the pounding of it as it ran through her veins, making her heart skip as if it just couldn't keep up with the pace of her pulse.

It was impossible to ignore her growing awareness of him,

the way he made her feel when he so much as looked at her with the dark censure of his eyes. She felt her skin rise in re-action every time, the soft hairs at the back of her neck stand-ing to attention as if waiting for his hand to reach out and touch her there.

She couldn't believe her own foolishness. She had fallen in love with a man who had nothing but hatred for her. Even if he found out the truth about who she really was, she knew he would never forgive her for deceiving him. How could he? She wasn't Georgia's mother. She could not give him what he wanted because what he wanted wasn't hers to give.

She gave the pillow another frustrated thump before flopping back down. This was hopeless. What she needed was exercise and plenty of it. She glanced at the bedside clock and grimaced when she saw it was well past midnight. Too late for a walk around the block. Then she thought about the gym and pool downstairs, and her legs were already over the side of the bed when she hesitated.

Could she risk it?

What if Marc heard her?

She rummaged for her faded bathing suit before she could change her mind. A long swim in the heated lap pool was just what she needed. It was a huge house, and besides, Marc was probably already deeply asleep.

She didn't bother with turning on the lights; instead she put the baby monitor remote on top of her towel on one of the com-fortable-looking loungers and slipped into the warm silvery moonlit water.

Her tense muscles began to unfurl as the water held her in its liquid embrace, the slip and slap of the water against the sides of the pool the only sound as she carved her way through length after length.

She stopped to re-tie her loosened hair and, blinking the water out of her eyes, looked up to see a pair of very male tanned legs standing on the pool deck. She slowly lifted her head and locked gazes with Marc.

He stood looking down at her for a long moment while the silence crawled around them.

'What's wrong, Nina?' he asked. 'Are you finding it difficult to get to sleep alone?'

She tilted her chin at him. 'No, are you?'

His eyes dipped to where the water was lapping against her breasts and she felt a shiver of reaction pass through her as if he had just brushed her there with his fingers. She felt her nipples begin to push against the worn Lycra of her bathing suit, the bare skin of her arms and legs prickling in awareness. She tried not to stare at his lean tanned body but it was incredibly difficult to ignore the flat plane of his stomach, the rippling muscles of his abdomen and the dark trail of hair that disappeared into his black shorts.

She craned her neck to maintain eye-contact, her stomach giving a little startled moth-like flutter when he began to lower himself into the water.

'W-what are you doing?' She shrank away.

'What do you think I am doing?' he asked.

She turned to get out but her foot slipped on the steps and she went under instead. She felt Marc's hands on her waist as he steadied her, his body so close behind her she could feel every ridge and plane as she came upright.

The air she desperately needed in order to take her next breath stopped somewhere in the middle of her throat as he slowly turned her around so she was facing him. She could feel the magnetic pull of his body, drawing her closer and closer, even as the rational part of her brain insisted she step out of his hold. His fingers spanning her waist tightened fractionally, and one of his hard muscled thighs came between her trembling ones.

'I don't think this is such a good idea,' she said, hoping he wouldn't notice the nervous up and down movement of her throat.

'What is not a good idea?' he asked, his eyes burning into hers.

'Th-think of what it could cost you...' Her eyes skittered away from his as she felt his hard thigh press even closer.

His hands slid upwards from her waist to hold her shoulders so he could secure her shifting gaze, his voice low and deep as if it had been dragged across gravel. 'Do you think I give a damn about the money?'

She moistened her lips and then wished she hadn't when his gaze dipped to her mouth and lingered there.

'It's a l-lot of money…and if it was doubled…' She stared at the line of his mouth, wondering if he was going to allow himself to kiss her. Just one kiss. That wouldn't be breaking his vow to keep the marriage unconsummated, would it?

His head came down slowly, his mouth stopping a mere breath away from the tingling surface of hers. Her eyelids fluttered closed as she felt herself rock towards him, her body seeking the hard warmth of his like a small iron filing did a too-powerful magnet.

At the first touch of his lips on hers heat licked like a hot tongue of flame, igniting her senses into a blazing roaring fire of need. He plundered her mouth, sending her head snapping back as his tongue thrust determinedly into her moist warmth, his arms pulling her into him where his body pulsed and throbbed.

Her hands went around his neck, her fingers plunging into the thickness of his hair, her breasts tight against his chest, their aching points nothing to the storm that had just erupted between her thighs. She could feel the dampness of need he'd awakened, the silk of sensual desire that called out for him with silent but fragrant pleas.

His hands came to her breasts, shaping them through the worn fabric, his warm palms covering her possessively, his mouth still determined on hers. He pushed the shoulder straps aside and uncovered her, the roughened edge of his fingertips running over her nipples until she ached to feel the rasp of his tongue there as well.

As if she had spoken her need out loud, he lifted his mouth off hers and bent his head to her exposed breasts, moving his mouth and tongue in tightening circles until she became unsteady on her feet.

He came back to her mouth, taking it with renewed pressure as if in tune with the fire of need he was fighting to control.

Her hands slipped down to his waist, her inexpert fingers skating over his shorts where they were distended, his erection reaching towards her, as if seeking her feathering touch.

He groaned into her mouth as she shaped him, and again, even more deeply, when her fingers slipped inside to where he pulsed with increasing urgency.

He tore his mouth off hers and stared down at her, his dark eyes burning with unrelieved need, his chest rising and falling against hers as he struggled to rein in his galloping breath.

'This is exactly what you planned, is it not?' he said through gritted teeth. 'You wanted to make me eat my words, every one of them.'

'No!' Her hands fell away from his body with a little splash. 'No, of course not.'

He gave a rough grunt of derision. 'It's another of your tricks. You like to play the innocent now and again to put me off the scent of your real motives.' He dropped his hold and stepped back from her, his eyes still scorching her with contempt.

'Marc...I—'

'I know what you are up to.' He launched himself out of the pool and turned around to glare down at her. 'You will not rest until you have me begging. That is what you want, isn't it, Nina? Your final triumph in the face of Andre's rejection would be to have his older brother on his knees, offering you anything you want in exchange for your body. That is why you did not ask for payment, isn't it? To make me think you were not after money when in fact you are after so much more.'

'But I'm not after—'

'Get out of my sight,' he barked at her. 'Take your lies and your deceptive little games out of my damn sight!'

Nina got out of the pool with quiet dignity, her sense of pride refusing to allow him to intimidate her with his fury. She could tell he was angrier with himself than with her. Angry that he wanted her in spite of all he'd said to the contrary. But she felt sure this wasn't just about the money, it was about pride—his pride.

'You can't order me about like that,' she said, standing in front of him. 'I won't allow you to.'

Something moved behind his eyes as he stepped towards her again. 'You will not *allow* me to?' he asked with a curl of his lip.

'No,' she said, holding his gaze. 'I won't allow you to speak to me in such a way.'

He drew himself up to his full height, his mouth tightening as he looked down at her. 'Tell me, Nina, how are you going to stop me?'

She moistened her lips, her stomach giving a tiny quiver at the fiery intensity of his gaze. 'I'll think of something.'

He threw his head back and laughed.

Nina pursed her lips and frowned at him. 'You have appalling manners. I suppose it comes from having so much money. You think you can get people to do what you want by writing a cheque or issuing autocratic demands.'

'Well, well, well,' he drawled. 'Look at the pretty little pot telling off the kettle for being black.'

'You know what your trouble is, Marc?' she said, incensed by his attitude. 'You don't like yourself. You keep blaming me for your brother's death but I get this distinct impression that you actually blame yourself. I might be a convenient scapegoat but I will not have you browbeat me to appease your own sense of inadequacy.'

It became instantly obvious to Nina that she'd hit him on a particularly raw nerve. She saw it in the sudden flare of anger in his black eyes and in the tight clench of his hands as he held them by his sides as if he didn't trust himself not to use them against her.

He didn't speak for a long time but his silence was more menacing than any blistering statement could be, she thought as she stood before him defiantly.

'Tell me something, Nina.' He tipped up her chin with one long determined finger. 'Tell me why you fell in love with my brother.'

She froze at his words, her eyes flaring in panic, her heart ramming against her ribcage as she did her best to hold his hard penetrating look.

'You did love him, did you not?' he asked when she didn't answer.

Nina lowered her gaze to concentrate on the beads of moisture still clinging to the strong column of his neck. She couldn't bring herself to tell him yet another lie.

'No,' she said softly. 'I didn't love him.'

Marc's dark eyes narrowed dangerously as her gaze came back to his. 'You callous bitch. You callous little money-hungry bitch.'

She closed her eyes to block out his fury.

'Look at me!' He grasped her arms roughly and gave her a little shake.

Her eyes sprang open in alarm, her stomach twisting with despair at the hatred shining in his.

'You destroyed his life!' His fingers bit into her arms. 'You hunted him down and destroyed him for what? *For what?*' he repeated bitterly.

'Marc, I need to tell you—' she began.

'I do not want to hear anything you have to say,' he snapped, cutting her off.

'Marc, please.' Her eyes misted over and her tone became pleading. 'You don't understand—'

'I understand all right. I understand that you were not happy that Andre left you stranded without money. That is why you twisted the knife by threatening to have Georgia adopted, was it not?' He gave her a disgusted look. 'You never had any intention of giving her up. You were just playing a game to get as much money as you could.'

'I have never wanted money from—'

'Do not lie to me!' he shouted. 'You have played this for all you are worth. Well, I will tell you something, Nina.' He lowered his voice but it was no less threatening. 'You can have your money. All of it. I will double your allowance as of tomorrow.'

She blinked up at him in confusion. 'But—'

'I have changed my mind about our marriage,' he said. 'I've decided we will no longer adhere to the rules I set down.'

'You can't mean that!'

He smiled a chilling smile. 'Why so worried, *cara?* You slept with my brother without loving him. Sleeping with me will not be beyond your capabilities, I'm sure.'

'I don't want to sleep with you!' She wrenched herself out of his hold and stood glaring at him, rubbing her arms where his fingers had been.

'I think we could more or less say I have paid dearly for the privilege,' he pointed out ruthlessly.

'I am not for sale,' she said. 'I don't care how much money you throw at my feet. I will not be bought.'

'You *have* been bought, Nina,' he said. 'You have already pocketed one instalment.'

'I don't want your money, Marc,' she insisted. 'I never wanted it.'

She could tell from his expression that he didn't believe her. His mouth was tight with cynicism and his eyes diamond-hard as they tethered hers.

'If you did not want it then why is it no longer in your account?' he asked.

Nina's eyes flared in anger. *'You checked?'*

He gave a single nod, his expression still unyielding.

'You had no right to do that!' Nina could feel the panic beating like an out of time drum in her chest. If Marc was watching her so closely it wouldn't take him long to find out the truth.

She'd only transferred the money less than an hour or two ago. What if he orchestrated a paper trail of her account to see where the money had been deposited?

'You keep saying you do not want money but what is it you *do* want, Nina?' Marc said, breaking the humming silence.

She couldn't answer. How could she tell him what she really wanted? She wanted him. She wanted him to make her feel alive as a woman. She wanted him to make her feel desirable, irresistible and precious. She wanted to feel him in the throes of uncontrollable passion for her, not for who she was pretending to be, but for her—Nina.

She held her breath as his hands ran down her arms to encircle her wrists.

'Is this what you really want, Nina?' he asked, tugging her up against him. 'Is this what you crave more than money, the thing that I too crave until I cannot think straight for my need of you?'

She moistened her lips with her tongue, her heart doing a fluttery dance in her chest when she saw the way his eyes glittered with purpose.

His head came down, the heat from his mouth storming its way into hers, lighting a fire within her that refused to be banked down. She felt it crawling up her legs to pool in between her thighs, the heavy pulse of her desire for him only fanning the flames even further.

His tongue circled hers sensuously, the thrust and stab movements inciting her responses in a way she had not thought possible. Her teeth nipped at his bottom lip, her tongue delved and her hands clung where they could to hold him to her. She heard him groan, a rough low growl of male primal need that made her feel incredibly feminine and vulnerable and yet strangely powerful at the same time.

She felt herself being carried along on a tide of need so strong she had no way of resisting even if she had wanted to. This scorching physical chemistry had been crackling between them from the very first day and it seemed that, in spite of Marc's determination to resist her, it was becoming clear he was no longer able to do so. The evidence of his desire for her was breathtakingly unmistakable; she could feel his hard male body pressed tightly against her softer one, his mouth working its magic on hers until she was like warmed honey in his arms.

She felt his hands at her bathing suit straps where they had slipped from her shoulders, and then the rush of air as he pulled the material from her like a sloughed skin. Her legs quivered as she stepped out of the pool of wet fabric at her feet, her mouth still locked with his, her heart thudding with the hectic pace of her fevered blood as he pressed her to the nearest cushioned lounger.

He came down on top of her heavily, his legs entrapping hers, his solid weight a welcome burden. She began to claw at his shorts but he shoved her hand away as he dealt with them himself. She gave a breathless gasp of anticipation when she felt him against her, the length and satin strength of him searching for the entry of her body with a desperation she could feel echoing deep within her.

He drove forward with a deep guttural groan which drowned out the sound of her bitten-off cry as he tore through her tender untried flesh. She sucked in a breath and tried not to cry out again as he thrust deeply, but her body resented the intrusion and made it impossible for her to hold back the sound of her discomfort. She gave one short sharp cry, biting down on her lip as soon as it escaped, but it was too late.

Marc stilled his movements and, easing his weight off her, looked down at her, his frown almost closing the space between his dark-as-night eyes.

Tears sprang to her eyes and her teeth sank even further into her bottom lip.

'*Cristo,*' he groaned and rolled off her in one movement.

Nina closed her eyes, her limbs suddenly feeling cold without the warmth of his.

'Nina...I—'

'Please don't say anything.' She scrambled to her feet without looking at him and reached for her towel.

'I am assuming from your reaction that you had rather a difficult delivery with Georgia,' he said, his voice flat and unemotional.

She wound the towel around her body without looking his way.

'Nina?'

'I don't want to talk about it.'

'We have to talk, whether you like it or not. I need to know.'

'What do you need to know?' She turned on him. 'Do you want to hear how Georgia was born after fifteen hours of labour without her father present? How her father refused to acknowledge her existence? Is that what you want to know?'

Marc stared at her, all of his carefully rehearsed accusations fading away.

'You have no right to cast judgement,' she continued. 'Do you have any idea of what it's like to be pregnant and alone? Do you?'

He drew in a breath and let it out on a sigh. 'No, I do not. You are right. I have no right to judge.'

'Georgia needed a father and my...I mean *I* needed someone to help me bring her into the world, but your brother wasn't interested.'

'He had not planned on having a child with you.'

'So what?' she asked. 'Whatever the motive when a child is conceived, it's up to both of the parents to jointly see to its welfare. Besides, accidents can happen.' She gave him a pointed look and added, 'I didn't happen to see you put on a condom just now.'

'I did not...you know...' He let his words trail off, a dull flush riding over his cheeks.

She raised her brows. 'Surely you know better than that? Pre-ejaculatory fluid contains thousands of sperm. You might very well be in exactly the same position as your brother.'

'If I am, I am prepared to meet my responsibilities. If we have conceived a child I will not walk away.'

'Even though you loathe me and can barely stand to look at me?'

He met her gaze without flinching. 'I will put my personal feelings aside if need be.'

Nina felt her heart tighten painfully at his words. He was so unlike his brother, who'd had his fun and had walked away without a backward glance. She knew Marc would stand by his word, even if it cost him dearly. How she wished she could tell him the truth!

She turned away before he could see the longing in her eyes. 'I wouldn't lose any sleep over it. I have no plans to get pregnant.'

'If it were to happen…' He raked a hand through his hair as he considered the prospect. 'You will tell me?'

She met his eyes for a brief moment. 'I would owe you that at the very least.'

His eyes fell away from hers first. 'I will check on Georgia. You should go to bed; you look…exhausted.'

She opened her mouth to deny it but stopped as she realised it was true. 'Thank you,' she said softly and moved towards the door.

'Nina?'

His voice stopped her hand from turning the handle and she slowly turned around to face him. 'Yes?'

His eyes didn't quite meet hers. 'I am sorry.'

Her hand on the doorknob fell away. 'For what?'

He dragged his gaze up to hers with an effort. 'I wish I had known the truth about Georgia's birth.'

She gave him a rueful little grimace and reached for the doorknob again. 'I wish you had, too. You can't imagine how much.'

Marc opened his mouth to call her back but the door closed on her exit, locking him inside with his guilt.

CHAPTER ELEVEN

THE first thing Nina saw when she came down with Georgia the next morning was a personal cheque made out to her lying on the kitchen bench, which was exactly double the allowance he had deposited in the bank the day before.

She wasn't sure whether to be angry or hurt. Was he paying off the bet out of guilt or to insult her even more? She scrunched it up and threw it at the nearest wall only to hear a reproving hiss behind her. She turned to see Lucia looking at her with her usual contempt, her dark eyes going to the ball of paper lying against the wall before coming back to hers.

'Do you wish me to clean that up, *signora*?'

Nina unthinkingly responded in Italian. '*No. Mi scusi.* I will see to it.'

Lucia stared at her, her mouth opening and closing like a fish.

Nina gave her a rueful look. 'I should have told you earlier. I speak and understand Italian.'

'Signore Marcello did not tell me,' Lucia said, her eyes narrowing slightly.

'Signore Marcello doesn't know.'

The housekeeper's dark eyebrows shot upwards. 'You have not told him?'

She shook her head and a little sigh escaped from her lips. 'There's a lot I haven't told him.' She turned to look at Georgia, who was sucking noisily on her fist. 'So very much I haven't told him.'

Nina became conscious of Lucia's lengthy, studied look.

'Signore Marcello told me to tell you that he has some business to see to. He will be home in time for us all to leave for the airport together.'

She gave the woman a faltering smile. '*Grazie,* Lucia.'

'He will be a good husband,' Lucia said after another little pause. 'You must give him time. He is still grieving; he is not himself at all.'

Nina inwardly smiled at the irony of the housekeeper's statement. Marc wasn't the only one who wasn't himself!

'Georgia is such a beautiful baby,' Lucia said, gazing down at the child. 'She has brought joy to Signore Marcello's life.'

Unlike her fake mother, Nina couldn't help thinking as she reached to tickle her niece's tiny fingers. 'She's my world, aren't you, Georgia?' She kissed each little finger in turn.

'You are a wonderful mother,' Lucia said. 'No one could doubt it for a moment.'

Nina looked around in surprise. The housekeeper had been nothing but hostile towards her for days. What had happened to bring about this sudden change?

Lucia's gaze was so intent and watchful that Nina had trouble maintaining eye contact. She looked away guiltily, unable to rid herself of the feeling that Lucia was starting to put some pieces of a rather complicated puzzle together in her head.

'There was a phone call for you while you were in the shower,' Lucia said into the sudden silence.

'Oh?' Nina tensed.

'I did not want the sound of your mobile phone waking Georgia so I answered it.' The housekeeper paused for a single heartbeat and added, 'I hope you do not mind.'

'No.' Nina swallowed. 'No, of course I don't mind.' She forced her voice to remain calm. 'Who...who was it?'

'She did not say, but for a moment I thought it was you. It was uncanny, really. Her voice sounded so similar.'

'Did…she leave a message?' Nina asked, staring at Georgia's starfish hands with fierce intent.

'She said she would call back some other time.'

'*Grazie.*'

There was another small pause.

'Signore Marcello has instructed me to help you pack for your trip.'

'It's all right, Lucia. I can manage. I haven't got much to pack anyway.'

The housekeeper gave her one last thoughtful look before moving away to complete her tasks. 'If I can help you with anything, Signora Marcello, you have only to ask. It will be my pleasure, I assure you.'

'*Grazie,* Lucia.'

Nina waited until the housekeeper had left the room before she released her breath. She sighed as she looked down at the chortling baby, muttering in an undertone, 'I'm in over my head, Georgia, and drowning fast.'

Georgia gave her a toothless grin and stuck her fist back in her mouth.

Marc was well aware of Nina's reluctance to establish eye contact with him as they prepared to leave for the airport later that day. She spoke politely to Lucia and was openly affectionate to Georgia as she settled her into the car, but each time her gaze swung to him it just as quickly shifted away, her cheeks turning a delicate shade of pink.

He slanted his gaze her way as they drove to the airport, frowning when he saw her hands moving restlessly in her lap and her bottom lip being nibbled by her teeth as she stared anxiously, almost fixedly, in front of her.

The memory of the intimacy they had shared the night before gnawed at him constantly, the feel of her body against his,

her soft mouth feeding off his, her flinching cries when he had
gone too deep for her.

He had been so confident he would be able to resist her but
in the end he had not stood a chance. Even though his brother
had walked away from her, Marc knew he was not going to find
doing so as easy as Andre had. In spite of everything he knew
about her, he still couldn't get her out of his mind. His every
waking thought was of her and only her; even his restless slum-
ber was haunted by his out of control need for her.

For years he had actively avoided becoming emotionally entangled with anyone. He didn't like feeling so vulnerable. It
made him uneasy that the power balance had subtly shifted,
leaving him open to the sort of hurt he had sworn he would
never expose himself to again.

He couldn't make her out. If she was truly the sort of woman
his brother had described why was she avoiding his eyes all the
time? Andre had described her as a wanton witch who would
do anything for his money or his attention. But after last night
he was totally confused. It didn't make sense. She'd supposedly had numerous affairs since the birth of Georgia; the papers had been full of her exploits. Yes, he had rushed things a
bit, but she had not given him any indication she wasn't with
him all the way. Unless someone had got their wires very
crossed, the Nina Selbourne he was married to was nothing like
the woman who had pursued and subsequently destroyed his
brother. He was the first to admit that people could change, but
the sort of change Nina had supposedly undergone defied all
reasonable belief.

'I am assuming from your continued silence that you are not
looking forward to the flight,' he said after another lengthy silence.

Nina unlocked her hands and, searching in the bag at her
feet, silently handed him the cheque he'd left that morning, her
eyes communicating her anger.

Marc looked down at the cheque for a moment. Was this
a trick?

He met her resentful gaze. 'I apologised for what happened last night. This trip will become even more unpleasant than it needs to be if you do not accept my remorse.'

'It's not your remorse I won't accept,' she bit out. 'It's your money.'

'I fail to see what you are so angry about. It was a bet, fair and square. I lost it and have paid up accordingly—or perhaps you are regretting settling for such a small amount.' His lip curled slightly. 'Would you like me to treble it to soothe your ire?'

Nina swung her head away from his hateful cynicism, her eyes smarting with angry tears.

'Come now, Nina,' he chided her softly. 'You have been paid for your charms before. Andre told me how much you enjoyed receiving gifts of jewellery and the like for your favours. That is, after all, the universal currency of mistresses. There is no point playing the affronted victim; it is just not you.'

No, Nina thought with a deep pang inside. It certainly wasn't.

A short time later their luggage was checked in and their documentation dealt with efficiently. Nina stood by Marc's side, wondering when the axe of officialdom was going to fall. She'd 'forgotten' Georgia's birth certificate, and if anyone asked for additional papers she was not quite sure what she would do, but to her immense relief no one did. They were waved through as if they were a normal, happily married couple travelling with their small child.

Marc's private jet was nothing like the aircraft Nina had travelled on previously. She settled into the luxurious seat as Marc dealt with Georgia beside her, his staff politely offering assistance and ensuring everything was to their liking.

As the jet taxied along the runway she sat with her fingers curled into her palms, her stomach churning in fear as the roar of gunned engines sent her backwards in her seat as the aircraft lifted off. She squeezed her eyes shut, panic making her skin break out in tiny beads of perspiration.

She felt Marc's hand reach for one of hers, the warm grasp of his long fingers incredibly soothing. She opened her eyes and encountered his deep dark gaze. She gave him a sheepish look and then looked down at their joined hands.

'I know it's silly, but I just can't help it.'

'It is not silly,' he said, giving her fingers a tiny squeeze. 'Close your eyes and try to sleep. Before you know it we will be there.'

She closed her eyes and willed herself to sleep but, as exhausted as she was, it was impossible to ignore Marc sitting so close beside her. She could smell his aftershave and even the fresh fragrance of his newly laundered shirt, and every time he moved in his seat she felt the gentle brush of his muscled arm against hers.

She caught him watching her once or twice, the slightly frowning thoughtful look in his eyes unsettling her deeply. Did he already suspect she wasn't who she had said she was? After last night he must surely be suspicious. She'd seen the same suspicion in Lucia's eyes this morning, the way she had looked at her as if seeing her for the first time.

When they finally arrived at the airport in Naples they were met by a member of the Marcello staff who had a car waiting. As they drove to Sorrento, Nina could pick up bits of the exchange between the driver and Marc.

'How is my father, Guido?'

'He is fading, Signore Marcello. He is living for the moment he sees Andre's child.'

'Yes…' Nina heard Marc's deep sigh, his tone immeasurably sad. 'I know.'

The Villa Marcello was situated a short distance out of Sorrento on top of a cliff overlooking the Bay of Naples, the surrounding hills densely wooded where olives and vines grew lushly along with lemon and orange groves. The villa was not old but it was built in the classical style and beautifully maintained with terraced gardens and cobbled walkways.

Nina looked around in quiet awe. The view across the water was nothing short of breathtaking; in the distance she could make out the shape of the Isle of Capri and the gulf of Positano and the warm summer air was scented with lemons and the salty tang of the sea.

She held Georgia close as Marc led her by the elbow towards the front entrance where another member of staff was chatting animatedly with Lucia, who had gone on ahead.

Lucia moved inside as the small Italian woman she had been speaking to turned and bowed respectfully to her employer.

'*Buon giorno*, Signore Marcello. Your father is waiting for you in the *salon*.'

'*Grazie*, Paloma.'

Paloma's dark eyes slid in Nina's direction but, instead of the frosty reception Nina had been expecting and mentally preparing herself for, the little woman smiled warmly. 'You are very welcome, Signora Marcello. My English is not good but I will try to be of help to you.'

'You are very kind,' Nina responded. '*Grazie.*'

Marc led the way into the *palazzo*, their footsteps echoing on the marble floors. Yet another member of staff was waiting outside the door of the *salon* and opened it as they approached.

Nina stepped into the room two steps behind Marc, her eyes going immediately to the figure seated in a wheelchair next to a large sofa.

'Papa.' Marc bent over his father and kissed both of his cheeks in turn. 'It is good to see you.'

Vito Marcello's thin hands gripped the sides of his chair as Marc brought Nina forward. 'Papa, this is Nina and your grand-child, Georgia.'

Nina held out her hand but the old man ignored it as his gaze
went to the baby perched on her hip. She saw the sheen of moisture in his eyes and the slight tremble of his chin as he reached
out a gnarled hand towards Georgia.

Georgia gurgled and dimpled at him, her tiny hands reaching down to him.

Nina had to fight back her own tears at the sight. She lowered the child to his lap and stepped aside, surreptitiously hunting for a tissue. She caught Marc's penetrating gaze and looked
away, pretending an interest in the view from the window.

'She is so like Andre...and your mother.' Vito spoke in
Italian, his voice husky with feeling.

Nina turned and saw the way Marc's throat moved up and
down as if swallowing the emotion his father's observation had
evoked.

'Yes.'

'For once you have done the right thing, Marc,' his father
went on in his own tongue. 'I know it is not what you want, to
be tied to such a woman, but it will soon be over. I have already
sought legal counsel. When the time comes you will have no
trouble taking the child off her.'

Nina had to fight hard not to reveal her comprehension. She
pretended an interest in the view, her spine stiffening with
anger.

'Papa, there are things we need to discuss, but not now,'
Marc said in a low tone, his gaze flicking to Nina standing rigidly by the window.

Vito's lip curled in derision. 'You think she understands a
word of our conversation? Then you are a fool, Marc. Andre told
me she is an uneducated empty-headed whore. Do not tell me you
doubt it? What has she done to you, talked her way into your bed?'

When Nina turned back around she saw the way Marc's jaw
tightened as a tinge of colour rose over his cheekbones but she
had no other choice than to school her features into a blank
mask when his eyes briefly sought hers.

'Do not forget what she has done!' Vito continued heatedly.

'I have not forgotten,' Marc said, turning back to reach for Georgia. 'It is time for Georgia's bedtime routine. We will leave you to rest before dinner.' He looked towards Nina once more and spoke in English. 'Come, Nina. We will need to settle Georgia and get changed for dinner.'

Nina gave Marc's father a small polite smile as she held out her hand to him. 'It was nice to meet you, Signore Marcello.'

For the second time that evening Vito Marcello ignored her hand.

'Papa?' Marc prompted with a frown down at his father.

Vito made some inaudible comment under his breath and briefly took Nina's hand. 'Thank you for agreeing to bring my granddaughter to see me. I have not much time. She is all we have left of Andre.'

Nina blinked back the moisture gathering at the back of her eyes. 'I am so sorry for what you have suffered.'

Vito pushed himself away in his chair, effectively dismissing her. 'You know nothing of my suffering. Nothing.'

Marc took her elbow and led her away, softly closing the *salon* door on their exit.

'I apologise for my father's rudeness,' he said as they moved towards the huge staircase leading to the upper floors. 'He is still grieving.' He hesitated for a moment before adding, 'I probably do not need to tell you that Andre was his favourite son.'

Nina came to a stop and looked up at him. 'It's all right, Marc. I do understand. This has been a terrible time for you all.'

He gave her a rare smile, tinged with sadness but, for all that, still a smile. 'I sometimes wonder what my mother would have made of you,' he mused.

'Your mother?'

He pointed to a portrait hanging on the mezzanine level a few feet away. 'My mother.'

Nina took the remaining steps to stand in front of a portrait of a beautiful dark-haired, porcelain-skinned petite woman, her soft brown eyes sparkling with exuberant life.

'She's very beautiful.'

'Yes…she was.'

The tone of his voice turned Nina's head around to look at him.

He held her gaze for a heartbeat before saying, 'My father has never forgiven me for leading her to her death.'

Nina made a tiny gasp but no words came out. He looked at her across the top of Georgia's downy head as she buried it into his broad chest, her tiny hands splayed across his shirt. 'I was late. We had arranged to meet but I was late. I called her to tell her to fill in the time until I got there.'

Nina felt her breath bank up in her chest. She could almost sense what was coming, the guilt and the blame that clung like lead weights to one's conscience—what could have been done differently if one had only known.

'She was across the street when she saw me. She waved and called out to me…a motor scooter clipped her as she stepped out.'

'Oh, Marc.'

'She didn't see the other car. Nor did I until it lifted her and tossed her like a rag doll towards me.' He turned back to the portrait and let out a ragged sigh. 'If I had been just a few seconds earlier…'

'No!' She clutched at his arm. 'No, you mustn't think that!'

He extricated himself from her hold, securing his niece against him as he continued up the stairs. 'You cannot change the past, Nina. You, of all people, should know that. We all do things on the spur of the moment that we regret later.'

Nina wished she had an answer at the ready but there was a ringing truth in what he had just said. Her own impulsive actions had already caused her incalculable regret. If only she had told him right from the first moment what was going on, maybe things would not be as they were now. He was a reasonable man, a good man, a man of sound moral principles. If she had only told him that very first day of her fears for Georgia's safety, of her worries about her sister's motives—surely he would not have taken Georgia out of her life without thinking of the impact it would have on her niece?

But it was too late now. She had taken a pathway that had led her to this—a lifetime of deception. She had no choice but to continue in it, the lies and deceit banking up behind her like a tide of inescapable debris that at some point would come pouring over her, weighing her down until she would surely be choked by the brackish filth of it.

'Marc?'

Marc turned to look down at her, his brother's child asleep in his arms. 'Nina, this is my father's last chance for peace. I know this is hard for you…'

'It is not hard for me,' she said, touching him gently on the arm. 'I owe this to the memory of your brother. In another life, in other circumstances, he might have gladly accepted Georgia as his own. The timing was wrong. You have taken on the role as her father. I am…her mother. It is up to us to make her life what it should be.'

'And you are happy with that for now?' he asked.

She looked at the infant cradled in the protective strength of his arms. 'I am happy with that.' A tiny sigh escaped from her lips as she raised her eyes back to his. 'For now.'

A small silence swirled around them for several moments. Nina couldn't tear her eyes away from the lingering pain reflected in his. Coming home had affected him deeply, the rush of memories no doubt reawakening the guilt he felt over his mother's death. Hadn't she experienced the very same pangs? Even though her mother had ultimately been responsible for her own death, Nina still felt as if in some way she had failed her. If only she had tried harder to get her into a clinic or had visited her more often, maybe the outcome would have been different.

'Come.' Marc's deep voice broke the silence. 'Lucia will be waiting to settle Georgia. My father does not like to be kept waiting.'

CHAPTER TWELVE

ONCE Georgia had been fed and bathed, Nina left her in Lucia's care and made her way to the room Paloma had prepared for her.

It was luxuriously furnished, the huge bed dominating the room with its array of brightly coloured pillows and cushions, the floor softly carpeted with priceless antique rugs. There was a large wardrobe and dressing table and two doors, one leading to an *en suite* bathroom, the other to another room which, Paloma had informed her earlier—exchanging a conspiratorial wink with the hovering Lucia as she did so—was Marc's suite.

Nina tore her eyes away from the firmly closed door and moved across the room to the bank of windows, looking out over the majestic slopes of Mount Vesuvius. A slight breeze disturbed the sheer curtains, carrying the scent of orange blossom and honeysuckle into the room.

There was the sound of a knock on the connecting door. She turned and issued the command to come in, her throat drying up when Marc stepped into the room. He was dressed formally, his dinner suit making him appear even taller and more commanding, the whiteness of his shirt highlighting the olive tan of his skin and the darkness of his eyes.

'My father likes to dress for dinner,' he explained. 'Do you have everything you need?'

'Yes.' She pointed to the dress Paloma had laid out earlier.

'I'm sorry, I won't be long. I wanted to make sure Georgia had settled first.'

'I will wait for you in my suite. Knock when you are ready to go down. It will take you a while to find your way around the villa.'

'Thank you.' She waited until he had closed the door behind him before she stepped out of her clothes, wishing she had time for a shower but deciding it wouldn't do to upset Marc's father by turning up late for dinner. She made do with a quick splash at the basin and a touch of subtle make-up, tying her hair up with a clip in a casually arranged knot that revealed the length of her neck. The dress she had packed was one of Nadia's and, while it was very close-fitting, it was elegantly simple, the candy-pink chiffon giving her skin a creamy glow.

She gave the connecting door a tentative knock and held her breath as she heard Marc's footsteps approach.

'Ready?' he asked, his eyes sweeping over her with un-masked approval.

She gave him a small nervous smile. 'Yes.'

The dining room was as sumptuously furnished as the rest of the villa. Crystal chandeliers hung from the high ceiling, and the walls were adorned with priceless works of art as well as several gilt-edged mirrors that made the room seem even larger. The long dining table was set at one end for three people, the best of glass and silverware laid out in elegant style, with a fragrant arrangement of roses as a centrepiece.

Vito Marcello was already seated at the end of the table, his dark brooding gaze boring into Nina as soon as she stepped into the room with Marc by her side.

'You are late, Marc,' he said in Italian, his tone reproving. 'Have you not yet taught your wife how to be punctual?'

Marc held out the chair for Nina as he met his father's scowling look. 'It was not Nina's fault that we are late,' he responded in his father's tongue. 'I had to make several calls. It was I who kept Nina waiting.'

Nina sat down and waited until Marc was seated opposite before sending him a grateful glance. He held her look for a long moment, a small shadow of puzzlement passing through his dark gaze as it rested on her.

Vito muttered something under his breath and reached for his wineglass and took a deep draught of the rich red wine. Nina saw Marc's eyes go to the glass in his father's hand and the almost empty carafe nearby, the small frown between his brows deepening.

'You have a very beautiful house, Signore Marcello,' she said to break the uncomfortable silence.

'It will be Georgia's one day,' Vito answered in English and beckoned to the hovering staff member to refill the carafe. 'That is unless Marc has a son. How about it, Marc?' He switched back to Italian and added insultingly, 'You could take up where Andre left off. I am sure your wife will not mind if you pay her enough. She has opened her legs for many others, why not you?'

Nina drew in a breath, her hands tightening in her lap in anger, her cheeks storming with colour.

'What is between Nina and me is between Nina and me and no other,' Marc said with implacable calm. 'I would prefer it, Papa, if you would refrain from insulting her in my presence. She is, after all, the mother of your only grandchild and surely deserves a modicum of respect.'

Vito's eyes flashed with fury. 'She is the reason your brother is dead! She must be made to pay.'

'How?' Marc asked evenly. 'By taunting her whenever you get the chance? By twisting the knife of guilt all the time like you do to me?'

Nina sat very still.

Vito's glass thumped on the table so heavily that the chandelier above their heads tinkled along with the rest of the glasses on the table. He glared back at his son, his cheeks almost puce and his lips white-tipped.

'It is true, is it not?' Marc continued in the same even tone. 'You have always blamed me for my mother's death because you do not want to face the truth of the role you played in it yourself.'

'You were late.' Vito's words were slurred. 'You killed her by being late!'

'No, Papa,' Marc insisted gently. 'You were the one who was late. Do you remember how I had to wait for you to turn up to sign the rest of the documents on the Milan deal? You had been drinking. I had to wait for you to sober up before you signed.'

Nina watched in anguish as the older man reached for his glass and downed the contents, his chin wobbling as if he was having trouble controlling his emotions.

'It is easy to blame someone else rather than face the pain of the truth,' Marc continued on the tail end of a sigh, his tone gentle. 'Perhaps we are both to blame. I should not have covered up your drinking for as long as I did, but I only did it to protect my mother. I would do differently now that I know the price we all had to pay for my silence.'

Vito pushed himself away from the table and gestured for the young man who had poured the drinks to wheel him from the room.

Marc got to his feet as a mark of respect as his father left. Nina stayed put, her throat raw with emotion at what Marc had had to deal with on top of his own grief.

Marc's eyes met hers across the width of the table. 'I am sorry you had to witness that.'

'It's all right.' She looked down at the table rather than hold his gaze. 'I understand...you have no idea how much.'

There was a stretching silence.

Nina hunted her brain for something to fill it but couldn't think of a thing to say. She was conscious of the weight of Marc's gaze, as if he was trying to solve some puzzle about her that had previously eluded him.

'How long have you spoken my language?' he asked, bringing her startled gaze back to his.

'I…I studied it at school and university.'

'And yet you did not think it necessary to inform me of this?'

'I had my reasons.'

'Yes,' he said with a hint of resentment. 'So you no doubt could hear what was being said about you to use against me later. Is there anything else you have neglected to tell me about yourself that I should know?'

Nina lowered her gaze. 'No.'

She heard him get to his feet, heard his approach, her breath halting when he took her chin between two fingers and turned her head to look at him.

'Why do I get the distinct impression you are lying to me, Nina?'

'I—I don't know,' she answered lamely.

He tilted her chin even further so her skittering gaze had nowhere else to go but lock with his probing one. 'You are an intriguing woman, *cara*,' he said softly, the pad of his thumb stroking along the curve of her bottom lip. 'I wonder what other secrets those grey eyes of yours are hiding from me.'

'Th-there are no secrets.' Her voice came out thinly. 'I don't have any secrets.'

His thumb moved back and forth until Nina couldn't think straight. Her lips were buzzing with the need to feel the hard pressure of his, her breasts already tightening in anticipation of his touch.

He drew her slowly but inexorably to her feet and brought her up close to his body, his hands at her waist, his thighs brushing hers as his head came down.

A soft sigh escaped from her lips into the warm cavern of his mouth as it captured hers, her whole body singing with delight at being in his arms once more. She felt the thrusting probe of his tongue and began to melt inside and out, her legs weakening as she clung to him unashamedly.

His hands slipped from her waist to her hips, bringing her even closer to his pulsing heat. She felt the hard ridge of his erection and stifled a gasp of pleasure when he moved against her.

Marc dragged his mouth off hers and stepped back from her, his eyes glittering with desire. 'I told myself I would not touch you. After last night…'

She was saved from having to respond by the staff coming in with their entrée. She resumed her seat, picked up her water glass and drank deeply, all the time doing her best to avoid Marc's dark watchful eyes.

She was relieved when the meal was finally over. They had eaten most of it in silence, only occasionally exchanging a comment or two over the various dishes that were brought out from time to time.

Marc got to his feet once the last of the plates were cleared and came around to Nina's chair to escort her from the table. She got unsteadily to her feet and took his proffered arm as he led her from the room, while the nerves in her stomach fluttered frantically.

He opened the door of her suite for her and looked down at her, his expression unfathomable. 'I would like you to think about our marriage becoming a real one.'

Nina stared back at him, her heart starting to gallop behind her breast.

'I want what is best for Georgia and, in spite of what my brother told me, I now believe that you do too. That is why I feel it would be best if we conduct ourselves in a normal manner so as to give her the best possible environment in which to grow up. It would not be good for her to be around parents who bicker and snipe at each other all the time.' He gave her a soft smile as he reached out to tuck a loose strand of her hair behind her ear. 'You are still jet-lagged. I will let you sleep in peace. For now.'

She didn't want to sleep in peace! She wanted to sleep with him, but how could she tell him that without revealing her true feelings?

'Go on, *cara,*' he said when she didn't move. 'I am trying to be a gentleman here but you are not making it easy for me.'

'I—I'm not?' She moistened her dry lips.

'No, you are not. I only have to look at you and I want to bury myself inside you. Go now while I still have the strength to resist you.'

Nina turned and went into her room with dragging steps, the door closing softly behind her.

She wasn't so sure she liked the thought of Marc being able to resist her, especially when she had no such strength where he was concerned. But then he wasn't in love with her, she reminded herself painfully. He hated her even though he desired her, but he had decided to put that hatred aside for Georgia's sake. How much more would he hate her if he ever found out who she really was?

CHAPTER THIRTEEN

NINA woke some time during the night with the familiar cramps that had plagued her on and off since puberty, the clawing fingers of pain tearing at her from the inside. She stifled a groan as she dragged herself from bed.

She made her way to the *en suite* bathroom and, after swallowing a couple of painkillers, sat on the edge of the bath, willing them to work before she made her way back to bed.

'Nina?' Marc's voice sounded from just outside the door. 'Are you all right?'

'I'm fine,' she answered.

'I thought I heard you groaning. Are you sick?'

'Not really.'

'Can I get you anything?'

She eased herself off the edge of the bath and opened the door. 'I'm fine. It's nothing I haven't had before.'

Marc frowned as realisation gradually dawned. 'You are having a period?'

'You're off the hook, Marc,' she said as she made to move past him. 'You're not going to be a father; aren't you pleased?'

He caught her wrist on the way past and turned her back to face him. 'You look pale. Are you sure you are all right?'

'Georgia is fast asleep, Marc. You don't have to pretend you are the least bit concerned for my welfare right now.'

'You are living under my family's roof and therefore under my protection,' he said. 'If you are sick you need to tell me.'

She pulled out of his hold. 'I am not sick! I just need to be left alone. Is that so much to ask?' She felt the blur of tears film her eyes and spun around for the door.

Marc caught the back of her over-sized nightwear and, like an elastic band, she bounced back towards him. He turned her around and looked into her streaming eyes, something deep inside him loosening as he saw the betraying wobble of her chin.

He brushed the pad of his thumb across her cheek where a tear was making a crystal pathway, the softness of her skin like velvet beneath his touch.

'You are crying,' he said, his tone sounding surprised.

'You don't say.' She gave a little choked sob and brushed at her eyes with her free hand.

'Why are you crying?'

She lifted her head to look at him. 'Do you have a law against it, Marc? Do I have to ask your permission before I have a good howl?'

'No…I was just asking.'

'I'm crying because I always cry when I have my period,' she sobbed. 'I can't help it. I get overly emotional and start blubbering over the stupidest things.' She blew her nose on the tissue he handed her from the box nearby and continued, 'I didn't mean to wake you. I'm sorry…but I…'

'Hey.' His hand cupped the back of her head and brought it into his chest, his fingers stroking through the silky strands of her hair in soft soothing strokes.

Nina buried her head into his warmth, her cheek pressed against the steady thump of his heart, her arms going around his waist before she could stop them.

'Shh,' he said softly. 'Don't cry.'

His kindness and gentleness only made it worse. Her guilt over all the lies she'd told him assailed her and she sobbed into his chest all the harder.

After a while Marc felt her settle against him, her crying bout over. He stood with her in the circle of his arms, his chin resting on the top of her head, his nostrils filling with the gardenia scent of her hair. He wished he could freeze time and stand here forever with her, holding her close to him, his body silently communicating the love he had been unable to stop himself feeling in spite of her past.

'I'm sorry.' She eased herself away from him and let her arms fall to her sides. 'I've made your shirt wet.'

He looked down at the damp patch and smiled. 'That's all right. I was just about to take it off anyway.'

Nina gave him a little embarrassed glance as her hand fluttered in the door's direction. 'I...I'd better go back to bed. It's late.'

'Nina.' He captured her fluttering hand and brought it up to his mouth, his lips brushing each of her fingertips as his eyes secured hers.

'Marc...I...' She swallowed as his lips closed over her little finger, the rasp of his tongue instantly curling her toes.

'Do not talk, Nina.'

'I don't think we—' She stopped when he pressed a finger to her mouth.

'No talking,' he insisted. 'I have changed my mind. I am taking you to bed, in my room.' He kept his finger on her lips as he continued, 'Not to have sex with you; that can wait. I just want to hold you.'

'W-why?' she asked as soon as his finger moved away from her mouth.

His eyes held hers for seemingly endless seconds before he answered. 'Because when I hold you I forget about my brother. I forget about my grief. I think of nothing except how you feel in my arms.'

She drew in a breath that got caught somewhere in the middle of her chest, her heart squeezing at the honesty in his dark gaze as it rested on her.

'All right.' She lowered her eyes. 'I will sleep with you.'

He led her out of the bathroom, his fingers curling loosely around hers as they walked down the passage to his bedroom, every step she took reminding Nina of every lie she'd told which had paved the pathway to this.

He thought she was Nadia and was attracted to the persona she'd projected, never once suspecting the woman he'd married was a fake, a total lying fake who had no business being in his life, let alone in his bed.

Marc pulled down the covers for her and she slipped between the cool sheets, carefully avoiding his eyes as she curled on her side.

She heard him in the *en suite* bathroom brushing his teeth and a few minutes later the sound of the shower running. She closed her eyes and willed herself to sleep before he joined her but her nerves were on high alert, finely tuned to pick up every single sound he made.

The bathroom door opened. She tightened her eyelids and, keeping herself to the furthest edge of the mattress, held her breath as he approached the bed.

She heard the soft rustle of cotton as he slid the covers back, felt the depression of the mattress as it took his weight and the sound of his small sigh of relief as his head finally met the pillow.

The silence seemed to be creeping towards her from every shadowed corner of the room, curling around her, making it impossible for her to relax enough to sleep. Her legs felt twitchy and uncomfortable and she longed to stretch the tension out of them but didn't want to encounter his long legs in doing so.

She squeezed her eyes shut and tried to count back from a thousand but she'd only got to nine hundred and twenty-seven when she heard Marc turn on the bedside lamp and felt him move towards her.

Her eyes sprang open to see him propped up on one elbow, his mouth tilted as he looked down at her. 'Are you always this restless in bed?' he asked.

'I'm not used to sleeping with—' She stopped mid-sentence as she realised what she'd just said, her cheeks heating from the inside out.

The smile went from his mouth. 'You mean that in the past you loved them and left them? Got the business done and moved on?'

'I wouldn't exactly put it like that.'

Marc wished he could control the tide of jealousy that assailed him every time he thought of her with his brother and God knew how many other men, but it ate at him regardless. He could just imagine how she had flitted from bed to bed on her hunt for the highest bidder. Hadn't his own experience with women taught him that in the past? Money was the biggest aphrodisiac for mercenary women and, although Nina was giving an Oscar-winning performance as a wide-eyed innocent, he had to remember it was an act, and it wasn't likely to last.

'How exactly would you put it?' he asked, unable to remove the contempt from his tone.

She moistened her lips and stared at the pulse beating in his neck rather than meet his eyes. 'I don't want to argue with you. I'm tired and it will only make things worse.'

'Did you ever spend a whole night with my brother or did you just service him and leave as quickly as you could?'

Nina flinched at his blunt crudity, her anger rising steadily within her. Her sister was promiscuous, yes, but she sure as hell wasn't a prostitute and she resented him implying it.

'That's a despicable thing to say,' she bit out.

'Did you ever spend a full night with him?' he asked again.

'It's none of your business.' She shut her eyes again and turned her back.

His hand came down on her shoulder and turned her over in one swift movement, his expression grimly determined as he held her gaze. 'Did he ever pay you for sex?'

'What do you think?' she said with a challenging edge to

her tone. 'You're the one who thinks he knows me better than Andre ever did. Do *you* think I would do something like that?'

Marc wanted to believe her incapable of such behaviour but everything his brother had said proclaimed her guilt. Besides, the allowance he had given her had disappeared almost as soon as it had been deposited.

After a tense moment that seemed like forever, he released her. He twisted round to snap off the bedside light and lay back down and closed his eyes, wishing he could wake up in the morning to find that the woman he had come to care for was someone else instead of the woman who had destroyed his brother's life.

'Marc?' Nina whispered in the darkness a few minutes later, but there was no answer except the deep even breathing indicating he had fallen asleep.

She flopped on her back and stared at the ceiling. If only she could fall asleep so easily, she thought with a touch of resentment. Her conscience was very likely to keep her awake for the rest of her life.

Some time during the early hours of the morning Nina became aware of strong arms holding her, the warmth of a large body behind her making her feel safe in a way she'd never felt before.

She moved one of her legs and felt the springy hair of Marc's legs where they lay entwined with hers. He mumbled something in his sleep and his hold tightened a fraction, one of his hands gently cupping her breast through her thin cotton nightshift.

She closed her eyes and tried to go back to sleep but it was impossible to ignore the heated probe of his growing arousal at her back. She felt it swelling against her, the heat coming off his body melting her like chocolate beneath a blowtorch. She felt her own body responding, the tightening of her breasts, the clench of her stomach muscles and the feathering feeling stirring between her thighs.

She drew in an unsteady breath as he began to nuzzle her neck, his mouth playing further havoc with her senses.

'Mmm,' he murmured against her skin, the movement of his mouth tickling her. 'You taste wonderful.'

'I—I do?' She gave a tiny shiver as his tongue unfolded in her ear.

'Mmm.' His mouth moved towards hers, hovering just above, the movement of air when he spoke caressing her lips. *'Delizioso.'*

She shut her eyes as he closed the distance, the soft press of his mouth on hers sending her back into the mattress with a deep sigh of pleasure. It was unlike all of his previous kisses in that it was slow and drugging, no hint of urgency, although no less tantalizing. She felt the slow melt of her bones in his loose embrace, the way her spine softened where it lay against the mattress, her legs gently tethered by the length and strength of his.

His kiss deepened with the soft stroke of his tongue, the sensuous movement sending shooting arrows of need to her core. She could feel her body clamouring for more, his pace two steps behind her need of him. She groaned against his mouth as he sent a hand to the soft swell of her hip, the splay of his fingers drawing her inexorably closer to where his erection pulsed with thick, passion-charged blood.

'I want you so badly,' he said against her mouth. 'I do not think I have ever wanted someone so much.'

She sucked in a breath as he lifted the hem of her nightshift, the slow glide of his hand up the length of her thigh instantly reminding her of why she was in his bed in the first place.

'I can't.' She captured his hand to stall him, an apology in her eyes as she met his. 'My period, remember?'

He looked at her for a long moment, his eyes so dark she felt herself drowning in their midnight depths.

'I did not have you picked as coy about such things,' he said at last. 'It is terribly old-fashioned to be so squeamish about a perfectly normal bodily function.'

'I know. I'm sorry.'

'You have been doing a lot of apologising just lately.' He gave her a wry smile. 'Is there anything else you need to get off your chest while you are at it?'

Nina's eyes skittered away from his, her cheeks instantly growing warm. 'No! No, of course not.'

'Just asking.' He brushed a strand of hair away from her mouth with a gentle touch which brought her troubled gaze back to his as he'd intended. 'Sometimes, Nina, I think you are holding something back from me. Something important.'

He watched her throat move up and down in a small swallow, the nervous shadow moving behind her grey eyes another indication of her increasing uneasiness around him.

'What could I possibly be hiding?'

'I don't know.' He watched the play of emotions flitting across her face. 'I have been trying to work out who the real Nina is but I keep drawing a blank.'

'I find it hard to be myself around you,' she said, absently plucking at the sheet with her fingers.

'Why?' he asked. 'Because of my brother?'

No, because of my sister, she wanted to say, but couldn't.

'You've been so angry at me all the time,' she said instead. 'I'm not used to dealing with such a barrage of negative emotion.'

She heard him release a heavy sigh. 'You are right. Andre's death on the top of my mother's knocked me sideways. I have not been myself for ages; sometimes I wonder if I ever will be again. But I meant what I said about a truce for Georgia's sake.'

She lifted her eyes to his, her expression soft with empathy. 'I do understand, you know.'

He gave her a twisted smile. 'Yes, I suppose you do. You lost him as well and, even though you say you did not love him, when all is said and done he was still the father of Georgia, and that must count for something, surely.'

'It counts for a lot,' she said softly.

Marc settled himself back down with another deep sigh.

'Better get some sleep, Nina,' he said with his eyes closed.

Nina watched him for a long moment. The normally harsh lines of his face were more relaxed than she had ever seen before. She wanted to reach out with her fingers and trace over his aristocratic eyebrows, feel the ridge of his nose where it looked as if it had been broken some time in the past. She wanted to press her lips to the line of his, feel the way his mouth responded to her, fought with her, mated with her.

'Marc?' She whispered his name in the silence.

'Mmm?'

'I want you to know that I think you're a wonderful substitute father for Georgia.'

She felt him reach for her hand, his long fingers squeezing hers momentarily. 'Thank you,' he said. 'I love her as if she were my own.'

'So do—' She stopped, her heart giving a hard ram against her ribcage at the slip of her tongue.

She waited in agonising silence for him to pick her up on it, her stomach rolling in panic, her heart racing until she could feel the blood thrumming in her ears. But his breathing had evened out, his chest rising and falling at neat intervals, indicating he was already asleep.

Nina eased herself back down beside him, her breathing gradually returning to normal as she realised that so far her secret was still safe.

But it had been close.

Far, far too close.

CHAPTER FOURTEEN

NINA woke the next morning to find Marc lying propped up on one elbow, silently watching her. She felt warm colour instantly flood her cheeks and wished she had the aplomb of her sister so that she could wake up next to a full-blooded man without blushing to the roots of her hair.

She made a move to leave the bed but his hand came down over hers and stalled her.

'No, don't run away. Lucia is caring for Georgia. You are entitled to a morning or two off. How are you feeling?'

She shifted her gaze. 'I'm fine. The cramps have gone.'

'Good.' She heard him get out of bed but didn't chance a glance his way, not sure she could cope with seeing his body without the shield of his clothes. 'I have plans for you.'

'Plans?' She met his eyes briefly.

He shrugged himself into a bathrobe. 'This is your first visit to Sorrento, is it not? I think it would be nice if we left Lucia with Georgia this morning while I show you around a bit. We can visit the church of San Francesco and have lunch at one of the restaurants in the centre of Sorrento at Piazza Tasso. Tomorrow we can explore the ruins of Pompeii and then drive to Positano for a late lunch.'

'Are you sure Georgia will be—'

'She will be fine,' he reassured her. 'My father will want to spend time with her, under Lucia's supervision, of course. In the light of what occurred last night, I think it is best if both of us are not there.'

Nina was inclined to agree but didn't voice it. She was still feeling terribly unsettled by the exchange between Marc and his father. Vito Marcello was undoubtedly an ill man and his drinking of obvious concern to Marc, but when she considered the back to back grief he had experienced so recently she could hardly hold it against him.

'If there's anything I can do...' she offered, lowering her gaze once more.

It seemed a long time before he responded. 'Just be yourself, Nina. You cannot do any more than that.'

His words were like a dagger to her heart. If only she could be herself!

The morning was sunny and clear, the cobbled streets filled with avid tourists intent on seeing this exquisite part of the Amalfi Coast. The view from the public gardens above the typical Italian square of Piazzo Tasso was spectacular and Nina couldn't help feeling as if all of her worries and fears were gradually disappearing on the light breeze that gently stirred her loose hair whenever she faced the sea.

Being in Marc's company was like a potent drug; the more she had, the more she wanted. She drank his presence in, filling her senses with everything she most loved about him: his tall commanding figure, his darker than night eyes that now held no trace of their previous hardness, the softer line of his mouth now that a smile had replaced its earlier line of contempt and the way his hand reached for hers, his long tanned fingers threading through hers as if he never wanted to let her go.

He walked beside her, his broad shoulder against hers as he pointed out various sites of interest, his deep voice stroking over her like a soft caress. 'According to legend, it was here at Sorrento that Ulysses heard the tempting song of the Sirens, the nymphs who tried to entice passing sailors.'

Nina looked out at the sparkling water, shielding her eyes from the bright sunlight as she tried to concentrate on what he was telling her instead of the way his lips moved when he spoke and how her stomach fluttered like a handful of butterflies every time he looked at her.

'It's so beautiful,' she said and, after a short pause, turned to look up at him. 'You must miss it terribly now that you live in Sydney.'

Marc's eyes left hers to gaze out over the water. 'Yes, but after my mother died I felt it necessary to get away.' He gave a small sigh and turned back to look down at her, leaning his back against the terrace railing. 'My father had decided Andre should set up the Sydney branch but it became clear after a while that he was not doing a good job of it.'

Nina held her breath, wondering if he was going to break his promise of a truce and blame her sister—and thereby her—for distracting Andre from his work, but to her surprise he didn't.

'Andre was a party animal, not a merchant banker, but my father refused to admit it. He resented the fact that I could handle business better than his favourite son,' he went on. 'But I think, given enough time, my over-indulged brother would have ended up very much like my father is now—a bitter, broken man with the crutch of alcohol doing a very poor job of keeping him going.'

She put her hand on his, her fingers curling around his, her expression empathetic as she held his gaze. 'Marc, I know you won't believe this, but I know what it is like to be the unfavoured child. It hurts so deeply to think that no matter how hard you try you can never quite please the one you love the most.'

Something briefly flickered in Marc's eyes and a small frown appeared on his forehead. He looked at her very intently and said, 'I thought you were an only child.'

Nina froze.

'How can you know what it is to be the unfavoured child when you are the *only* child?' he asked when she didn't respond.

The silence seemed endless as she hunted frantically for something to say.

'I—I meant I can imagine what it must be like…you don't have to have personal experience of something to understand what it is like—might be to feel that way…' Her fractured sentence trailed helplessly away.

It was only a second or two at the most before he responded, but to Nina it felt as if a century had passed.

'We should get back,' he said, pushing off the railing and taking her arm. 'The sun is starting to burn your face. I should have thought to tell you to bring a hat.'

Nina walked on unsteady legs as he led the way back to the car, her heart-rate all over the place at how close she had been to giving the game away.

The next few days passed in the same manner. Each morning Nina woke with Marc's arms around her, his body warm and protective, although he did not touch her intimately, even though her body ached for his possession. After breakfast he would take her out for the morning while Lucia cared for Georgia so Vito could spend time with her in his favourite private garden on one of the many terraces.

Nina was fascinated by the site of Pompeii. The crumbling buildings with their tragic history, the ancient relics, including bodies frozen in time by volcanic ash, chilled her blood as she stood silently looking at them, wondering how the people must have felt trying to escape the fury of Mount Vesuvius.

'It's just so sad,' she said when they came back out to the sunshine. 'To think that they had no time to escape, nowhere to run and hide, no hope of protecting their loved ones…'

Marc looked down at her troubled expression as she gazed out over the vista of ancient ruins. It was hard at times like this to imagine her as anything other than a thoughtful caring young woman with a soft heart for those who suffered. Where was the selfish little whore now? he wondered.

During the first few evenings Vito Marcello ate alone in his suite, sending word down, usually at the last minute, that he did not wish to join them, but on the fourth evening when Nina came downstairs a short time after Marc she found both Marc and his father waiting for her in the dining room.

At first the meal was a somewhat stilted affair but it became apparent to Nina that Vito Marcello was doing his best to make up for his rudeness on the first evening she'd arrived at the villa. He also seemed to be making an effort not to drink to excess.

'Georgia is a beautiful child,' he said at one point. 'I have enjoyed my time with her each morning. Thank you for allowing me the privilege of getting to know her.'

'I'm glad you have enjoyed her, Signore Marcello,' Nina said softly. 'She is very special.'

He gave her a lengthy look and added, 'Lucia has told me what a good mother you are. And, since my son has informed me you speak our language, I must beg your forgiveness for speaking of you so insultingly the other night.'

'It doesn't matter. I've forgotten all about it.'

He cleared his throat and continued. 'I must also apologise for the letter I sent you. Some of the things I said were…unforgivable. I am surprised you still agreed to marry Marc when you had such a weapon to use against us.'

Nina sat very still. Nadia had briefly mentioned a letter from Andre's father but she hadn't shown her the contents. Was Vito right? Had there been a way out of marrying Marc that her sister had deliberately kept hidden from her?

She felt Marc's suddenly intent gaze and turned back to his father. 'We all do and say things on the spur of the moment.'

'You are very gracious,' Vito said. 'I had not thought you

capable of it. I am afraid Andre did not paint a pretty picture of your personality.'

Nina found it almost impossible to hold the older man's gaze. Lying to an old man, a dying one at that, seemed to her to be morally reprehensible no matter how altruistic the motivation behind it. She looked down at her plate, wondering how on earth she was going to get through the rest of the meal, when there was a knock at the door and one of the staff members came in at Vito's command and politely informed Nina that there was a telephone call for her.

She felt the full weight of Marc's gaze as she rose from the table, her legs threatening to give way beneath her as she made her way to the nearest telephone extension in the library down the hall. She closed the door behind her and, taking a deep breath, picked up the phone and held it to her ear. 'Hello?'

'Nina, it's me, your alter ego,' Nadia said with a giggle.

Nina's hand tightened on the receiver. 'How did you get this number? I told you not to call me! It's dangerous.'

'Surely I can call my own sister,' Nadia said sulkily. 'My married-to-a-billionaire sister,' she added with a suggestive drawl.

'You planned this, didn't you? You purposely didn't show me that letter.' Nina asked. 'You let me think I had no choice but to do as Marc and his father said, not telling me I had an escape route all the time.'

Nadia gave an amused chuckle. 'You fell for it so easily. Now who is the smarter twin? You think you're so clever with your university degree and gift with languages but you couldn't even get out of the Marcellos' plan for revenge.'

'What do you want?' Nina snapped. 'I've transferred the money into your account. Don't tell me you've already spent it.'

'I have, actually,' Nadia replied. 'That's why I'm calling you. I want more.'

'*More?*' Nina choked on the word.

'You heard me, Nina. I want regular instalments, starting tomorrow.'

'But I don't have—'

'Ask your husband to up your allowance.' Nadia cut her off. 'I want you to give me the bulk of it. That's only fair, don't you think? You have my baby so I should have your allowance.'

'I can't believe I'm hearing this. What's happened to Bryce Falkirk and your big film career?'

'Like most of the men I've been involved with, he's shown his true colours and left me high and dry,' Nadia said. 'That is why I'm relying on you to turn my life around.'

'Surely that is up to you?'

'One phone call, Nina,' Nadia reminded her coldly. 'That's all it will take. Or maybe I will pay your husband a visit. That would be even more effective, wouldn't you agree?'

'You wouldn't dare,' Nina said through gritted teeth.

'Oh, wouldn't I?' Nadia goaded.

'He would take Georgia off me without a moment's hesitation,' Nina said. 'She would be devastated; she thinks I'm her mother now.'

'Do you think I care what happens to that kid? This is about money, Nina. Just do what you are told and your little secret will be safe. *Ciao* for now.'

Nina replaced the receiver and made her way back to the dining room with a sinking heart. She knew she had no choice but to tell Marc the truth before her sister got there first, but she couldn't imagine how she should go about it. How could she frame the words in any way that would not incite his bitter anger? He had every right to be furious at what she had done.

Marc rose from the table as she approached. 'Is everything all right, Nina? You look as if you have heard bad news.'

'No…nothing important.' She forced her stiff lips into a smile that encompassed both Marc and his father. 'I'm sorry for interrupting dinner.'

'Not at all,' Vito said, gesturing to the staff member nearby. 'I am retiring early anyway. I am very tired. *Buonanotte.*'

Marc waited until his father had left before reaching for her hand across the table, his eyes holding hers. 'Do you know what I think we should do, *cara*?'

'N-no…what should we do?'

He gave a slow smile and rose from the table, pulling her with him. 'I think we should do the same as my father and retire early. While you were on the phone Lucia assured me Georgia is still sleeping peacefully so we have the rest of the night to be together. It is time to commence our marriage in the proper sense of the word.'

'Marc…I…' She stopped mid-sentence. One night in his arms, and then she would tell him. Surely that wasn't too much to ask? She would spend the rest of her life regretting it if she didn't have him make love to her properly just this once.

'I will not hurt you this time,' he said, stroking a finger over her anxious brow.

She stepped closer, loving the feel of his arms going around her, trusting him with all her heart. 'I know.'

He led her upstairs, his arm around her waist as they made their way to his suite, her heart picking up its pace when he closed and locked the door once they were inside.

He brushed his mouth with hers, once, twice, three times. His hands skated over her, his touch light but warm as he gently removed her clothes while she fumblingly did the same to his.

He pulled back the covers of the bed and sat down, tugging her down beside him, turning her so that she was beneath him as he pressed her backwards with a heated kiss. Her body responded hotly with each tantalizing thrust of his tongue, reminding her of the intimacy of the union she craved. He moved his mouth from hers and caressed each of her breasts in turn, the warm moistness of his mouth stirring her into a mindless frenzy of need.

She drew in a breath as his fingers splayed over her intimately, the possessive touch thrilling her even as it terrified her.

He inserted one finger, slowly but surely, waiting until her body accepted him before going further. She writhed under his caress, her limbs becoming boneless when he explored her shape and form. She felt the tingling of her flesh as his fingers played with her, the tightening of nerves that threatened to explode with feeling.

'Relax for me, Nina,' Marc said softly. 'Let go.'

Nina closed her eyes and let herself fly with the feelings he had evoked, her mind going completely blank as wave after wave surged through and over her. She vaguely registered the gasping cries of someone and then, with a shock of sharp awareness, realised they had sprung from her own mouth. She floated back down, her body feeling as if it had been melted into a sun-warmed flow of golden honey.

Marc waited until she was totally relaxed before he moved over her carefully, his weight supported by his arms so as not to crush her.

Nina looked up at him wonderingly, her eyes wide and luminous as he eased himself into her with such gentleness she felt like crying.

'Are you all right?' he asked, stalling for a moment.

She wrapped her arms around him and drew him closer, relishing the feel of his satin strength stretching her.

'I'm fine...you feel so...so...right.'

He fought for control as her body gripped him, her words so in tune with what he was feeling it was uncanny. He'd made love many times, perhaps not as often as his less particular brother, but enough times to know when the chemistry was right. But with Nina it was more than just right—it felt perfect.

He bit down on his tongue when she moved beneath him, her small body fitting so snugly he thought he was going to go over the edge before he could stop himself. He felt the ripples of her muscles along him, the silk of her warmth caressing him as she held him close. He plunged deeper, muttering a silent curse under his breath in case he'd hurt her, but she simply sighed with pleasure, her head going back, her eyes dreamy.

He kissed her again, relishing the feel of her soft mouth submitting to the invasion of his tongue, the shy darts of her own making him swell even further.

In spite of her inexperience Nina could feel the struggle Marc was having. She could sense it in the way he held back from her, as if he was unused to letting go completely. She wanted him to let go, she wanted him to groan her name as he filled her, she wanted to soar with him.

She kissed him fervently, her fingers burying in his thick hair, her legs moving apart even further to make him go deeper.

He groaned as his thrusts increased their pace and depth, the muscles of his back tightening when her hands moved over them. She wriggled beneath him, her body instinctively seeking the intimate abrasion of his.

She sucked in a breath when his hand came down to touch her, his fingers seeking the pulse of her body with heart-stopping accuracy.

Now it was she losing control. She felt it building all over again, deeper and more intense with the swell of his maleness invading her, her muscles clenching at him to keep him hard and hot within her.

She felt the first tingle, and then the second before the avalanche hit her, stunning her with its totally devastating impact on her senses.

She felt Marc suddenly tense, the momentary stillness of his body heralding his subsequent cataclysmic plunge into paradise. She felt him empty himself inside her, the spilling warmth of his essence binding her to him in the most primal way imaginable.

She held him to her, relishing the feeling of him as close as could possibly be, the silence between them settling like breeze-driven blossoms falling softly to the ground.

She felt him move, the long stretch of his legs against hers reminding her of how intimately entwined she was, and not just physically. Her love for him seemed to fill every space in her body. She could barely take a breath without feeling it tug on her somewhere, a painful little tug that warned her that he did not care for her at all. His priority was Georgia and always would be.

She turned her head to look at him, the words of her confession already forming in her head, when she realised he was asleep.

'Marc?' She gave him a little shake.

There was no answer.

She gave a soft sigh and curled back into his warmth; she would tell him in the morning, but for tonight she would remain in his arms where she hoped with all her heart to stay for ever.

Nina knew something was terribly wrong as soon as she opened her eyes the next morning. The space beside her in the bed was empty and she could hear voices, urgent upset voices, echoing all through the villa. Her eyes went to the baby monitor but it showed no signs of being activated through the night.

She scrambled out of bed and threw on some clothes and rushed to Georgia's nursery where she found her niece just starting to wake, her tiny hands unfolding as she heard Nina come in. She gathered the baby close and turned around to see Paloma enter the room with a stricken expression.

'Whatever is the matter, Paloma?'

The Italian woman sank to a nearby chair, her face ashen. 'Signore Marcello passed away in his sleep last night. Marc is with him now.'

'Oh, no!' Nina cried.

'It has been expected for a long time but it is so sad,' Paloma said. 'For all his faults, all the staff members were very fond of him.'

'Is there anything I can do?'

Paloma gave her a sad smile. 'You have already made such a difference in the short time you have been here, *signora*. He died a happier, more peaceful man for having met his only grandchild.'

Nina found the next few days excruciatingly painful as she watched Marc deal with his grief over his father's passing whilst maintaining the family business and household affairs. Her plan to tell him of her deception was unthinkable now. He was barely able to cope with the stress of seeing to his father's funeral arrangements and the steady influx of calls of condolence from all over the world. She did what she could where she could, trying to take some of the burden from him, holding him in bed at night while he lost himself in her arms, again and again, as if their physical union was the only salve he could find to ease the sting of his loss. But during the day he often retreated into himself, reminding Nina of a lone wolf who trusted no one to come too close.

The day after the funeral Paloma informed her that Marc wished to speak with her in the study where he had been sorting through his father's papers.

He looked up as she came in, rising from the desk as she closed the door behind her. She was shocked at how tired he looked, his normally olive skin looked more sallow than tanned and his dark eyes had lines at the corners she hadn't noticed before.

'You wanted to see me, Marc?'

'I have been doing some thinking. I want to talk to you about Georgia's future.'

She felt her heart give a sudden lurch. Surely he wasn't thinking of a divorce so soon? Perhaps the death of his father had made him realise he could no longer tie himself in a loveless marriage indefinitely.

'W-what about her future?' she asked warily.

'I want to formally adopt Georgia.'

She swallowed, hunting for her voice, but when she found it she couldn't get it past the lump of panic in her throat.

'I want to be her father, not her uncle,' he went on. 'Nothing I can do will ever bring her real father back, and in time I will tell her about him, but for now I want to be her father in every way possible.'

Nina didn't know what to say. She saw the way Marc interacted with her niece, his dark eyes warm with deep affection as he cradled her in his arms or played with her, murmuring endearments to her in his own tongue. No one could question his ability to be a wonderful father, but she could hardly give the go-ahead for a formal adoption when she wasn't even the child's mother. And the thought of telling him now, after all he had been through…

'You don't seem all that enthusiastic,' he observed after a too long silence.

'I—I don't think it's such a good idea.'

'Why not?'

'No one can take Andre's place. He is her father even though he is no longer…here… I don't want to confuse her with you.'

'Cristo, Nina, I am doing everything a father would do. I am providing for her and protecting her. I do not see why she has to call me Uncle for the rest of her life when all I want is to be her father.'

'You are not her father.'

'Do you think I do not know that?'

She met his eyes briefly, trying to think of a reason to put him off. 'I don't trust you enough to let you take that step.'

He let out a sigh of exasperation. 'I married you, did I not? That's more than my brother did.'

'You only did it out of a sense of duty.'

'So what is wrong with that? Surely you were not expecting me to fall in love with you and promise you forever?'

Her eyes fell away from his. 'No, of course not, but I can't help thinking you have a hidden agenda. As soon as I let my guard slip you're going to snatch Georgia away from me. You've threatened me with it numerous times.'

He let out another deep sigh. 'I can understand your fears and I apologise for threatening you in such a way, but believe me, I had to ensure Georgia's safety. I had heard so much about you and I did not trust you to look after her in the way she needs.'

'What about now?' she asked, returning her gaze to his. 'Do you trust me now?'

He gave her a studied look before answering. 'My earlier misgivings have been somewhat resolved. However, I would be happier if I were officially documented as Georgia's father.'

'I'll think about it,' she said, buying for time.

'I suppose I will have to be satisfied with that for the time being, but I am warning you, Nina, I will not rest until I get what I want.'

Nina knew he meant every word. She saw it in the hard glitter of his eyes and the determined thrust of his chin. The only trouble was, she was in the way of him achieving his goal. He could never be Georgia's legal father, not unless he was to become fully aware of her deception. The web of lies she'd spun was threatening to choke her, each tiny gossamer thread pulling painfully on her heart as she thought about losing not only Georgia but Marc as well.

'There's something else I wish to tell you,' he said after a short tense silence. 'I have a business dinner tonight in Positano. I can't get out of it—there are people who wish to see me before I return to Sydney. I know it is short notice, but I would like you to come with me. Lucia will mind Georgia; I have already cleared it with her.'

Nina hesitated.

'Have you got something else planned?' he asked, his tone sharpening a fraction.

'No. No, of course not.'

'We will leave at seven. Wear something long; it is a formal affair.'

* * *

Lucia gave Nina an approving smile as she came down the stairs later that evening dressed in clinging black satin, her long hair twisted into a casual but stylish knot on top of her head, the escaping tendrils drifting over her cheeks giving her a softly sensual look.

'Will I do?' She twirled in front of the housekeeper.

'He will not be able to resist you tonight, Nina,' Lucia said.

Nina felt her cheeks heating and hastily covered her embarrassment by plucking at a tiny thread on her shoulder strap.

'You of all people know why he married me, Lucia.'

'Yes, but things have changed, have they not? You share his bed like a proper wife. That is good.'

Nina met the housekeeper's dark eyes. 'He doesn't love me. He hates me for what…for what I did to his brother.'

'But you didn't do anything to his brother, did you, Nina?' Lucia asked, her dark gaze never once leaving hers.

A tiny footstep of apprehension stepped on to a nerve in her spine. 'What do you mean?'

Lucia smiled a knowing smile. 'You might have fooled Signore Marcello but I am not so easily duped. It took me a few days to work it out but you are not Georgia's mother, are you?'

Nina's hand tightened a fraction on the banister. 'W-what makes you say that?'

'You could not possibly be the woman who seduced Andre.'

'W-why not?'

'Because I have met the woman you are pretending to be.'

Nina stared at her in shock, her hand falling away from the banister. *'You've met Nadia?'*

Lucia nodded. 'Yes. She came to the house to see Andre. I had stayed later than usual and ran into her. She was everything I had expected her to be: shallow and vain. She didn't even acknowledge me; I was just a nameless servant to her. Those first few days after you came I was confused. You acted like her, looked like her and even sounded like her. Then I had my suspicions, and when that phone call came and the voice sounded so like you I finally realised what was going on. I have twin sons myself. They are all grown up now but they often used to switch places for sheer devilment.'

Nina swallowed painfully. 'Have you told Marc?'

'No. I thought I would leave that to you.'

Nina caught her lip between her teeth for a moment.

'You have to tell him, you know,' Lucia said.

'I know.' She gave the housekeeper an agonised look. 'I just don't know how to do it. He has been through so much just lately…I didn't want to hurt him any more. I feel so guilty.'

'That guilt belongs to Nadia, not you. I suppose she left you with Georgia?'

'Yes. Believe me, it's the habit of a lifetime.' She gave a ragged sigh. 'Our mother was exactly the same: restless, moody, impulsive and irresponsible with a propensity to chase after totally unsuitable men.'

'He will understand,' Lucia assured her. 'He is a good man, Nina. He will be good to you once he knows who you really are.'

Nina wished she had her confidence. Somehow she didn't see Marc taking the news that well. No man liked to be made a fool of, and she had done that and more.

She heard the sound of his voice as he spoke to one of the staff as he came down the hall and she sent the housekeeper a tremulous smile as she tucked a strand of hair behind one ear. 'Wish me luck, Lucia.'

'Just be you, Nina,' Lucia advised. 'That is all you need to do.'

The dinner was held in a small but elegant hotel, the function room decked out with fragrant summer flowers and candelabra, the majority of the guests suited men with the occasional wife thrown in here and there. Nina had never felt less like socialising. She stayed close to Marc's side, her arm linked through his and smiled her way through the many introductions, but her heart wasn't in it and she couldn't wait for the night to be over.

After the meal was over a small band began to play and several couples got up to dance. Nina excused herself from the table and made her way to the ladies' room, more to escape the prospect of Marc's arms going around her on the dance floor than any other reason.

She locked herself in a cubicle and took several calming breaths, garnering up the courage for what she had to say to him as soon as they returned home.

She suddenly became aware of two women speaking just outside her cubicle, their voices rising above the sound of the hand dryer next to the basins. Though they spoke in Italian Nina was able to understand every damning word.

'I heard she was a topless dancer at a nightclub when his brother met her first. Apparently they had a hot affair for a while but then Andre Marcello decided he had better return to the respectability of his fiancée's arms.'

'I heard she'd had a baby,' another female voice said.

'Yes, rumour has it that's why Marc agreed to marry her. He wants his brother's child and marrying its mother was the only way to get it.'

'I hope he doesn't live to regret it. Women like Nadia Selbourne are trouble.'

'Apparently she goes by the name Nina now,' the other woman said with a little snicker. 'No doubt she wants to distance herself from her foray into blue movies. Apparently there was some other scandal that was hushed up too. Mind you, she has a great body considering she's not long had a baby. I wonder if Marc has been tempted to sample her for himself?'

'They're married, aren't they?'

Nina heard the cap of a lipstick tube being replaced.

'Marc Marcello is known to be highly selective in the women he chooses to sleep with,' the woman said. 'He only married her to get access to the child. But you know what they say about men: they don't think with their brains but what's between their legs.'

'I wouldn't mind having a look at what he's got between his legs,' the other woman said as they left the ladies' room.

Nina put her head in her hands and stifled a groan. Could it get any worse?

Marc rose when she came back to the table, his hand cupping her elbow. 'Would you like to dance?'

She wished she could think of an excuse but decided it was better to be on the dance floor with him than sitting at the table with the rest of the party who had heard God knew what else about her sister.

'All right,' she said. 'But I must warn you, I have two left feet.'

Marc led her to a less crowded corner of the dance floor and drew her closer, his chest brushing up against hers from time to time as he manoeuvred her around the other dancers.

'Andre told me you were a phenomenal dancer,' he said as he deftly turned her out of the way of another couple.

Nina quickly untied her feet. 'I don't know about that.' She sucked in a breath as he pulled her closer, her eyes skating away from his.

He frowned down at her. 'You have been on edge all evening. What is wrong? Are you worried about having to stay in Sorrento longer than we planned? I am sorry but there was nothing I could do. I have to tie up things here before we can return.'

She shook her head. 'No, it's not that.' She lifted her eyes to his, finally coming to a decision. 'Can we go home? I really need to talk to you—alone.'

He slid his hands down her arms and brought her closer. 'Is that what you want?'

'Yes.'

He turned her towards the table where his jacket and her bag were and, after a few brief farewells, escorted her towards the exit.

Marc barely spoke on the way home and Nina didn't know whether to be worried or grateful for his silence. She sat twisting her hands in her lap, pretending an interest in the passing view of twinkling lights in the distance. He pulled into the driveway a few minutes later and she waited until he came around to open her door, her heart thumping in apprehension as she got out.

'You looked very beautiful tonight,' he said, taking her hand as she got out of the car, his eyes holding hers as his thumb moved back and forth on the sensitive skin of her wrist.

'Marc...' She moistened her mouth, her throat closing over when his head came down, her breath stalling as his lips found hers.

His kiss was gentle at first, his hands light on her as he drew her even closer. Nina felt herself melting against him, her limbs loosening as his kiss became more insistent and his tongue more demanding as it mated sensually with hers.

Her hands found their way to his hair, her fingers burying in the black silk while her chest pushed against his with the urgency of her fast-growing need for more. She felt his hands at her breasts, shaping her, caressing her through the slippery fabric of her gown, the slide of silk over her tingling flesh an added delight to her highly tuned senses.

His groan as he pressed her back against the car stirred her into a frenzy of wanting. She ached for his hard thick presence and reached to touch him intimately, her fingers going to his waistband and releasing it to explore his jutting contours. He was hot and hard and heavy in her hands, his breathing becoming ragged as she explored him boldly.

His hand reached for the fall of her dress, sliding it up over her hips to bunch at her waist as his long fingers sought her liquid warmth. She gasped as he shifted the tiny lace panties out of his way, his fingers touching her tenderly but masterfully until she was breathless with the building sensations that were ricocheting through her.

She clung to him as he withdrew his fingers, replacing them with his solid length in one deep thrust that arched her backwards against the car. She felt her inner muscles clench him tightly, the shockwaves of delight coursing through her as he moved within her deeply and possessively, his building urgency inciting her own.

A cry burst from her lips as she neared the summit, her hips rocking with the motion of his to take her that final step. Her breath whooshed out of her when she finally made it, the earth-shattering feelings cascading through her veins like bubbles of champagne instead of blood. She felt light-headed and disconnected, her brain floating on a sea of pleasure, the receding tide washing over her in soft strokes like the lace of a foamy wave.

She opened her eyes to see the dark intensity of Marc's looking at her as he neared his own pinnacle of pleasure, his face contorted with the anticipation of rapidly approaching ecstasy. She held him as he shuddered against her, his body spilling into hers, his deeply muttered groans of release making her skin tingle with vicarious pleasure.

He was still breathing hard when he stepped back from her, his hands readjusting his trousers, his eyes still lit from behind as he held her gaze without speaking.

Nina smoothed down her gown and put a hand to her tumbling hair, her eyes falling away from his as she bent to retrieve the bag that had slipped to the floor at her feet.

His hand reached her bag first and they straightened together, Nina doing her best to appear unaffected by what had happened between them even though her legs were still shaking with reaction.

Marc tipped up her chin and forced her to look at him. 'Do not hide from me, Nina. I like to see the light of pleasure in your eyes.'

'I'm not hiding from you.' She took a breath and twisted out of his hold. 'Let's go inside. I feel cold.'

Marc let her go, following her into the house with a small frown etched between his brows.

Lucia was hovering in the foyer as soon as Nina opened the door, Marc just a few steps behind.

'What's wrong?' Nina asked, her blood running cold at the worried look on the housekeeper's face. 'Is Georgia all right?'

'Georgia is fine.' Lucia's hands twisted together as her eyes flicked towards the *salon* leading off the foyer.

'What is going on?' Marc asked as he closed the door behind him.

The housekeeper sent Nina an agonised look before turning to her employer. 'Signora Marcello has a visitor,' she announced.

Nina felt her colour drain away, her limbs going weak and her head swimming with panic.

'Who is it?' Marc asked as he shrugged himself out of his dinner jacket. 'Anyone I would know?'

There was a sound as the *salon* door opened and Marc looked up to see a mirror image of his wife framed in the doorway.

'Hello, Marc,' Nadia purred.

Nina felt the full force of Marc's dark eyes as they sought hers, his mouth a rigid line of incredulity, shock and unmistakable anger.

'Are you going to tell me what the hell is going on or am I supposed to guess?' His voice was razor-sharp.

Nina gave a convulsive swallow. 'I was going to tell you—'

Nadia stepped forward with a seductive sway of her hips, cutting her sister off mid-sentence. 'Isn't she a naughty little thing, Marc? Pretending to be me so she could get her hands on Georgia's inheritance.'

Nina gasped and grabbed Marc's arm to make him look at her. 'That's not true!'

He looked down at her hand on his sleeve, his expression one of distaste as he peeled it off, finger by finger.

He turned to his housekeeper and politely asked her to leave. Lucia gave Nina one last worried glance and made her way down the hall with slow steps that communicated her reluctance.

'Both of you.' Marc indicated the door of the *salon*. 'In here—now.'

Nadia sashayed her way back into the room, casting a sultry look over her shoulder at Marc as she did so.

Nina clenched her jaw and followed stiffly in her wake, her stomach twisting in despair.

Marc waited until the door was closed behind him before he spoke. 'Now, let us start from the beginning. Which of you is Georgia's mother?'

'I am.' Nadia stepped forward. 'I left her with Nina for a short period only to find she had stepped into my shoes while my back was turned.'

Nina's eyes flared in anger. 'I did no such thing! You abandoned her!'

'Don't listen to her.' Nadia's eyes glistened with ready tears. 'I love my daughter; she's all I have left of Andre. Nina was jealous. All she's ever wanted was to get married and have a baby. She tricked you into marrying her.'

'Marc!' Nina swung to face him. 'You mustn't listen to her! She's making it up!'

He looked at her for a brief moment before turning back to Nadia. 'I would like to speak to my…Nina alone for a moment. Will you excuse us?'

Nadia lifted her chin. 'She'll only tell more lies to cover her back. She did it for the money, you know. In spite of what she says, that's what she's after.'

Marc's hold on Nina's arm bit into her flesh as he led her out of the room, his face tight and his usually full mouth thin-lipped.

Nina didn't speak as he escorted her upstairs. She took one

look at the rage on his features and decided to wait until they were out of earshot of her twin.

Marc pushed open the door of his room and ushered her in, snapping it shut behind them.

His eyes hit hers—hard.

'You had better have a very good explanation for your behaviour or I swear to God you will wish you had never been born.'

'I was going to tell you—'

'When?' he barked at her. 'When were you going to tell me you had deceived me in such a despicable way?'

'I didn't do it deliberately—' she began.

'Do not lie to me!' he shouted. 'You played me for a fool from the start.' He shoved a hand through his hair and stepped away from her, shaking his head in disbelief. 'I cannot believe you would stoop so low.' He turned back to glare at her. 'Was it worth it? Did you have a good laugh behind my back at how you had tricked me?'

'No! I—'

'Damn you, Nina,' he ground out darkly as he came towards her, his hands clenched by his sides. 'You made a fool out of me and that I will not forgive.'

'Marc...please let me explain.' She twisted her hands in front of her in agitation. 'I didn't mean it to go this far. When you arrived at my flat that day I was so concerned you were going to take Georgia away. I had to do something! I didn't know it would lead to this, I swear I didn't.'

'Why did you not come clean when you had the chance?' he asked. 'You have strung me along with a web of lies the whole time. You have had numerous opportunities to tell me and yet you did not.'

'I know! I'm sorry...I was frightened. I thought you wouldn't let me see Georgia any more. You kept threatening to take her away; I had no choice.'

He gave a disgusted sound at the back of his throat and

turned away from her. 'You must think me the biggest fool, but don't forget I know that as soon as that money was put in your account you spent it.'

'I didn't spend it! I gave it to Nadia as she insist—'

'You cooked this up together, did you not?' His eyes grew dark and dangerous.

'What?' She looked at him in bewilderment.

He gave a cynical snort. 'I can see what you have been up to. The twin routine is an old one but effective if played well. And you certainly played it very well, very well indeed. You switched personalities with the blink of an eye.'

'I'm not proud of what I did but I—'

His venomous look cut her off. 'Was it fun, Nina? Was it fun making a fool out of me? Did you enjoy yourself? Did you get off on the fact that I could not help myself, that I slept with you in spite of my determination not to?'

'I never intended sleeping with you. You have to believe that.'

'I believe nothing of what you say!' he spat. 'How can I, after all you have done?'

'I didn't mean to hurt you.'

'Hurt me?' He gave her an imperious look. 'You would have to try much harder, Nina, if you wanted to hurt me. I am well used to the perfidious nature of women like you and know how to protect myself.' He swung away to open the door, indicating he was finished with her. 'I will give you until midday tomorrow to get out of my house. I will send the divorce papers to you as soon as you provide me with a forwarding address.'

Nina stared at him, shock rendering her immobile, her legs refusing to take her even one step forward.

'Did you not hear me?' he asked.

'I want to see Georgia regularly,' she said, trying to keep the tears back.

A tiny nerve pulsed at the corner of his mouth. 'That will depend entirely on her mother.'

'Nadia doesn't care for Georgia. She only cares for herself. She abused her. I know it for a fact. And she'll do it again just as our mother did.'

'Your sister is Georgia's mother and therefore her legal guardian. You have no say in what happens to her.'

'Nor do you,' she pointed out.

'Your sister and I will no doubt come to some mutually satisfying arrangement.'

'As long as there is plenty of money involved, Nadia will be very satisfied,' she said bitterly. 'But you should think twice before you leave her alone with Georgia. She is not to be trusted.'

'And you think you have the market cornered on trust?' he sneered. 'You, who lied to me every time you could? Why should I believe a single word you say?'

'I wanted what was best for Georgia. That was my only motivation. I don't care if you don't believe me; you can't make it untrue just by not believing what I say.'

He gave her a brittle look. 'I would prefer it if I did not have to see you again. I will arrange for a car to take you to the airport tomorrow but as far as I am concerned I never want to set eyes on you again.'

Nina knew she was beaten. She saw it in the hard glitter of his eyes and in the tight set of his mouth. Hatred seeped from every pore of his body towards her, stinging her in its intensity.

She stalked past him, refusing to allow him to see how broken she really was. She kept her expression blank, her shoulders straight and her head at a devil-may-care angle.

She made it to her room just in time, the tears flowing from so deep inside her she couldn't stem the flow. She lay face down on the bed and sobbed until her throat was raw and her eyes swollen. After a few minutes she dragged herself up and, stuffing what she could into a small bag, hoisted it over her shoulder. She crept into Georgia's room and stood looking down at her for a few heart-wrenching moments.

She touched the baby's petal-like cheek with her fingers. 'Goodbye, darling, I will never forget you as long as I live. I'd do anything to keep you, but Marc…' She bit her lip. 'Marc doesn't want me.' She choked back a sob and continued. 'He loves you, sweetie. He loves you a lot. I know he will be a wonderful father to you. I know that with every beat of my heart.'

Nina closed the door softly and made her way down the stairs and, with barely a sound, walked out of the house and out of Marc's life as if she had never been.

Marc had returned to the *salon,* where Nadia Selbourne was helping herself to a large tumbler of his best brandy. She gave him a seductive smile and raised her glass in a toast as he came in.

'Sorted out everything, Marc? Did she confess?'

He compressed his lips and ran a hand through his hair in a distracted manner without answering.

'She's always been jealous of me, you know,' Nadia continued. 'I've always been the one with the boyfriends but no one takes a second look at her because she's too shy. Pathetic, don't you think? I mean she's still a bloody virgin, unless you've dealt with that. At twenty-four! Can you believe it?'

Marc froze.

Nadia sat down and crossed her long legs, her eyes running over him speculatively. 'I take it you want to keep Georgia?'

He finally located his voice. 'Yes.'

She gave him a look from beneath her lashes, the glass in her hand making a slight ringing noise as she ran her fingertip around the rim. 'I can't give her what you can give her.' She made a little moue with her lips. 'But if you want to adopt her…well…' She gave a streetwise smile. 'I won't stand in your way if the price is right, so to speak.'

Marc forced himself to concentrate on what she was saying, even though his mind was flying off at disturbing tangents.

'Name your price.'

She named a figure that would have shocked him under any other circumstances.

'I'll have the legal papers drawn up in the morning,' he said.

Nadia uncrossed then re-crossed her legs, a little smile still playing about her mouth. 'Why not give me an advance right now? I need to find somewhere to stay—unless you have a bed I could use?'

Marc ground his teeth behind his cool polite smile. 'How much?' he asked, reaching for his wallet.

She got up from the sofa and floated over to him, her talon-tipped fingers taking the wad of notes he held out to her. 'You know…' She tiptoed her fingertips up the front of his shirt. 'You are so much nicer than your brother. He wouldn't give me anything in the end.'

Marc removed her hand. 'He gave you a child.'

She gave another pout. 'I never wanted her. I only went through with it because Nina insisted.'

Marc fought with himself not to physically throw her out. He couldn't believe how two sisters, and twins at that, could be so different. Nadia was everything Nina was not. And, fool that he was, he hadn't realised it till now.

'I will call you a cab,' he said, moving towards the phone.

'Are you sure you don't want me to stay and keep you company?' She gave him a little wink as she slid a hand down her hip in a seductive manner.

'No.' He held the door open for her. 'I will see you out.'

Once Nadia had left, Marc went upstairs in search of Nina, his apology already rehearsed in his head. How could he have got it so wrong? Of course Nina would have done whatever she could to protect Georgia—including marrying a man she didn't know—rather than allow her niece to suffer being brought up by a totally selfish mother.

How had he not guessed? She was nothing like Nadia. She

was loyal and devoted, selfless and shy, and—he gave a pain-ful swallow—she had been a virgin.

'Nina?' He knocked at her door but there was no answer. He opened it but it was empty except for a few scattered articles of clothing suggesting she had packed in a hurry, not bother-ing to take everything with her.

'Nina!' He called out louder as he went through to the nurs-ery, the door swinging back against the wall in his haste.

Georgia awoke with a start and immediately began crying, her tiny frightened sobs galvanizing him out of his temporary stasis.

'Hey there, little one,' he soothed as he picked her up, hold-ing her over his shoulder, stroking her as he made his way back through the rest of the villa in search of Nina.

Georgia was inconsolable, her cries growing louder and more frantic, as if she sensed the panic coming off him in waves.

'Do not cry,' he pleaded as he searched the downstairs rooms. 'We will find her, do not worry. We *have* to find her.'

After twenty minutes he knew he was beaten. Nina was gone and he was left holding the baby—a very unhappy baby who was crying out for the mother she had come to know as her own.

CHAPTER FIFTEEN

NINA decided against using the airport at Naples and hailed a cab to take her to Rome instead. She took the first available flight, arriving in Sydney bleary-eyed and broken-hearted. She stayed with Elizabeth for a week, hardly coming out of her room, her eyes red from bouts of weeping, her slim build visibly shrinking as each day passed.

Elizabeth sat on the end of her bed on the seventh day and frowned in concern. 'Come on, Nina. Don't take this lying down. Go and see him and tell him how you feel. Yesterday's paper said he's back in town now.'

'I can't,' Nina sobbed.

'Yes, you can,' her friend insisted. 'You love him and you love Georgia. He needs to know.'

'He hates me.'

'How do you know that? Things might have changed by now. Who knows? A full dose of Nadia might have set him straight.'

Nina rolled on to her back and scrubbed at her eyes. 'It's my fault for not telling him the truth from the start. He has every right to be angry. He married the wrong woman.'

'What rubbish!' Elizabeth said. 'He married the right one, if you ask me. You are everything he needs. You are loyal and faithful and would rather suffer yourself than hurt someone else. What more could a man ask for?'

Nina's chin wobbled. 'I just wish I could tell him how I feel.'

Elizabeth got to her feet. 'Do it.' She handed her the phone from the bedside table. 'Call him now and ask to see him.'

Nina stared at the phone for a long moment.

'Go on,' she urged. 'What's his number and I'll dial it for you.'

Nina took the phone with an unsteady hand. 'No…no, I'll call him.'

'Good girl.' Elizabeth gave her an encouraging smile. 'I'll leave you to it.' She went to the door and turned back to add, 'Good luck.'

Nina gave her a tremulous smile and, although she'd only said she'd call Marc to get her friend off her back, she looked down at the phone in her hands, surprised to see she had pressed more than half the numbers in already. She took a shaky breath and pressed the last three.

'Nina?' Lucia answered on the second ring. '*Dio!* Where are you? We have been so worried! Georgia is not sleeping and Marc is—'

'Is she all right?' Nina gasped.

'She is missing her mother,' Lucia said.

'Where is Nadia?'

Lucia made a noise of disgust in the back of her throat. 'Not that mother—you. Your sister took the money and left.'

'What money?'

'The money she asked for in exchange for Georgia,' Lucia informed her.

Nina closed her eyes. 'And…Marc? How…how is he?'

'He is angry.'

'I know.' Nina bit her lip. 'I don't blame him.'

'Where are you?' Lucia asked. 'He will want to see you.'

'He told me he never wanted to see me again.'

'That was then, this is now. Come around tonight. I will take Georgia home with me so you can have the evening together to sort things out.'

'I don't know if it can be sorted out.'

'Just come home, Nina. This is where you belong.'

Nina was sitting on the edge of the sofa in Marc's house when she heard his car come up the drive. She'd spent an hour with Georgia before Lucia had taken her with her, the baby settling as if by magic as soon as Nina tucked her into the baby seat in the back of the housekeeper's car.

She heard Marc swear as he entered the house, the rough expletive cutting through the air like a knife. She rose to her feet as the lounge room door was pushed open, her hands in a tight knot in front of her body, her eyes hesitantly searching for his.

He came to a complete halt as his eyes met hers, his colour draining away as if he'd just been given the shock of his life.

'Nina?' He stepped towards her, then stopped. 'It is you?'

'Yes, it's me.'

'I was not sure…' He pushed a hand through his hair, making it even more untidy than it already was. 'I was expecting your sister. She called today, asking for more money.'

'What did you say to her?'

He gave her a quick glance before looking away. 'There is not much I can say until the adoption papers are processed.'

'She's letting you adopt Georgia?'

'Yes, for a price, of course.'

'Of course.'

He met her eyes once more, his expression guarded. 'Why are you here?'

'I wanted to see Georgia.'

He held her gaze for an interminable second or two. 'Is that all?'

'No.' She took another breath and added softly, 'I wanted to see you.'

'Why?' His one word held a note of accusation as if he thought she too was after his money.

'I wanted to tell you that I'm sorry for what I did. I thought I was doing the best thing for Georgia but…I can see now how terribly wrong it was. I thought you would take her away from me but I know you are not the hard man you pretend to be. You are…' She tripped over a little sob. 'You are the most wonderful man I have ever met.'

'You are her mother in ways your sister could never be,' he said, his voice suddenly rough with emotion. 'I was wrong to speak to you the way I did. I was so angry at how you had deceived me. I never once stopped to think of what you had sacrificed in order to protect Georgia from Nadia.'

'W-what do you mean?'

A shadow of a smile haunted his mouth. 'You gave yourself to me. I had no idea what you were doing at the time. I simply assumed you had had a difficult birth with Georgia, never once suspecting that not only were you not her mother but that you were also a virgin.'

Colour seeped into her cheeks and she had to look away.

'No.' He stepped towards her, taking her by the shoulders in a gentle hold so she had no choice but to meet his eyes. 'Do not hide the truth from me any longer. You gave yourself to me and I want to know why.'

'I…' Her eyes fell away from his. 'I couldn't help it. I had never felt that way before.' She lifted her eyes back to his. 'I think I fell in love with you that first day when you came to my flat. You picked up Georgia and you had tears in your eyes. I know you were grieving the loss of your brother but you still had room for her in your heart and were prepared to do anything to protect her. I had the very same feelings. It made me realise we were more alike than different. I couldn't help falling in love with you.'

He swallowed convulsively as he reached for her, burying his head into her neck. 'I have wronged you so abominably. How can you love me?'

She felt the moisture of his eyes against her skin and hugged him tightly. 'I just do. No rhyme or reason. I just do.'

He pulled back from her, his expression tortured. 'I cannot believe I am hearing this. You mean you forgive me for what I said to you?'

'You were angry.'

'Not just angry,' he admitted ruefully. 'I was so hurt. I imagined you laughing behind my back at how you had hood-winked me.'

She gave him a quizzical look. 'I thought you said you never allowed yourself to get hurt?'

He smiled. 'You are not the only one who can tell lies, you know. Of course I was hurt. In spite of what I believed to be true of you, I had fallen in love with you. I wanted to believe you were not capable of the behaviour that had led to my brother's death, but every now and again you would remind me of it by acting like your sister. I had no choice but to think you were one and the same.'

'And yet you fell in love with me?'

He gathered her closer. 'How could I not? You were always so loving towards Georgia and you responded to me so delight-fully. I ached for you day and night and, while I hated myself for my weakness, there was nothing I could do to stop myself from touching you.'

She sighed against the solid warmth of his chest. 'I can't be-lieve you love me.'

He stroked a hand through her hair, pressing her to his heart. 'You had better believe it. I have been out of my mind these last few days trying to find you. I have not slept or eaten in days.'

She smiled up at him. 'Me neither. I missed you so much.'

He gave her a suddenly serious look. 'I have lain awake at night agonising over the ways I have insulted you. Do you know how wretched I feel? You are the most beautiful person, your nature is gentle and loving and your natural shyness so endearing. I have been such a fool for not seeing it from the first. If I had been thinking clearly I would have, but I was torn apart by Andre's death and my father's demands to claim Georgia no matter what the cost. I knew he was dying, time was running out and I had to do whatever I could to fulfil his last wish.'

Nina stroked his jaw tenderly, her eyes shining with moisture. 'Don't be so hard on yourself. I was the one in the wrong. I should have told you right at the beginning when you came to my flat but I was frightened you'd take Georgia away. I didn't think. I just acted on impulse and then it was too late to back out.'

'I railroaded you, *cara*,' he said with regret. 'I can see that now. I was determined to show you for the money-hungry opportunist I believed you to be. I didn't allow for any other explanation.'

'But it's over now,' she said. 'We have each other and we have Georgia.'

'But you have been cheated out of so many things.' His expression turned serious again. 'A proper church wedding, for one thing, and a honeymoon. I do not know how I am going to even begin to make it up to you.'

She gave him a twinkling smile and nestled close. 'I don't mind so much about the wedding but I do mind about the honeymoon. How soon can we go on one?'

Marc smiled as he scooped her up in his arms and carried her towards the door. 'How about now?'

THE ITALIAN'S
GP BRIDE

Kate Hardy

Kate Hardy lives in Norwich, in the east of England, with her husband, two young children, one bouncy spaniel, and too many books to count! When she's not busy writing romance or researching local history, she helps out at her children's schools; she's a school governor and chair of the PTA. She also loves cooking—see if you can spot the recipes sneaked into her books! (They're also on her website, along with extracts and stories behind the books.)

Writing for Mills & Boon® has been a dream come true for Kate—something she wanted to do ever since she was twelve. She's been writing Medical Romance™ for nearly five years now, and also writes for the Riva™ series. She says it's the best of both worlds, because she gets to learn lots of new things when she's researching the background to a book; add a touch of passion, drama and danger, a new gorgeous hero every time, and it's the perfect job!

Kate's always delighted to hear from readers, so do drop in to her website at www.katehardy.com

For Fi, with much love
(and thanks for the asparagus!)

CHAPTER ONE

'IF THERE'S a doctor on the plane, please could you make yourself known to the flight attendants by switching on the light above your head.'

The announcement that every doctor secretly dreaded. Especially on a plane, where space was so tight that it was difficult to work. Eleanor knew that the crew were trained in basic life support, so the problem was obviously something more complicated than that. They needed her help—her knowledge, her experience in emergency medicine. She switched on her light, and one of the flight attendants came over to her.

'One of our passengers has collapsed. Would you be able to take a look at her, please?' she asked in a low voice.

'Of course,' Eleanor said, keeping her voice equally low. She knew some people wouldn't want to get involved, but she'd never stand by and leave someone needing medical help. And in a way this was going to help her, too: instead of spending the whole of the flight from London to Naples wondering just what she was letting herself in for and worrying that maybe she wasn't doing the right thing, she had something to keep her mind occupied.

'Oh—do you have any identification?' The flight attendant swallowed hard. 'Sorry, I should've asked you that first.'

'No problem,' Eleanor said. Either the flight attendant was new to the job, or the emergency was something that had thrown her. Eleanor really hoped it was the former. The cramped aisle of an aeroplane, several thousand feet up in the air and half an hour from an ambulance wasn't the ideal place to deal with something major. 'You need proof that I'm a qualified doctor.' Luckily she kept her hospital ID card in her credit-card holder. She fished it out and showed it to the flight attendant, who looked relieved.

'Would you come this way, please, Dr Forrest? One of my colleagues is fetching the emergency kit.'

Eleanor followed her up the aisle to where a middle-aged, plump woman was slumped in her seat. A quick check told her that the patient wasn't breathing and didn't have a pulse. She needed to get the woman flat and start CPR *now*.

'Did she bang her head at all?' she asked the woman seated next to her patient, who was sobbing.

The answer was a flow of Italian that Eleanor really couldn't follow.

Ah, hell. The chances were that the patient hadn't hit her head so there wasn't a risk of a spinal injury, and right now the most important thing was resuscitation. Just as she was about to ask the flight attendant to find someone who could speak Italian *and* English, to translate for her and get some help in moving the woman so Eleanor could start giving CPR, a man made his way down the aisle, following another flight attendant.

'Orlando de Luca, family doctor,' he introduced himself. 'May I help?'

His English was perfect, not halting in the slightest, though she was aware of his Italian accent. And he had the most beautiful mouth she'd ever seen.

Though now was absolutely *not* the time to be thinking

about that. They had a patient to save. And right now she needed his skills—language as well as medical. 'Eleanor Forrest, emergency registrar,' she replied. 'Thank you. Her pulse and respiration are flat, so we need to start—'

'CPR,' he finished, nodding.

Good. They were on the same wavelength.

'I don't speak much Italian. The patient's travelling companion either doesn't speak English or is too upset to cope in a different language. Can you ask her if our patient hit her head, is taking any medication or has any medical conditions?'

'Of course. But first…' He turned to the flight attendant who'd brought him to the patient. 'We need your help, please, to fetch supplies. Do you have an Ambubag and a defibrillator? It should be kept with the captain.'

'I'll check,' she said, and hurried away.

Then he spoke to their patient's travelling companion in Italian much too rapid for Eleanor to follow, given the basic Italian she'd started learning two weeks before. The only word she could catch was '*dolore*'—what was that? Sorrow?

And then she heard him say '*l'infarto*'—it sounded close enough to 'infarct', she guessed, for it to mean 'heart attack'. Usually if a patient was unconscious and there was no pulse, it meant a cardiac arrest—though it could also be a *grand mal* epileptic seizure.

As if Orlando had guessed what she was thinking, he said, 'Our patient's name is Giulietta Russo. She's travelling back to Napoli—Naples—with her daughter Fabiola. Giulietta complained of a pain in her chest and then collapsed. No history of epilepsy, no history of angina, no other medical condition Fabiola can think of, and she didn't hit her head when she collapsed.'

So far, so good. 'Can you ask Fabiola if her mother has a pacemaker?' she asked.

Another burst of rapid Italian. 'No,' he confirmed.

At the same time, Orlando and Eleanor moved the unconscious woman to the aisle and laid her flat. Gently, Eleanor tilted the patient's head and lifted her chin so she could check the airways. 'No sign of blockage. Airway's clear.' But the B and C of 'ABC' were a problem: Giulietta still wasn't breathing and there was still no pulse: no sign of circulation.

'Then we start CPR,' Orlando said. 'You bag and I do the chest compressions, yes? Five compressions to one breath?'

'Thank you,' Eleanor said.

At that moment, the flight attendant arrived with an Ambubag. 'We're still checking for the defibrillator and the drugs kit,' she said.

Eleanor really hoped there was a defibrillator on board. Otherwise their patient had no chance, because even if they landed at the nearest airport it'd take too long to get the help she needed. Without defibrillation, even with CPR, their patient's chances of survival dropped drastically with every minute.

'Thanks,' she said. At least the Ambubag meant that they could give their patient positive pressure ventilation. But when their patient recovered consciousness, she'd need oxygen—more than that available from the aircraft's emergency oxygen masks. 'Is there any supplemental oxygen, please?'

'I'll check,' the flight attendant said, and hurried away again, quickly returning with the defibrillator.

'I'll attach the defibrillator. Do you mind carrying on with the CPR?' she asked Orlando.

They both knew that you couldn't stop the CPR except for the moment when she was ready to administer a shock—if this was a case where she could use a defibrillator. If the monitor showed a different heart rhythm from VF, they were in real trouble.

'No problem,' Orlando said.

Lord, he had a gorgeous smile. The sort that would've made her weak at the knees if she hadn't already been kneeling next to their patient. She glanced up at the flight attendant. 'I need your help to keep doing the breathing while I attach the defibrillator,' she said. 'If Dr de Luca tells you what to do, can you keep going for me, please?'

The other flight attendant nodded, and followed Orlando's instructions while Eleanor attached the defibrillator and checked the monitor reading.

'She's in VF,' she told Orlando, hoping that the abbreviation was the same in his language. Certainly the words would be: ventricular fibrillation, where the heart wasn't contracting properly and was just quivering instead of beating.

She really needed access to Giulietta's neck veins to administer the adrenaline, but in the confines of the aisle space she didn't want to interfere with ventilation. 'I'm going for IV access in the right subclavian vein,' she said to Orlando. 'Administering one milligram of adrenaline. Six-oh-six p.m.'

'Got you.' Although he was a family doctor—a GP—obviously he knew the protocol in this sort of case: one milligram of adrenaline every three minutes. He smiled at her, and kept directing the flight attendant while Eleanor put the paddles of the defibrillator in place.

'Shocking at two hundred joules. Clear,' she said.

As soon as Orlando and the flight attendant had taken their hands off the patient, she administered the shock and continued looking at the readout. 'Still in VF. Charging to two hundred. And clear.'

Another shock. Still no change. 'Still VF. Charging to three-sixty.'

'Mamma?' Fabiola asked.

'Um, *bene.* Soon,' Eleanor said, trying to remember the

Italian phrases she'd learned and hoping that her voice sounded soothing enough for Fabiola to understand what she meant.

She didn't have time to react to the amusement in Orlando's eyes. 'And clear.'

This time, to her relief, Giulietta responded.

'Sinus rhythm. Can you tell Fabiola that it will be all right? We just need to get her mother to the hospital.'

Orlando nodded, and turned to the flight attendant. 'Can you ask the captain if he can divert the plane to the nearest airport? And talk to the *pronto soccorso* at the hospital—we need the paramedics on standby. *Autoambulanza*,' he added.

Then he talked to Fabiola again in Italian.

'I've explained that her mother needs to go to hospital,' he told Eleanor. 'And we will stay with her until the paramedics can stabilise her.'

It was part and parcel of being a good Samaritan—if there was an emergency and you were present simply as a passer-by and not officially as a doctor, you didn't charge for your service and you stayed with the patient until he or she was stabilised or a doctor with equivalent or higher training took over. Eleanor had heard horror stories of doctors being sued for good Samaritan acts, but she knew if you kept to the protocol and de-livered as near to hospital-standard care as you could, you'd be indemnified by either the travel company or your medical union.

The flight attendant who'd been acting as runner came back. 'Captain says he'll land us at Milan. We have clearance, so we should be on the ground in about twenty minutes. The airport's contacting the hospital for us. Oh, and the supplemen-tal oxygen…?'

'Excellent work.' Orlando said with a smile. 'Thank you, *signorina*…?'

The flight attendant blushed. 'Melanie.'

Orlando de Luca was living up to the stereotype, Eleanor thought. Charming every female in the vicinity.

Just like Jeremy.

Well, she wasn't falling for that sort of charm again. Anyway, this relationship was strictly emergency. And strictly medicine. It shouldn't bother her who Orlando de Luca flirted with. It was nothing to do with her.

She busied herself fitting the mask over Giulietta's face.

'Eleanor, your party must be wondering what happened to you.'

Party? Oh. He meant travelling companions. 'It's not a problem, Dr de Luca.'

'Orlando, please.'

Even his name sounded sexy. Her best friend's words echoed in her head: *Even if this thing doesn't work out, a week in Italy will do you good. What you need is some Italian glamour...and a fling with a gorgeous man to get that sleazebag Jeremy out of your head.*

Tamsin would definitely describe Orlando de Luca as gorgeous. Her exact words would be along the lines of 'sex on legs'. Eleanor couldn't help smiling at the thought.

'My name makes you laugh?'

'No.' Though she certainly wasn't going to explain why she was smiling. What was 'sorry', again? *'Mi dispiace.'*

'You speak some Italian.'

She needed to turn this back to business. Fast. 'A little. But not enough to help Fabiola. Thank you for that. *Grazie.*'

'Prego.' He inclined his head.

At that moment, Giulietta recovered full consciousness and pulled at the mask.

Immediately, Orlando went back into doctor mode, taking her hand and calming her and speaking to her gently in Italian.

Eleanor guessed he was telling Giulietta what had happened and where she was going as soon as they reached Milan. She caught the words '*Inglese*' and '*dottoressa*'—clearly he was explaining who she was, too.

The flight attendants managed to persuade people in the aisle seats to change places with Eleanor and Orlando, so they could continue monitoring Giulietta throughout the descent—both of them were aware that she could easily go back into VF and need shocking again.

But at last they were at the airport. The paramedics boarded the plane with a trolley, and Orlando gave them the full handover details in rapid Italian, pausing every so often to check readings with Eleanor. Fabiola accompanied her mother off the plane, and Eleanor returned to her seat—at the opposite end of the plane to Orlando's.

She wasn't sure whether she was relieved or disappointed when he didn't suggest changing places and sitting with her. Relieved, because then she wouldn't have to make polite conversation and her stomach was already in knots with her impending meeting tomorrow. Yet disappointed, because there was something calming about Orlando—the way he'd assessed the situation, acknowledged that she was the one with emergency experience and hadn't made a fuss about her leading, and had gently turned Fabiola's reaction from panic to understanding. He was the kind of man who made people feel *safe*.

But then again, she knew her judgement in men was lousy. Just because he was a good doctor, it didn't mean he was a good man: Jeremy certainly wasn't. And Orlando was probably married anyway. A man that good-looking couldn't possibly be single. Even if Eleanor was going to act on Tamsin's suggestion of having a holiday fling—which she had no intention of doing—Orlando de Luca wasn't the one for her.

Their paths would probably never cross again, so there was no point in dwelling on it. Besides, she had something else to think about.

Her meeting tomorrow, with the man who might just turn out to be her real father.

And maybe, just maybe, she'd have a family to belong to again. Wouldn't be alone any more.

CHAPTER TWO

THEY were two hours late getting to the airport at Naples. And then there was the wait for the luggage to arrive...except Eleanor couldn't see her suitcase at all.

Maybe she'd just missed it, taken her eye off the conveyor belt during the moment it had passed her, and the suitcase would be there the second time round.

Except it wasn't. Or the third time.

Oh, great. Not only was she late—tired, and in need of a shower and a cup of decent coffee—now her luggage was missing. Thank God she'd put the most important things in her hand luggage. She still had the original photographs back in England, so she could've had replacement copies made, but she'd wanted to hand them over in person.

And although, yes, she could go into the centre of Naples and replace most of her luggage first thing tomorrow morning, she already had plans. A meeting to which she didn't want to go wearing travel-stained clothes. Even if she rinsed her clothes out in her hotel room tonight, they'd be crumpled and scruffy and...

Oh-h-h.

She could have howled with frustration. The shops were probably closed by now and, even if she got up really early tomorrow morning, she wouldn't have enough time to find the shops, buy new clothes and be on time to meet Bartolomeo.

First impressions were important. Especially in this case. This really, really wasn't fair.

'Problems, Dottoressa Eleanor?'

Orlando's voice was like melted chocolate. Soothing and comforting and sinful, all at the same time.

And she really shouldn't give in to the urge to lean on him. She was perfectly capable of sorting things out on her own. She had a phrasebook in her bag—given a little time and effort, she'd be able to make herself understood. Luggage must go missing all the time. It was probably just mislaid, on the wrong carousel or something. And when she got to the hotel, she could talk to someone in the reception area and ask where she should go to buy clothes and shoes tomorrow. She could call Bartolomeo and put back their meeting by an hour, if need be.

'I'm just waiting for my luggage,' she said.

'It hasn't arrived yet?'

He was carrying a small, stylish case. And there were only three cases left on the conveyor belt—none of which was hers.

'I was just about to go and ask.'

'Let me,' he said.

Before she could protest, he added, 'You said on the plane that you didn't speak much Italian. So let me help you.'

Italian was his native tongue and he spoke perfect English, too: it made sense to let him interpret for her instead of struggling. '*Grazie*.' Though she still had reservations. 'But won't it make you really late home? Especially as our flight was delayed.'

He shrugged. '*Non importa*. It doesn't matter.'

'It's not fair to your family, to keep them waiting even longer.'

He spread his hands. 'Nobody's waiting for me. I live alone.'

Now, that she hadn't expected. She'd been so sure a man like

Orlando de Luca—capable, practical and gorgeous—would be married to a wife who adored him, with several children who adored him even more and a menagerie of dogs and cats he'd rescued over the years.

'I won't be long. What does your bag look like?'

'It's a trolley suitcase—about so big.' She described the size with her hands. 'And it's, um, bright pink.'

'Bright pink,' he echoed. His voice was completely deadpan, but there was a sparkle of amusement in his eyes—as if he thought she'd chosen something completely frivolous and un-doctor-like.

She wished now she'd bought her luggage in a neutral colour. Grey, beige or black. She'd just thought that a bright suitcase would be easier to spot at the airport.

He smiled at her and went over to one of the airport staff. During the conversation, the man nodded, looked over at Eleanor with an expression of respect, said something to Orlando, and then strode away.

'He's going to check for you,' Orlando confirmed when he returned. 'I explained that our flight was late in because of a medical emergency on the plane. You saved the patient's life and we should be looking after you, not losing your baggage.'

She felt colour flood into her face. 'I didn't save Giulietta's life on my own. You did the chest compressions and got a patient history from her daughter. I couldn't have done it without you.'

'Teamwork, then. We worked well together.' His eyes narrowed as he glanced at her. 'You look tired. You've had a long journey, plus the stress of dealing with a cardiac arrest in a cramped space without the kind of equipment you're used to, and now your baggage has disappeared. Come and sit down. I will get you some coffee.'

He was taking over and Eleanor knew she should be standing

up for herself, telling him that she appreciated the offer but she really didn't need looking after. Her feelings must have shown on her face because he said gently, 'It may be a while until they locate your luggage. Why stand around waiting and getting stressed, when the coffee-shop is just here, to our right, and you can sit down in comfort and relax?'

And he was right. She *was* tired. Caffeine was just what she needed to get her through the rest of this evening until she got to the hotel.

'Do you take milk, sugar?' he asked when he'd settled her at a table.

'Just milk, please.'

There was something about the English *dottoressa*. Orlando couldn't define it or even begin to put his finger on it, but something about her made him want to get to know her better.

Much better.

He'd liked the way she'd been so cool and calm on the plane, got on with her job without barking orders or being rude to the flight attendants, and had even tried speaking the little Italian she knew to help reassure Giulietta's daughter. There was a warmth to Eleanor Forrest that attracted him.

A warmth that had suddenly shut off when he'd asked her a personal question.

And he wanted to know why.

He ordered coffee and *cantuccini*, then carried a tray over to their table.

'Biscuits?' she asked.

'Because I missed them in England,' he said simply. 'Your English biscuits fall apart when you dip them in coffee. These don't.' He smiled at her. 'They're nice dipped in *vin santo*, too, but I think for now coffee is what you need.'

'Thanks. Odd how just sitting around can make you feel tired.'

'Don't forget you saved a life in the middle of all that,' he reminded her.

She ignored his comment. 'How much do I owe you for the coffee?'

An independent woman. One who'd insist on paying her way. He liked that, too: she wouldn't take anyone for granted. She was the kind of woman who'd want an equal. 'My suggestion, my bill.'

He caught the expression on her face just before she masked it. Someone had obviously hurt her—hurt her so badly that she wouldn't even accept a cup of coffee from a man she barely knew, and saw strangers as a potential for hurt instead of a potential friend.

Softly, he added, 'That puts you under no obligation to me at all, Eleanor. Whatever you might have heard about Italian men, I can assure you I'm not expecting anything from you. I haven't put anything in your coffee and you're not going to wake up tomorrow morning in a room you can't remember seeing before with no clothes, no money and one hell of a headache.'

'I... I'm sorry. And I didn't mean to insult you or your countrymen,' she said, looking awkward and embarrassed.

'No offence taken. You're quite right to be wary of strangers offering drinks. But I'm a doctor buying a mug of coffee for a fellow professional. And this really is just coffee.'

'And it's appreciated.'

He settled opposite her. 'So, are you on holiday in Naples?'

'Sort of.'

Not a straight yes or no. And she didn't offer any details, he noticed. He had a feeling she'd clam up completely if he pushed her, so he tried for levity instead. 'Your *mamma* told you never to talk to strangers, is that it?'

'No.' Her voice went very quiet. 'Actually, my mother died just before Christmas.'

Six months ago. And the pain was clearly still raw. '*Mi dispiace*, Eleanor,' he said softly. 'I didn't intend to hurt you.'

'You weren't to know. It's not a problem.'

But he noticed she didn't explain any further. And those beautiful brown eyes were filled with sadness. He had a feeling it was more than just grief at losing her mother. Something to do with the man who'd made her wary of strangers, perhaps?

Yet she'd put her feelings aside and gone straight to help a stranger when the flight attendants had asked for a doctor. Eleanor Forrest was an intriguing mixture. And Orlando wanted to know what made her tick.

He switched to a safer topic. 'You're an emergency doctor?'

'Yes.'

OK. He'd try the professional route: say nothing, just smile, and give her space to answer more fully. Just like he did with his shyer patients. If he waited long enough, she'd break the silence.

She did. 'I work in a London hospital.'

Something else they had in common. Good. 'London's a beautiful city. I've just spent a few days there with the doctor I used to share a flat with, Max. It was his son's christening.'

There was the tiniest crinkle round her eyes. 'I don't know if I dare ask. Were you the…?'

'*Padrino?* The godfather, you mean?' So under her reserve there was a sense of fun. He liked that. Enough to want to see more of it. He hummed the opening bars of the theme tune to the film. 'Yes, I was.'

Though seeing the expression on Max's face when he looked at his wife and baby had made Orlando ache. Orlando had stopped believing in love, long ago, when his mother's fifth marriage had crumbled: every time she'd thought she'd found

The One, she'd been disillusioned. But Max was so happy with Rachel and little Connor, it had made Orlando think again. Wonder if maybe love really *did* exist.

Except he didn't have a clue where to start looking for it. And he wasn't sure that he wanted to spend his life searching and yearning and getting more and more disappointed, the way his mother did. So he'd decided to stick to the way he'd lived for the last five years—smile, keep his relationships light, just for fun, and put his energy into his work.

'You work in London, too?' she asked.

'Not any more. I did, for a couple of years, on a children's ward.' He spread his hands. 'But then I discovered I wanted to see my patients grow up—not forget about them once they'd left the hospital. I wanted to treat them, just as I'd treated their parents and their grandparents and would treat their children. I wanted to see them with their families.'

Strange, really, when he didn't have a family of his own. Just his mother, a few ex-stepfathers and ex-stepsiblings he hadn't kept in touch with. The only way he'd get an extended family now was to get married: and that was a risk he wasn't prepared to take.

Keep it light, he reminded himself. 'And I missed the lemon groves. I missed the sea.'

'And the sunshine,' she said with a wry smile.

'I don't mind London rain. But I admit, although I like visiting London, it's good to be back under the Italian sun. And I love being a family doctor.'

She smiled, and he caught his breath. Her serious manner masked her beauty—when she smiled, Eleanor Forrest was absolutely stunning. Perfect teeth and a wide smile and those amazing deep brown eyes.

It made him want to touch her. Trace the outline of her face with the tips of his fingers. Rub his thumb against her lower lip. And then dip his head to hers, claiming her mouth.

Then he became aware she was speaking. Oh, lord. He really hoped he hadn't ignored a question or something. She must think he was a real idiot.

'My best friend at medical school, Tamsin, did the same thing,' Eleanor said. 'She started in paediatrics and became a GP because she wanted to care for the whole family.'

'There's a lot to be said for it.' But they were talking about him. He wanted to know about *her*. 'You prefer the buzz of emergency medicine?'

'I like knowing I've made a difference,' she said simply.

She'd make a difference all right, he thought. Whatever branch of medicine she worked in. But before he could say anything, the man he'd spoken to about Eleanor's luggage came over, carrying one bright pink case.

'I am sorry for the wait, Dottoressa Forrest,' he said politely.

'No problem. *Grazie,*' she said, taking the case and checking the label. 'Yes, this is mine.'

He left after some pleasantries, and Eleanor stood up. 'Thank you for the coffee, Dottore de Luca.'

'You haven't finished it yet.'

She made a face. 'It's getting late. I really ought to check into my hotel.'

He didn't want her to walk out of his life. Not yet. And there was one way he could keep her talking to him for a little longer. 'You could be waiting a while for a taxi, and although public transport is good in Naples, you have baggage with you. I'll give you a lift.'

She shook her head. 'Thank you, but you've already been kind enough. I'd rather not impose.'

He wasn't sure what was going on here—he'd never experienced this weird, unexplainable feeling before—but what he knew for definite was that if he let her walk out of his life now, he'd regret it. Somehow he needed to persuade her to trust him. And to spend time with him so they could get to know each other.

Max had said he'd known the instant he'd met Rachel that she was the one he wanted to spend the rest of his life with. Orlando had scoffed, saying it was just lust and luckily he'd found friendship as well. But now he wasn't so sure. *Was* it possible to fall in love with someone at first sight? Did 'The One' exist? Was this odd feeling love? And was Eleanor Forrest the one he'd been waiting for?

He needed to know.

Needed to keep her with him.

'Eleanor, I know I'm a stranger, but you're a fellow doctor and you've helped save the life of one of my countrymen. Don't they say in England, one good turn deserves another?'

Eleanor couldn't help smiling at the old-fashioned phrase. 'You've already bought me coffee and sorted out my luggage for me. I think we're quits.'

'Let me put this another way. You could take a taxi, but why spend money you could spend on…' he waved an impatient hand '…oh, good coffee or ice cream or something frivolous to make your time here in Italy fun, when I can give you a lift?'

Lord, it was tempting. But she knew it would be a bad idea. Orlando de Luca might be the most attractive man she'd met in a long while—probably ever, if she thought about it—but that didn't mean she should act on the attraction. She'd already proved her judgement in men was lousy. Spectacularly lousy. OK, so Jeremy had caught her at an acutely vulnerable moment, but she'd still swallowed every single lie. Not just hook, line and sinker—more like the whole fishing rod. 'We might not be going the same way.'

'Then again, we might.'

The man should've been a lawyer. He had an answer for everything.

'So where are you going?' he asked.

A direct question. One she was reluctant to answer.

He lifted an eyebrow. 'Is it all strangers, all men, or just me?'

She frowned. 'How do you mean?'

'I make you nervous, Eleanor.'

'No.' Actually, that wasn't quite true. He *did* make her nervous. Because she was aware of the chemistry between them. And she remembered what had happened last time she'd acted on chemistry. Cue one broken heart. And she was still picking up the pieces.

'There's another saying in your country, is there not?' he asked softly. 'Trust me, I'm a doctor.'

Ha. Jeremy had proved that one to be false in the extreme. He was a doctor—and most definitely not to be trusted.

She faced Orlando, ready to be firm and say thank you but, no—she was getting a taxi. And then she saw the challenge in his eyes. As if he dared her to take the risk. Let him drive her to the hotel.

They'd worked well together on the plane. She'd trusted him then. Could she trust him now?

'I won't expect you to invite me in for a nightcap, if that's what you're worrying about.'

She felt the colour shoot into her face. 'Actually, that didn't occur to me.' Though Orlando had already told her he was single. And he was the most gorgeous man she'd seen in years, with those unruly dark curls, dark expressive eyes and a mouth that promised all kinds of pleasure. And she couldn't get Tamsin's suggestion out of her head: that a holiday fling with a gorgeous man would do her good…

He folded his arms. 'So are you going to stand in a long, long queue, Dottoressa Eleanor, or are you going to let me drop you off on my way home?'

She gave in to temptation. 'If you're sure it's no trouble, then thank you. A lift would be nice.'

His smile was breathtaking. And it made every single one of her nerve-endings feel as if it were purring.

'Then let's go through Customs, *tesoro*,' he said softly.

The queues at the customs area and passport control had died down, and they moved through the airport surprisingly quickly. She followed Orlando into the car park—just as she could've guessed, he drove a low-slung, shiny black car. A convertible, to be exact. Men and their toys. And didn't they say that all Italian men wanted to be racing-car drivers?

As if her thoughts were written all over her face, he laughed and stowed her case in the boot next to his. 'I have only myself to please, Eleanor. And I love driving along the coast road with the hood down and the wind in my hair and the scent of the sea and lemon groves everywhere. If you have time in your schedule here, maybe you'd like to come with me some time.'

He made it sound so inviting.

And it made her knees go weak to imagine it: Orlando, wearing a black T-shirt and black jeans, a pair of dark glasses covering his eyes, at the wheel of the open-topped car.

'So, your hotel?'

She told him the name, and before she could tell him the address he told her exactly where it was. Clearly he knew his home city well. 'And just to stop you feeling guilty about taking me out of my way, it's on my side of the city. On my way home, to be precise. It's within walking distance of my apartment, in the Old Quarter.' He opened the passenger door for her, an old-fashioned gesture of courtesy she found charming.

Though some nervousness must have shown on her face because he added, 'I assure you, Eleanor, you will be perfectly safe. I am a good driver.'

He proved it. Though he was also a very fast driver, and her knuckles were white by the time he pulled up outside her hotel.

'We are both in one piece,' he said with a grin. 'Relax.'

She wasn't sure if it was the way he'd driven—exactly the same as all the other people on the road, taking advantage of every little gap in the traffic—or being so close to him in such a small space, but relaxing was the last thing she felt like doing right now.

'Enjoy your stay in Italy, Eleanor.' When he'd taken her case from the back of his car and carried it up the steps to the entrance of the hotel, he took a card from his wallet, and scribbled a number on the back of it. 'If you have some spare time while you are in Naples, maybe we could have dinner. My surgery number is on the front. The one I've written on the back is my mobile. Call me.'

It wasn't a question.

'Call me,' he said again, his voice soft, and raised her hand to his mouth.

The brush of his lips against her skin was momentary. It was a mere courtesy, she knew, the Italian way of doing things. It didn't mean anything. But there was heat in his eyes. Heat matched by the flicker of desire rising up her spine.

Calling him would be way too dangerous for her peace of mind. But she wasn't going to argue over it now. Instead, she smiled politely. 'Thank you for the lift, Dottore de Luca.'

'Orlando,' he corrected. '*Prego.*' He smiled, sketched a bow, ran lightly down the steps to his car and drove off.

CHAPTER THREE

ONCE Eleanor had signed the register and been shown to her room, she unpacked swiftly and took a shower. She was too tired and it was too late to eat a proper meal, so she ordered a milky hot chocolate from room service. She started to text her mum to say she'd arrived safely, then realised what she was doing halfway through, blinked away the tears, reminded herself to stop being over-emotional and texted Tamsin instead.

When she'd finished her hot chocolate, she slid into bed and curled into a ball. The sheets were cool and smooth and the bed was comfortable, but despite the milky drink she couldn't sleep.

Because she couldn't get a certain face out of her mind. Orlando de Luca. Every time she closed her eyes she saw his face. His smile. That hot look in his eyes.

Which was crazy.

Right now she wasn't in the market for a relationship. She knew she needed to get over Jeremy's betrayal and move on with her life, but was having a holiday fling with a gorgeous man really the right way to do that? And anyway there must be some reason why Orlando was single.

She didn't think it was a personality flaw—the way he'd worked with her was nothing like the way Jeremy worked, being so charming that you didn't realise until it was too late that he'd taken the credit for everything. Orlando was genuine. A nice guy, as well as one of the most attractive he'd ever met.

So why? He'd said he'd worked as a paediatrician then turned to family medicine. So was he still building his career and putting his love life on hold until he was where he wanted to be? Was he the sort who was dedicated to his career and didn't want the commitment to a relationship? In that case he would be the perfect fling—and maybe she should call him…

But not until after her meeting tomorrow. Her stomach tightened with nerves. What would Bartolomeo Conti be like? He'd sounded nice, on the phone. The photograph he'd emailed to her was that of a man in his mid-fifties with a charming smile. But she knew firsthand that charm often covered something far less pleasant. And her mother hadn't stayed with Bartolomeo. So was the man who might be her father a snake beneath the smile? Or was she judging him unfairly?

Finally, Eleanor fell asleep; the next morning, the alarm woke her, and by the time she'd showered her stomach was in knots. She couldn't face even the usual light Italian breakfast of a crumbly pastry, just a frothy cappuccino—and she checked her watch what turned out to be every thirty seconds to make sure she wasn't going to be late.

After one last glance in the mirror in her room to check she looked respectable, she headed for the hotel lounge. The second she walked in, a tall man stood up and waved to her. She recognised him instantly from the photo he'd emailed her—just as he'd clearly recognised her.

A moment of panic. What did she call him? 'Signor Conti?'

'Bartolomeo,' he corrected. 'And I hope you will let me call you Eleanor.' He enveloped her in a hug. 'Thank you so much for coming to see me—and all this way, from London.'

'*Prego.*'

He looked delighted that she'd made the effort to speak his language. 'We are both early.' His smile turned slightly wry. 'I slept badly.'

'Me, too,' she admitted.

He put his hands on her shoulders and looked closely at her. 'I thought it from your photo, and now I know for sure. You look so much like my Costanza. Constance Firth,' he corrected, 'the woman I fell in love with, thirty years ago.' He added softly, 'But your colouring is all mine.'

Constance Forrest had been fair-haired and Tim Forrest had had sandy hair; both had been blue-eyed. What were the chances of them producing a brown-eyed, dark-haired child— one with olive skin that didn't burn, rather than an English rose? Whereas Bartolomeo Conti, the man whose initial had been at the bottom of the love letter she'd found among her mother's things, had hair, skin and eyes the same colour as her own. Coincidence? Or was he her biological father?

'Have you had breakfast, Eleanor?' he asked.

She shook her head. 'I was too nervous to eat.'

'Me, too. Let's go and have a late breakfast and watch the world go by.'

He took her to a little caffè-bar and ordered them both coffee and *sfogliatelle*. 'You will like these, Eleanor—they are a Neapolitan speciality. Sweet pastry shaped like a shell and filled with sweetened ricotta cheese and candied orange rind.' His smile was full of memories. 'I bought these for your *mamma,* the first time we went to a *caffè* together.'

She had so many questions. But they had time.

'I thought you might like to see these,' Eleanor said when they'd sat down, handing him an envelope.

Bartolomeo leafed through them. 'Yes, this is how I

remember my Costanza,' he said softly. 'And she grew into a very, very beautiful woman. This one of her in the garden…' There was a catch in his voice. 'And this is you as a *bambina*?' He smiled. 'You look so much like my sisters Luisella and Federica when they were *bambini*. Those dimples… May I borrow these to make copies?'

'Keep them. I did this set for you,' Eleanor explained.

He reached over the table and hugged her. 'I never thought I would be blessed with children. And now…' He shook his head in wonder. 'And now it seems I have a daughter. A daughter I would very much like to get to know. If your *papà* does not mind?'

She appreciated the fact he'd asked. Even though strictly speaking it didn't matter any more. 'Dad had a stroke the year after I graduated as a doctor.' Though at least Tim Forrest had been there for her graduation. He'd shared that particular triumph with her. 'There's only me now.'

'You are alone in the world?' Bartolomeo looked shocked. 'What of Costanza's *famiglia*? Her mother, her father?'

'I never knew them.'

He frowned. 'Are you telling me they disowned Costanza because she had you when she was not married?'

Eleanor shook her head. 'I don't really know anything about them. The only grandparents I remember were dad's parents, but he was twenty years older than Mum and they died when I was in my early teens.' She'd often wondered about her grandparents but hadn't wanted to hurt her mother by asking. And, thirty years ago, being pregnant and unmarried had still had a bit of a stigma. So maybe Bartolomeo's theory was right. 'You really had no idea I existed?'

'None,' he said firmly. 'Had I known my Costanza was carrying my baby, I would have flown straight to England and married her.'

'So what happened?' She needed to know. Why had her mother gone back to England alone?

Bartolomeo sighed. 'I don't come out of it very well, but I want to be honest with you from the start. I fell in love with your mother, but I wasn't really free to do so.' He looked awkward. 'I wasn't formally betrothed to Mariella, the daughter of my father's business partner, but we'd grown up together and our families both expected us to get married. Except then I met Costanza. She was on holiday. It was springtime. I drove past her and caught her in a shower from a puddle. I stopped and took her for a coffee to apologise and that was it. Love at first sight.'

Something she didn't believe in—in her view, you had to get to know someone properly first—so why couldn't she get Orlando de Luca out of her head?

Memories softened Bartolomeo's face. 'Your mother was so warm, so vibrant—nothing like the cool English rose I thought she would be when I first heard her accent. She made me laugh, and I fell in love with her smile. We were inseparable in the days after that. Everything happened very fast, and I knew I wanted to marry her. I told my parents that I could not marry Mariella, that I wanted my bright English girl. And it was made very clear to me that I would have to choose between my family and Costanza.'

'So you chose your family.' Eleanor could understand that. She would've hated being cut off from her parents.

'Not at all. I told them if they were going to insist I had to choose, then I would choose my Costanza.' Bartolomeo's face tightened. 'But she had already made the decision for me. I went to her hotel and she was gone. She'd left me a letter, saying she would not come between me and my family. She was going back to England and she wasn't going to see me again. And I was to marry Mariella, as everyone expected, and be happy.'

Which had given him a neat get-out. And even though Bartolomeo had warned her he didn't come out of it well, disappointment seeped through her. 'Didn't you even *try* to get in touch with her?'

'Of course I did. But I didn't have a telephone number for her, only an address.' He frowned. 'I wrote to her but my letters were returned unopened.'

'And that was it? You just gave up?'

He smiled wryly. 'You have to remember, I wasn't that old. I was twenty-two. So I did the impulsive thing and flew over to England. I thought that I could make her change her mind if I saw her—but when I arrived your grandparents told me she had moved out and they wouldn't give me a forwarding address. I didn't know who her friends were, where she worked, where even to start finding her. And then I thought, clearly, she meant it. She really didn't want to see me again or she would have left me clues.' He looked sad. 'And now I know I was right. She decided to keep it a clean break. Otherwise she would have told me about you. My Costanza was never a liar.'

'But she never told *me* about *you*. I grew up thinking Dad was…' She shrugged. 'Well, my dad. I only started wondering when I bought my house and the bank queried the fact my birth certificate had my surname as Firth. Mum said it was just an admin thing. Then, when I was clearing out her things afterwards, I found the papers: they changed my name from Firth to Forrest by deed poll after they married.'

'So her husband brought you up as his own.' Bartolomeo looked anxious. 'She was happy with him? He treated her well? Treated you both well?'

There was a lump in Eleanor's throat as she remembered. 'They loved each other very, very much. And, yes, they were happy. *We* were happy. We were a family.' The perfect family. And how she missed them.

'I am glad.' Her surprise must have shown on her face because he said, 'I would not want my Costanza to be sad. And I would want your childhood to be full of smiles.'

'It was. Tim obviously wasn't my biological father, but he was my dad. He read me bedtime stories, taught me to ride a bike and drive a car, grilled my boyfriends and grounded me when I was late home, helped me with my homework and opened the champagne when I got my exam results. He was always there any time I needed to talk—always there with a hug and a smile and sheer common sense when I was full of teenage angst. Mum was, too.' She swallowed back the tears, the aching loss. The knowledge that Tim would've seen through Jeremy and gently made her see the truth. 'And you? You were happy with Mariella?'

'We married, but it was a mistake.' He sighed. 'I loved her, but not in the way I loved Costanza—there wasn't the same spark, the same passion I found with Costanza. We were more…friends. I tried to be a good husband, worked hard to provide for her and build up my family's business. Too hard, maybe, because she thought I neglected her.' He shrugged. 'She found love in someone else's arms.'

'I'm sorry.'

He sipped his coffee. 'No matter. But I've had my work, and my sisters are close to me. And I have two nieces to spoil.' He smiled. 'And you? You have a husband, a *fidanzato*?'

She'd had a fiancé. Five months ago. 'No. I'm single.'

'A beautiful *ragazza* like you? Why?'

'There was someone,' she admitted.

'What happened?'

'He was wrong for me.' She wasn't prepared to tell

Bartolomeo just how close she'd been to making the biggest mistake of her life. If she hadn't met Penelope and found out the truth… She pushed the thought away. 'So what made you send that message to the radio station?'

'To find my lost love? I've reached that age when you look back at your life and you wonder what you would have done differently.' He spread his hands. 'I am just lucky you heard the *Lost Loves* programme.'

'And put the pieces together.' She nodded. 'That song always made Mum cry. And the dates fitted—the summer before I was born. I never even knew she'd been to Italy.'

'I regret that I never knew you as a baby.' His voice softened. 'I can't change the past. But we can change the future. And I would very much like you to be part of my future, Eleanor. Part of my family.'

Longing tugged at her. To be part of a family again…how could she say no?

Before Eleanor knew it, it was lunchtime. She and Bartolomeo ate a leisurely *panini* and fruit and ordered more coffee, and spent their time talking and catching up.

Finally she glanced at her watch. 'I'm sorry—have I made you late for an appointment?'

Bartolomeo smiled. 'I kept my diary free today.'

But he looked pale, tired. 'Are you all right?' she asked.

'Just getting old—at the stage in my life where I need a *son-nelino*, a nap.'

But Bartolomeo could only be in his early fifties. If he'd been twenty-two when her mother had fallen pregnant, that would make him fifty-three now. He was too young to feel this tired, this early in the day.

'Come to dinner tonight,' he said. He took a business card

from a small leather case, and wrote swiftly on the back. 'This is my address. My sisters and their husbands usually come over for supper on a Tuesday evening. Come and meet them.'

Eleanor wasn't sure. 'It's the evening you spend with your family.'

'You are my daughter. So they are your family, too.' He smiled and squeezed her hand. 'It's nothing formal—a simple supper. Please come.'

'I…'

'Please?'

How could she resist that beseeching look? 'All right.'

He beamed at her. 'Then I will see you at seven, yes?'

Once his taxi had driven off, Eleanor headed into the centre of Naples. For a mad moment she thought about calling Orlando—but he was probably in surgery right now. And anyway, she wasn't there to have a holiday fling: she was there to find out the truth about her father. She really didn't need the extra complication.

She wasn't sure whether the etiquette of dinner parties was the same in Italy as it was in England, but she bought wine and chocolates to take with her anyway. She'd just finished changing when the phone in her room rang.

'Dottoressa Forrest? I have a call for you,' the receptionist said.

Odd. If it was Tamsin, the call would've come through on her mobile phone. Who would call her at the hotel? Bartolomeo, to cancel this evening? 'Thank you. I'll take it,' she said quietly.

'Hello, Eleanor?'

She recognised the voice immediately, and a shiver of pure pleasure ran down her spine. 'Orlando?'

'I was just passing your hotel on my way home. Do you have time to have a drink with me in the bar?'

She glanced at her watch. Fifteen minutes until she needed to catch the metro. Fifteen minutes when she could sit on her own and worry about whether Bartolomeo's family would accept her, or... 'I have to leave in about fifteen minutes,' she said.

'Then you do have time. *Bene.* What would you like to drink?'

She knew that alcohol wasn't the right way to soothe her nerves: she didn't want to turn up at dinner reeking of wine the first time she met the Conti family. 'Mineral water would be lovely. Sparkling, please. I'll be right down.'

She replaced the receiver, picked up the things she wanted to take with her to Bartolomeo's, and went to join Orlando in the bar. He was sitting at a table on his own, skimming through a newspaper and seemingly oblivious to the admiring glances of the women sitting in the bar. Including her own. In a well-cut dark suit with a sober tie and a white shirt, he looked absolutely edible. As she reached the table, he put down the newspaper and stood up. 'Thank you for joining me, Eleanor.'

Old-fashioned etiquette. Funny how it made her knees weak.

'I assumed you'd like ice and lemon,' he said, indicating the glass at the place opposite him.

'*Grazie,*' she said, sitting down.

'*Prego.*' He smiled at her, sat down and poured water from the bottle into her glass. 'I rang the hospital in Milan today. I thought you'd like to know that Giulietta Russo is doing just fine and they expect her to make a full recovery from her heart attack.'

She smiled back. 'That's great news. Thanks for telling me.'

'Though I admit, it wasn't the only reason I called by.' He took a sip of his own drink—also mineral water, she noticed. 'I wondered if you might be free the day after tomorrow—if you'd like to come to Pompeii with me.'

He was asking her on a date?

Her first thought was, *Yes, please.* Her second was more

sensible: despite Tamsin's suggestion, she really wasn't here in Naples to have a fling. And the fact that she hadn't been able to stop thinking about Orlando meant she really ought to steer clear: things could get way too complicated, and right now there were enough complications in her life.

She took a sip of iced water to give her a breathing space. The answer was no—but nicely. Because in other circumstances it would definitely have been yes.

'It's very kind of you to ask,' she said, 'but I'm not in the market for a date.'

He looked pointedly at her left hand. 'Not married. So you're involved with someone at home—someone who couldn't join you here in Italy?'

'No. I'm single,' she admitted.

'As am I. So what's the harm? You're here on holiday, yes?'

'Not exactly,' she hedged.

'Business, then?'

She shook her head. 'It's personal. But I can't really talk about it right now. I need to get some things straight in my head.'

'It sounds,' Orlando said thoughtfully, 'as if you could use a friend. A sounding-board, you could say. Someone who's not involved.'

Lord, he was acute. That was exactly what she needed. Someone who was objective, who could see things more clearly than she could right now.

'You barely know me, I admit—but I think we could be friends. And, as a *medico di famiglia*, I'm a good listener.' He spread his hands. 'Come to Pompeii with me. We can potter around among the ruins and eat *gelati*…and you can talk to me, knowing that whatever you tell me won't go any further.'

Tempting. So tempting

But Eleanor wasn't sure she could handle the beginning of

a relationship as well as everything else—even if it was just temporary, a holiday fling.

'As friends,' he added, almost as if he'd guessed why she was stalling. 'No pressure.'

She nodded. 'Then thank you. I'd like that.'

'Good.' His eyes glittered. 'I'll pick you up here the day after tomorrow, at half past ten. Do you have good walking shoes?'

'Yes.'

'Wear them.' Then, to take the edge off the command, he gave her one of those slow, sensual, knee-buckling smiles—a smile that made her very glad she was sitting down. 'Of course, you could wear high heels if you prefer. But you'd end up with blisters.'

Which he, as a doctor, would insist on treating. The idea of his fingers stroking her skin—even if it was only to put a protective plaster around a blister—made desire flicker through her.

He glanced at his watch. 'My fifteen minutes is up. Unless you can be late?'

She shook her head. 'Not this time. It's…complicated.'

'You don't have to explain, *bella mia*.' He reached across the table, took her hand, raised it to his lips and kissed it—just the way he had the previous day, when he'd dropped her off at the hotel.

Every nerve-ending seemed to heat, and, shockingly, she found herself wondering what it would be like to feel his mouth against her own instead of her hand.

Oh, lord.

'Thank you for the drink,' she said politely. 'And I'm sorry I didn't, um, have a chance to finish it.'

'*Non importa.* You warned me we only had fifteen minutes.' He smiled at her. 'Have a pleasant evening. And I will see you on Thursday morning, yes?'

'Thursday.' And she really hoped her voice didn't sound as croaky to him as it did to her.

CHAPTER FOUR

THE evening went better than Eleanor had expected: Bartolomeo's sisters were a little wary of her to start with, but gradually started to thaw. She spent Wednesday morning exploring the city and the afternoon with Bartolomeo.

And then it was Thursday morning.

Her date-that-wasn't-a-date with Orlando.

She knew the second that he walked into the hotel foyer—even though she was reading a guidebook to Pompeii rather than watching the door—because the air in the room changed. Became electric.

And she noticed that just about every woman in the room was watching him as he walked towards her. His movements were fluid, graceful—almost like a dancer's. Beautiful. Yet he didn't seem aware of the turned heads. He just came to a stop in front of her and smiled.

'*Buon giorno*, Eleanor. You are ready?'

'Sure.' She closed the guidebook and stuffed it into her handbag.

'Then let's go.' He held his hand out to pull her to her feet. 'So, today—on your holiday that isn't exactly a holiday—you are officially on holiday, yes?'

The convoluted phrasing made her laugh—and made her

realise how ridiculous she was being. There was no need to be
cagey about why she was there. And, given what Orlando did
for a living…she could do with a second medical opinion to
confirm her suspicions. 'Yes.'

'*Bene.*' He ushered her down the steps to where he'd parked
the car, and opened the door for her. She hid a smile. All the
women were staring at them and envying her for being with
someone so gorgeous. And all the men were staring at them
and envying her for climbing into a car that gorgeous. Well,
they were probably envying Orlando, actually, for being behind
the wheel.

'What?' Orlando asked as he closed the driver's door.

'Nothing.'

He tipped his head on one side. 'Nothing?'

'Your car's attracting attention, that's all.'

He shrugged. 'There are plenty of cars like this in Italy.'

A low-slung, sleek black convertible. 'Flashy.'

He slanted her a grin. 'I prefer to use the word "fun".'

He would. 'Why are we driving there? The tourist guide said
the best way to get to Pompeii is by train.' Driving in Naples
would be a nightmare. Full of traffic jams—worse even than
London, she thought.

'Ah, so you were reading while you were waiting for me?'
He laughed. 'It's true—but I wanted to take you along the coast
afterwards. So this saves time coming back to Naples. This is
your first time in Naples, I take it?'

'My first time in Italy, full stop,' she said.

He smiled. 'You chose the best place. Rome is flashy. Venice
is…' he made a noise of contempt '…flooded.'

She laughed. 'Isn't that the point?'

'Maybe, but they also have *alta acqua*. Which is very far
from pleasant, believe me.' He shuddered. 'Naples—now, we

have Vesuvius. And the bay. We have the most beautiful churches in Italy. Oh, and the best pizza. Best *gelati*, too.'

She grinned. 'I'll take it as read that you love your home city, then.'

'That's why I came back,' he said simply. 'Don't get me wrong—I was happy in London. But this is home.'

'It's sort of my home too, in a way.'

'How so?'

He sounded interested, yet not pushy, and she found herself telling him. 'I never knew but my mother came here the year before I was born. She fell in love with someone. It didn't work out. But then I heard my mother's name on this radio programme—one of these ones where people search for their lost loves—and it was the man she'd fallen in love with. So I got in touch.'

'And you're here to meet him?'

'Yes.' She paused. 'That's why I said I wasn't really here on holiday. Because it turns out that he's my biological father.'

'And you had no idea?'

'Not until after my mother died, no. I mean, you hear of these "secret babies"—but you don't expect to find out that you're one of them.'

'It must have been a shock for you,' he said, sounding sympathetic. 'You were meeting him for the first time the other night?'

'Second,' she said. 'This time, I met his family.'

'Ouch. Difficult for you,' he said.

'More difficult for them—this English girl appearing out of nowhere after thirty years and claiming to be related.'

'We have warm hearts and big families over here. Give it time. They'll get used to the idea.' He reached over with his right hand and squeezed her hand. 'You're very brave to come all this way on your own. You told me about your mother, but you have no brothers, no sisters?'

'Just me. And my dad—the man who brought me up, the man I've always thought of as my dad—died the year after I graduated.'

Orlando left his hand curled round hers. 'So this man— your biological father—is now your only family.'

'Something like that.'

'So what about your friend, the one who's a GP? Wouldn't she come with you?'

'She would have done—but she's six months pregnant.'

The penny clearly dropped. 'So no travelling.'

She shrugged. 'There's just me.'

'Just you,' he said softly.

She swallowed hard. 'Except… Can I ask your advice?'

'Of course.'

'Bartolomeo said he'd just reached that age when he's curious about what might have been—that's why he tried to find Mum. But I think there's more to it than that. He isn't *that* old— he's in his early fifties, the prime of his life. And yet he's tiring easily, he's pale and I've noticed that he gets a little out of breath when he walks. That's not normal. So I'm thinking either a heart condition or maybe AML.' Without examining him herself, she couldn't give a proper diagnosis. But the symptoms she'd noticed were definitely worrying. 'And I was wondering…maybe he wanted to find Mum to make his peace with her. Before…' Her throat closed up and she couldn't say the words.

Orlando clearly knew what she meant, because the pressure of his hand tightened briefly around hers. 'It might be a post-viral illness—he might be recovering, not becoming sicker,' he said. 'But I think you need to talk to him about it. Be open about it. Get him to put your mind at rest.'

'Or let me prepare for the worst.'

'You,' Orlando told her, 'are looking on the dark side. It might not be what you think. You know as well as I do that the symptoms you listed apply to other illnesses that can be cured, or at least controlled. The breathlessness could be asthma—which can start at any age, so it could be recent and he's not used to taking his inhalers yet.'

'Maybe.'

'Talk to him,' Orlando advised. 'And although my medical textbooks are in Italian so they won't be much use to you, if you need them for research I can translate for you.'

'That's a very generous offer.' She was glad that her sunglasses hid her need to blink back tears.

'We're friends. Well, maybe we're more acquaintances, at the moment,' he told her, 'but we're going to be friends. And friends look out for each other, yes?'

'Thank you. *Grazie*.'

He smiled. 'My pleasure, *tesoro*. And now I want you to stop worrying. Until you've talked to him and found more information, there's nothing you can do. So relax. Enjoy the sunshine. Things have a way of working out.'

He squeezed her hand once more, then placed his hand back on the steering-wheel. This time he drove a little more sedately than he had from the airport. And then she noticed the music playing softly in the background. A string quartet: something she didn't recognise, but it was soothing—and very pretty. 'What's the music?' she asked

'Vivaldi.'

'It's lovely.'

'Well, of course. It's Italian.' He gave her a wicked look. 'We do have more than just "O Sole Mio", you know.'

'You listen to mainly classical music?'

'Depends on my mood. I'll sing along with Lucio Battisti or Andrea Bocelli—or sometimes I just like the regularity of Vivaldi or Corelli in the background. Had I been a surgeon, I think I would choose this for the operating theatre.' He paused. 'And you?'

She shrugged. 'Whatever's on the radio. Something I can hum along to.'

'If you want to change the music, help yourself.'

Jeremy had teased her about singing out of key: no way was she going to sing along in the car beside a man she barely knew. A man she was finding more and more attractive, the more time she spent with him. Today Orlando was wearing casual clothes—pale linen trousers and a white T-shirt—and yet he looked utterly gorgeous. Even more so than he had in a formal suit—because casual meant *touchable*.

And he'd just been holding her hand.

She gripped the edges of her sunhat to keep herself from temptation.

'I'm glad you don't have long hair,' Orlando said.

Not what the rest of the world had said when she'd gone from hair that was almost waist-length to an urchin cut. 'Oh?'

'Because it's beautiful outside,' he said. 'Beautiful enough to have the top down—but if your hair were long and loose, that wouldn't be much fun for you.'

'Is that a hint?'

'Would you mind? I know it's hot, but we're not that far from Pompeii so you shouldn't get a headache from the sun. Though I would advise you to remove your hat.'

She did as he suggested. *'Prego.'*

He pressed a button: moments later, the hood was down and folded away. Automatic. Impressive.

'Now you're showing off,' she said.

He laughed. 'It's called "having fun".'

When they reached Pompeii, Orlando put the hood back up, and took two bottles of water from the glove compartment.

'You need to keep properly hydrated in this climate,' he said.

'Thanks. I didn't think about that.'

He shrugged. 'At least you remembered a hat and sunglasses. That's more than many people would.'

'And as you drove us here,' she told him when they joined the queue for tickets, 'I'm paying the entrance fee.'

'No. This was my idea. And in my world women don't pay on a date.'

'This isn't a date,' she reminded him. 'We're here as friends. I pay for the tickets, or no deal.'

He laughed. 'You're independent and impossible. And I want the pleasure of showing you Pompeii, so what choice do I have?' He held his hand out for her to shake. 'OK, it's a deal. Provided you let me buy you a *gelati*.'

She shook his hand, and her palm tingled at the contact. 'Deal,' she said, hearing the huskiness in her own voice and hoping that Orlando hadn't noticed.

When she'd paid for their tickets, they wandered through into the old town. There were beautiful frescoes and mosaic floors everywhere. 'It's gorgeous. You wouldn't think this place was over two thousand years old,' she said, full of wonder.

'Nearer three,' Orlando said, 'as it was first occupied in the eighth century BC. Some of the ruined buildings were actually ruins before the eruption.'

'Incredible.' Though there was something that made her uncomfortable. 'Those bodies on the floor…where did they come from?'

'They're plaster casts,' he told her. 'The ash from the volcano fell and buried the people and animals, then hardened round them. The bodies decomposed and left a space behind in the ash. In the nineteenth century, the archaeologist Giuseppi Fiorelli had the idea of pumping plaster in to the cavities so we could see what was under the ash.'

'That's a bit ghoulish,' Eleanor said. 'I mean, these were people—we're witnessing how they suffered, their last agonies. It's a bit…well, not very nice, don't you think?'

He gave her a perceptive look. 'Is that why you became an emergency doctor? To stop people hurting?'

She nodded. 'Neither of my parents were medics. Dad was a history teacher and Mum taught music.'

'Your father would have enjoyed it here, then.'

'Loved it,' she confirmed. 'He used to research local history for fun and would spend hours in the archives. He did some research in the National Archives at Kew while I was training in London. I remember he met me from lectures and we had dinner together.' The memories were good, but they still made tears clog her throat—because they made her realise how much she missed her parents.

'You were close to your parents?' Orlando asked.

She nodded. 'Very. I miss them.' She shook herself. 'How about you? Are your parents medics?'

He shrugged. 'My mother is in property.'

He didn't say anything about his father, she noticed, and there were lines of tension around his mouth. Clearly she'd just prodded a very sore point. Maybe, she thought, his father had died when Orlando had been young.

On impulse, she took his hand and squeezed it. '*Mi dispiace*, Orlando. I was being nosy. I'm sorry if I've said something that brought back sad memories.'

'*Non importa*. It doesn't matter.'

But he laced his fingers through hers and didn't let her hand go. Oddly, it felt *right*. If someone had said to her a week ago that she'd been strolling hand in hand with a gorgeous Italian between Vesuvius and the sea, she would've laughed—but it was happening.

She'd learned that making plans—as she had with Jeremy—didn't work for her. So from now she was going to do the opposite: take things as they came. Enjoy life as she experienced it.

And sauntering through Pompeii with Orlando was fantastic. Especially as he seemed to know everything about the site—pointed out little things that she wouldn't have noticed and which she couldn't remember seeing in the guide book she'd started reading the previous evening.

The streets were rough; she stumbled slightly on a paving slab, and Orlando steadied her against him. 'OK?' he asked.

Very OK. Holding hands with Orlando—even though she knew that it didn't mean anything—sent a warm glow through her. Something about his strength, his steadiness. Orlando de Luca was the kind of man who'd never let you down. 'I'm fine.'

'Good.' He didn't let go of her hand. 'The roads used to flood here, so they made special pedestrian crossings of raised stones to make it easier for people to cross the road. Look, there's one here.'

'How do you know so much about the place?' she asked.

'I did some work on here.'

'What sort of work?' A tour guide in the summer holidays when he was a student, perhaps?

His answer surprised her. 'I wrote a couple of articles about the medicine of Pompeii. This place has fascinated me right from when I was a tiny child and came here with my nanny.'

Not with his mother, she noticed. 'Did you ever think about becoming an archaeologist?'

He nodded. 'But, like you, I wanted to make people better. I had to make the choice between studying medicine and studying archaeology. I think I made the right choice: this way I get the best of both worlds, with a job I love and a place to escape.'

'Have your papers been trans—?'

Eleanor didn't get the chance to finish asking her question, because they heard a cry and saw a man in front of them stagger and lean against the wall, clutching his stomach with one hand and gripping the wall with the other.

'*C'è un problema?*' Orlando asked.

'Not…speak…Italian,' the man gasped. 'American.'

Orlando switched to English. 'What's wrong?'

'Feel dizzy. Sick. Stomach hurts.' The man dragged in a breath. 'Can't see properly.'

'Do you have any pain anywhere, apart from your stomach?' Eleanor asked.

'My head,' he croaked.

Eleanor checked his pulse: it was racing and thumping. His forehead was hot, even allowing for the weather—and it was dry rather than sweaty.

She exchanged a glance with Orlando.

He mouthed, 'Heatstroke?'

It wasn't something she saw much of in England—except in a rare heatwave—but the symptoms certainly seemed like it. They needed to get the man out of the sun and start to cool him down—now. Gently, she took the tourist's arm. 'We're both doctors. Let's get you into the shade so we can have a look at you.' She led him into a cool, quiet area where he could sit down.

'Are you on your own or with a group of people?' Orlando asked.

'MedAm tours,' he said. 'I lost my party. Stopped to look at something. They'd gone.'

'I'll go and find your guide,' Orlando said. 'And get a medical kit. I didn't put mine in the car today but the office here should have something.' He took a handkerchief from his pocket—clean, folded and uncrumpled—and handed it to Eleanor, along with his bottle of water. 'Eleanor's an emergency doctor, so I'm leaving you in good hands,' he said gently. 'Don't worry. We'll get help for you.'

'What's your name?' Eleanor asked.

'Jed Baynes.'

'Pleased to meet you, Jed. I'm Eleanor Forrest.'

"I'm not drunk,' Jed said to Eleanor when Orlando had left. 'Don't even drink. But my head *hurts*. Like a killer hangover.'

She noticed he wasn't wearing a hat. And he didn't appear to be carrying any water with him. 'Have you been in the sun long?' she asked.

'No, just since first thing this morning.'

She glanced at her watch. It was nearly half past twelve, so he'd probably been out in the sun for at least three hours. And right now it was the hottest part of the day. 'No hat?'

'Forgot it. Wanted to see the ruins.' He grimaced. 'Didn't think.'

'Have you stopped for a drink?'

'No.'

And in this heat he'd be dehydrated even before he felt thirsty. Not good. 'OK. I think you've just been in the sun too long. You need some water.' She unscrewed the lid from her water bottle, wiped the neck with Orlando's handkerchief and handed it to Jed. 'Take a sip. Not lots of gulps, or you'll bring it back up again—just take it nice and slowly. One sip at a time.' She opened Orlando's water and dampened the handkerchief with it, then gently dabbed it across Jed's face. 'We need to cool you down a bit,' she said softly. At least he was wearing loose shorts and a shirt, so his clothing wasn't going to make things worse. 'Have you ever had anything like this before?'

'No.'

'When Dr de Luca's back, hopefully he'll have a thermometer with him. I think you've got a temperature—and we might need to get you to hospital to help you cool down.'

'I don't want to make a fuss!'

'It's no trouble,' she reassured him, and dampened the handkerchief again. A quick glance showed her that Jed's pupils weren't dilated, so hopefully they'd caught him before his condition spiralled out of control.

Within a few minutes Orlando had returned with a medical kit. 'They're getting in touch with the tour leader on his mobile phone. I told them exactly where to find us.' He handed Eleanor the thermometer.

'Would you mind just popping this under your tongue for me?' Eleanor wiped the thermometer, then handed it to Jed. As soon as it beeped, she checked the electronic reading. 'Your temperature's very high—almost forty-one.'

Orlando said in low tones, 'If you've been cooling him down since I left you, then I'm really not happy. It's still way too high. He could end up having a fit.' He sat down on the other side of Jed and took his hand. 'Are you taking any medication?'

'My blood pressure's a bit high,' Jed said. 'I'm on tablets for it.'

'Diuretics—water tablets?' Orlando asked.

'That's right.'

'And you've been taking them regularly?'

'Just like the doctor ordered.'

'That's really good, Jed,' Eleanor said, 'but the tablets you've been taking are a type that makes you more susceptible to heatstroke.'

'So we'd be much happier if we get you to hospital and get you checked over—your blood pressure needs checking, too. I'll call the ambulance now,' Orlando said.

Jed looked embarrassed. 'I'll be all right. Just need to sit in the shade. I don't want to make a fuss.'

Eleanor stroked his hand. 'You're not making a fuss—but you're not used to this kind of heat. Being English, neither am I. If you don't sit down now and cool down properly, you could end up being very ill indeed. You might even collapse and fall unconscious—and that would make even more of a fuss, wouldn't it?'

Orlando spoke rapid Italian into his mobile phone. Eleanor caught the words *'febbre'*, *'mal di testa'* and *'il colpo di sole'* and guessed that Orlando was giving a list of Jed's symptoms and diagnosis.

Jed's hand tightened around Eleanor's. 'But I can't go to hospital. I don't speak Italian. I won't know what they're saying.' He swallowed hard. 'And they won't understand me.'

Orlando exchanged a glance with Eleanor as he ended his call. 'Don't worry, Jed. We'll come with you. I'll translate,' he said.

Jed frowned. 'But I'm spoiling your honeymoon.'

Eleanor blinked. 'Um, we're not married.'

Jed flushed. 'I'm sorry. The way you look at each other…I thought you were…'

'Confusion's all part of heatstroke,' Orlando said to Eleanor in low tones.

True. But they had been holding hands when they'd first gone to Jed's rescue. And Eleanor knew exactly what Jed meant: she and Orlando had been looking at each other like that since the moment they'd met on the plane.

Hot.

Wanting.

Like lovers.

Except they weren't.

Yet. The word shimmered into her mind. The attraction was there. Mutual. They were both single. Would they…?

'The ambulance will be here in about ten minutes,' Orlando said. 'You go in the ambulance with Jed, Eleanor. I'll follow in my car.'

'You speak Italian?' Jed asked her hopefully.

'A little.' Not enough to translate for him in the ambulance. 'Surely it'd make more sense for you to go in the ambulance and translate?' she asked Orlando.

Orlando shook his head. 'You don't know the way to the hospital—and I'd hate you to get lost.'

She laughed. 'Listen to him, Jed. He's got this flash Italian sports car. Sounds to me like he doesn't want me to drive it.'

Orlando snorted. 'In that case, when we've got Jed settled at the hospital, you can drive us home.'

Eleanor backtracked fast. 'I was teasing.'

'No, it was a definite challenge. Don't you think, Jed?'

Jed tried to smile, but he was clearly in pain. Eleanor encouraged him to take small sips of water. 'Not long now, honey.'

'Cos'è?' A man came hurrying towards them. 'Mr Baynes? What's happened?'

Orlando explained quickly while Eleanor continued trying to cool Jed down; by the time Orlando had finished explaining, the paramedics had arrived. He went through the handover, then said to Eleanor, 'I've given them a patient history. I told them you're an English emergency specialist who doesn't speak much Italian, but you will know what they are doing and will help to explain to Jed.'

'I will get in touch with your family, Mr Baynes, and tell them what's happening,' the tour leader said, 'and then I will get someone to take over from me and I will join you at the hospital.'

Eleanor persuaded Jed to allow the paramedics to carry him to the ambulance—it would be quicker and avoid him rushing and making the heatstroke worse. But Orlando's grim prediction came true in the ambulance when Jed went into convulsions.

The paramedics immediately gave him diazepam, to control the fitting, and an oxygen mask.

'At the moment your body's too hot and it's making you have a fit,' she explained to Jed, holding his hand. 'They've given you some drugs to stop you having a fit. And the oxygen's to help you breathe more easily.' Diazepam could depress respiration, but Jed was worried enough: he didn't need something else to panic about.

'When you get to hospital, they'll cool you down properly,' she explained. 'They'll probably spray you with tepid water and blow fans over you.' Immersion in cool water wasn't an option in this case, as he'd already had a fit and the potential resuscitation problems made it unworkable. 'They might put cool packs in your armpits, over your neck and scalp, and in your groin area.'

Jed looked askance and lifted the mask from his face. 'My groin?'

'Put this back because you need the oxygen right now,' she said quietly, helping him settle the mask back in place. 'The packs will help to cool you more quickly. It's standard treatment, so try not to worry. They might give you some more drugs to stop you having another fit or feeling sick, and they'll take some blood so they can check the chemicals in your blood are all as they should be and give you something to help if they're not.'

When they got to the emergency department, Orlando was already there.

'You drive like a maniac,' she said. 'I think we should bet on him to win the next Grand Prix, Jed.'

Orlando just laughed. 'How are you feeling, Jed?' he asked.

'Terrible.'

'You'll be feeling much better soon,' Orlando promised.

Orlando translated everything that the medics were doing for Jed's benefit, and by the time the MedAm tour leader arrived, Jed's condition had stabilised enough for them to be happy to leave him with the tour leader.

'You take care. And enjoy the rest of your holiday,' Orlando said, patting Jed's shoulder.

Jed nodded. 'Thank you. I don't know how to repay you for the way you looked after me.'

Orlando shrugged. 'We're doctors. This is what we do. Just have good memories of my country—that will be enough for me.'

Eleanor followed Orlando into the car park. He leaned against his car door and took the keys from his pocket. 'So. I drive like a maniac, do I?'

She rubbed a hand against her face. 'No, just a bit faster than I'm used to.'

'A maniac, you said.' He raised an eyebrow. 'Right. Let's see what you can do.' He tossed the keys towards her.

She caught them automatically—and then froze. 'Orlando, I can't do this. I'm not insured.'

'Under the terms of my insurance, anyone over the age of twenty-five can drive, with my permission.' His eyes sparkled. 'And I give you my permission, Eleanor.'

'I've never driven a left-hand-drive car before.'

'So?' He spread his hands. 'You're perfectly capable. You can do anything you want to, if you try.'

'You're really going to let me drive your car?'

'Uh-huh.' He smiled at her. 'We've already established that we make a good team. Tell you what, you drive, I'll direct you, and we'll stop somewhere for a late lunch.'

She'd get to drive this gorgeous car with the top down and music playing and the sunlight sparkling on the sea. Amazing.

And then her elation faded as she took in what he'd said. 'You're going to make me drive through Naples?'

'When you're used to the car, maybe. The traffic here's even crazier than it is in London. For now, we'll take the quieter roads. Relax. Enjoy.' He gestured to the car. 'And I'm hungry. So can you, please, get in and drive?'

She climbed into the driver's side and put the key into the ignition. Orlando put the roof down again, and stretched his arm along the back of her seat. Close enough to touch her.

But that was fine. She'd promised herself she'd stop fussing and planning and let things just happen as they would.

He directed her out of the hospital car park and along the coast road. When they were on the open road, he switched programmes on his MP3 player; she recognised the singer as Andrea Bocelli. By the third song Orlando was singing along—and he had a beautiful voice, a rich tenor. Better still, he sang in tune.

Good music, good company, good weather, and a fast car that responded perfectly to her. She couldn't remember when she'd last enjoyed herself this much.

'My singing is that bad?' Orlando asked.

She frowned. 'No, it's fine. Why do you ask?'

'You had a pained expression on your face. Why?'

She shrugged. 'Nothing, really.'

'Tell me,' he invited.

Well, he'd asked. She may as well tell him. 'It's the first time I can remember enjoying myself like this for a long, long time.'

His fingers brushed against the nape of her neck. 'Then stop thinking about it, *tesoro*, and enjoy. Because it's only going to get better.'

CHAPTER FIVE

ORLANDO directed Eleanor down a narrow road on the side of a cliff, full of hairpin bends; he knew that she was having to concentrate on the drive and that the sheer drop on her right-hand side was definitely occupying her, but he thought she'd agree that their destination was worth it.

'Next turn on the right,' he said, directing her into a car park.

She pulled up and gazed at the view over the sea. 'Wow. That's stunning.'

'One of my favourite places,' he said. 'And the food's even better than the view.'

It was only a few minutes before they were seated in a shady spot overlooking the sea, with hunks of good bread, a bowl of green salad and two steaming plates of monkfish in a garlicky tomato sauce.

'This has to be the best fish I've ever eaten,' Eleanor said. 'And the best sauce.'

'It's *ragù Napoletana*. Of course it's the best,' he said with a grin.

'Thank you.'

'My pleasure. And I'm so glad you're not one of these women who only eats a tiny morsel and says she couldn't possibly manage any more.'

'Not when the food's this good.'

When they'd mopped the last of the sauce from their plates, she opted for a *lattè* rather than pudding. Then she was aware of his expression.

'What?'

'How can you possibly drink *lattè* after a meal?'

She smiled. 'Because I prefer *lattès* to the lukewarm, incredibly strong stuff you drink.'

'It's the way we drink coffee here.'

'And I'm a tourist,' she reminded him.

He laughed. 'Ah. I forgot. Because you look so Italian. You *are* Italian.'

'Half Italian, half English,' she corrected him. 'And I'll be going halves with you on the bill for lunch.'

Not if he could help it. He'd pay for it without telling her— and then, when the waitress told her that Dottore de Luca had already settled the bill, he had a good excuse to have lunch with her again later in the week. A little underhand, perhaps, but he wanted to spend time with her, and she had this ridiculous idea about imposing on people so she'd probably refuse a second invitation to lunch. Doing it this way neatly circumvented the problem.

But then she went quiet on him. Was she worried about her father—or was there more to it than that? Why was a woman as lovely as Eleanor Forrest—kind, beautiful, funny and clever—alone? And why was she so adamant about paying her way for things, about not being beholden to anyone?

He placed his hand over hers and rubbed his thumb over the back of her hand. Lord, her skin was soft. Touching her made his blood fizz through his veins; it made him want to touch her more intimately. Much more intimately.

'Penny for them?' he asked.

'I'm fine.'

'That's not what your eyes are saying. If I promise you the protection of the Hippocratic oath…?' He squeezed her hand gently. 'Talk to me, *bella mia*. Tell me why you're sad. It's not just concern about your father, is it?'

'No. I was thinking about the choices we make. If my mother had chosen differently, I might have grown up around here.'

He was pretty sure there was more to it than that. So he waited. And finally she filled the silence. 'I made a really bad choice last year.'

'How?' he prompted softly.

'I fell in love. With someone at work. I thought he was in love with me.'

From the expression on her face, she'd clearly been wrong.

'We were going to move in together, but we hadn't quite sorted it out. He bought me an engagement ring—said it was only a cheap one because he had to support his mum since she'd lost her job. She'd supported him through med school so he thought it was his turn to support her.'

The man was obviously a confidence trickster. One who knew exactly which buttons to press. Eleanor believed in sharing and fairness and family. Those words would've gone straight to her heart.

'I didn't mind. Jewellery doesn't bother me and I'd rather be with someone who cared about his family than someone who spent loads of money on fripperies.'

Exactly as he'd guessed. 'So what happened? His family came between you?'

Her face tightened. 'Hardly. He wasn't supporting his mother.'

'So what was he doing with the money? He'd invested badly? Addicted to online poker games?' No, Eleanor wouldn't be hard on someone who'd made a mistake. It had to be more serious than that. 'He had a drug habit?'

She shook her head. 'He was supporting someone. Except she was his girlfriend.'

'The man you loved cheated on you?'

She dragged in a breath. 'She didn't work at the hospital so he'd managed to keep her secret. But she'd finally had enough of him messing about and promising her things he wouldn't deliver. Especially as she was three months into her pregnancy.'

'Oh, no. The...' He switched to Italian, not wanting to offend her but needing to vent his disgust. 'What happened?'

'She confronted me.' Eleanor closed her eyes. 'Luckily it was *before* I'd signed the paperwork to open a joint bank account with him. So if he'd been planning to transfer my funds, it didn't happen.'

'Ellie, I'm so sorry.' His hand rested over hers again, squeezed it comfortingly. 'He preyed on you when you were vulnerable.'

'My mum was my only family after Dad died. So when she was diagnosed with cancer—with secondaries—I was...' She swallowed hard. 'Jeremy was just *there*. He let me lean on him. I'd known him vaguely for a while, danced with him at parties and what have you. I'd heard rumours that he was a bit ambitious, but he was always perfectly charming when he came to the department to discuss a patient. And he was, um, rather nice-looking.'

Was that white-hot flare at the base of his spine *jealousy*? Orlando was too shocked to say anything.

Luckily she seemed to misread his silence, as if he'd accused her of being shallow. 'It wasn't just me. Most of the female staff really fancied him. And when he asked me out I was... I dunno. Flattered. Glad to have something else to think about other than the fact that my mum was dying.'

And clearly she'd been twice as disillusioned when she'd found out the truth—that the man she'd loved hadn't loved her. The bastard had tried to take advantage of her instead. Worse, he'd done it when he'd been committed elsewhere.

'I thought Jeremy loved me. I thought I loved him,' she said softly. 'I thought he was the one.'

He laced his fingers through hers. 'Maybe this "The One" thing is a myth. Love doesn't really exist like that.'

'How do you mean?'

He stared out to sea. 'My mother is always searching for The One. And she never finds him. She's been divorced five times. Is it really worth all the pain and disappointment?'

She frowned. 'So what are you saying? That people shouldn't even bother looking?'

'Just that they shouldn't be blinded by an impossible ideal when they choose their partner.'

'You mean, have an arranged marriage?'

'Maybe.' He formulated the words carefully. 'If you're good friends, that's an excellent basis for a relationship. It means you'll never be disappointed in each other. You'll have something to keep you together when the first flush of passion fades.'

Eleanor shook her head. 'There's more to love than just friendship or sex.'

He wished she hadn't used that particular word. Because right now he could imagine Eleanor lying in the grass in a lemon grove, giving him that sensual smile as he slowly, slowly stroked the clothes from her body and explored her skin with his mouth.

'My parents were happy,' she continued. 'They loved each other. And my best friend's happily married.'

'So how do you know when you find this "love", then?' Orlando asked.

She shrugged. 'I don't know. I assume you meet someone

and you know you want to be with them for the rest of your life. You want to wake up with them. You want to go to sleep in their arms.'

'That's just sexual attraction,' Orlando corrected.

'That,' she said, shaking her head in apparent disbelief, 'is outrageously cynical.'

'Realistic,' he countered. 'And sexual attraction wears off. When it's over, what do you have left? Unless, as I said, you're friends to start with.'

'So you'd marry someone who was a friend?'

'If I liked them enough. If I thought we'd make a good life together.'

She removed her hand from his, propped her elbows on the table and rested her chin on her linked hands. 'There's a flaw in your argument, you know. A huge one.'

'Which is?'

'You're not actually married,' she pointed out.

'Because I'm picky.'

'More like, if you explained your views on marriage to any woman you were thinking of asking to marry you, she'd shove you in the nearest puddle and tell you what to do with your ring.'

'I've never explained it to anyone before.' He'd never wanted to get married. His affairs had always been for mutual pleasure and he'd made it clear right from the start, so nobody had got hurt. 'I probably didn't make a good job of explaining it just now.'

A corner of her mouth quirked. 'I do hope you're not going to claim that your English was too poor for you to explain your theory to me.'

'When I lived in England for a couple of years? Hardly. I might miss a few of the more obscure idioms, but…' He smiled back at her. 'No, I just phrased it badly. What I mean is that these people who claim they've found The One are just infatuated. They have this grand idea of what love should be and they're determined to find it. They're expecting rainbows and fireworks and a thousand balloons to float through the sky every time they kiss—and that really doesn't last for ever. If they're not good friends with their lover to start with, once the infatuation wears off there's nothing left to keep them together. No shared interests, no jointly held views on life, no real bond.'

'So how do you explain my parents? They were married for over twenty years. They really believed in "till death us do part".'

'Maybe they were lucky.' He shrugged. 'Maybe the infatuation didn't wear off.'

'They loved each other, Orlando.' She stared at him. 'I can't believe you're such a cynic. You're *Italian*. And Italians are meant to be the most romantic race on earth. Look at Romeo and Juliet.'

'Who didn't live happily ever after, if you remember,' he pointed out.

'But they loved each other.'

'So did Dante's Paolo and Francesca. And Manzoni's Renzo and Lucia. And Petrarca and whatever the woman's name was that he wrote all those sonnets to.' He spread his hands. 'They're *fictional*, Eleanor. Just like love. A figment of a poet's imagination.'

'So you're saying you don't believe in love?'

'I believe in friendship. And in sexual attraction. But love…that's a con.'

She raised an eyebrow. 'Some people believe men and women can't be friends. That sex always gets in the way.'

'Not true. We're friends, aren't we? Or on our way to becoming friends.'

'Maybe.'

She didn't tackle the other question, he noticed. About sexual attraction.

He was definitely attracted to Eleanor. Had been, right from the first time he'd seen her. That mouth was just made for kissing. He wanted to slide his fingers through her short dark hair, feel just how silky and soft it was. Wanted to stroke her skin until she was boneless with pleasure.

And he liked her, too. He liked her no-nonsense practicality. He liked the warmth of her smile. And when they'd held hands this morning in Pompeii, he'd been close to kissing her. Probably would have kissed her under a lemon tree overlooking the sea—had they not ended up rescuing a fellow tourist.

He was pretty sure the attraction was mutual. There was heat in her dark eyes when she looked at him. He'd felt the pulse throbbing when he'd linked his fingers through hers—a little too hard, a little too fast.

But love?

Who the hell knew what love was, anyway?

'So how long are you planning to stay in Italy?' he asked.

'A few days. Maybe a couple of weeks. Enough to get to know Bartolomeo a little better.'

'And then you're going back to England—back to the hospital to work in the emergency department?'

She took a sip of her *lattè*. 'Probably. Though right now I'm not sure if I want to go back to emergency medicine.'

'Because you'll have to face this Jeremy?'

'It's been a bit hideous at work,' she admitted. 'He's a surgeon, so we don't exactly work together—but obviously everyone knows what happened, and I've really hated being pitied by my colleagues. Poor Ellie, who got taken for a ride. Jeremy's baby's due in a couple of weeks so the sympathy's been a bit choking lately. But something else will knock me off the hospital grapevine soon enough. By the time I get back, hopefully everyone will have forgotten about it.'

'So if it's not embarrassment, why don't you want to go back?'

She sighed. 'What you said about wanting to see your patients grow up—sometimes I think that's what I want, too. Or maybe it's because I've lost my family and I miss them and I want to get that feeling back—and working in family medicine would give me that feeling again. I don't know. Right now I don't trust my judgement in anything except a clinical situation.'

He knew he was storing up trouble, but he couldn't help himself. 'I have a suggestion for you.'

'What?'

'I assume you'd like to see a lot of Bartolomeo, as he's your only blood family now.'

She nodded. 'But I can't keep flying between UK and Italy.'

'Why don't you stay out here for a while? Talk to your boss, take a sabbatical. And if money's a problem, you're a qualified doctor—we could do with a hand in our practice.'

'But I'm qualified in England.'

'A qualification that is valid here, too.'

She shook her head. 'I'm hospital-trained. I haven't done a GP rotation. And I haven't got the right paperwork.'

He shrugged. 'We can work around it. And the paperwork will be easy enough to sort out.'

'My Italian isn't good enough to deal with patients.'

'That,' he said, 'is temporary. And you can always start by helping expats and tourists—look at today. Your language skills and your medical skills were perfect. You really helped Jed.'

'You had to do the handover. I couldn't have told the paramedics what was going on.'

'It's a matter of vocabulary. You're bright: you'll pick up the language quickly.' He paused. Now this would definitely mean they'd have to spend time together. 'I can teach you. Test you on your vocabulary, if you like.'

She frowned. 'Why? Why me?'

'Why not you? I like you, Eleanor. I've seen the way you work in an emergency—twice now. You're good with people and I think you'd be an excellent family doctor. Think about it. You could spend the summer in Italy. Have the chance to see if this is the kind of medicine you want to do, without taking any risks. And take the opportunity to get to know Bartolomeo.'

And get to know me, he added silently. See if this thing between us is real. See if you're right and I'm wrong.

She rubbed a hand across her face. 'I could talk to my boss. See if I can take some time off. Though I don't want to live in a hotel.'

'You don't have to.' He just about stopped himself from offering her a room at his place. He didn't want to rush her, he wanted them to get to know each other. Properly. Living together would only get in the way. 'I can help you find an apartment.'

'I'll think about it.'

'It's an open offer.' He finished his espresso. 'Would you like another coffee—well, a fat-laden excuse for coffee, in your case?'

She laughed. 'Another *lattè* would be lovely. Thank you.' Her eyes crinkled at the corners. '*Grazie*, Orlando.'

Lord, he loved it when she spoke his language. And how he'd like to hear her say—

No. He really shouldn't rush her. Especially because she was so vulnerable right now. She'd already been hurt badly. He wasn't going to make it worse by pushing her into something she wasn't ready for. 'I'll go and order it.'

He paid the bill at the same time. And just as he'd expected, Eleanor was annoyed about it when she found out.

'You're not under any obligation to me,' he reminded her. 'Lunch was my idea.'

She folded her arms. 'You know how I feel about paying my way.'

'If it makes you feel better, you can buy me lunch some other time.' He kept the suggestion very light, very casual. 'I have a clinic this evening, so I'd better drive us back.' He opened the passenger door for her. What he really wanted to do was to kiss her. But if he pushed her too hard, too fast, he knew she'd walk away. She needed time to think. And he wanted her to stay in Italy for a while.

'Are you seeing Bartolomeo tomorrow?' he asked when he parked outside the hotel.

'We haven't made any arrangements.'

'Then, unless you have anything pressing to do, you're very welcome to shadow me for the day. See how our practice works. And if you like what you see, and your boss will let you have a sabbatical out here, I can help you sort out the paperwork later in the week.'

Again, he waited, knowing that it had to be her decision.

Finally, she nodded. 'Thank you, Orlando. I'd like that.'

'Then I will see you tomorrow,' he said. 'Unless you call me to tell me you're busy, I'll pick you up at eight. Will that give you enough time for breakfast?'

She nodded. 'It doesn't take that long to drink coffee and eat toast.'

He'd missed an opportunity there: he should've suggested taking her to a *caffè* overlooking the sea for breakfast—coffee and brioches, maybe some fruit. But maybe he was being greedy. At least she'd agreed to spend the day with him. '*A domani.* See you tomorrow.'

'See you tomorrow,' she echoed.

On impulse, he leaned forward and kissed her on the cheek. His lips actually tingled at the contact, and it took all his self-control not to yank her into his arms and kiss her properly. On the mouth.

CHAPTER SIX

THE next morning, Orlando was already waiting for Eleanor in the hotel foyer. He was dressed formally in a suit and tie, and he was the subject of more than a few nudges and glances and whispers. Again, he seemed oblivious of the female interest in him; he merely stood up when he saw Eleanor and gave her a tiny bow.

She noticed the disappointment on the faces around them when they realised he was indeed waiting for someone. Ha. They'd be even more disappointed if they found out he didn't believe in love. Whereas it suited her fine.

'Sorry—am I late?' she asked.

'No.' His eyes crinkled at the corners. 'I'm early. Ready?'

'Yes. And thank you for doing this, Orlando. I appreciate it.'

'Believe me, we'll appreciate you just as much if you decide to join us for the summer,' he told her. 'We're a busy practice.'

They took the metro to his consulting rooms. 'Right. I'll introduce you to everyone and show you where everything is,' he said.

'You're sure your partner in the practice doesn't mind?'

'Partners,' he said. 'They're looking forward to meeting you. Though they'll drive you mad because they'll try to practise their English on you.'

'You're the senior partner?' she asked.

'No. We're all equals. Actually, we're more or less the same age. Alessandro's married to Serafina, our practice nurse, and Giacomo's getting married in September.' He grimaced. 'So they will also drive you mad, trying to pair you off with me.'

'Why would they try to do that?'

He rubbed a hand across his face. 'Because they're a little *pazzo*. Crazy. They're in love and think everyone else should be, too.'

She laughed. 'You mean, you haven't told them your theory?'

'They don't believe me. They can't pair me off with a patient because it's unethical, our receptionist Chiara is old enough to be my mother, and I've resisted every single one of the little dinner parties they hold to introduce me to a suitable woman who will reform me.' He rolled his eyes. 'You're in the right age group—so in their eyes you'll be a suitable woman.'

'All cats being grey in the dark, you mean?'

He looked quizzically at her. 'That's not a phrase I'm familiar with.'

'Any port in a storm.'

'Ha.' He smiled and ruffled her hair. 'I'm almost tempted to tease them and… No. That wouldn't be fair to you. But if they go on about it, I'll kiss you in front of them and you can pretend to faint. Then they'll leave us alone and we can get on with our work.'

She coughed. 'Orlando, you're something else.'

'I think I'll take that as a compliment.' He smiled. 'Welcome to our practice, Dottoressa Forrest.'

Alessandro and Giacomo were both charming. Serafina looked as angelic as her name; she glanced at Eleanor and then Orlando, and broke into a wide smile before whispering something to her husband. And Chiara rolled her eyes, shooed them all away and gave Eleanor a cup of coffee before showing her around the building and making sure that she was comfortable.

It felt, Eleanor thought with a pang, like being part of a big, noisy family. They were clearly close to each other—behind the banter and the teasing she could tell that they all cared deeply about each other.

Orlando shepherded her through to his consulting room for the beginning of morning surgery; when each patient arrived, he introduced them to Eleanor and asked their permission for her to remain during the consultation, explaining that she might be staying to join the practice. And although Eleanor couldn't follow all the conversations, she picked up odd words during the consultation that, coupled with the kind of tests he did, made her realise exactly what each medical problem was.

She noticed that Orlando was particularly good with the children who came to see him. He was careful in the way he conducted the hearing test and then checked inside one little boy's ears with the otoscope: a case of glue ear, she guessed, because Orlando's gestures when he spoke to the mother showed that the little boy's hearing was slightly better on the right side and it'd be easier for the little boy if people who talked to him came down to his level and kept sentences short and simple. He made the little boy laugh by doing magic tricks and making a coin appear from behind his ear, followed up with a sticker with a smiley face saying '*Coraggioso*'—the equivalent of the 'I was *this* brave' stickers she gave out at the emergency department.

She'd just bet he'd been the most popular doctor on his ward when he'd worked in paediatrics, charming the parents as well as the patients. The little girl who came in wheezing left with a smile as well as an inhaler to help her asthma. And Eleanor could just imagine him with a little girl of his own, cuddling her on his lap and telling her stories. A little girl with long curly hair, just as Eleanor herself had once been…

Oh, lord. Now, there was a fantasy she really ought to stop right now. Constance Firth had fallen in love with a Neapolitan man and it had all gone pear-shaped. Eleanor wasn't about to follow in her mother's footsteps. She and Orlando were friends. Nothing more. And marriage and children really weren't on the agenda for her anyway.

During a coffee-break, Serafina made a point of looking at Eleanor's left hand. She said something in Italian to Alessandro, who smiled and agreed.

Orlando groaned. 'Apart from the fact that it's really rude to speak only Italian when Eleanor can't follow, will you two, please, stop it? We're just friends.'

'I've heard that one before,' Giacomo said with a grin. 'Just *good* friends, is it?'

'Right. That's it.' Orlando marched over to Eleanor, grabbed her hand, yanked her into his arms, bent her over backwards and kissed her.

It was meant to be a kiss for show. They'd even discussed it beforehand.

But he hadn't expected this.

Time stopped and the room dissolved. There was nobody else there, just the two of them. Kissing. For real. Because her hands had slid into his hair, and as he nibbled at her lower lip her mouth opened, letting him deepen the kiss. He could hear the blood roaring in his ears and he felt as if he were falling very slowly from a very great height.

When Orlando broke the kiss, he was disorientated at first. All he could focus on was Eleanor. Her pupils were huge and her mouth looked as if she'd just been very thoroughly kissed.

Well, she had.

Oh, hell. That wasn't meant to happen. She'd run a mile if

she had any idea of the crazy thoughts whirling through his mind. Crazy thoughts, like picking her up, carrying her into his office, locking the door behind them and continuing from where they'd just left off.

And heaven only knew what his colleagues were thinking after witnessing that.

His *colleagues*.

Um.

Head still swimming, he lifted his chin and raised an eyebrow at Alessandro, Giacomo and Serafina, who were staring at them in apparent disbelief. 'Let that,' he said in a voice that didn't really sound to him like his own, 'be an end to the gossip.'

'*Porca miseria!*' Serafina fanned herself. 'No more questions. I promise. Alessandro, why don't you kiss me like that?' she demanded.

'In public, you mean? Because, *mia innamorata*, it would not be good for the blood pressure of our patients. Or our colleagues,' Alessandro teased, taking her hand and kissing the backs of her fingers.

Giacomo assumed an angelic posture. 'I'm saying nothing.' But his smile said it all for him. *You've found The One.*

Ridiculous. It was a myth Orlando didn't subscribe to.

So why was adrenaline racing round his system like this?

Eleanor didn't remember anything more from the coffee-break, even though there was an empty cup of coffee in her hand, which she'd presumably drunk. The kiss had been for show—Orlando had even warned her before they'd left the car that his colleagues would drive them crazy and he'd probably have to kiss her to shut them up—but when he'd been supporting her, she hadn't been acting. At all. Her knees really *had* gone weak.

And she'd never reacted like that to anyone before. Not even

Jeremy, and she'd thought she'd loved him. Now she knew it hadn't been love at all. Because what she felt for Orlando was so much stronger. One kiss, and her head was spinning.

This was mad. Completely mad. It couldn't possibly work out between them. Orlando was as damaged as she was—more so, in fact, because he didn't believe that love even existed. But, lord, the man could kiss.

'Are you all right, Eleanor?' Orlando asked when they were back in his consulting room. 'Sorry. Was I too rough with you?'

'No, it's not a problem.' Not quite the truth. But her brain wasn't quite working in synch with her mouth after that kiss. Worse, she wanted him to do it again. This time in private. When they wouldn't have to stop.

'You look a bit…'

Stunned? Shocked? Yeah, that was exactly how she felt. She hadn't expected that surge of emotion when he'd kissed her. Hadn't expected the world to melt away. Hadn't expected to find herself kissing him back.

'Maybe working together isn't such a good idea,' she said carefully.

Orlando's eyes widened. 'No, no, no.' He crossed his hands rapidly in front of him. 'That kiss was just to shut them up. For show. I did warn you it was the only way.'

Mmm. But she hadn't expected a kiss for show to be so—well—mind-blowing.

'Don't worry, I'm not going to pounce on you. You're perfectly safe.'

She should have been relieved. Instead, she felt disappointed.

When the last patient from the morning's surgery had left, Orlando finished writing up his notes.

'Time for lunch,' he said.

'Only if I pay. Seeing as you were sneaky about yesterday.'

He folded his arms. 'Hmm. You've been shadowing me today. Either I have to pay you for your work today—or you let me buy you lunch.'

'I haven't exactly done any work,' she protested.

'You will, this afternoon—we have house calls. And I'm starving.'

So am I, Eleanor thought. Though not for food.

'So, Dottoressa Forrest, are you going to let me buy you a ham and fontina *panini* and one of your touristy *lattès*?'

She could only nod.

Orlando led her through the maze of tiny streets, pointing out buildings of interest and the best *gelati* shop in Naples. They ended up at a little *caffè* where he ordered their lunch.

'So, what do you think of family medicine? Is it the sort of thing you'd like to practise?'

'Maybe. I can see why you enjoy it. And you're good with children.'

He smiled. 'I like children.'

So did he want any of his own? Was he looking to settle down and get married—to someone he considered a friend? And why should the idea of it make jealousy flicker in her stomach?

She concentrated on her coffee and the *panini*. But it didn't help. She kept finding herself glancing at Orlando—and catching him glancing at her.

The attraction was definitely mutual. But she was also aware that if she gave in to the impulse to suggest a mad affair and get it out of their systems, it would make life impossible. There was no way she could spend a summer here, working with him, when their affair ended—which it would. Because Orlando didn't believe in love or commitment.

After lunch, he took a detour to a florist's shop and purchased a bunch of bright summery flowers.

At her questioning look, he said, 'I've known our next patient, Vittoria Moretti, since I was a child. She was my teacher at primary school.' He shrugged. 'Her family has moved to Rome. She's lonely. So when I call on her, I like to brighten her day a little.'

How typical of Orlando. A little kindness to make an old lady happy: he cared. He was a good man, whatever he claimed to think about love. Because he really did care.

'So tell me about our house calls. About Vittoria.'

'As I said, she taught me when I was tiny. She has an ulcerated leg.'

'Venous?' she asked.

He nodded. 'She had a clot in her leg.'

Typical presentation, Eleanor thought. She'd come across a few of them in the emergency department, when an elderly patient hadn't wanted to make a fuss and left it until the ulcer actually became painful or spread so much that someone noticed.

They took one of the funicular railways up one of the steeper hills, then he led them into a quiet street, rang the bell and then opened the front door. 'Signora Moretti? Vittoria?'

'Orlando! *Come va*?' She hobbled over to meet them, then hugged him when he gave her the flowers and rattled off something in Italian that Eleanor couldn't follow before putting the flowers immediately in water.

'Vittoria, this is Eleanor Forrest. She's an English doctor who might join our practice for the summer,' Orlando explained in Italian.

'Elenora.' Vittoria pronounced the name the Italian way. 'My English…very little.'

'I'll translate,' Orlando said with a smile. He looked at Vittoria. 'May Eleanor examine your leg and treat you?'

'*Si.*'

Gently, Eleanor removed the dressing and looked at the ulcer. The skin was darker and thicker around the area just above her ankle, and there was some swelling. 'Does it hurt at all?' she asked.

'She says it aches a bit and it's worse when she's been standing. But she hates sitting around and doing nothing,' Orlando translated.

Eleanor knew the type. The kind of elderly lady who liked to keep busy and tended to look about twenty years younger than she really was, because she kept active. 'Tell her it's a good idea to keep up gentle exercise,' she said, 'but emphasise the "gentle". Definitely no climbing these hills. And she needs to rest every so often and put her leg up on a cushion—if she keeps her leg higher than her hip, gravity will help pull the blood in the right direction, towards the heart. That will reduce the pressure of blood in her leg veins, and ease the swelling.'

Orlando translated, then laughed. 'She says she's not going to sit with her leg up on a cushion all day. She's far too busy.'

Eleanor smiled. 'Three or four times a day,' she said, 'for half an hour at a time. Tell her to lie on the sofa and put her foot on a couple of pillows.' She glanced at the bookshelves. 'It's a good excuse to read. Doctor's orders. But, yes, if she keeps moving about the rest of the time, it will help her leg heal.'

'*Bene,*' Vittoria said when Orlando had explained.

Eleanor gently cleaned the ulcer; it was at the earliest stage, when it was still moist and there was a lot of pus, so she took a non-adhesive absorbent dressing from Orlando's bag. 'We need to change the dressing daily until the ulcer has healed and dried.'

Vittoria clearly caught the word 'daily', and indicated that she didn't want a fuss.

'Tell her if we don't do that, the ulcer will take a lot longer to heal. But if we change the dressing daily and she wears elastic bandages, it will speed the healing.'

'You've done this before, haven't you?' Orlando asked.

'My speciality when I was a house officer,' she said. 'Geriatric medicine. I'm good at checking for diabetic foot, too.'

Deftly, she started applying elastic bandages over the dressing. 'Tell Vittoria it's not meant to hurt—if she feels any pain, I need to know right now because it means the compression's too tight and it will affect her circulation.'

'She says it's fine,' Orlando translated.

'Good.' She pursed her lips in frustration. 'I hate having to ask you to speak for me. It's wrong. I should be able to talk to my patient myself. Reassure her, listen to her, answer any questions she might have and second-guess what she's not asking me.'

Orlando smiled at her. 'You're a good doctor, Eleanor.'

'Not right now, I'm not. Can you tell Vittoria that she'll feel more pressure at the ankle and less towards the knee? And explain that this is to help counteract the raised pressure in the leg veins.' The pressure that had caused the problem in the first place.

When she'd put the third layer of bandages on, she checked that Vittoria could still move her ankle around. '*Più dolore*, um, *pede*?' she said to Vittoria, pointing to her foot, and mimed telephoning before pointing to herself.

'*Piede,*' Vittoria corrected with a smile, patting her hand. '*Bene.*'

'*Febbre,*' Eleanor said, remembering what Orlando had said about Jed's sunstroke, and mimed the phone again.

Vittoria laughed, and said something to Orlando.

'She says you're stubborn. And she likes the fact you're trying to speak Italian,' he informed Eleanor.

'Just confirm that if it starts to hurt more, or her foot feels hotter or colder or changes colour, she needs to call me straight away. I mean, call you,' she amended.

'Us,' Orlando said, 'and we will check her foot.' He quickly gave Vittoria Eleanor's instructions.

'And in the meantime, there's an exercise she can do sitting down.' She sat next to Vittoria and moved her foot in a circle, then up and down, then pointed to Vittoria. *'E lei?'*

Once she'd checked that Vittoria could do the exercise, she smiled. *'Una volta, due, ora?'*

Vittoria nodded, held up one finger and then a second, then mimed the minute hand going round her watch once.

Do it once or twice an hour. Exactly. *'Bene,'* Eleanor said, smiling.

Vittoria said something to Orlando, who nodded. 'She says you'll do,' he told Eleanor. 'You'll do just fine.'

And something in his eyes told her that he agreed.

CHAPTER SEVEN

ELEANOR rang her boss in England the next morning to see if she could arrange a sabbatical. When she'd explained the situation with Bartolomeo, Ian said immediately, 'Take as much time as you need. We can get locum cover for you here.'

'I feel as if I'm letting you down.'

'No, you're not. The last year's been pretty rough for you, and you're a marvel to have got through it as well as you have. Now you've got a chance to meet the family you never even knew existed, I think you should go for it. Spend some time with them.'

'There's a bit more to it than that,' she admitted. 'I've, um, had the offer of working over here. Temporarily.'

'And you want to do it?'

'Yes. So I'd better give you my resignation, hadn't I?'

'Not necessarily. You're a good registrar and we don't want to lose you,' Ian said. 'Anyway, working abroad would be good experience for you. Call it job enrichment, if you like. I'll sort out the admin side this end. If you need a reference, just let me know.'

Tears pricked her eyelids. 'I really appreciate this, Ian.' Especially the feeling that she belonged somewhere. That they'd keep her place open for her. Maybe her thoughts about leaving emergency medicine were just a knee-jerk reaction to the fact she missed her family. And maybe working in family medicine for a while would make her realise how much she loved her real job.

She heard the faint sound of a bleep on the other end of the phone. 'Ah, I'm needed in Resus. Gotta go. You take care, Ellie. Ring me if you need anything,' Ian said. 'And stay in touch. Let us know how you're getting on and when you're ready to come home.'

'Thanks, Ian.'

So now she could stay in Italy as long as she liked. Instead of the three weeks she'd planned, it could be the whole summer. Getting to know her father. Getting to know Orlando.

Even at her lowest point, she'd believed there would eventually be light at the end of the tunnel. Right now, it was blazing away like the Mediterranean sun itself.

For the next week, Eleanor spent her afternoons getting to know her father and her mornings shadowing Orlando in the surgery. The rest of the practice seemed to accept her as part of the team immediately: Serafina roped her in to help with the minor injuries clinic; Alessandro and Giacomo quizzed her about the way things were run in England and asked her opinion about setting up specialist clinics for their diabetic patients; Orlando talked about the possibility of setting up an expat clinic; and Chiara took Eleanor under her wing, making coffee exactly how Eleanor liked it without having to ask.

It was strange how she felt so at home in Naples—and so quickly.

And the more time she spent with Orlando, the more she liked him. He was funny, he was clever, and he cared.

But since that kiss in the surgery he'd kept an emotional distance between them. As if he was running scared.

She met Bartolomeo on the Friday for lunch in the city after the morning surgery ended, then spent the afternoon with him poring over his old family photographs, Bartolomeo explained who everyone was and told her little anecdotes that made her laugh. He also had some old ciné film that he'd had transferred to DVD format, and she had to swallow hard as she saw her mother at the age of twenty-one. Constance looked so beautiful, so vibrant.

'If only,' Eleanor said wistfully, 'the film had sound—so I could have heard Mum's voice just once more.'

'I know. It makes me feel that way, too,' Bartolomeo said, squeezing her hand. 'It reminds me of all the opportunities I missed. But I'm glad she had a happy life. I would have hated my Costanza to be sad.'

'Would you…? Could I, please, have a copy of the disc?' she asked. 'I'm more than happy to pay for it.'

'It will be my pleasure. And there's no need to pay. I can do it for you myself.' He smiled at her. 'In fact, I can do it today. And this evening I will scan in the photographs for you and make you a CD of the stills.' He forestalled her protest with a lifted finger. 'It will amuse me to do it. And what's the point of having good computer equipment if you don't use it?'

Later that afternoon, when they were sitting on his terrace with coffee and pastries, Eleanor decided to tackle him about his health. Find out the truth. She'd hoped to be able to piece it together from the little bits she'd managed to get him to admit, but so far the diagnosis eluded her. Bartolomeo had avoided her gentle probing, so now she had to change tactics and ask him straight.

'So are you going to tell me what the problem is?' she asked. 'With your health, I mean?'

Bartolomeo waved a dismissive hand. 'Nothing is wrong, Eleanor.'

Obviously they were going to have to do this the hard way. 'I'm thirty, so that would make you...what...fifty-three?'

He nodded.

'And you're tired all the time.'

He shrugged. 'It's my age.'

No, it wasn't. 'And I suppose it's because of your age that you became breathless when we walking along the bay the other day?'

He smiled. 'Exactly so. I had a job where I sat down all day, every day. And even though I've sold the company now and I have time on my hands, I still don't exercise enough. I really should go to the gym.'

Eleanor scoffed. 'I'm a doctor, Bartolomeo. I add things together. Like the way you bruise easily—you're wearing short sleeves today so I can see the bruises.' Bruises in certain places that made her wonder if they'd been caused by a needle. 'And your gums were bleeding over lunch today.'

He made another dismissive gesture. 'Because the bread was a little too crusty.'

'It still shouldn't have made your gums bleed,' she said. 'And you're too young to be tired and breathless like this. I think your platelet count might be low. Are you going to tell me the truth about this, or do I have to nag you?'

He sighed. 'Your mother was sharp, like you. She noticed things. All right. The doctors say I have anaemia.'

Simple iron deficiency wouldn't have caused Bartolomeo's symptoms. There had to be more to it than that. 'What sort?'

'Aplastic.'

That explained a huge amount. The anaemia accounted for Bartolomeo's pallor—but aplastic anaemia was serious and couldn't be treated just by a course of iron tablets and changing his diet. The way he got tired so quickly and became short of breath was caused by low numbers of red cells in his blood. The way he bruised easily and his gums bled were due to low platelet levels, and she'd just bet, because his white cells weren't high enough either, that he picked up every cold and infection going. And it confirmed her suspicion that those bruises on his arms—bruises that seemed to appear between one day and the next—were due to transfusions into his arm. 'How long have you had it?'

He leaned back in his chair. 'Four months or so. Maybe a little longer before we found out what it was.'

In severe cases of aplastic anaemia, she knew that the chance of survival after six months of having the condition was less than fifty per cent. So her guess was right. Bartolomeo was dying. He clearly knew he was on borrowed time, and that was why he'd tried to find Constance Firth. To make his peace with her before he died.

No. This wasn't fair. After thinking she was all alone in the world, Eleanor had found after all that she did have someone. Her biological father. In the few days they'd spent together she'd found that she liked him—liked him a lot—and she wanted to get to know him better.

But now she might not get the chance. Because the aplastic anaemia might take him from her. Way, way too quickly.

Well, she wasn't going to stand by and let it happen. There had to be something she could do.

'Do you know the cause?' she asked carefully.

'The consultant said there was no cause—it just happened.'

From what she could remember about the condition, it was an auto-immune reaction, caused when the body's immune system became confused and started to attack the body's own tissues; it damaged the bone marrow, and around two-thirds of cases had no known underlying cause. 'What treatment are you having?' she asked.

'Blood transfusions, antibiotics.'

They were standard treatments for the symptom of a low blood count, but they clearly weren't working well enough. 'What about a bone-marrow transplant?'

Bartolomeo closed his eyes. 'My sisters had the test to see if their tissues were compatible with mine. It seems that tissues aren't the same as blood type.'

She nodded. 'We inherit three antigens from each parent.' She drew a swift diagram on the back of a napkin, with a stick woman and a stick man; she added two blocks of three numbers underneath the woman and two blocks of three letters underneath the man. 'If you inherited 1, 2 and 3 from your mother and A, B and C from your father, that leaves 4, 5 and 6 and C, D and E that don't match your tissue type.' She drew a circle round each block of three antigens, then drew lines from each to show potential matches. 'You see? That gives you a one in four chance of the tissues matching.'

He smiled. 'Like a probability tree. You inherited my talent for maths, then.'

'Yes.' She smiled back, but her heart was heavy. A one in four chance. Twenty-five per cent. The odds were too low. 'I take it they didn't match?'

'They match each other because they're twins—but, no, they don't match me. My consultant has put me on the waiting list for a donor, but…'

He didn't have to say any more. 'It's the same in my country. There aren't enough donors.' But when Bartolomeo had been put on the waiting list, the situation had been different. Then, he'd thought there was nobody in the family with his tissue type. Now he knew he had a child. One who would have inherited three of his antigens. Which meant a tissue match. 'We need to talk to Orlando.'

'Orlando?' Bartolomeo looked puzzled.

'I told you about him—the family doctor I'm working with right now.'

Bartolomeo's eyes narrowed. 'You haven't said that much about him. Or that you were working here, come to that. I thought you were here on holiday?'

'I met him on the plane on the way over,' Eleanor explained. 'We worked together to help a fellow passenger who'd had a heart attack. We became friends.'

'Friends?' Bartolomeo sounded suspicious.

She sighed. 'He gave me a lift from the airport. And he took me to Pompeii.'

'On a date?'

'As *friends*.' Lord. Anyone would think she was thirteen, not thirty!

Though they had ended up walking hand in hand at Pompeii. And had they not rescued the American tourist, Orlando might well have kissed her in the shadow of Vesuvius. Exactly the same way he'd kissed her in the surgery. And then…

Oh, she had to get a grip. 'I've been thinking about maybe retraining and doing family medicine. Orlando's a *medico di famiglia*, so he offered me a chance to work with him while I'm over here to see if family medicine suits me. And my boss said I can have a sabbatical. Which means I get the chance to spend the whole summer over here.'

'The whole summer?' Bartolomeo smiled. 'We would have more time together.'

'I'd like that,' she said.

'And this man, Orlando—he knows something about aplastic anaemia?'

'Probably as much as most family doctors,' Eleanor admitted. 'But the thing is, he worked in England for a couple of years. His English is perfect, so he'll know the medical terms in your language and mine—and he can help me talk to the consultant and find out what I need to know. But we'll need your permission to discuss your condition with your doctor.'

'Hmm,' Bartolomeo said, looking faintly suspicious. 'I don't know the man.'

'I do. And he's a good man. A good doctor.' Eleanor paused. 'Maybe we could have a drink together—a coffee, perhaps. And then you could decide, once you've met him.' She glanced at her watch. 'He might still be at his surgery, if he's not on a house call. I'll ring him now.'

Bartolomeo laughed. 'Something else you inherited from me. You're bossy.'

She smiled back. 'No, I'm efficient.'

His smile faded and he took her hand. 'Eleanor, I know I'm on borrowed time. I have you now, and I just want to enjoy you in the time I have left. It might be weeks, it might be months—and we might be very lucky and it will be longer.'

'And on the other hand we might not be lucky. I've just found you—and I'm not giving you up without a fight. I want time to get to know you.' She lifted her chin fiercely. 'I have my mother's genes, too. So that makes me stubborn.'

'I can see that.' His eyes glittered with amusement.

'This isn't a condition I deal with in the emergency department. But I know where to start looking for the answers. I want to do some research on this and see what we can do. You're not in this on your own any more.' She squeezed his hand gently. 'You're with me. And together we're going to fight this.'

The glitter in his eyes was no longer amusement: she could see the tears forming.

'So will you meet Orlando? Talk to him?'

Bartolomeo dragged in a breath. 'All right.'

Still holding his hand with one of hers, she fumbled for her mobile phone, and flicked through the directory until she found the surgery number.

Chiara answered.

'*Buona sera*, Chiara. It's Eleanor. May I speak with Orlando?'

'*Un minuto*, Eleanor.' There was a pause. 'No, he has left for house calls. He has surgery later, at—ah, yes, four.'

'Can you ask him to call me, please? Tell him it's about…about Bartolomeo.' Good as Chiara's English was, Eleanor doubted that she'd be able to translate the English condition to Italian either—and she didn't want to involve Alessandro or Giacomo.

'Of course. *A presto.*'

'*A presto,*' Eleanor echoed. '*Grazie*, Chiara.' She cut the connection and flicked through to Orlando's mobile number. The chances were his phone would be switched to divert or voicemail—but if it was the latter she could at least leave him a message.

To her relief, it was voicemail. 'Orlando, it's Eleanor. Please can you ring me?' She left him her number.

Bartolomeo finished his coffee. 'Eleanor, *cara*, I hate to say it but…'

'You're tired,' she said gently. She could see that. 'You need some rest. I'll leave you in peace.'

He smiled ruefully. 'Once I could walk through Naples all day and dance all night.'

She squeezed his hand. 'I don't think I could do that, and I'm younger than you!'

'What will you do with yourself this afternoon?'

'Be a tourist,' she said. 'Visit churches and museums and eat cake.' Actually, she had other plans, ones which involved finding an internet café so she could do some research. 'And maybe tomorrow you can eat *gelati* with me. Show me where they sell the best *gelati* in Naples and introduce me to your favourite flavours.'

Eleanor took the metro back to her hotel and asked for directions to the nearest internet café. Armed with coffee—which she ordered *molto caldo*, not caring that it marked her as a tourist because she really didn't like her coffee the lukewarm Italian way—a pen and paper and two hours' credit, she started her research, moving from journal to journal and paper to paper until she found what she was looking for.

She was halfway through when her mobile phone rang.

'Eleanor Forrest,' she answered crisply.

'It's Orlando. Chiara gave me your message. What's up?'

'I've found out what's wrong with Bartolomeo.'

'And it's serious?' His voice radiated concern.

'Aplastic anaemia.'

There was a pause. 'I don't know much about the condition, *tesoro*. I can look it up in my books for you, but you really need to talk to a specialist. A haematologist.'

'That's why I need your help.' She paused. 'I know you have surgery now, so could we meet this evening?' It was Friday so he'd probably be busy, but she crossed her fingers and said, 'After dinner? Say, nineish?'

'Fine. I'll meet you at your hotel, then we'll go to a bar or somewhere we can talk.'

'Thank you.'

Eleanor read through the last few papers online, then headed back to the hotel. It was still hard to take in: the fact that she'd found a family to belong to again, and was going to have it snatched away before she'd even had the chance to get to know Bartolomeo properly.

Even a quick chat with Tamsin didn't lift her spirits. Despite her best friend's teasing.

'So have you found a gorgeous man for your fling yet, then?'

Yes. 'No.'

'Ah, I get it—you're walking around with your eyes closed. Because we both know that Italian men are gorgeous, with a capital G.'

'Mmm.'

'Seriously, are you having a good time in Italy?'

'Yeah.'

There was a pause. 'What's wrong, hon? You said Bartolomeo was nice. Or were you just saying that to stop me worrying about you?'

'Bartolomeo's lovely. But…' Eleanor dragged in a breath, then told Tamsin what she'd discovered.

'Oh, no. That's *so* unfair.' Sympathy radiated through Tamsin's voice. 'Look, do you want me to come over?'

'They wouldn't allow you to fly, seeing as you're in the last trimester of pregnancy—and, no, I don't want you taking the risk and telling the airline staff you're just fat. I'll be fine. But thanks anyway.'

'You call me whenever you need to talk. Well, I know you know that, but it doesn't hurt to say so. And, Ellie, just for the record, Bruce and I think of you as family. That's why we asked you to be godmother to our baby. So you're not alone. You've got us.'

Eleanor had to blink away the tears. 'Tam, you're making me cry.'

'All right, so no airline will take me as a passenger. But flying isn't the only way to get to Italy. I can get the ferry across to France and drive—'

'No, Tam. Honestly, I'll be fine. But thanks for the support. I appreciate it.'

'And I've got a friend who works in Haematology—I'll give her a ring and see if she can give me some ideas. We'll talk tomorrow, OK?'

'Yeah. Thanks, Tam.'

'Any time. And I mean that.'

At precisely nine o'clock that evening, Orlando walked through the revolving doors into the hotel foyer. Eleanor was just walking down the stairs—his eyes were drawn to her straight away. Wearing a simple black dress and mid-height heels, and carrying the tiniest handbag, she looked stunning. And with her dark hair cut short, she reminded him of a 1950s film star. All she needed was a pair of elbow-length gloves, a chiffon stole and a set of matched pearls.

Dio, she was beautiful.

And was it his imagination, or were her dark eyes full of tears?

Her voice had sounded so flat on the phone. Given that she'd recently lost her mother, the news of Bartolomeo's illness—and its likely prognosis—must be particularly hard for her to take.

He wanted to pull her into his arms, hold her close, comfort her—but here and now wasn't the place or the time. He held himself in check and simply joined her at the foot of the stairs. '*Buona sera*, Eleanor.'

She didn't return his smile. 'Good evening, Orlando.'

He didn't ask her what was wrong. He already knew. 'Let's go somewhere we can talk,' he said, and shepherded her out of the hotel to a small bar just down the street. It was crowded and noisy—but it was anonymous. Everyone was too busy to look at them or join in their conversation. Just what they needed.

'May I get you a drink?'

'Thanks.'

'What would you like?'

'Oh…' She spread her hands, as if thinking about what to drink was too much effort. He could understand that: she'd had a bombshell today, and her mind was probably churning round and round the issues. 'Anything,' she said finally, shaking her head as if she really didn't care.

He played it safe and bought her a glass of pinot grigio; he ordered a double espresso for himself. He had a feeling he was going to need the caffeine hit.

'*Grazie,*' she said when he returned to their table. She took a sip of wine, then turned the stem of the glass round and round between her fingers. 'I've only just found him. And now I'm going to lose him, Orlando. It's so bloody *unfair.*'

'Is he on the list for a bone-marrow donor?'

Her face tightened. 'You know as well as I do there aren't enough donors. It's hard enough to get people to give blood, let alone bone marrow—especially as giving bone marrow or stem cells is a hell of a lot more complicated than giving a pint of blood.' She dragged in a breath. 'I can't bear this. Just when I thought maybe I wasn't alone in the world after all, I have to…' She covered her face with her hands. 'I have to deal with it all over again. Losing the last person in the world who shares my blood.'

Seeing her pain made his own heart feel as if someone had taken it and wrung it out. And he couldn't stand by and just watch her crying. He scooped her onto his lap and wrapped his arms round her, holding her close to him. 'Ah, *mia bella.*'

He rested his cheek against her hair—lord, how soft it was and how sweet she smelled, like spring flowers—and stroked her back comfortingly. 'It will be all right, *piccolo.*' Though he knew he was lying to her. Without a transplant, the outlook for Bartolomeo was bleak. It was just a matter of time. But Orlando needed to reassure her, comfort her, make her feel better.

He shifted to kiss the top of her head. She burrowed closer. And suddenly his senses all went haywire.

Ah, hell. He shouldn't be so damned selfish. Her heart was breaking and all he could think of was how much he wanted her, how much his body was going up in flames, how much he wanted to carry her to her bed. What kind of man was he?

But then she shifted again so her cheek was against his. He could feel the dampness against his skin—what could he do but kiss her tears away? His mouth brushed against her cheek, moved lower, brushed against hers.

And then she was kissing him back. Just as she had when he'd kissed her for show in the staffroom. A proper kiss. Urgent and hot. The crowded bar just melted away as the kiss deepened. There was just the two of them…

Guilt kicked in sharply and he broke the kiss. 'I'm sorry, *tesoro*. I shouldn't be pressuring you like this. It isn't fair.' He should be protecting her, comforting her—not thinking about making love with her and losing himself inside her.

Her hands were shaking as she stroked his cheek. 'It wasn't just you. I was there, too.'

Again, the chatter in the bar faded to a distant hum. All he was aware of was Eleanor.

'Orlando…I don't want to be alone right now,' she told him. 'I'm so sick of being alone.'

Was she asking him to…? Ah, hell. He felt like the worst kind of bastard—right now he was taking advantage of her when she needed comfort. He needed to take a step back. Before it was too late. Before they both regretted it. 'Eleanor, listen to me. This is a bad idea. I can't promise you for ever. I don't believe in l—'

She put her finger over his lips, silencing him. 'I know,' she said huskily. 'And I understand.'

Did she? He wasn't so sure. She wanted a family to belong to—a family he couldn't give her.

'And I'm not asking for for ever.' She swallowed hard. 'I don't do this sort of thing. I don't…proposition men. But tonight…I need you tonight, Orlando. Stay with me tonight. Make me forget all this.'

His self-control was splintering rapidly by the second. 'This is a seriously bad idea,' he said, while he still had the strength to resist the appeal in her dark, dark eyes. 'You're upset, and I'm not going to take advantage of you. I'll see you back safely to the hotel.' A vision of their bodies tangled together between clean white sheets made his head spin. No, he didn't dare take her to the door of her room. He didn't trust himself enough. 'I'll escort you to the foyer.' He was speaking slowly, he knew— very slowly—but every word was an extreme effort: most of his energy was concentrated in trying not to kiss her. 'And I'll call you tomorrow morning.'

In answer, she leaned in and kissed him.

'Eleanor, God help me, I'm trying to do the honourable thing,' he told her when she broke the kiss. Every word, every breath was a struggle. His body was screaming out to carry her to her bed.

'What if I don't want you to be honourable?'

Oh, lord. He couldn't even try thinking of clinical chemistry and reference intervals to distract his body because his mind had simply stopped functioning.

She wanted him as much as he wanted her.

With a huge effort, he managed to say, 'So, as you said yesterday, all cats are grey in the dark?'

'No. I just want you.' She swallowed hard. 'I don't do this sort of thing. But I haven't been able to stop thinking about you since last week. Since you kissed me.'

'It was meant to be for show.'

'It didn't feel like it.'

'You kissed me back,' he pointed out.

She dragged in a breath. 'I don't even remember much of the rest of the day after that.'

'Neither do I,' he admitted. 'Eleanor, I don't think I have any blood left in my head. It's all gone south. But while I can still just about string a sentence together, let me tell you that I don't sleep around.'

'Neither do I.'

'So if we're going to...' Heaven help him, there was no 'if' about it. They were going to make love. Soon. Very soon.

Not soon enough, because every one of his nerve-endings was on fire.

'We need to get something?' she said.

'Yes.' With his last bit of self-control, he asked her, 'Are you sure about this?'

'Stop talking,' she said huskily, 'and kiss me.'

CHAPTER EIGHT

ELEANOR didn't remember going back to the hotel. She knew they must have called at a late-opening pharmacy or something on the way, because Orlando had mentioned the need for protection—but all she was aware of was his arms holding her close, the hard warmth of his body against hers, his clean masculine scent.

When the lift arrived, to her relief, they were the only ones waiting.

'Which floor?' Orlando asked, his voice husky with desire.

'Third.' She could barely force the word out. Couldn't think straight, she wanted him so badly.

He pressed the button; as the doors closed behind them, he rested his hands either side of her on the wall of the lift and bent his head to hers. The walls were mirrored, so she could see their reflections kissing, stretched out in an infinite line.

Right now she didn't want this to stop. Ever.

The lift glided to a halt and the doors opened again.

He broke the kiss and stared at her, looking dazed. His mouth was reddened and slightly swollen; she knew that hers would be in a similar state. That it would be obvious to anyone who saw them that they'd just been kissing each other stupid.

And she didn't care. She wanted him to kiss her again. And again. Until she forgot the whole world.

'Room…uh…number?'

Ha. He couldn't string a sentence together either, then.

As if he'd guessed her thoughts, he kissed her again, and her mind went blank. 'Number?' Ah. Key. It would be on the key. She fumbled with the zip on her tiny handbag and took the cardkey. 'Three-oh-five.'

To her shock, he scooped her up into his arms and carried her down the corridor; she was forced to slide her arms round his neck for balance. Eleanor was about to protest and ask him to put her down when he stopped outside her door. He brushed his mouth against hers, then let her slide all the way down his body until her feet touched the floor again.

She was aware that they were in a public place—that it was obvious to anyone who saw them exactly what was going to happen, the minute her door closed behind them—but the desire that flooded through her pushed everything else out of its way. And, judging from the hardness of Orlando's body, it was the same for him, too. Need. Urgency.

Key. Where was the cardkey? Oh, yeah. She was still holding it. She nearly dropped it, then it wouldn't fit into place and she almost growled with frustration. She didn't want to wait another second. She needed Orlando right now. Needed to feel his body inside her. Needed him to make her forget the world.

'Oh, why won't this bloody key work?' The words ripped from her in frustration.

'Relax, *piccolo*,' Orlando whispered against her ear, the warmth of his breath sending a shiver of pure lust down her spine. He took the cardkey from her and pushed it into the slot. And at last, at long last, the door swung open.

'*Dio*, I am glad your bed isn't a single,' he said as he

switched on the overhead light and pushed the door shut behind them. 'I need space for what I have in mind. And a light that's a little less harsh than this.'

The curtains were already closed; Orlando worked rapidly through the bank of switches next to the bed until the soft glow of the bedside light came on and the glare of the overhead light disappeared.

'Better. Much better,' he whispered, and pulled Eleanor back into his arms. His mouth dipped down to hers, taking tiny nibbles until she was practically whimpering, and then he deepened the kiss, exploring and teasing and inciting.

In the lift, she'd thought her desire was at a peak.

She'd thought wrong.

Orlando's mouth was stoking her desire higher and higher, and his hands were stroking the curve of her bottom, moulding her against him so she could feel the heat and hardness of his erection against her. It left her in no doubt that this thing between them was driving him just as crazy.

When he broke the kiss, he traced a path of kisses along the curve of her jaw. She tipped her head back, wanting more, and he nibbled his way down her throat to her collar-bones. She gasped as the tip of his tongue pressed against the pulse beating madly in her throat.

'Orlando. I need… Please…'

'Shh, *bella mia*.' Gently, he laid one finger over her lips. 'We have time. And I don't want to rush this.'

Unable to resist, she took the tip of his finger into her mouth and sucked it.

His eyes widened and he shuddered. '*Porca miseria!* Do you have any idea what you do to me, Eleanor?'

'The same as what you do to me,' she admitted. 'I hope.'

'Eleanor, I want this to be good for you, too. But you drive me so crazy, I don't think my self-control is going to last very long.' He stole another kiss. 'I want to touch you and taste you and look at you and fill my senses with you.'

Italian charm. She knew that was all it was. But, oh, it worked. More than worked. He blew her mind.

His English was still perfect, but voice was deeper now and his accent had become more Italian. She'd never heard anything so sexy.

Slowly, he unzipped her dress and eased it down over her shoulders to her waist.

'*Dio*, your curves,' he breathed, looking at her with his hands resting on her shoulders. 'So beautiful.' His hands skated over her shoulders, sliding her bra straps down her arms. 'You're amazing. Soft and sweet and the sexiest woman I've ever met.' His breathing was shallow and his hands were shaking as he touched her. His voice was a ragged whisper as he added, 'And I want you so badly, *tesoro*, it actually hurts.'

He traced the edge of the cups of her bra with one finger, making her shiver with need. This wasn't enough. She needed him to touch her much more intimately. Ease the ache. Tip her over the edge of fulfilment.

'I'm going to enjoy every second of this,' he told her. 'Every touch and every taste and every whisper of your voice. I want it to last a long, long time—yet at the same time I'm going to go crazy if you don't rip my clothes off right now and take me to your bed.'

Oh, so tempting. How she wanted to. She even placed her palms flat against his chest, ready to slide her fingers into the edges of his shirt and pull. But the feel of the soft silk shimmering against her skin made her stop. 'Your beautiful shirt. I can't treat it like that.' With shaking hands, she undid the buttons and slid it from his shoulders, the same way he'd pushed her dress down to her waist.

Lord, he was perfect. Broad shoulders, defined musculature, a light sprinkle of hair on his chest that arrowed down towards a very visible erection. Perfect. And all hers, for tonight.

She hung his shirt over the back of the chair; he followed her, slid his arms round her waist and pulled her back against him. His mouth grazed along the sensitive curve between her shoulder and her neck, making her shiver and lean back against him.

He dealt with the catch of her bra and let the garment fall to the floor. Her breasts spilled into his hands; she gasped as his thumb dragged across the tips of her nipples. The friction was good, but it wasn't enough. Not nearly enough.

'Orlando. Please. I need…' She couldn't get the words out. Could hardly breathe, she wanted him so much.

His mouth brushed the nape of her neck. 'Me, too, *tesoro*.'

She twisted round in his arms and kissed him, sliding her hands into his hair. The dark curls were fine, silky beneath her fingertips. Every inch of her skin felt sensitized, and even though his touch was light, it made her burn.

She wasn't sure who removed whose clothing, or when, or how. The next thing she knew they were both naked and he was carrying her to the bed. He pushed the cover to one side and laid her down on the cool smooth sheets, then knelt between her thighs.

'*Bella mia*,' he said softly. 'I ache for you.'

She ached for him, too. He was beautiful—built like an athlete, sturdy and muscular, no hint of fat. Just strong, ardent male.

'I want you so badly, Orlando de Luca,' she whispered. 'Make love with me. Please.'

'*Con piacere*.' His voice was actually shaking. 'With pleasure.' His fingers splayed over her stomach; his hands moved with feather-light touches, yet it didn't tickle. Her skin just felt hotter and hotter where he touched her. As if she were slowly being consumed by desire.

'You're so beautiful, Eleanor. All curves.' He skated around the edge of her breast with the tip of his index finger, and she tipped her head back against the pillow.

'More,' she murmured.

She reminded him of a medieval princess, lying back and commanding him to touch her. All she needed was the long hair spread over the pillow and a tiara. He couldn't help smiling.

'What?' she asked, frowning slightly.

'You remind me of a *principessa*—a princess. We really should have the four-poster and the velvet drapes.'

'Sir Orlando. I can imagine you coming home from the battlefield on your white charger.' She sat up and stroked his cheek. 'Was there a Sir Orlando?'

'In Italian literature, there's *Orlando Innamorato*—the tale of the knight Roland, who fell in love with the beautiful princess Angelica and tried to win her favours.' Just as he was winning Eleanor's. 'Though he went mad when she fell in love with another man., and was finally restored to sanity by a magician.' He turned his head slightly to the side so that he could kiss her palm. 'That story's called *Orlando Furioso*. "The Madness of Orlando." And right now I'm a little crazy, too, Eleanor. I need to touch you. Taste you.'

In answer, she brought her other hand up to his face, slid her fingers into his hair, and drew his mouth down to hers.

He couldn't remember the last time he'd wanted someone so much. Everything about Eleanor Forrest attracted him— body, mind and heart. Her skin was so soft, she smelled good, and the need he felt for her made him dizzy.

He broke the kiss, and gently lowered her back to the bed. Kissed the curve of her neck, the hollows of her collar-bones, and nuzzled his way down the valley between her breasts.

He teased one nipple with the tip of his tongue, until she arched on the bed and slid her fingers back into his hair. He smiled against her skin, then took her nipple into his mouth and sucked.

Her breathing had changed, he noticed, become needy little gasps. Good. He planned to make her forget everything except him. He kissed his way over her abdomen and slid one hand up her thigh. When she shivered, he cupped her sex with one hand.

'Yes. Oh, please.'

Hot and wet and so ready for him. He touched and teased and explored until she was shuddering, almost hyperventilating. Her eyes were tightly shut.

Was she thinking about Jeremy, the man who'd asked her to marry him when he'd already been committed elsewhere?

Well, he was going to drive that image right out of her head. Starting now.

'Open your eyes, *innamorata*,' he commanded softly. He wanted her to see him. So the next time she closed her eyes in pleasure, it would be his face she saw in her mind. 'Open your eyes.'

She did—and he saw the very second that her climax hit her. Saw the way her gaze became opaque. Heard her gasp his name. Saw the shudder of pleasure that rocked right through her.

So he'd been able to make her forget the world, forget her worries—forget everything except the fever pitch of desire between them.

Bene.

When Eleanor finally floated back to earth, she found herself lying in Orlando's arms. He'd tucked her protectively into his body; her head was resting on his shoulder and her arm was draped round his waist.

She could hardly believe he'd been so generous. He'd made sure that she was satisfied and had left himself frustrated. Given her time.

'Orlando. *Innamora*—' She stumbled over the word

He smiled and brushed a kiss against her mouth. '*Innamorato* is what you say to me.'

'Like the title of the poem,' she remembered aloud.

'Exactly like that. Except I think you're much more beautiful than the princess Angelica.' He stroked her face. 'And you're certainly not spoiled.'

Wasn't she? 'Orlando...I wasn't expecting that. That you'd...' She swallowed hard, trying to work out how to say it.

'Make sure you came first? *Tesoro*, I'm not quite that unselfish.' His laugh was wry. 'That's why I told you to open your eyes. So you'd see me and know that I was the one making you feel that way.'

She shivered. 'I wasn't thinking of Jeremy.'

'Good. But just in case you were...' Gently, he manoeuvred her onto her back and slid his hand between her thighs again.

She was shocked to discover how quickly he could arouse her again. When he kissed her, she matched him hunger for hunger, bite for bite, stroke for stroke.

Exploring his body was a revelation. Jeremy had always seemed faintly embarrassed about sex. Orlando clearly enjoyed it, encouraged her to touch him and even showed her exactly how he liked being touched. And because he was so bold about it, Eleanor wasn't in the least self-conscious: she even found herself enjoying it, discovering how to make his breathing become faster and shallower and how to make him arch in pleasure, his fists curling round the headboard.

He murmured something in Italian—something she couldn't quite catch.

'Orlando?'

His eyes snapped open and he stared at her. 'What?'

Tension radiated from him. Did he think she'd changed her mind and was going to tell him to stop? 'You spoke in Italian,' she explained. 'I'm sorry, I couldn't follow.'

Immediately, his tension dissolved, and he smiled. '*Mi dispiace, tesoro.* Oh, hell. Here I go again. I'm sorry. I, um, forgot to think in English.'

'What did you say? I mean, I understood that last bit. It's the bit before where you lost me.'

A slow smile spread across his face. 'Ah. That.'

'Orlando?'

'It might shock you.' He kissed her, a sweet kiss that turned into a slow burn of pleasure. 'What I said was, "I need to be inside you, Eleanor,"' he said huskily.

She nibbled at his lower lip. 'Guess what? I need you inside me.'

He slid his hand between her thighs. 'Now?'

'Right here, right now,' she confirmed.

He moved to unwrap a condom and roll it on. Then he frowned. 'You're smiling. What?'

'Just thinking.'

'Tell me.'

'You don't actually keep a stock of condoms on you.'

His frown deepened. 'No, I already told you I don't. That's why I had to buy some.'

'So you don't take, um, every opportunity that comes your way.' And with a man as gorgeous as Orlando, there would be opportunities. Plenty of opportunities.

'I told you before, I'm picky.'

'Mmm, and you're beautiful.'

This time, he laughed. 'You can't tell a man he's beautiful.'

'Oh, yes, I can. Look at you. Like one of the gorgeous statues you see in the museums and art galleries here. Perfect.'

Her fingertips trailed across his skin, down his chest to his abdomen, and he groaned. 'Don't tease me, Eleanor. I can't wait any more.'

'Neither,' she said, 'can I.'

And she stopped thinking as his body eased into hers.

CHAPTER NINE

THE next morning, Orlando woke to find himself wrapped around Eleanor, with a sheet half covering them and half on the floor. The rest of the bedclothes were probably also on the floor; and he realised with a flicker of guilt that she was balanced virtually on the edge of the bed. He had the lion's share of the pillows, too.

Last night had been...amazing. He knew he should've left last night—or at least in the early hours of the morning. But she'd asked him to stay with her. Hold her until she slept. And, heaven help him, he hadn't been able to tear himself away. Even worse, he hadn't *wanted* to stay away—if she hadn't asked him to stay, he would've suggested it.

And they'd woken twice in the night, feasted on each other.

They'd gone through a whole packet of condoms.

Oh, this was *bad*.

He'd told Eleanor he didn't do relationships. That he didn't believe in 'The One' or love or happy ever after.

She'd said it didn't matter.

But had she, with that weird female logic, decided that maybe she could change his mind? Would she expect him to stick around this morning? Would she think that what they'd shared last night meant he'd decided that maybe love did exist?

What really scared Orlando was that he was beginning to wonder it himself.

Oh, lord. He needed a cold shower to shock some common sense back into his head.

From where he was curled around Eleanor, he could see the clock on the bedside table. Nearly seven o'clock. It was his turn to run the practice's Saturday morning surgery this week. He could hardly turn up dressed in what he'd worn last night—besides, his doctor's bag was at home. He needed to leave. Now.

Eleanor seemed to be sleeping soundly. If he was careful, he'd be able to untangle himself from her, get dressed, write her a note and leave her sleeping. Avoid all that horrible morning-after awkwardness. And then maybe they could meet for dinner. Back on the old footing. And everything would be just fine.

He was just starting to move away from her, very gently, when Eleanor rolled onto her back and opened her eyes.

'Good morning, Orlando.' She gave him a soft, trusting smile that made him feel like a real louse. Oh, lord. How could he possibly leave now?

And, for his own peace of mind, how could he possibly stay?

Orlando definitely had a rabbit-in-headlights look on his face, Eleanor thought. Frozen in panic and desperate to run.

'I…' He swallowed hard. 'Good morning, Eleanor.'

It was clear to her that he regretted what had happened last night. Though she hadn't exactly given him a chance to refuse, had she? She'd cried all over him in the bar and asked him to stay with her because she was tired of being alone. She'd actually begged him to make her forget the world.

He had.

What they'd shared last night had been amazing. And she was sure that it had been mutual. But this morning the real world had come back to smack them both in the face. Orlando had made it clear he didn't do relationships—and nothing had changed.

'I…um, I'm on duty this morning,' Orlando muttered. 'At the surgery.'

Oh, for goodness' sake. Did he really have to make such an obvious excuse? Embarrassment flooded through her, making her temples throb.

'Listen…about last night,' Orlando said.

Oh, no. That was one of the most cringe-making phrases in the English language. The one that made people apologise and shuffle their feet and offer excuses. It made her want to bury her face in the pillow and howl. Instead, she strove for coolness. Never again after Jeremy would she let a man know he'd hurt her. And weren't the English meant to be good at this stiff-upper-lip business? 'Don't worry about it.' She yanked the sheet up to cover herself. 'We both know where we stand.'

He rubbed a hand over his face. 'Eleanor, I—'

Don't let him say he was sorry. She couldn't bear hearing that. 'I know. You need to go home and change. I'll, um, catch you later. And don't worry, I won't look while you're getting dressed.'

Disappointment made her voice catch. She'd thought there was something between them. That Orlando felt the same pull of attraction she did. Or maybe he was one of those men who just liked the thrill of the chase without the manacles of commitment. Hadn't the fiasco with Jeremy already proved beyond reasonable doubt that her judgement in men was lousy?

'Eleanor, I really do have to work. It's not an excuse. It's my turn to do the Saturday morning surgery and I need to collect my doctor's bag from home first. And I need to change into the sort of clothes our patients expect me to wear.'

She didn't dare meet his gaze.

'I'm not expecting you to shadow me today. Not on a Saturday.'

That definitely sounded as if he wanted some distance between them.

'Maybe we could, I don't know, have a late lunch somewhere overlooking the sea?'

Eleanor had a nasty feeling that this was his way of softening what he wanted to say. Over lunch, he'd give her the 'Dear Jane' speech about how it wasn't her, it was his fault and he was a louse, yada yada yada.

Well, she didn't want to hear it.

If he thought it was a mistake and it shouldn't have happened, then she wanted to be the one to say it first. She still had *some* pride left. 'You really don't need to do that. I'm a big girl and I can take responsibility for my own actions.' She took a deep breath. 'We both know last night shouldn't have happened. I was upset and I took advantage of your good nature.'

'*Cara*, *I* am the one who took advantage of *you*.'

'No, you didn't.' She still couldn't bring herself to meet his eyes. 'I'm the one who asked you to stay. And I'm not under any illusion that you're going to declare undying love for me. You were honest with me from the start. You told me you don't believe in love.'

There was a long, long pause. 'So where does it leave us now?' he asked.

'As we were. Fr—' She changed her mind in mid-sentence. 'Acquaintances.'

'And colleagues?'

It'd be hard to explain to Serafina, Alessandro, Chiara and Giacomo why she'd suddenly vanished from the practice. Though, at the same time, how could she work with him now?

Complicated.

Or maybe it'd be easier if they did work together: a working relationship would slot a nice neat barrier between them, pre-cluding a more personal relationship.

'The offer to work in our practice is still open,' he said. 'You were planning to stay in Italy for a while. And I'm not intend-ing to break my promise to help you with the paperwork and to find a place to live.'

'I'll sort something out myself.' She took a deep breath. 'But there is something I need your help with.'

'Of course,' he said immediately.

Relieved that she'd let him off the hook so easily? It stung, so she couldn't help saying, 'Careful, you don't know what I'm going to ask you.'

'Ask me, then.'

This time, she did look at him. 'Will you come to Bartolomeo's house this afternoon? Talk to us—as a doctor—about the aplastic anaemia.'

He frowned slightly. 'His doctor might not be too happy about that.'

'I'll deal with that when I have to. Will you help me?'

He nodded.

'What time can you make it?'

'Three?' he suggested.

'Perfect. I'll see you then.' She found a piece of paper and scribbled Bartolomeo's address on it. 'Have a good morning at the surgery.'

He opened his mouth as if to say something, then closed it again. She turned away as he slid out of the bed and feigned interest in a guidebook about Naples while he dressed.

'I'll see you later, then,' he said at the doorway.

'*A presto.*' She didn't look up from her book until she heard the door click behind him. Then she sat up in bed, drew her knees up to her chin and wrapped her arms round her legs. What a mess. She didn't regret last night—how could she, when she'd discovered so much pleasure in his arms?—but she really, *really* regretted this morning. She regretted the awkwardness between them. And most of all she regretted the knowledge that she'd been stupid enough to hope for something more than Orlando was prepared to offer her.

At five to three, Eleanor answered the door to Orlando. 'Come in,' she said. She ushered him through to the terrace where Bartolomeo was sitting and introduced them quickly. 'I'll fetch coffee,' she said.

It had finished brewing—just—when she walked into the kitchen. And when she returned to the terrace with the tray of coffee she could virtually see the tension between Bartolomeo and Orlando. They were speaking so rapidly that she couldn't follow what they were saying, but she could tell by the tone that things were getting a little heated.

'Perhaps one of you could be courteous enough to translate for me?' she asked, pouring them both a cup of coffee.

They exchanged a glance, and then Bartolomeo said ruefully, 'Orlando was telling me that if you could understand what I was saying, you'd go bananas because you're an independent woman who's perfectly capable of making her own decisions and doesn't need her father to grill a man about his intentions towards her.'

Bartolomeo was playing the heavy father?

And Orlando was doing the angry-young-man thing?

She looked at them both in disbelief, and then burst out laughing. 'Oh, honestly! The pair of you!'

'I'm glad you can see the funny side,' Orlando said dryly. 'But your father accepts now that we are colleagues and this is a professional matter.'

Which pretty much summed up their relationship. That morning she'd called him an acquaintance. He'd referred to her just now as a colleague. Last night had been…an aberration. Something they wouldn't repeat.

'Eleanor's qualified medically but she needs my help as a translator—someone who understands both languages and medical terminology. So may we have your permission to talk to your consultant about your condition?' Orlando asked.

Bartolomeo looked at both of them, and sighed. '*Si*. All right.'

'That's settled. Good.' Eleanor folded her arms and looked at Orlando. 'We could sit here and be polite. But I think it's better if I say it straight.'

For a second, alarm flitted over his face. Did he really think she was going to bring up last night? She didn't want Bartolomeo knowing just how naïve and foolish she'd been. 'We need to talk about a bone-marrow transplant. My bone marrow will be compatible with my father's.'

Orlando sucked in a breath. 'You're saying you want to donate bone marrow?'

Bartolomeo's hand shook as he replaced his coffee-cup in the saucer, making the china clatter. 'Eleanor, *piccolina,* you can't do this.'

'Yes, I can,' she said. 'We already know the supportive therapy isn't going to cure you. It's helping—but clearly it's not helping enough, because you're still tired. My best friend Tamsin is a GP—a *medico di famiglia*, like Orlando—and she has a friend who works in haematology.' For Bartolomeo's benefit she added, 'Disorders of the blood, like thalassaemia and aplastic anaemia. They talked last night and Tamsin called me this morning. She says that definitive therapy—in other words, a bone-marrow transplant—will restore healthy, working bone marrow. And then you won't need the blood transfusions any more.'

Orlando held up a hand in protest. 'Hang on—you're rushing things. There's Bartolomeo's age to consider, and transplants are usually done from a brother or sister or a matched unrelated donor.'

Eleanor's mouth tightened. 'Bartolomeo's sisters are not a match. He has no brothers. And you know as well as I do, the risks of rejection are much lower in an allogenic transplant from a blood relative than they are in a transplant from an unrelated donor. Which means me.'

Bartolomeo frowned. 'I'm not happy about this. What about the risks to you?'

'They're low,' Eleanor reassured him. 'I'm thirty years old, I'm perfectly healthy, and I'll recover quickly.'

'How quickly?' Bartolomeo asked.

'That depends on how the marrow is harvested,' she admitted. She didn't want to lie to him. But she didn't want him worrying either. 'You know how a transplant works?'

He wrinkled his nose. 'Vaguely.'

Which meant he didn't. Probably nobody had explained it to him because nobody had thought it was an option. Until now. 'There are three parts to your blood—red blood cells that carry oxygen round your body, white cells that fight infection, and platelets that help stop you bleeding. The blood is made with stem cells in your bone marrow—that's the spongy stuff in the middle of your bones. If your bone marrow isn't working properly, your body can't produce blood. So right now you need a transplant of bone marrow to help your body make the blood cells.'

'How it would work,' Orlando chipped in, 'is that we test the donor's blood to see if the tissue type matches yours. If it does, then we would give the donor a full medical examination and counselling.'

Eleanor rolled her eyes. 'There's no "if" about it. I'm Bartolomeo's daughter. You can even see the family resemblance, for goodness' sake! As his daughter, I've inherited three out of my six antigens from him. So our tissue types will match.'

'You would still have to undergo counselling,' Orlando said.

'I don't *need* counselling over this.' Didn't he realise? Wasn't he listening? 'Bartolomeo is my father.' Her only living blood relative. Who was dying. And it was in her power to save him. 'I want to do this. And, yes, of course I need to undergo a medical examination, but I can tell you now the results will be fine.'

'You need counselling,' Orlando repeated stubbornly.

'Then help me fast-track it. Because I'm not going to change my mind,' Eleanor informed him coolly.

Orlando glared at her, then turned to Bartolomeo. 'For a week or so before the bone marrow is taken from the donor, we give him or her injections of growth factor to produce lots of stem cells in the bone marrow.'

'So it hurts?' Bartolomeo asked.

'No,' Eleanor reassured him. 'The injections are done in the arm or the leg.' And sometimes in the abdomen, but she thought it politic not to mention that. She grinned. 'Hey, I'm a doctor and I work in the emergency department, so I see needles all the time. I'm not scared of needles.'

'I loathe needles,' Bartolomeo muttered. 'So then they take out the bone marrow? How? Does it hurt?'

'The donor has a general anaesthetic,' Orlando said. 'The operation lasts for an hour, maybe two, and the surgeon collects the marrow cells from the pelvis with a needle and syringe.'

'There's no cutting or stitching involved, and I'd be able to leave hospital the next day,' Eleanor said. 'Then the bone marrow would be given to you in the same kind of way as you have a blood transfusion—there's a thin plastic tube called a Hickman line that the surgeon would put in your neck or your groin, and the healthy marrow travels through your body and settles in the spaces in the middle of your large bones. Then hopefully in the next fortnight to a month your body will accept the new bone marrow and start producing new healthy blood cells.'

Bartolomeo looked impressed. 'I thought you said you were an emergency doctor? I didn't think you did that sort of operation in the emergency department.'

'I am, and we don't,' Eleanor said. 'But I've been researching the procedures since you told me about the aplastic anaemia, and my best friend's haematology colleague filled in the gaps for me.' She smiled at him. 'It's pretty straightforward. Though before the operation you'll need radiotherapy or chemotherapy to destroy your remaining bone marrow cells, so there's less risk of your body rejecting the donated cells.'

Orlando frowned. 'That's not suitable for all patients, Eleanor. And it might be too stressful for Bartolomeo's body.'

Given his age, she knew that was true. 'There are other ways,' Eleanor countered. 'Such as a non-myeloablative stem cell transplant, with smaller doses of drugs and chemo to lower his immune system enough to accept the donor cells.'

Bartolomeo waved both hands. 'Hello, I am still here! Don't talk over me—I'm not following half of what you're saying now. Non-mye—what?'

'Non-myeloablative,' Eleanor said. 'Sorry. I didn't mean to talk over you. Or talk jargon.' She'd just wanted Orlando to realise that she knew exactly what she was getting into. She needed him on her side. Needed him to help her convince the consultant to give her father the life-saving treatment he so desperately required. 'Non-myeloablative just means treatment that won't destroy your bone marrow. Normally if a cell goes into your body that your body doesn't recognise as its own, your immune system will kick in to destroy the invader—so if we don't lower your immune system before the transplant, you'll be at risk from something called "graft versus host disease".' She smiled at him. 'If we lower your immune system, it won't attack the bone marrow cells from my system when we transplant them to your body. For a while, our cells will be mixed, and eventually mine will replace yours.'

'After the transplant, you'll need medication to stimulate the production of blood cells, and you'll have blood tests to check the new bone marrow is working,' Orlando said.

'More needles,' Bartolomeo said wryly.

'Though I should warn you that while you recover, you're likely to pick up infections because your immune system will be so low,' Eleanor continued. 'You need to avoid anyone coming near you who has a cold.'

'We can try to minimise it by giving you antibiotics, so the infections don't get a chance to take hold,' Orlando said. 'But as well as the medication, you'll still need blood transfusions to maintain the right level of blood cells in your body until the new bone marrow is working. It's demanding, Bartolomeo—very demanding, physically and emotionally. And it can take a long time to recover.'

'How long?' Bartolomeo asked.

Orlando took a deep breath. 'I have to be honest with you. It could take as much as a year.'

Eleanor glanced at her father. A year's recovery was a much better prospect than having no time at all, in her eyes. Did he feel the same? Oh, please. He had to. She couldn't bear the idea of losing him so soon after she'd found him. 'Often it's less than that,' she said.

'And you, Eleanor?' Bartolomeo asked. 'What side effects will it have on you?'

'Hardly anything,' Eleanor said swiftly.

Bartolomeo scoffed. 'Orlando, you took the Hippocratic oath, yes? So tell me the truth. Tell me what Eleanor is trying not to tell me.'

She tried kicking Orlando's ankle under the table, but he ignored her. 'A donor might have bruising and soreness in the lower back and in the place where the bone marrow was taken. It'll last for a few weeks. And while the bone marrow renews itself the donor will feel tired and should avoid strenuous exertion. It may take a week or so to recover.'

'That's if we go for a traditional bone-marrow harvest under a general anaesthetic,' Eleanor argued. 'There's a newer procedure called PBSC, which stands for peripheral blood stem cell donation. What that means is that I'd have daily injections of a growth factor to increase the number of stem cells and make them move out of my bone marrow and into my general circulation. Then the surgeons simply hook me up to a special machine that separates out the stem calls from the rest of my blood cells. The procedure's called leukapheresis. Basically the blood goes out of one arm, gets filtered, and goes back into the other arm. The doctors collect the cells in two separate sessions, each lasting about four or five hours, so I won't need to stay in hospital overnight. I won't need any anaesthetic either—definitely not a general and not even a spinal block, so you can take out a huge chunk of risks there.'

Bartolomeo folded his arms. 'And the side effects?'

Eleanor smiled. 'I might feel a bit fluey, but a donor can go back to their normal job within twenty-four hours of a PBSC.'

'The success rate is good?' Bartolomeo asked.

'Between forty per cent and seventy per cent,' Orlando said.

'And it's getting better,' Eleanor added.

Bartolomeo looked thoughtful. 'So how new is this process?'

'It's becoming more and more common,' Eleanor said. 'And it's much better for the donor and the person receiving the stem cells. On the donor's side, it's not an invasive procedure, doesn't involve a general anaesthetic and has a shorter recovery period. On your side, it means you'll spend a shorter time in hospital, and your white blood and platelet counts return to normal more quickly so there's less of a chance of complications.'

'It still doesn't mean you can definitely do it,' Orlando warned. 'You inherited one set of haplotypes from Bartolomeo and one from your mother—if your mother's haplotypes are a bad mismatch for Bartolomeo's…'

Eleanor's jaw set. 'Only one way to find out. I want that blood test. First thing tomorrow morning.'

Orlando shook his head. 'Tomorrow's Sunday. You're not going to get a test on Sunday.'

'Then we'll do it Monday. I'll pay for a private test if it's quicker.'

Bartolomeo put his hand over hers and squeezed it. 'I can't ask you to do this for me.'

'You're not asking,' Eleanor pointed out. 'I'm offering. We've been through this, Bartolomeo. You're my only blood family, I've just found you, and I'm not prepared to stand by and lose you before I get the chance to know you properly. If donating a few of my stem cells will keep you around a bit longer, I want to do it. And do it *now*.'

Bartolomeo stared helplessly at her. 'I don't know how to thank you.'

'You don't have to. You're my family.'

CHAPTER TEN

THEY managed small talk for another half an hour, then Eleanor, noticing how tired her father looked, called a halt. 'You need a rest,' she said gently. 'I'll leave you.'

'I'll see you back to the hotel,' Orlando said.

'No, it's fine. I'm sure you have things to do.'

'I said,' he repeated, 'I'll see you back safely to the hotel.'

It was fairly obvious he wanted to talk to her about something—something he didn't want to say in front of Bartolomeo. Well, if he wanted a fight, he'd get it. She was still furious with him for spelling out the bleakest side of the bone-marrow donation and worrying her father. *'Grazie,'* she said quietly, hugged Bartolomeo goodbye and followed Orlando outside.

As soon as they were seated on the metro, Orlando shot her a sidelong look. 'You really sprang that one on me.'

She folded her arms. 'Don't be ridiculous. I told you I needed your help talking to my father's consultant about the aplastic anaemia. And that I'd been researching it.'

'But you didn't warn me you were going to offer to be a donor.'

She rolled her eyes. 'Oh, come off it. Isn't it the obvious solution?'

Orlando mirrored her stance, arms folded. 'May I point out that you only met the man a few days ago? And you're proposing to undergo a very painful operation for someone you barely know.'

She glared at him in outrage. 'How can you say that? He's my *father*!'

'You told me yourself you didn't even know he existed until a couple of weeks ago.'

She shook her head in disbelief. 'I know you've got a problem with families, Orlando, but don't dump your insecurities on me.'

He gave a mirthless laugh. 'I don't have any insecurities.'

'No?' They'd shared the ultimate closeness the previous night, and the way he'd walked out on her so easily this morning still rankled. 'The way I see it, Orlando, you can't understand why anyone might want to show some commitment to another human being, because you can't do it yourself.'

He rolled his eyes. 'Don't tell me you think this is about last night.'

'Isn't it?'

'No,' Orlando snapped. 'This is about *you*. About the fact you're rushing in to something without thinking it through properly. You said yourself, a bone marrow donation is complicated—that's why it's hard to get donors. It isn't an easy option, Eleanor. It's not like giving blood.'

She lifted her chin. 'A PBSC is. Virtually.'

'It's more complicated than that, and you know it. It takes a lot longer, your blood is filtered, you have to take drugs beforehand, and you can't just get up and carry on as normal after a cup of tea and a biscuit. And you're proposing to do this,' he repeated, 'for someone you barely know.'

He really, really didn't get this, did he? She frowned. 'If I were donating blood marrow to someone on the transplant list, it'd be to someone I didn't know. What's the difference?'

'The difference is you're vulnerable right now and you're setting yourself up for heartbreak because there's no guarantee it's going to work. If you were an unrelated donor, there wouldn't be the emotional involvement: you'd be sad if it didn't work, yes, but it wouldn't really affect you. In this case, if it doesn't work, you'll be devastated. You're pinning all your hopes on something that isn't one hundred per cent guaranteed—on something that basically has a fifty-fifty chance of working, if you look at it objectively.' He raked a hand through his hair. 'And before you bring it up, I'm not proud of the way I took advantage of you last night. I've already apologised for that.'

He didn't say it, but she could see the question in his eyes. *What else do you want from me?*

He'd told her the truth, right from the start. He didn't do commitment, didn't believe in love. What was the point in asking him for something he couldn't give?

She swallowed the lump in her throat. 'I'm sorry. I'm just…'

'I know.' He reached out and stroked her cheek. 'I'm sorry, too. But you need to think about what you're doing here, Eleanor. Don't rush in blindly.'

She knew he was right, and it made the comment sting even more. And the gentleness of his touch… It hurt. Because she knew he couldn't give her more, and she was ashamed of herself for wanting more. She pulled away from him. 'So what am I supposed to do? Bartolomeo is my only living blood relative. Am I supposed to just stand by and watch him die slowly?'

'No, of course not.'

'His sisters aren't a match, there isn't a matched unrelated donor available, and the chances are that my bone marrow will be a match for his. Yes, you're right in that I haven't known him long. But I want time to *get* to know him. The only way I'll get that time is if he has a bone-marrow donation. From me. What other way is there?'

He was silent, and her rage died as quickly as it had blown up. 'I'm sorry. I'm upset about the situation and I shouldn't take it out on you. But you need to understand where I'm coming from, Orlando.'

'I do.'

'Really?' She didn't think so. 'I'm completely alone in the world. I have good friends, and I'm grateful for that, but it's not the same as having someone to belong to. It's not the same as being part of a family.'

'And that's what you want?'

'Doesn't everyone? Don't you?'

He shrugged. 'I don't need that. I'm happy as I am.'

'Are you? I mean, *really*? Don't you look at your friends— at Serafina and Alessandro, at your friends in London with your godson—and wonder what that special something is they have?'

'No.'

She stared at him. 'You're unbelievable. Are you seriously telling me you think they're going to split up?'

'No. Just that confetti doesn't last for ever. Honeymoons end. After that, you just have to make the best of it.'

'You're horribly cynical.'

'I'm a realist, *tesoro*.'

'So last night…'

He flinched. 'How many times are you going to make me apologise for that, Eleanor?'

She shook her head. 'That's not what I was going to say. Last night there was a connection between us.' She felt the colour seep into her face. 'Apart from the physical, I mean. Are you telling me it wasn't the same for you?'

There was a long, long, pause. 'I don't know,' he admitted finally.

'Then why did you agree to help me?'

'Because I'm a nice guy?' he suggested.

She shook her head. 'You could've pleaded pressure of work. Or maybe put me in contact with a specialist you know. But you haven't. You came with me to meet Bartolomeo yourself. You're giving me support.'

'As I would any colleague.'

She reached over to run her thumb over his lower lip. 'If you were the kind of man you're trying to make me believe you are, this wouldn't affect you. But your pupils just dilated.'

'That's merely a physical reaction.'

She shook her head. 'There's more to it than that, and you know it. It isn't just sexual attraction. When you kissed me at the surgery. When you held my hand at Pompeii. Every time you're near me. I know how it makes me feel—and I think it's the same for you. Or are you going to lie to me as well as to yourself?'

He didn't answer, and as they reached her stop, she stood up. 'I'll see myself back.'

'I said I'd see you back, and I keep my word. Look, I'm trying to be completely honest with you,' Orlando said, following her off the train.

'Honest?' she scoffed.

'Yes. I like you, Eleanor. A lot. And I find you attractive. The way I feel about you…' He swallowed hard. 'All right. You want honesty? I've never felt like this about anyone before. If you must know, it scares the hell out of me because I've no idea what I'm doing. Though what I do know is that I'm making a complete mess of things,' he added wryly.

'What do *you* want, Orlando?'

He shook his head. 'How can I answer that? I don't believe in love. I've seen my mother like this, so sure her current love was The One—the man she wanted to spend the rest of her life with. And then I watched the disillusionment set in when she realised he wasn't, and saw a good relationship sour into contempt and hatred. Time and time again. She's been divorced five times, and in and out of love more often than I can count. I don't want that to happen to me. To *us*.' He took a deep breath. 'Look, I know you want to be part of a family. I can tell you now mine's a mess. Stepsiblings and ex-stepfathers I don't see, a father I can barely remember from my childhood. I don't know if I can give you what you want out of life.'

'Then it's simple,' she said as they reached hotel. 'Don't bother.'

Orlando watched her disappear through the revolving doors, feeling as guilty as hell. What was wrong with him that he couldn't just tell her that he wanted to take the chance—to see if their relationship could grow and develop into something really special? Tell her that he was beginning to believe in 'The One'—and that she was it, for him?

'You,' he informed himself as he walked home, 'need your head examined.'

No. What he really needed to do was apologise. Ask her if they could start again.

It was just a question of working out how.

Eleanor spent a restless night, not sure whether she was more furious with Orlando for being difficult or with herself for having such lousy judgement in men.

She'd just dragged herself out of the shower the next morning when there was a knock at the door.

Huh? She hadn't ordered room service.

Pulling her dressing-gown tighter, she opened the door a crack.

'Dottoressa Forrest? I have a delivery for you.'

It was the most beautiful hand-tied bouquet of roses and freesias. She frowned. 'Are you sure it's for me?'

In answer, the maid handed her an envelope addressed to Dottoressa Forrest.

'Thank you,' she said, accepting the flowers with a smile and then fumbling for her purse so she could tip the maid. 'Um, where would I be able to buy a vase?'

'I can bring one for you,' the maid said with a smile. 'I'll get it now.'

'*Grazie.*' Eleanor set the arrangement on the dressing-table and opened the envelope. There was a small card inside.

I apologise. We need to talk. Please meet me for breakfast. I will be waiting for you in the foyer. Orlando.

Right at that moment she wasn't sure she wanted to see him. But she got dressed anyway. When the maid had brought the vase, Eleanor arranged the flowers. So Orlando wanted to see her. And he was waiting downstairs in the foyer. Did this mean he'd brought the flowers himself? Come to think of it, florists didn't usually deliver on a Sunday.

So he must have been waiting for at least ten minutes.

Good.

He could wait a bit longer.

She managed to hang it out for another fifteen minutes before she went downstairs. Immaculately made up, so he wouldn't be able to see the shadows under her eyes and guess that she'd slept badly. She was going to play this so cool she'd be the queen of the Antarctic.

He was sitting in one of the chairs, ostensibly absorbed in a newspaper. But she could tell that he had one eye on the stairs,

because the moment she started walking down them he folded
the newspaper and stood up.

'*Buon giorno*, Eleanor.'

'Good morning, Orlando.' She wasn't in the mood to compromise. Even though he had sent her flowers. 'Thank you for
the flowers,' she added politely.

'They were the least I could do.'

'I didn't think florists were open on Sunday mornings.'

'The Mercarto dei Fiori—the flower market—by the Castel
Nuovo is open at sunrise every morning.'

'So you picked these yourself?'

A slight smile curved his mouth. 'Yes, but I admit that the
stall-holder arranged them for me. Hand-tying a bouquet is a
little beyond my skills.' His smile faded. 'I owe you an apology.
I'm sorry, Eleanor.'

She inclined her head in acknowledgement.

'Will you join me for *la prima colazione*—for breakfast?'

His eyes were huge; he looked as guilty as a puppy who'd
been caught chewing a favourite pair of shoes. And when he
gave her a smile that beautiful... Even though she was still
angry with him, how could she say no? 'All right.'

'*Bene.* Would you prefer to stay here, or go to a little place
I know round the corner that does the best almost croissants
in Naples?'

She'd bought pastries to go with morning coffee at the
practice a couple of times the previous week, so he knew her
weakness for them. Particularly almond croissants. She made
the effort to sound cool, calm and collected. 'As you wish.'

'Then let's go.'

When they were ensconced in the little *caffè*, with a *lattè* each
and a plate of almond croissants between them, he looked at her.

'You look as bad as I feel.'

She stared at him for a moment, not quite believing what she'd just heard. Was this his idea of a truce? 'Oh, thank you.'

He noticed the acid edge to her tone and winced. 'That came out wrong.' He raked a hand through his hair. 'I used to be good with people. No, I *am* good with people. With patients. It's just…you.'

She'd noticed. But she also knew he wasn't going to say the words. And, without those, she definitely wasn't playing.

'Let me start again. I feel horrible about the way I behaved towards you yesterday.' He took a deep breath. 'I'm not offering any excuses. I don't do relationships—well, only the very lightest ones—and the fact I'd even consider something different with you scares me stupid.'

She opened her mouth to speak, and he lifted a hand to forestall her. 'No, Eleanor, please, hear me out. I've been thinking about what you're doing, and even though I don't agree with you completely I can understand why you want to do it. But you can't do it on your own—even though your Italian's come on in leaps and bounds, you might feel groggy in the hospital and not be able to follow what people are saying or make them understand what you want. You need someone with you. A support person. So I'm proposing…'

Her heart did a funny sort of wiggle and she dug her nails into her palms. He didn't mean *that* sort of proposal, and she knew it.

'I'm proposing that I'm that person. Your support person,' he emphasised.

When she said nothing, he continued, 'I made some phone calls this morning. Certain people owe me favours. So I called them in. I've arranged tissue typing. I'll take the blood from you myself, first thing tomorrow morning—any future procedure will be done by the doctor at the hospital, but if we wait to register you with another doctor the paperwork will take for ever. Time I know you don't want to waste.' He paused. 'And it's your decision whether you spend your mornings at the practice or not this week. No pressure.'

She could only focus on the first bit. He'd arranged tissue typing. He was going to support her, help her as much as he could with the bone-marrow donation. 'You'll do the blood test,' she echoed.

'And I'll take the blood over to the hospital in my lunch-break. It takes five days to get the results, so if I'm there by about half past one we'll have the results on Saturday afternoon. In the meantime, I'll register you with the practice, so Alessandro or Giacomo can be your doctor—not me, because it's not ethical.'

'They're my colleagues, too,' she pointed out. 'So are you saying things are different between us—that you don't see me just as a colleague?'

A muscle tightened in his jaw. 'Don't interrupt.'

'You can't run from this for ever.'

'I'm trying to focus on practical things, Eleanor.'

'Do you or do you not see me as just a colleague.'

'What do you want, blood?' He gritted his teeth. 'All right. I admit I don't see you just as a colleague. But don't give me a hard time over this, because right now I'm not in the mood for dealing with it,' he told her. 'Now, as I was saying, we can arrange a full medical examination—with your permission—to save time when we get the results back.'

'If I'm a match.'

'If. But, as you say, Bartolomeo is your father. Unless your mother's haplotypes clash badly with his, the odds are that you will be a match.' He looked at her. 'This is going to be a big deal, Eleanor. Physically and emotionally. You're not going to have room in your life for…other stuff.'

Other stuff. He meant the attraction between them. The way they hadn't been able to keep their hands off each other on Friday night. The way he'd kissed her in the surgery. The way their hands had kept touching, the way they'd kept looking at each other and wondering. 'That's a cop-out.'

He smiled wryly. 'Maybe.'

'Come on. You know it is.'

'It is also, perhaps, buying time.'

She frowned. 'How do you mean?'

'My head's all over the place right now. But I do know one thing I definitely don't want.'

She was almost afraid to ask. 'What's that?'

'For you to walk out of my life. That's a first for me. I've never felt that about anyone before.'

'And you want to take things slowly.'

'Until I'm sure,' he said. 'Look, you've been badly hurt. It's going to take time for you to trust again. And I never trusted in the first place. It's going to take time for me to learn.'

'Time. Which Bartolomeo doesn't have,' she said.

'Exactly. If the transplant goes ahead, the procedure will take days, weeks. Time when we have space to think, to sort things out in our heads—well, *my* head,' he admitted, 'but we're not apart either.'

'That sounds suspiciously like having your cake and eating it.'

'I'm not that arrogant.' He spread his hands. 'I don't want to hurt you, Eleanor. If we rush this, it's going to go wrong. Badly. We both need time to get to know each other better, be sure what we both want. This will give us that time.'

He was being sensible, she knew. Though it hurt that they'd shared the ultimate closeness and he still wasn't sure how he felt about her.

'Eleanor?'

She considered it. What other option did she have? Finally, she nodded. 'All right. The other stuff goes on hold. Until Bartolomeo's had the transplant and we know whether it was successful.'

'And I'll support you through this.' He held her gaze. 'As your friend.'

CHAPTER ELEVEN

ON MONDAY morning, twenty minutes before Orlando's first patient was due in, Eleanor sat on the chair next to his desk with her arm propped on a pillow, exposing her inner elbow.

'Before we do this, I need to know something because it might affect the results,' Orlando said. 'Have you had a blood transfusion recently?'

'No. For the record, I've never had a transfusion.'

'That's good. Now, make a fist for me.'

He used his thumb to probe for the vein in her inner elbow; although the gesture was completely impersonal and professional, one she'd done herself countless times, the touch of his skin against hers still made her heart beat faster.

Stop being so pathetic, she told herself silently.

'I thought you said you weren't scared of needles?'

'I'm not.'

He gave her a half-smile. 'That's not what your veins are saying. They've gone into hiding. Squeeze and release your fist. And again. And again.' His smile broadened. '*Bene*. You'll feel a sharp scratch.' And then he was fitting a test tube to the end of the syringe, and deep red liquid was trickling into it.

Eleanor was silent while he took the blood sample, then

switched to a second test tube and then a third. She tried to crack a joke. 'How much do you want, a whole armful?'

He regarded her seriously. 'You're having a full medical as well as tissue typing. We're looking at Us and Es, full blood count, glucose—the usual blood work-ups. We need to check your renal function and your liver and your thyroid.'

'There's nothing wrong with my kidneys or my liver or my thyroid.'

He ignored her. 'And we need to be sure you haven't picked up anything that might compromise Bartolomeo's system.'

'I was teasing about the armful.'

He gave her a half-shrug, finished taking the sample, then placed a pad of cotton wool over the injection site before removing the needle. 'Press on that. It'll mean you're less likely to bruise.'

She already knew that, but assumed it was his way of trying to put some professional distance between them—treating her as if she were a patient. And talking about procedures was safe. It meant she'd concentrate on work instead of emotions—it'd help her ignore the way her skin tingled when he touched her, even as impersonally as taking a blood sample. 'So what happens now?'

'For the tissue typing, the haematologist will look at about ten different DNA markers. The important ones are the recognition ones—the antigens that tell the immune system whether to attack or leave them.'

'So they'll be looking at chromosome six,' Eleanor said. 'The MHC—the major histocompatibility complex. And there are a large number of proteins involved, so it's rare to find a perfect match with the human leucocyte antigens.'

'It doesn't need to be a perfect match,' Orlando reminded her. 'Just good enough. Remember Bartolomeo has had several blood transfusions, so he'll already have a large number of antibodies circulating against HLAs. When they test the HLAs, if your A, B and DR ones match, we'll be fine.' He paused. 'Your blood groups need to be compatible, too. If your blood group is O, it's the universal group so you can help anyone.'

Eleanor knew what he'd left unsaid: if her blood group clashed with Bartolomeo's, it wouldn't work. Her blood group wasn't a rare type, though: it was the second most common. 'I already know my blood group. It's A,' she said. She dragged in a breath. 'Don't say we're going to fall at the first hurdle. I know that my blood group means that his has to be A or AB for this to work.'

Orlando picked up his phone and handed it to her. 'Call him. Find out. And if it's A…'

'Check if he's positive or negative. I know.'

Two minutes later, she had the answer. 'A-positive. Same as mine.'

'*Bene.* Had you been O, it would still have worked. Except he would have acquired your blood group because your bone marrow will be making his blood cells in the future.'

'You've done a lot of research on this, haven't you?'

'I checked a few extra things yesterday,' he admitted. 'Like you, I was able to get access to a haematologist.'

'And he was helpful?' The question was out before she could stop herself.

Orlando clearly knew exactly what she was asking. 'Yes, *she* was,' he said coolly. 'And, just for the record, she's old enough to be my mother.'

Eleanor flushed. 'I…' Oh, lord. Talk about putting her foot in her mouth. And what gave her the right to be jealous anyway? They weren't officially an item.

'This is what happens when you put emotions into things.

It gets messy,' Orlando said dryly. He labelled the test tubes and took them to the practice nurse's room to store it in the samples fridge. 'I'll take this over myself at lunchtime,' he said. 'And you are going to have to be patient for the next five days. I've already pulled strings so the test results will be available on Saturday—we would normally have to wait until Monday.'

'Thank you.'

'It's not just the HLA we're looking at—I'm asking for other blood tests as well. You work in emergency medicine.' He looked grim. 'I should have asked you this before. Have you ever had a needlestick injury?'

'No.'

'Good. Any scares of any sort?'

'I'm not with you.'

'Maybe there was an emergency—maybe a case like the one on the plane, where you didn't have the right equipment with you but you were morally bound to help. Say you rushed in to help someone, didn't have gloves on, they were bleeding and maybe there was a cut on your hand—and obviously you wouldn't know if your patient was HIV-positive when you treated them. So have you been exposed to blood that might have been infected?'

'No.'

'Good. So, Eleanor.' He leaned back against his chair. 'Are you spending your mornings here this week?'

'I've been thinking about that all weekend,' she admitted. 'Working with you is going to be a strain.'

'Unless you keep your emotions out of it and treat me as you would any other colleague.'

She wasn't sure she could do that. And he'd admitted that he didn't see her as just a colleague, either. 'If I have to wait for five whole days with nothing to do except wonder what the results of the tissue-typing and medical tests will be, I'll go crazy. I need to keep busy.'

'Then the decision is easy. Work with me. Our first patient is due in about...' he glanced at his watch '...five minutes. Do you need a plaster for your arm?'

She stopped pressing on the cotton wool and removed it. No telltale oozing of blood. 'No, I'm fine.'

'And no bruise.'

Which was a good thing. Because she might not have been able to stop herself asking him to kiss it better.

When their first patient came in, Orlando introduced Eleanor. 'Signora Giordano, this is Dottoressa Forrest—she is an English doctor, working with me for the summer. Would you mind if she sat in on our consultation?'

Signora Giordano smiled shyly. 'No.'

'She might ask questions, but I will translate for you,' Orlando reassured her. 'Would you step on the scales for me?'

Signora Giordano sighed. 'I've been trying to lose weight, really I have. I walk the dog twice a day.' She took the pedometer from the waistband of her skirt. 'Ten thousand steps a day. And still the weight won't come off.'

'I know you're trying hard,' he reassured her.

Eleanor read the display on the scales and tapped the figures into Orlando's computer. 'No change since last month,' she said quietly.

Orlando translated rapidly, then took Signora Giordano's blood pressure. 'Still a bit on the high side,' he said. 'If it's like this next month, we'll need to change your drugs. How are you feeling in yourself?'

'A bit low,' she admitted. 'My family say I've lost my sense of humour. And sometimes I cry—but I just need to pull myself together.'

Low mood, struggling with her weight—Eleanor had heard this before. Tamsin's mother had had a similar problem. And, like Signora Giordano, she'd worn a cardigan even though it had been quite warm outside. And her eyes seemed slightly protuberant, too.

'May I look at the back of your hand?' she asked. At Signora Giordano's nod, she examined the woman's skin. 'It seems very dry. Do you need to use more hand cream than usual?'

'*Si*. And it doesn't really work any more.'

'And your periods, your *flusso mestruale*—how are they?'

Signora Giordano made a face. 'I haven't wanted to bother Dottore de Luca with it because it's not really an illness, but I have to get up a couple of times at night to…' She flapped an embarrassed hand. 'To change.'

Orlando exchanged a glance with Eleanor, as if he knew exactly where her questioning was going. 'And your energy, Signora Giordano?'

'I get tired,' she admitted. 'I go to bed earlier than I used to. But that's my age.' She put a hand to her mouth. 'I'm too young for the menopause, surely!'

Eleanor glanced at the screen to check Signora Giordano's date of birth. Forty-two. 'Unless your mother and sisters went through the change very early, yes, you're a little young for that. *Permesso*, it's a very personal question, but making love with your husband is, um, less than it used to be?'

Signora Giordano blushed. 'We work hard. We're too tired.'

The symptoms were really adding up. 'I'm sorry, these questions must be embarrassing for you, but is there any change in your toilet habits?'

'It's more difficult to go, yes—the pharmacist said I needed to drink more and do more exercise.'

'That's better than using laxatives, yes,' Eleanor agreed, 'but if it's not working you need to talk to us about it. I would like

Dottore de Luca to give you a blood test, because I think you may have an underactive thyroid.'

'Your thyroid is a gland in your throat, just below your voicebox,' Orlando explained. He reached over to touch Eleanor's throat in demonstration, and her skin felt hot where he touched her. 'It regulates your energy—as Dottoressa Forrest says, we need to do a blood test to check, but I agree with her that your thyroid is probably underactive. Your symptoms all add up to a clinical picture.'

'But they're all such silly things. I didn't want to waste your time,' Signora Giordano protested.

'Singly, they're little things, but together they add up,' Eleanor said gently. 'Heavy periods, constipation, tiredness, dry skin, lower libido and slight depression. I think your thyroid isn't working as it should, and the earlier we spot it the earlier we can do something to make you feel better. We can treat it with tablets—we'll have to increase the dose gradually until we get the right one, or you'll feel really ill.'

Orlando swiftly took a blood sample. 'Come back and see us next week when the results are back,' he said. 'And then we can talk about your treatment.' He smiled at her. 'And I can promise you, you'll soon start to feel a lot better.'

'*Grazie*, Dottore de Luca—Dottoressa Forrest,' Signora Giordano said.

'*Prego,*' they said in unison.

'Good call,' Orlando said when their patient had left. 'You're a natural with family medicine. Have you come across this before?'

'My best friend's mum had it. I remember her symptoms,' Eleanor said. 'And you picked up on what I was thinking.'

'We work well together,' he said. 'A good team.'

Yes. But was that going to be enough? Eleanor wondered.

* * *

On Wednesday afternoon, Orlando went with Eleanor to see Bartolomeo.

'We won't know whether the tissue is a match until at least Monday,' Orlando warned. He'd agreed with Eleanor that they'd tell Bartolomeo the later date, so he wouldn't be uptight, waiting for the results, if they were late.

'But there's a chance. Hope,' the older man said, his eyes glittering.

'Well, I'm staying here in Italy for a while, regardless of what the tests show,' Eleanor said. 'So I'm going to look for a place to rent.'

'I have a spare room—more than one. And you're my daughter. You can stay here with me,' Bartolomeo said.

She stroked his hand. 'That's a lovely offer—but I'm used to having my own space,' she said quietly. 'So thank you, but no.'

'There are hardly any places to rent around this part of Naples,' Bartolomeo said, 'and I won't have you staying in a rough part of the city.'

'I won't move to a rough part,' she promised. 'Orlando will help me find somewhere—he'll tell me which areas I should avoid.'

The older man's eyes narrowed as he looked at Orlando. 'You won't let her move somewhere bad?'

'Of course not.'

'I'd still be happier if you moved in with me, Eleanor,' Bartolomeo said, his mouth compressed.

There was a solution. One that was going to test Orlando's self-control to the limit. One that was really a very bad idea indeed, given that he wanted to take things slowly. But the words came out anyway. 'I, too, have a spare room.'

Eleanor's eyes widened. 'You're suggesting that I move in with *you*?'

'That way, you're not far from your father but you have

your independence. And if this transplant goes ahead, I'd rather you were staying with someone, not in an apartment on your own,' he said. 'I would recommend having someone to keep an eye on you for a few days.'

Bartolomeo's eyes widened. 'So there are risks with this procedure after all? Eleanor might be ill afterwards?'

'No, there aren't.' She glared at Orlando. 'He's scaremongering.'

'Actually,' Orlando said, trying to keep his tone as reasonable as possible, 'anyone who knows you, Eleanor, also knows you're likely to overdo things instead of resting the first couple of days. That's why I think someone should keep an eye on you. And who better than a fellow doctor?'

He'd told her he wanted time to think about things. Space between them. And what was he doing? Making sure she spent even more time around him. He must be crazy.

She clearly thought so, too, because she brought it up when he took her back to her hotel. 'I can't possibly move in with you.'

'Yes, you can. Look, do it for Bartolomeo's sake. He's worrying about you. And that means he's stressed. He already has enough stress lined up for when the transplant goes through.' Oh, lord. She had him at it now. Saying 'when' instead of 'if'. 'Think about it. It's the sensible option. And you, Eleanor Forrest, are a sensible woman.'

'Why does that sound like an insult?'

'Because your imagination is playing tricks on you. Look, it will stop your father worrying.'

'So I just move into your house.'

'To my spare room. You will have your own key, so you will be completely independent. Come and go as you please.'

'Won't I get in your way? Disturb you?'

She'd disturb him all right. Though not in the way she meant.

'No,' he fibbed. 'And when I am not on house calls, my car is at your disposal.'

'That's too generous. I'm perfectly capable of using public transport.'

She waved a dismissive hand—the sheer Italian-ness of the gesture amused him, but he didn't want her to get the wrong idea so he propped his elbow on the table and rested his chin on his hand, making sure to cover his face so she couldn't see him smiling.

'I have a weekly ticket,' she continued, 'so I can catch the metro, a bus, a tram, a funicular railway. No problem.'

'True. And I live reasonably near a metro station. But the offer is there. You might want to take Bartolomeo for a drive along the coast or something.'

She was silent for a while. 'If I move in—and I mean *if*— then I insist on paying you rent.'

He smiled. 'That's not necessary. I said I would support you through this.'

'Emotionally. You don't need to do it financially. I'm, um— look, my parents left me a house and money. I don't need support in that way. And I would still expect to do my share. You know, chores in the house.'

He made a dismissive gesture. 'No need. I have a cleaner.'

'Cooking, then.'

'We'll negotiate that later.' He paused. 'So. Do I have a house guest?'

'Yes. *Grazie.*'

'OK. Do you want to check out now or tomorrow morning?'

She gaped. 'That's a bit fast!'

'It's Wednesday. If we get the results back on Saturday afternoon and if they're the right ones, you'll be starting treatment on Monday. Whatever we've said to your father, we don't know how you're going to feel. So it makes sense to move now, have a couple of days to settle in, just in case you start to feel rough.'

He was pushing her. He knew it. And he also knew it was crazy. If anything, he should be thinking up reasons why she *shouldn't* move in. Reasons to keep his distance.

But he yearned for her to be near.

And this was a way of doing it without having to explain how he felt or probe the emotions he normally kept at bay.

'I need time to pack my things,' she said.

'Pack them. I'll go back to the surgery for a couple of hours and do some admin work, then I'll fetch the car and pick you up.' He glanced at his watch. 'I'll see you at five. *A presto.*'

CHAPTER TWELVE

At FIVE o'clock exactly, Eleanor opened the door to Orlando's knock. 'Nearly done,' she said. 'I've finished packing. I just need to settle the bill.'

'Bene. I'll load your things into the car, then.' He smiled at her. 'Hold out your hand.'

She frowned, but did as he asked. He dropped two keys onto it. 'It's obvious which is which,' he told her. 'One is for the car and one is for the front door.'

'Thank you.' She took her keychain from her handbag and added Orlando's keys to it. It felt oddly intimate, having his keys nestle against hers. He trusted her with his keys. Would he trust her with his heart?

As soon as she'd settled the bill, she joined Orlando in the car and he drove them to his apartment. 'I live on the fifth floor,' he said, taking her baggage from the car and gesturing to the enormous ancient building in front of them. 'There is a lift.'

'This place is amazing,' she said as they travelled up. 'It's a *palazzo*, yes?'

'Yes. It dates from the fifteenth century, though it was converted into flats years ago, and my apartment was renovated not long before I bought it. One of these days I'm going to research it, find out who lived here.' He shrugged. 'I like it. It's convenient for work and convenient for the city.'

Smack in the middle of the city; she'd noticed plenty of shops and *caffès* on their way here. And yet the area wasn't that noisy: the palazzo overlooked a large pedestrianised square.

'Welcome to *mia casa*—my home,' he said softly, and opened the front door. 'I'll show you around.' He set her cases down in the hallway. 'This is the kitchen.' It was very modern, with stainless-steel appliances, maple cabinets with long tubular brushed aluminium handles, granite worktops and a dark slate floor, but it was definitely a kitchen for use rather than a kitchen for show. Pans hung from a rail, and there were fresh herbs growing in pots on the window-sill.

'Living room, dining room.' There was an arch between the two rooms; the walls were painted a bright sunny yellow, and the curtains at the large windows were white voile. Again, it was very modern—a glass-topped dining table with white leather chairs, with a state-of-the-art plasma TV and beige leather sofas in the living room. On the walls were framed prints of Whistler nocturnes.

But there was nothing personal there, she noticed. No photographs of family, no children's drawings made especially for a favourite uncle, not even any friends' wedding photographs. Nothing to give away who Orlando was.

And it was very much a single person's home—a young, single, urban professional person's home, she thought. Underlining the fact that Orlando wasn't a family man. Just like his consulting room in the medical practice, the room was incredibly neat: everything in its place. This wasn't an apartment that would echo with the laughter of children and have crayoned pictures stuck onto the fridge with magnets. There wouldn't be toys and books and socks scattered everywhere. Orlando was

good with children—she'd seen him at work—but it was clear
to her that he liked to keep them at a professional distance.

'My study.' It was painted a paler yellow, with a large desk,
a state-of-the-art computer and tightly crammed bookshelves
covering one wall. 'If you want to read anything, feel free to
help yourself. I'm afraid I don't have many books in English,
but you're welcome to use my library card—they have a reasonable foreign section.'

'Thank you.' She smiled wryly. 'It feels odd, thinking of
English as a foreign language.'

'It is, here,' he pointed out. 'Feel free to use my computer,
too—you don't need to find an internet café to research
anything or check your email.'

'*Grazie.*' And she really was grateful for that: it meant she
could have better contact with Tamsin, as well as researching
extra information about Bartolomeo's condition.

'If you need to call anyone in England—your boss, your
friends—you know the dialling codes from here.' He gestured
to the phone. 'As they say in Italy, *mia casa è sua casa.*'

Tears pricked her eyelids. 'I really appreciate this,' she said,
hoping her voice didn't sound as cracked to him as it did to her.

He continued with the tour, dismissing the next door with a
wave. 'My room and bathroom.' He led her to the door opposite.
'And your room and bathroom.'

It was gorgeous, Eleanor thought. White walls with the
faintest hint of peach, white voile curtains and a wrought-iron
bedstead with white covers. Like that in the rest of the apartment, the flooring was beech—the real thing, not laminate.
The bathroom walls were a rich turquoise, teamed with a black
and white diamond-tiled floor and a white suite.

Orlando either liked things very simple, or had found an
interior designer whose tastes he could live with.

And how.

'Wow,' she said, feeling her eyes widen in pleasure.

But he'd left the best to last. A terrace with wrought-iron balustrading overlooking the piazza, with views of Vesuvius and the Bay of Naples. 'This,' she said softly, 'is incredible.' The perfect spot to linger with a mug of coffee or a glass of freshly squeezed orange juice. There were olive trees growing in terracotta pots in the corners of the terrace, terracotta troughs with a jumble of red and white geraniums between them, and a granite-topped bistro table with two wrought-iron chairs.

'Would you like to eat out here tonight?' he asked.

She blinked. 'Eat?'

'Uh-huh. I was planning to cook for us. If that's OK with you. Why don't you unpack while I sort something out?'

'Um, shouldn't I be helping you in the kitchen?'

'No need.' He smiled at her. 'And it's not a chore. I enjoy cooking. It helps me relax.'

Which meant he'd be good at it. Orlando, she thought, was good at everything he did.

Including making love.

Which she'd promised herself she wouldn't think about.

By the time she'd finished unpacking, the aromas emanating from the kitchen were making her seriously hungry. She followed her nose.

He looked up and smiled at her. '*Bene.* You've finished.' He handed her a glass of wine. 'Go and sit on the terrace. Take a book, if you want. I'll bring the antipasti through when it's ready.'

'Thanks.' She walked into his office. As he'd said, he had few English books. Though the bookshelves were clearly in some sort of order—medical textbooks, novels, poetry. Including *Orlando Furioso*.

Oh, lord. Her grip tightened on the stem of the wineglass as she remembered that night. *Orlando Innamorato.*

Except he wasn't, was he? He'd offered her a place to stay. As a friend, not as his lover.

In the end, she went onto the terrace and just sat gazing out at the view. She was so lost in thought that she didn't hear Orlando join her, and jumped when he spoke to her.

'What are you thinking of, Eleanor?'

She shook her head. 'Nothing important.'

'Worrying about your father? We are doing what we can. What will be will be.'

'Just don't break into the Doris Day version,' she said wryly.

He laughed and hummed, '*Que sera, sera*'. 'Have some food, Eleanor. Everything always seems better when you're not hungry.'

She felt her eyes widen as he placed the food in front of her. 'This looks gorgeous—and complicated.'

He spread his hands. 'It takes *ages*. Possibly—oh-h-h—ninety seconds' preparation.'

'You're kidding.'

'The hardest part is cutting the prosciutto into strips. Wrap it around the asparagus, add a thin slice of *dolcelatte*, put it in the oven for ten minutes, and that's it.' He shrugged. 'The simplest things are often the best.'

'It's gorgeous,' she said after the first mouthful.

He'd made an equally simple second course: grilled chicken and salad. Followed by a bowl of fresh strawberries and a pot of melted white chocolate for dipping. And then the ubiquitous espresso.

'Don't tell me. It's half-cold,' she said before he'd even poured it out.

'No. I know you prefer your coffee the English way.'

'Whereas Italians like the buzz of caffeine.'

He laughed. 'That's why you never see an Italian sitting in a *caffè*. Waste of time.' He spread his hands. 'Pay for your coffee, get your receipt, have it made for you, and down it on your way out. It's the way here in Napoli.'

'I noticed. And if you order a *lattè* or a *macchiato* after breakfast-time, they look at you as if you have two heads. It's easier to go to a tourist coffee-shop.'

'And pay four times as much for the privilege.'

Easy banter. But there was nothing easy between them; Eleanor knew that they were both aware of the undercurrent. Both avoiding the real issues.

And that night she lay awake in the wide double bed, knowing that he was sleeping just the other side of the wall. How easy it would be to walk into his room, climb into his bed and just ask him to hold her.

And how bad an idea that would be, too. He needed time— time to get used to the idea that maybe they had a future. That he wouldn't be like his mother, searching fruitlessly for The One and leaving a trail of broken hearts behind him. That she wouldn't be like his mother either and walk out on him when he failed to live up to whatever impossible ideal she had in her head. He'd let her this far into his life. She just needed to be patient.

Eleanor was surprised at how easily she'd settled in to life at Orlando's apartment. And on Friday afternoon, when Bartolomeo was too tired for company, she did a little shopping in the tiny delicatessens and speciality shops nearby, tried her hand bartering in the market, and finally pottered around the apartment before giving in to the impulse to call Tamsin.

'Right. Now you're talking to me, you can spill the beans.

All of them,' Tamsin demanded. 'You are on your own right now, aren't you?'

'Yes. There's nothing to it. Orlando's just being a good friend.'

Tamsin groaned. 'I told you to have a fling with a gorgeous man, not go and live with him!'

'I'm not living with him. I'm staying in his guest room,' Eleanor corrected her.

'You're eating together and you're spending time in the evenings together—that counts as living together in my book. And you've already admitted he's drop-dead gorgeous.'

'We're just *friends*.'

'Yeah, right,' Tamsin said dryly. 'Just make sure you wait until I've had this baby before you announce you're staying in Italy with him. And I'm telling you now, if I'm not chief brides-maid and wedding planner, you're in major trouble.'

'Number one, you're married and pregnant, so you'd be matron of honour,' Eleanor said.

'Stop splitting hairs.'

'And, number two, we're not getting married.'

'Living in sin, then. But you don't move over there perma-nently until I've had a chance to inspect him and made sure he's good enough for you,' Tamsin said darkly.

'Tam, it's not like that.'

'Hmm. We'll see.'

'So you really don't have to worry. Everything's fine,' Eleanor said, hoping that she sounded rather more convinc-ing than she felt. She distracted Tamsin with talk about babies, but when she finally replaced the receiver her edginess returned.

Tomorrow was results day.

Please, please, let them be the right ones.

And if she didn't keep herself busy, she'd go crazy. She took the recipe she'd downloaded from the Internet and headed for Orlando's kitchen.

Orlando could smell the aroma of tomatoes and fresh herbs all the way down the corridor. He'd planned to take Eleanor out to dinner that night, to distract her from the fact that the results were due tomorrow, but clearly she'd been feeling antsy and taken matters into her own hands.

He closed the front door behind him, then walked quietly to the kitchen. He leaned against the doorjamb for a moment, just watching Eleanor as she chopped and stirred and tasted. Lord, she was beautiful. The way she moved... It was all he could do to stop himself striding over to her, yanking her into his arms and kissing her senseless. He just about managed to keep himself in check, then he said softly, '*Buona sera*, Eleanor. Something smells good.'

She looked over at him and smiled. 'Hi. I hope you don't mind me taking over your kitchen.'

'No.'

'I thought you might...' She bit her lip. 'Well, you don't like sharing your space.'

'I admit, it's strange,' he said. 'Coming home after surgery to a flat that isn't completely silent and empty—knowing the door's unlocked and you'll be curled up on the sofa with a book or listening to music. Domesticated.'

She looked faintly worried. 'And you hate that.'

The words slipped out before he could stop them. 'It's different with you.'

'How do you mean?'

'I... Nothing.' He made a dismissive gesture. 'Just ignore me.'

'Bit difficult when you're standing three feet away from me,' she pointed out. 'So how's it different with me?'

She wasn't going to let him get away with this one, was she? He sucked in a breath. 'OK. I admit, I like you being around.'

'And?'

Could she read his mind, or was it that obvious? 'And it scares me stupid at the same time,' he admitted. 'Because when this is all over, it's going to be messy. We're both going to get hurt.'

'You're assuming it will be over.'

She was calling him on this? He lifted his chin. 'My experience of families tells me that, yes, it'll end.'

'Not necessarily. My experience of families is different: it tells me that things *can* work out. My parents were together for well over twenty years. And if they'd both lived they'd still be together now.'

'That,' Orlando said, leaning back against the wall, 'is what scares me. How can I live up to that? How can I give you what they gave each other when I don't know how it's done—when I haven't had an example to show me the way?'

She took the pan off the heat and walked over to him. Took his hand and raised it to her lips. Brushed her mouth, oh, so lightly over his palm. It made his whole body feel as if it had turned to flame. She curled his fingers over the place where she'd kissed him. 'Why don't you try trusting yourself? See where this takes us?'

Because he'd already seen what happened when people did that. Seen the tears and the wreck of the relationship. Too many times. 'I don't want to see you hurt when I let you down.' Just as his mother's husbands had never lived up to her expectations.

She frowned. 'You're here now, when I need you. What's going to change?'

'I can't answer that. I just know that one day we'll both wake up and everything will seem different. And I don't want to hurt you, Eleanor. The longer this goes on, the more it's going to hurt—me, as well as you.'

'This is all your decision. Don't I get a say in it?'

'No.'

'Why not?' she asked, her voice very soft.

'Because right now you've got a lot on your mind. You're vulnerable and you're not thinking straight.'

'And you are?'

Probably not. He found it very difficult to think straight when she was around. But he wasn't going to admit *that*.

At his silence, she dropped his hand and took one step backwards. 'So do you want me to leave?'

'Of course not. I'm not going to throw you out at a time like this. You're waiting for the test results. If all goes well, you'll probably be on treatment next week. And...' He raked a hand through his hair. 'I said I'd support you through this. I'm not the kind of man who goes back on my word.' He dragged in a breath. 'And that's why I can't promise you a relationship and say that it will last for ever and ever. I can't make a promise that I don't know if I can keep. Eleanor, I can offer you my friendship and my support. And that's all.'

'I'd better get on with dinner, then.' She walked over to the hob again and continued with the sauce she'd been making when he'd come home.

He was about to protest that he didn't want to hurt her—but he knew he already had. Her British stiff upper lip was firmly in place. Brisk, no-nonsense. 'Eleanor. I'm sorry. I wish I could be different. I like you—I like you a lot—and I admit there's a physical attraction between us. But until I can promise you undying love, it's not fair to either of us to act on that. Let's get through the transplant. And then we'll have time to concentrate on us.'

'Sure.'

She didn't sound sure at all. She sounded utterly miserable—rejected, unwanted, unloved.

Lonely.

Ah, hell.

He couldn't leave it like this. He joined her at the stove, took the pan off the heat again and pulled her into his arms. Held her close, rested his cheek against her hair, breathed in her sweet scent. 'I'm trying to get my head around this. I swear, I'm trying.' And, lord, he was trying to be the man she needed him to be. He so wanted to be that man.

But could he?

Would he be enough for her?

'I just need more time, *tesoro*.' He let himself hold her for a few seconds longer. 'I just,' he whispered, 'need time.'

With a huge effort he let her go again. She was rigid, as if trying to hold her own emotions in check.

Domestic. Routine. That was what he needed right now. Something everyday that he could focus on, help him put his emotions back behind the fence where he normally kept them. 'How long is dinner going to be?'

'Soon.' She was clearly in the same state as he was, the way she was stirring that sauce when both of them could see it didn't need stirring.

'Shall I open some wine?'

'I'll do it. I meant to surprise you. Make dinner the same way you did for me.' She went to the fridge, took out a bottle of wine and poured him a glass. 'Go and sit on the terrace.'

His fingers touched hers as she handed him the glass and it felt like an electric shock. He knew he was being a coward, but he was glad to escape to the terrace and stare out at Vesuvius. Hell, the way she made him feel, his emotions were like the volcano in mid-eruption. Turbulent. Hot. Overwhelming.

Why couldn't he let himself believe? In her—in himself—in love?

The breathing space did them both good, because when she reappeared on the terrace, carrying a platter, he was able to smile calmly at her, and she no longer looked near to tears.

'I cheated with the antipasti,' she said. 'There was this gorgeous little deli round the corner.'

She'd brought out a plate with an arrangement of his favourites. Black olives, chargrilled artichokes, sun-dried tomatoes and grilled sweet peppers. She'd included tiny cornets of cured ham, anchovies and slices of *scamorza*.

'It's perfect,' he said.

The main course was even better. 'An authentic Napoletana sauce, too,' he noted. 'I'm impressed.'

'It's not hard to follow a recipe.'

'Even so.' He raised his glass to her. 'It's lovely. *Grazie*.'

Although his head was telling him he really needed to get some distance between them—that he should make some excuse to skulk in his office for the rest of the evening—his heart reminded him that she needed the company. Needed the distraction. Tomorrow could make or break her.

There was one thing that would distract both of them…

But no. The timing was wrong. He wasn't that much of a louse, to put his needs first. So he sat with her. Talked to her. Taught her a few Italian phrases, introduced her to some of his favourite music. Just about managed to stop himself kissing her goodnight.

Though he slept badly. And from the shadows under her eyes at breakfast the next morning, so had she.

As the minutes dragged by, the tension in her body racked up until he could almost see waves of it flowing out from her.

'Come on. We'll go to the hospital. The long way round,' he

said, 'because waiting there for the results will be even worse. We'll play tourist on the way, have an early lunch out.'

'Mmm-hmm.'

She was too tense even to be polite, he noticed. Well, he wouldn't take it personally. What she really needed, he thought, was a hug. But he didn't trust himself to stop at a friendly hug. A walk and negotiating the public transport system would help him get his impulses back under control again.

Although he pointed out particularly interesting architecture and told her little snippets about the bits of Naples they passed through, she didn't seem to take anything in. She barely touched lunch. And by the time they reached the hospital, the strain was really showing on her face: she'd lost all colour on her face and her expression was pinched. Haunted.

Right now she needed him. He slid his arm round her shoulders as they made their way to the consultant's office. Maybe she'd find comfort in the warmth of his body; maybe she'd find strength in his strength.

'Dottoressa Forrest? Gilberto Marino. A pleasure to meet you.' The consultant extended his hand to her.

'Dottore Marino. A pleasure to meet you, too.' She shook his hand and smiled politely, but Orlando could feel a tiny tremor of fear running through her.

This was it.

And if the answer was no...

Please, don't let it be no. Don't let her hopes be smashed.

'Now, our friend Orlando here has given you a thorough medical. Everything's clear, and I expect you already know you've not been exposed to HIV, hepatitis or syphilis,' Gilberto told her.

'Of course I do.' She dragged in a breath. 'Dottore Marino,

I'm going crazy here. I really need to know.' There was a note of desperation in her voice. 'Can we go ahead with the transplant? Please?'

Time slowed down to the point where every second seemed to take an hour.

And then Gilberto smiled. 'It's a good match. Yes.'

Eleanor clapped a hand to her mouth. 'Oh, thank God,' she said brokenly. 'Thank God.'

She wasn't sure if she was crying or shaking or laughing hysterically or if Vesuvius had just decided to erupt again: the world had gone mad. For a moment she felt herself teetering on the edge of an abyss. And then Orlando's arms were wrapped tightly round her again and her face was buried in his shoulder.

'It's going to be all right, Eleanor,' he soothed, stroking her hair. 'Everything's going to be fine.'

She could feel his heart beating, strong and sure and steady, and gradually the trembling stopped. When Orlando guided her to a chair and sat next to her, she could see a wet patch on his shirt.

Just as well she hadn't been wearing make-up today.

Oh, lord. Last time she'd cried all over him, they'd...

She dragged in a breath. That wasn't going to happen again. Though Orlando kept one of her hands sandwiched between his, his thumb rubbing reassuringly against the back of her hand. Telling her without words that he was there for her.

Gilberto explained what was going to happen next. Eleanor couldn't follow much of what the consultant was saying, so Orlando translated for her. Though nothing seemed to stay in her head—the only thing she could think about was that the transplant would go ahead.

Bartolomeo had a much, much better chance of staying around.

And she would still have a family to belong to.

CHAPTER THIRTEEN

'DON'T you have surgery this morning?' Eleanor asked Orlando on Monday.

'Alessandro and Giacomo are splitting my list between them until I get there. I'm buying them *gelati* every day this week as a payback,' Orlando explained.

'Why aren't you doing your list yourself?'

He rolled his eyes. 'Why do you think, *tesoro*? I'm going with you to the hospital.'

'There's no need. I'll be fine.' She waved a dismissive hand. 'It's only an injection.'

'It's the first injection of granuloctye-colony stimulating factor,' Orlando said, folding his arms. 'You don't know how you're going to react to the G-CSF, so I'm taking you myself to make sure you're all right. Plus this is a huge thing you're doing. Even though you know what's going on, it's a lot to take in and you'd be struggling with it in your own language, let alone Italian. You need someone with you who can speak medical jargon *and* Italian. Which is what we agreed last week, yes?'

'Yes.'

'And that person is me.'

'Yes.' Though she was still feeling a little edgy with him. He'd held her close, comforted her, on several occasions over the weekend, and it was driving her crazy, being so close to him and yet *not* close to him at the same time, because he'd behaved with impeccable propriety rather than carrying her to his bed and making her forget the rest of the world. 'But you have your patients.'

'As I said, it's not a problem. Though if we could rearrange the rest of the injections this week for the gap between surgery and house calls, that would make my life a little easier,' he admitted.

'I can go to the hospital by myself.'

'You're perfectly capable of doing so, I agree,' Orlando said, 'but you're still not doing it. I said I'd support you, and I will.'

The first injection went without a hitch, though when the specialist started talking to her and asking her questions, Eleanor had to admit she was glad Orlando had insisted on coming with her, because for some reason her brain had turned to mush and she could barely string two words together in Italian. Orlando also managed to arrange her appointments to fit in with surgery hours.

By the middle of the week she was bone-achingly tired. Literally. She'd known in advance that she might feel some degree of bone pain because of the way the G-CSF worked on her body, but she'd bought some paracetamol from the local pharmacy to deal with it. Except it wasn't quite strong enough to deal with the pain.

'You look terrible,' Orlando said when he walked into Serafina's room after the Wednesday morning list, where Eleanor had elected to work in the baby clinic. 'Serafina, why didn't you tell me that Eleanor was feeling so ill?'

Serafina waved a dismissive hand at him. 'Because you would have made her go home and she would've sat brooding all day and getting miserable on her own. Which isn't a good thing.'

'And sitting here in pain is?' he asked scathingly.

'Everything's fine—isn't it, Ellie?' Serafina asked.

'Yup.'

But Eleanor's tone was too short to fool Orlando. 'You feel as bad as you look, don't you?' he asked gently. 'As if you need to sleep for a month. And you ache like hell.'

Yes. But if she admitted that, she knew he'd make her go back to his apartment. Right now she didn't want to be on her own. And she wasn't going to tell Orlando about the tingling either. She'd been given an anticoagulant to stop her blood clotting during the treatment, and she knew the tingling would stop shortly after she'd stopped having the G-CSF.

She lifted her chin. 'I'm not putting any of the patients at risk, if that's what you're worrying about. If I think my diagnosis or treatment skills aren't up to the job, I'll ask for help. I'm not that stupid.'

'Nobody's saying you are. But there's a limit to bravery. You're stopping for lunch right now,' Orlando said. 'And we'll see how you are tomorrow morning. If you're feeling any rougher than this, you're staying put. In bed.'

In bed. She wished he hadn't used that phrase. Because the idea of drifting off to sleep with him wrapped round her was more than appealing right now. And it made her want to cry. 'I won't be feeling rough,' she lied.

'If she's feeling under the weather, she can just sit in with me,' Serafina chipped in. 'Or with Chiara. I don't want Ellie to be on her own. She can't spend the mornings with Bartolomeo or he'll start worrying about her, and he needs to be as stress-free as possible for next week. She's better off here with us.'

'Hmm,' Orlando said, sounding completely unconvinced, and shepherded Eleanor out of the room.

* * *

The following morning, she was still feeling lousy, but not admitting to it. Orlando said nothing over breakfast, but he clearly guessed exactly how she was feeling. When they reached the surgery, he said, 'You're in with me today. Where I can keep an eye on you. And if I tell you to go into the staffroom and lie down for half an hour, you do it. Understood?'

She scowled. 'Stop bossing me about.'

'Those are the terms. Take them or go home. Your choice.'

She didn't have the energy to argue any more. 'OK. I'll stay here.'

She allowed Orlando to take the lead in all the cases that morning, until Paolo Barese walked in, complaining of chest pain. This was something she was used to dealing with.

'My call,' she said to Orlando. 'Signor Barese—'

'Paolo,' the middle-aged man insisted.

She smiled at him. 'Paolo. Tell me about the pain.'

'It's like someone pushing on my chest. It goes on for a few minutes, but it goes away if I sit down. I thought it was indigestion, but...' he grimaced '...the tablets don't make it go away.'

She had a fair idea what this was, but she needed to be sure. 'Do you get the pain often?' she asked.

'I've been getting it a couple of times a day. In the afternoons, mostly.'

'What are you doing when it happens?' she asked.

'Lifting furniture. I'm a carpenter,' he explained.

'Do you smoke at all?'

He looked rueful. 'Used to. My wife made me gave it up.'

Orlando already had the notes up on the computer and tilted the screen so she could see it. As she'd half suspected, she saw that Paolo's last blood-pressure measurement had been on the high side.

'Has anyone in your family ever had heart disease?' she asked gently.

'My father died of a heart attack in his fifties.' Paolo went white. 'Oh, *dio*. Am I going to die?'

'You're not having a heart attack,' she reassured him. 'I think you're suffering from something called angina. It happens when little lumps of fat called plaques build up on the lining inside the arteries leading to your heart. That makes the arteries narrow and not enough blood gets through to your heart—in turn, that means your heart doesn't get enough oxygen. That's what causes the pain—a bit like if you get a cramp in your leg, yes?'

He nodded.

'You might find you get the pain when you do something active, like moving furniture around or going up stairs,' she said.

'It can also happen if you're feeling stressed or angry, or if you've eaten a big meal,' Orlando added.

'Or even if you go out on a very cold day,' Eleanor finished. 'It's good that you've stopped smoking because that will help. I need to listen to your heart, if I may?'

Orlando was already holding out the stethoscope. She listened to Paolo's heart, the arteries in his neck and his lungs. 'No murmurs, no cardiac bruit and chest clear,' she told Orlando, who typed rapidly into the computer. 'It's all looking good so far, Paolo.'

His blood pressure wasn't so good—even if she made allowances for the fact that he was clearly worried, plus the 'white coat hypertension' patients tended to experience when an unfamiliar doctor took their blood pressure. 'We're going to need to start you on medication to keep this under control,' she said. His pulse was a little fast for her liking, too. 'Would you stand on the scales for me, please?'

Paolo patted his rotund stomach. 'You don't need to weigh me. I already know I need to lose a few pounds.'

'For your heart's sake, yes.'

'Am I going to have a heart attack?'

She wasn't going to lie to him. 'Hopefully not, but this is a warning that you need to look after yourself. You can carry on life as normal for the time being, but I'm going to send you to hospital for some tests.' She looked at Orlando. 'Which I'm sure Dottore de Luca can arrange for you.'

'I'll write the letters today,' Orlando said.

'I'm going to send you for an ECG—that's an electrocardiogram and it shows the activity of your heart on a graph,' she told Paolo. 'You'll also need a stress test—that's where you walk on a treadmill for ten minutes or as long as you can and you'll have some wires attached so the doctors can measure what your heart is doing, And you'll need an angiograph—that's where they give you a special kind of X-ray using dye to see your arteries, so they can see where there are any blockages.' She looked at Orlando. 'Start with diuretics for the blood pressure, yes?'

He nodded. 'And GTN.'

She turned to Paolo again. 'We're going to give you some tablets that you'll need to take every morning—water tablets, which will help reduce the pressure of your blood in your veins. And we're going to give you a spray called glyceryl trinitrate—GTN for short—that you can put under your tongue when you have any pain. It'll taste disgusting, but it will ease the pain.'

'But if it doesn't work or you need to use it more and more, you need to come back and see us,' Orlando warned. He printed off the prescriptions and signed them. 'The pharmacist should fill this for you while you wait. You'll get a letter from the hospital about the tests, and I'd like to see you again in a month to see how you're getting on. Chiara will make the appointment. If you need to come back before then, that's fine.'

'Thank you, *dottore, dottoressa*.' Paolo took the prescriptions, smiled at them both and left the room.

'I imagine you have a lot of chest pain cases in the emergency department,' Orlando said.

'And quite a few of them turn out to be angina rather than a full-blown MI. So yes, I'm used to spotting the signs,' she admitted.

'You handled that well—you did a fair bit of that in Italian, on your own,' he said.

'Because you've been coaching me.'

'We make a good team,' he said.

'That's not the first time you've said that.' She smiled wryly. 'It's just a pity that you're so obstinate.'

He frowned. 'How do you mean?'

'Think about it. If we can work as a team here, we can work as a team *outside* here.'

Orlando folded his arms, looking grim. 'We're in the middle of surgery. We have patients waiting. Now is *not* the time to discuss this, Eleanor.'

Yet again he was backing off. And she was sick of waiting. 'So when will you be ready to discuss it?'

'We've already agreed that. After the transplant.'

Give me strength, she thought. 'In the meantime, there's something you might like to think about.'

He frowned. 'What's that?'

'You,' she said quietly, 'are your own person. Your mother's given you half her genes, but even if you happen to look like her— and I have no idea, since you have nothing personal whatsoever in your flat—you're not her carbon copy. The way she reacts to things isn't necessarily the same way you react to things.'

Orlando rubbed his jaw. 'There's nothing wrong with my apartment. It's perfectly comfortable. It's well furnished.'

'But it could belong to anyone. It looks like something an interior designer dreamed up.'

He spread his hands. 'And that's wrong *how*, precisely?'

Did he really not know?

And then she realised how neatly he'd sidestepped the issue she'd brought up. Distracted her into talking about his flat instead of the real problem—his conviction that he was like his mother. 'You're impossible.'

'Yeah, yeah. Let's see our next patient.' And before she could protest, he pressed the button to call in the next patient on the list.

Finally, on the following Tuesday, the stem cells were harvested. Four hours of being hooked up to a machine with a cannula in each arm, watching the blood flow out of one arm and into the separator before flowing back into her other arm. Orlando insisted on staying with Eleanor throughout the procedure. Holding her hand, the pressure firm enough to let her know she had his support but light enough not to hurt her.

This was more than just friendship. It had to be. He wouldn't be here for her like this if he didn't care. If he didn't feel the same way she did. If he didn't love her.

Would he?

That evening, Eleanor had to admit to an appalling headache.

'I guessed this would happen.' Orlando led her through to the dining room. 'It's one of the most likely side effects. Sit down and close your eyes.'

She frowned. 'Why?'

'Because it's easier to do this if you're sitting on a straight-backed chair.' He stood behind her, and she felt his fingers slide into her hair.

'Scalp massage?' she asked as his fingertips began to make tiny circles against her skin.

'Works well for headaches, because it increases the blood flow to your scalp. As does brushing your hair. Standard self-help advice for migraines, actually,' he said sagely. 'I should have thought to get some lavender scented oil. Massaged into your temples, it can help with headaches.'

'Hang on. You're a family doctor. And you're advocating alternative remedies?'

'Some of them are excellent. Aromatherapy's been used as a supportive treatment for cancer patients—the trial reports I've seen are positive—and I often refer patients to acupuncture for relief of chronic pain.' He laughed. 'Of course, some alternative treatments are quackery—pure superstition with no clinical evidence to back up the claims. But a patient's belief can do a lot of things. Look at all the studies on placebos.'

'True.' And this was making her feel good—the warmth of his hands, the firm yet gentle pressure against her skin.

She wanted more. Much more. She wanted to feel his hands stroking her bare skin. Teasing her, raising her desire to such a pitch that she forgot everything except his touch.

The only way it would happen would be if she begged him. Even then he might say no. Might still want to keep his distance.

And her pride wouldn't let her risk that. Because how could she carry on staying here if he turned her down?

'Better?' he asked a couple of minutes later.

'Better,' she admitted.

'I'd prescribe paracetamol and an early night.' He fetched her the paracetamol and a glass of water and made sure she took them. Then, for a brief second, he touched the backs of his fingers to her cheek. 'Sleep well, *tesoro*,' he said softly.

She'd sleep a lot better if it was in his arms.

But she didn't want to risk him turning her down. 'Good night,' she said.

Orlando took the next day off so he could wait with Eleanor while Bartolomeo had the transplant. The plan was, he'd be there with her if she needed him and fade into the background if she didn't. And although the transplant went well and the earliest signs were positive, Eleanor's mood was bleak.

Over the next two weeks, while Bartolomeo was in hospital, her mood grew darker, though she kept up a bright, cheerful aspect when she visited her father in the afternoons. Visiting was restricted for the first couple of weeks, when Bartolomeo's immune system was at its lowest, because of the risk of picking up an infection, so Orlando waited for her outside the room in the evenings. But he noticed on the way home that she stopped smiling and barely spoke.

And one day he came home from work to find her crying, huddled on the sofa.

'Eleanor? What's wrong?' His heart felt as if it had stopped for a moment. No. Bartolomeo couldn't have gone downhill that fast. And she would've called him from the hospital, surely, told him what was happening?

Ice trickled down his spine when she didn't answer; she was clearly struggling to keep the tears back. 'Do you want me to call anyone?'

He could've kicked himself for asking such a stupid question. Of course not. She didn't have anyone any more—only Bartolomeo. Except... 'What about your friend, Tamsin? Do you want me to call her?'

'No. Ignore me.' She dragged in a breath. 'I'll be OK.'

He couldn't bear it, seeing her so upset. No way could he

keep his distance from her—not when she needed him. He sat on the sofa next to her, then scooped her onto his lap and held her close. 'Tell me,' he said softly, cradling her. 'I'm here.'

'Seeing him in hospital…it reminds me of visiting my mum.' Her voice was so quiet he could barely hear the words, though he could feel her shuddering breaths, the way she was clearly trying not to break down completely. 'The chemo and the radiotherapy, and he's so sick—just like she was. I'm so scared, Orlando. I'm so scared he's going to die before I get the chance to know him properly. I'm so scared we're not going to get our time together.'

'Hey, he's doing well.'

'But what if he develops graft versus host disease?' She buried her face in his shoulder. 'As part of the transplant, he's got cells from my immune system. They'll see his cells as invaders and attack them.'

'Not necessarily. He doesn't have a rash, does he? Or jaundice? So your cells haven't attacked the tissues of his skin or his liver.'

'What about his gut? The nausea and the vomiting—'

'Are probably down to the chemo,' Orlando reminded her. 'It's not a sign that your cells are attacking his gut.'

'You know as well as I do there's a higher risk of GVHD because of his age and because it's not a completely perfect match.'

'It's still a better match than an unrelated donor. And if he does develop GVHD, there are lots of things doctors can do nowadays. We can treat him with steroids, or an anti-thymocyte globulin, which will reduce the number of T-cells involved.' He stroked her face. 'And think of the other risks that increase the chances of developing GVHD—risks we can rule out immediately. One of the biggest is if the donor's had a transfusion, which you haven't. Or if the donor's been pregnant…'

His voice trailed off. Eleanor hadn't told him that much about Jeremy, and she certainly hadn't mentioned pregnancy. Had she carried another man's child?

The surge of jealousy was so powerful it shocked him.

'I've never been pregnant.'

And why that should make him so pleased…? He pushed his emotions aside. Now wasn't the time. 'So there you go. They're the two biggest risks and we can rule them out. It's going to be fine, Eleanor.'

'He had a sore mouth today.'

'Which happens with anyone who's had a transplant. And they find it painful to swallow at first.' He stroked her hair. 'And you know this perfectly well, but your brain's temporarily forgotten it because Bartolomeo is your father.'

'And I'm too close to the case.' She swallowed hard. 'He has mouthwashes. And tablets to stop the candida infection.'

'Exactly.'

'What about cytomegalovirus? Supposing he picked up CMV in hospital, and it turns to interstitial—'

'Pneumonitis?' Orlando finished wryly. '*Mia bella*, you're going to drive yourself crazy if you start thinking of every single complication, and every possible complication that leads off from that.'

'He's my father!' She lifted her chin and glared at him. 'I can't help worrying.'

'I know. But you know too much. And, as with any medic, you're focusing on the worst possible scenarios. Rare complications. This isn't good for your peace of mind.' He brushed his mouth against hers, intending it to be for comfort. But the first touch of her lips against his sent him up in flames, made him kiss her again. And again.

It was entirely mutual, because she was matching him kiss for kiss, touch for touch. And all his good intentions of waiting until Bartolomeo had recovered before sorting out what was happening between them went straight out of his head.

It was only when Eleanor had finished undoing his shirt and slid it from his shoulders and he was lying on the sofa with her on top of him that the tiniest, tiniest bit of common sense leaked back into his brain.

Just enough to make him stop.

He broke the kiss and gently manoeuvred them both into a sitting position. 'Eleanor.' He stroked her face, desperately wanting to kiss her again but knowing it was a bad idea. 'We can't do this.'

She dragged in a breath. 'Orlando…'

'We could give each other comfort, I admit. But we'll both regret it tomorrow.'

'You mean, *you'd* regret it.'

'I…' He exhaled sharply. 'Don't put words into my mouth. It's not the action I'd regret. It's the timing.'

'The time's never going to be right for you, is it?' She shook her head in exasperation. 'You're as bad as Jeremy.'

'No, I'm not.' The comment stung enough for him to say, 'I'm not sleeping with anyone else behind your back.'

She went white and stood up. 'That's low.'

He could see how much he'd hurt her and guilt flooded through him. He stood up, reached a hand towards her. 'I'm sorry. I didn't mean that. It wasn't my intention to open old wounds.'

She didn't take his hand. 'Your problem is, you don't know what you want.'

'I do. But I need time to get my head straight.'

'Time. It's always time with you. How much time do you want, Orlando?' She held up one hand, shaking her head. 'Don't answer that. Excuse me. I'm going to have an early night. Alone.'

And as she walked out of the room, the sun seemed to dim. He wanted her. How he wanted her. But supposing it all went wrong? Supposing he was like his mother, building up something in his head and finding that the real thing just didn't match up to it, and he ended up hurting Eleanor? It would be better to stop now than let her down.

Though there was this weird sensation in his chest. As if his heart—despite the fact he knew it was anatomically impossible—was splintering.

CHAPTER FOURTEEN

SOMEHOW, Eleanor got through the next week. And at last, when Bartolomeo was out of hospital and the preliminary tests showed that the new bone marrow was working—that he was starting to produce healthy blood cells—she knew everything was going to be all right. There was still a way to go, but the chances were loaded in Bartolomeo's favour.

Orlando was still being supportive, while keeping an emotional distance between them. And she'd begun to realise that, however much time she gave him, he was always going to need more. He couldn't learn to trust in love. Couldn't give them that chance.

Which left her two choices—stay in Italy and break her heart, or go back to England and break her heart.

So close to the choice her mother had made thirty years before. To leave the man she loved—for both their sakes.

And although Eleanor was growing to love Bartolomeo, she didn't belong here. It was time to go home.

A few minutes later it was all done. Ian was expecting her back on early shift tomorrow. Her flight was booked back to London. An afternoon flight. Orlando would be on house calls in the early afternoon and then go straight back to the practice for late afternoon surgery, she knew. And because she'd chosen to spend the last couple of days with her father rather than at the practice, he wouldn't call at the apartment to check that she was all right.

Then it was the hard part. Saying goodbye to Bartolomeo. 'I have to go back to London. Back to work,' she said softly. 'I'm sorry I can't stay longer.'

'Eleanor. My new-found daughter. The one who gave me my life back—who gave me my hope back.' He held her close. 'I shall miss you so much.'

'I'll miss you, too. But I'll call you every day,' she promised. 'And I'll visit often. And when you're feeling up to it, you can come and stay with me. I can show you where I grew up.'

'And, if you would not mind, I can put flowers on your mother's grave. Flowers I wish I'd been able to give her while you were growing up.' He stroked her hair. 'Ring me when you get home. So I know you're safe.'

'I will.'

He brushed away the tears spilling down her cheek. 'Don't cry. This is *a presto*, not goodbye.'

To him, yes.

To Orlando... No. She couldn't think about that. Or she'd crumble completely.

'*Arrivederci.* And you do what the doctor tells you, OK?'

She went back to the flat. And then all she had to do was pick up her luggage, leave the letter propped up where Orlando would see it and get a taxi to the airport. She'd already made arrangements with the local chocolatier to deliver a large box of chocolates to the surgery, with a card she'd written to Serafina, Chiara, Alessandro and Giacomo to thank them for their hospitality.

At least Orlando's front door was on the type of latch you could lock without having to use the key. She'd left the keys in the envelope with the letter.

'I wish,' she said softly, 'that it could've been different. That you'd get into your stubborn skull that love really does exist—that we could've been happy together. But it's time I faced facts. It's not going to happen. I've given you time. Nothing's changed. So there's no point in waiting and hoping.'

She closed the door behind her, checked that it was locked firmly and headed for the airport.

Unease prickled down Orlando's spine as he unlocked the front door. He'd expected Eleanor to be back from her father's; he knew that Bartolomeo usually had a nap at this time of day. Yet the flat was silent.

Something didn't seem quite right. He couldn't put his finger on it: just that something was different. Something felt *missing*.

He found out what when he walked into the kitchen to make himself a cup of coffee and saw the envelope propped against the kettle. His name was written on the outside in Eleanor's handwriting.

A note?

Why on earth would she have left him a note?

He ripped open the envelope and scanned it swiftly. She'd written in English. Formally.

Dear Orlando,
    Thank you for all your help during my stay in Italy. My father's well on the way to recovery now, so I am re-turning home to England.
    I'm sorry I didn't say goodbye personally, but I think it's easier this way. For both of us.
    I wish you a long and happy life.
    Eleanor

He stared at the note in disbelief, reading it and trying to make the words sink in.

She'd left Italy?

She couldn't have gone. She just *couldn't*. He flung the door to her room open.

She'd stripped the bedclothes—knowing Eleanor, she'd probably put them in the washing machine—and all the surfaces were clean and bare.

The drawers were empty.

The wardrobe was empty.

All her things had gone from the bathroom.

Holding onto the end of the bed, Orlando sat down heavily. She'd gone. And without her the apartment felt empty. Hollow. As if the centre had gone, leaving just a husk.

Without her…

And then it hit him. He couldn't be without her. Didn't want to be without her.

The One existed all right.

And he'd been stupid enough to drive her away. He might just as well have booked her flight himself.

'You stupid, stupid…' He cursed himself for being all kinds of fool, even as he picked up the phone and dialled the airport.

Please, God, don't let him be too late.

When he put the phone down again, his teeth were gritted so hard that they hurt. Eleanor's flight had left three hours ago. She'd be back in England by now. It would take her an hour, maybe two, to get home from the airport.

Except he had no idea where 'home' for Eleanor was. London was a huge place. And even if he called every single E. Forrest in the telephone directory, it wouldn't guarantee that he'd find her. She might be ex-directory. Or Eleanor might even be her middle name—so she wouldn't be listed under E. Forrest in the first place.

Stupidly, the one time he'd called her mobile phone, he hadn't stored the number. Chiara was on an efficiency drive, so a scribbled note from weeks ago would no longer exist. He had no way of contacting her.

There was only one person who could help him.

And this was something that definitely couldn't be done on the phone.

There was still enough rush-hour traffic left for it to be quicker to take public transport. And, oh, how slowly time could crawl. Orlando was almost beside himself by the time he reached the stop nearest to Bartolomeo's house.

'Orlando? I wasn't expecting to see you. Not now…' The old man's eyes glittered suspiciously. 'But I am glad. Tonight…I need company.'

Me, too, Orlando thought. Because I think we're both missing her like hell. 'I'll make us some coffee,' he said. *'Permesso?'*

'Sure.'

When Orlando returned with two mugs, Bartolomeo took one mouthful and gagged. 'What the hell did you put in this?' he asked.

Orlando spread his hands. 'Coffee.'

'About half a ton per cup,' Bartolomeo spluttered.

'Mi dispiace.' Orlando sighed. 'I'm…' He raked a hand through his hair. 'Hell. I can't think straight. Because she's gone.'

Bartolomeo frowned, as if suddenly realising something. 'Didn't you know she was going?'

'Not until I read the note she left me.' He took a sip of the coffee—probably the vilest he'd ever tasted. But it suited his mood. 'Do you have her phone number in England, please?'

Bartolomeo's frown deepened. 'Did you two have a fight?

Because if she didn't choose to give you her number, I don't feel I can go against her wishes.'

Oh, brilliant. He'd just made things a hundred times worse. 'I didn't have a fight with her.' He rubbed his hand across his eyes. 'Look, I know it's not fair to ask you because you're still recuperating from the transplant and you should be protected from anything that might worry you. But I've just made the biggest mistake of my life and you're the only one I know who can help me fix it.'

'What sort of mistake?' Bartolomeo probed.

'I let Eleanor go back to London without telling her something important.' He sucked in a breath. 'I love your daughter. And, before you ask, yes—I can assure you my intentions towards her are honourable.'

Too late. Bartolomeo was already in defensive father mode. 'How honourable?'

'Marriage. *If* she'll have me,' Orlando said bleakly. 'I want to grow old with her, to have children with her—to wake up every day knowing the world's a better place because she's in my life.'

'That's how I felt about my Costanza,' Bartolomeo said softly. 'So I know how you're feeling right now. Knowing she's gone for good. So why didn't you tell Ellie you loved her before she left?' He tipped his head on one side. 'Or *did* you tell her, and that's why she went so quickly?'

Orlando shook his head. 'It's complicated. And I'm entirely to blame—it's not her. But I don't want to waste any more time. I need to find her. Talk to her. Tell her how I feel—tell her how stupid I've been to let her go.' Orlando propped his elbows on the table and rested his chin on his linked hands. 'I'm asking for your help. But if you choose not to, that's fine, too. Because I'm flying to England tonight, and if I have to visit every single hospital within a thirty-mile radius of Greater London to find her, then I'll do it.'

'If you catch a flight to London now…' Bartolomeo glanced at his watch.

Orlando did the same and realised what the older man meant. 'After I've gone back to my flat to pick up my passport, called for a taxi to the airport, taken a three-hour flight to England and then however long it takes to get to her, I'll be there at stupid o'clock. When she really won't appreciate a visitor.'

'Especially as she's back on duty tomorrow,' Bartolomeo said. 'She works in the emergency department at the Albert Memorial Hospital in Chelsea—you'll have to look up the address.'

'Thank you.' Orlando gave in to an impulse and hugged him.

'So does this mean you're bringing her back with you to Italy?'

'I don't know.' Orlando smiled wryly. 'I hope so. But if she'd rather stay in England, then I'll move there. I don't care where I live, as long as it's with her.' And, please, God, don't let him have left it too late.

It was raining in England. Which suited her mood perfectly, Eleanor thought. She'd called Bartolomeo from the airport to let him know she'd landed safely, and sent him a text when she got home, not wanting to disturb him in case he was resting.

How lonely the house felt. How empty. And even though she busied herself unpacking and opening windows to let the stuffy air out and cleaning the place until it shone, she was still lonely. Bone-deep lonely.

Orlando would have found her note by now. Ha. And what was she expecting him to do? Call her and beg her to change her mind? Hardly. Apart from the fact that she hadn't left him her number, he'd just take it as further proof that love was a myth.

It took Eleanor a long, long time before she fell asleep that night, and her eyes felt gritty the next morning.

And she nearly cried her eyes out when she walked into the staffroom at work and there were banners everywhere saying, 'Welcome back, Ellie.' Cards. And a huge bunch of flowers from the whole ward.

'We missed you.' Sheena Redmond, the charge nurse, hugged her hard.

'Welcome back,' Ian said, ruffling her hair. 'Are you sure you're OK to work? I mean, you had a lot of travelling yesterday, and...'

She raised an eyebrow. 'And you've told everyone what I was doing in Italy?'

'No, but I got it out of him yesterday when he told us you were coming back,' Sheena said. 'You dope. You should've told us. One of us could've come out and—well—helped you recuperate.'

'It was a PBSC, so it wasn't invasive and I could've gone back to work within a day of the leukapheresis,' Eleanor said. 'I'm fine. And you know me—I'm happiest when I'm busy.'

'I'll remind you of that next time you haven't had a break for six hours and the patients are six deep in Reception,' Sheena said wryly. She hugged Eleanor again. 'It's good to have you back, Ellie.'

'Thanks.' She just about managed not to cry. At least she belonged *here*.

This was definitely one of the times when Orlando wished he was a multi-millionaire. Or knew one who had a private jet anyway. Even though this was the red-eye flight, the earliest one in the day from Naples to London, it wasn't soon enough for him.

At least he wouldn't have to wait at the other end. The only luggage he had with him was his passport, his wallet and his mobile phone, so he could go straight through customs.

Three hours. Three hours in which he hid behind a newspaper because he didn't feel like making polite conversation with the passenger in the seat next to him. Three hours to wait and fret and wonder if Eleanor would even agree to see him, let alone speak to him.

Customs didn't take long. Then he went for the fastest train he could get to London—and because he'd missed the last one by three minutes, he had twelve more minutes to wait before the next train, and then half an hour until he was in Victoria. And then the tube…

Finally he walked into the Albert Memorial hospital in Chelsea. Found the reception area for the emergency department. So near. Oh, please let her listen to him. Listen to what he had to say.

'May I see Dr Forrest, please?' he asked politely.

'Sorry, we can't guarantee a specific doctor. All our staff are highly trained and professional,' the receptionist told him.

'Perhaps I didn't make myself clear. I need to see Dr Eleanor Forrest, please.'

'I'm sorry, I can't guarantee a specific doctor,' the receptionist repeated. 'If you'd like to tell me your name so I can log you in to the system, a doctor will be with you as soon as possible.'

He didn't want a doctor. He wanted *Eleanor*. He was about to open his mouth to explain it was personal when one of the nursing staff came over.

Sheena Redmond, charge nurse, according to her badge.

'Is there a problem?' she asked, folding her arms and looking stern.

A woman who would brook no nonsense. He only hoped that she also had compassion. 'I'm not here to make trouble,' he said quietly. 'I just need to see Eleanor.'

'I'm afraid we can't guarantee you'll see—'

'A specific doctor,' he finished. 'Your receptionist told me. I'm not injured. It's personal.' He smiled wryly. 'Actually, it's good to know her friends here are looking out for her.'

Sheena's eyes narrowed. 'What do you mean, personal?'

'May I speak to you in private, please?' he asked, aware of the curious glance of the receptionist.

Sheena frowned, but led him into her office. 'Right. And this had better be good. Who are you?'

'My name is Orlando de Luca. I am a family doctor—what you would call a GP—in Italy.'

'Her father's doctor?'

He shook his head. 'I met Eleanor on the plane from London. We worked together when a fellow passenger had a heart attack. And I fell in love with her.' He took a deep breath. 'She's the love of my life. I was stupid enough not to tell her before she left Italy. And I need to tell her now.'

'Hmm. If you turn out to be another Jeremy—' Sheena warned.

'Hardly,' Orlando cut in gently. Then he grimaced. 'Oh, hell. When I left Naples, even the flower market wasn't open, let alone the shops. And I was so focused on catching my flight, getting here to see her, I didn't— Look, is there somewhere in the hospital I can buy flowers? Chocolates? Anything?' He raked a hand through his hair. '*Porca miseria!* I have no English money either—I paid for my train ticket by credit card. And hospital shops don't take credit cards, do they?' He looked beseechingly at her. '*Dio.* The only thing I can offer her right now is an apology and my heart. And that's...' He shook his head in misery. 'That might not be enough.'

Sheena patted his shoulder. 'All right. Go into cubicle three and wait. I'll have a word with her. See if she wants to talk to you.'

'Next?' Eleanor asked when she'd finished writing up the set of notes and put them on the trolley for filing.

'Cubicle three,' Sheena directed. 'Fracture.'

'OK.' Eleanor smiled, and walked over to the cubicle. When she twitched the curtain back and saw who was sitting on the bed, panic flared through her and she grabbed the end of the bed to steady herself. 'Orlando? What are you doing here? Is it Bartolomeo? Is he all right?'

'He's fine,' Orlando reassured her.

She felt her eyes narrow. 'So why are you here?'

'For emergency treatment.'

She frowned. 'I'm not with you.'

'I require emergency treatment,' he said.

He had dark shadows under his eyes and looked a bit rough around the edges, but that was as far as it went. She couldn't see anything that looked like a fracture or a wound that needed dressing. 'For what, precisely?' she asked crisply.

'A broken heart.'

'A *what*?' She stared at him.

'And, as a doctor, I already know the cure,' he said softly. 'You.'

She shook her head. 'You're the man who doesn't believe in love. Who thinks it's all a myth.'

'And I was wrong. I admit it freely. It's not a myth. I love you, Eleanor.'

She wasn't sure she was hearing this. 'How did you get here?'

'I caught an early flight from Naples this morning.'

Her frown deepened. 'How did you know where to find me?'

'Bartolomeo told me where you worked. He lost your mother—and I don't want that to happen to me. To us. I don't want to spend the rest of my life regretting that I didn't have the courage to tell you how I feel.' He raised a hand to forestall her protest. 'No, hear me out. The minute I walked into the apartment and realised you'd gone, it was as if someone had switched off the sun. And it was—oh, so *empty*. Without you, it wasn't my home any more, it was just a

place to live. That's when I realised how wrong I've been.'
He swallowed hard. 'So I came to find you. To tell you
what's been under my nose since the minute I met you—
what you told me and told me and told me but I was too
stupid and stubborn to take in. That there is just one special
person for me—and that's you. I want to spend the rest of
my life with you.'

'You want to spend the rest of your life with me,' she echoed,
looking stunned.

He coughed. 'I've been eating a fair bit of humble pie.
Serafina has been having a fine time at my expense.'

Her eyes widened. 'Oh, lord—the surgery. Your patients!'

'They're being looked after by my very capable partners.
Who are also enjoying themselves hugely, making me eat my
words,' he said dryly. 'In fact, they made me say it several
times, pretending they couldn't hear me. Serafina even suggested that I put it in writing.'

To his relief, a smile tugged at the corner of her mouth. So it
amused her, too. Good. At least the idea of him loving her
hadn't sent her screaming for cover. Maybe he had a chance.
'I want to be with you, Eleanor. I love you.'

'You love me.' She looked as if she didn't quite believe him.

Hardly surprising, in the circumstances. 'I admit I've been
very stupid. I've made you wait and wait and wait. And I
wouldn't blame you for telling me to get lost because I'm too
late. But the minute I found your note and realised you'd
walked out on me, it hit me. Without you, my life doesn't feel
right. There's an empty space, like a black hole, right where
my heart should be. Your letter...' He dragged in a breath.
'You said you wished me a long and happy life. Without you,
it'll be long—every second will last a lifetime—but it won't

be happy. Because, without you, the better part of me is missing. I love you.'

'You love me,' she repeated, still looking stunned.

'I love you,' he repeated. 'And I'm going to keep telling you that until you realise it's true.'

'How can I be sure?' she demanded. 'How do I know you're not going to change your mind and it's all going to end in tears?'

He smiled wryly. 'I think that was my line. Or it used to be, until I knew better. Because you taught me to believe.'

'Believe?' she echoed, frowning. 'Believe in what?'

'Believe in love. Believe in you. Believe in *us*.' He swallowed hard. 'You're right. I'm not my mother. I don't want you to change, to live up to some impossible ideal in my head— because you're already what I want. You're funny and you're clever and you're kind—and you're so damn sexy I have a hard time keeping my hands off you.'

'You managed it in your flat,' she pointed out.

'I was trying to be honourable.' He moistened his lower lip. 'Though if this means I need to make it up to you, we'd better go to a desert island for our honeymoon.'

'What honeymoon?'

'*Our* honeymoon. We're getting married.'

She coughed. 'I don't remember you asking me.'

He made a dismissive gesture with his hand. 'That's a tiny detail.'

'It's a big deal,' she corrected.

'Eleanor, I flew out from Naples at stupid o'clock when all the shops were closed. I've got no English money on me, so right at this second I can't give you a proposal with flowers and chocolates and a big sparkling diamond. If that's what you want, I'll meet you for lunch. I'll set up the champagne and the violin-player and the ring under a silver platter instead of your pudding. Whatever you want, I'll do it.' He looked at her. 'But right now, all I can give you is an apology. And my heart.'

'You're giving me your heart.'

'Yes. *Ti amo. Voglio passare il resto della mia vita con te.*'

'I love you,' she translated. 'I want to spend…the rest of my life?' At his nod, she continued, 'With you.'

He smiled. 'Good. I hoped you felt the same way.'

'I was transla—' She shook her head and sat on the bed next to him. 'You're impossible, Orlando. You've spent weeks keeping me at a distance. I've been so miserable about it. And now you're telling me you love me after all.'

'I do. It just took me time to get my head around it.'

'Time.' She rolled her eyes.

'I did warn you I needed time. And I could point out that you were the one who decided not to wait.'

'How much longer did you need, Orlando?'

He grimaced. 'I admit, you were right. It was when you *weren't* there that I realised what life would be like without you—what it *was* like without you. And I hated it. I want to be with you. I don't care whether it's here or Italy. The only place that feels home to me is where you are. So I'm telling you what I should have told you a long time ago. I love you, Eleanor Forrest.' It was time to take the risk. He slid off the bed and dropped to one knee. 'I meant what I said—in Italian as well as in English. I want to spend the rest of my life with you. Will you do me the honour of marrying me—being my love, my life, my one and only for the rest of my days?'

She didn't answer, and he felt himself freezing from the inside out.

He'd left it too late.

She wasn't going to give him the chance to make it up to her.

He was about to haul himself to his feet and leave when she spoke, her voice so soft that he could barely hear her. 'Are you saying, Orlando, that I am The One?'

'Yes. You were right. The One exists—and you are that person, for me.' His voice was equally soft. 'And this is a temporary proposal—until lunchtime, when I can do it with the flowers and the champagne and all the rest of it.'

'No.'

He'd thought it had hurt before. But this—this was as if his heart was being ground into the finest sand.

She wasn't going to marry him.

'Then I apologise, Dottoressa Forrest,' he said formally. 'I'll get out of your way.'

Before he could get up and leave, she took his hand. 'I meant no to the temporary proposal. Like you said, that stuff's just trappings. It doesn't last. Champagne goes flat, cut flowers wither, and diamonds…well, hit one in the right place with the right pressure and you'll fracture it.'

Hope began to flicker. 'So you'll marry me?'

'You're offering marriage. Which means…what?'

This was a test, he knew. The most important one of his life. If he failed, he wouldn't get another chance—because this was already his second chance. His *last* chance.

'It means a family,' he said carefully. 'Someone to belong to. You and me. And, in time, *bambini*—our children, who'll grow up secure and happy and knowing right from the start what I didn't… What you had to teach me. That love exists. That it's real. That it's good.'

'Then ask me again.' Her eyes glittered. '*Not* a temporary proposal.'

'I love you, Eleanor. My one and only. Will you marry me—make my life whole?'

She smiled and tugged him to his feet. 'Yes, I'll marry you, my one and only. And I'll love you for the rest of our days.'

THE ITALIAN'S
DEFIANT MISTRESS

India Grey

A self-confessed romance junkie, **India Grey** was just thirteen years old when she first sent off for the Mills & Boon® Writers' Guidelines. She can still recall the thrill of getting the large brown envelope with its distinctive logo through the letterbox, and subsequently whiled away many a dull school-day staring out of the window and dreaming of the perfect hero. She kept those guidelines with her for the next ten years, tucking them carefully inside the cover of each new diary in January, and beginning every list of New Year's Resolutions with the words *Start Novel*. In the meantime she also gained a degree in English Literature from Manchester University, and, in a stroke of genius on the part of the gods of romance, met her gorgeous future husband on the very last night of their three years there. The last fifteen years have been spent blissfully buried in domesticity and heaps of pink washing generated by three small daughters, but she has never really stopped daydreaming about romance. She's just profoundly grateful to have finally got an excuse to do it legitimately!

This is India's glitteringly emotional first book!

For Penny, a real-life fairy godmother,
who showed me how to make the
dream come true

CHAPTER ONE

'I CAN'T do this.'

Eve's voice was little more than a whisper as the icy hand of fear gripped her throat and trailed its chilly fingers down her spine. She wanted to run, but was suddenly too panic-stricken to move. Besides, in the stiletto-heeled thigh-length boots she probably wouldn't get very far.

On the other side of the curtains the ballroom of Florence's grandest *palazzo* was packed with five hundred of the world's most wealthy and beautiful, who had come to pay homage to the man who had been dressing them for half a century. Only the cream of Antonio di Lazaro's client list had been invited to attend this exclusive fiftieth anniversary retrospective, and any celebrities not sitting out there in the glittering ballroom waiting for the show to begin were backstage, getting ready to model some of the legendary Lazaro label's most iconic designs.

Sienna Swift, current supermodel darling of the international fashion scene, looked up briefly from the magazine she was reading and gave Eve her famously dazzling smile.

'Course you can. You'll be fine.'

'But I'm a…a journalist.' The dishonesty of the statement made Eve falter as she said it. 'My friend Lou was supposed to be doing this article—she'd have been fantastic, but I've never done anything like this in my life. I don't know the first thing about modelling!'

Sienna turned the page. 'Well, babe, you've got the legs for it. And better boobs than the rest of us put together. What's to know? It's hardly rocket science.' She paused to scrutinise a photograph of one of her closest rivals before adding, 'It's all about sex, I suppose.'

'Sex?' Eve wailed, her spirits sinking even further. 'Why sex? Where I come from sex is not something you do in front of five hundred people and photographers from every major publication around the globe.'

Apparently. She couldn't very well say she didn't know the first thing about that either.

Sienna sighed and put the magazine down.

'OK, we haven't got long, so let's make this as simple as possible. All you have to do is find someone to focus on. You're up there on the catwalk, right? And you just fix your eyes on some bloke and forget everyone else. Watch.'

The model took a couple of steps back, thrusting her hips forward in classic catwalk style and placing her hands on them. Looking around for a likely candidate, she fixed her smoky gaze on the singer from Italy's hottest new boy band, who'd just come offstage.

'You walk towards him and you never take your eyes off him,' she murmured through sultry, pouted lips. 'Not for a second. This is lust at first sight. You're looking at him as if he's the sexiest man alive and you're going to go right up to him and strip his clothes off there and then.' She swung back to Eve with a wicked smile. 'That's all there is to it!' And to the obvious dismay of the blushing singer she picked up the magazine again and resumed her study of it.

Eve squirmed uncomfortably in the transparent PVC mini-dress, and tugged it down over her bottom. It would be a lot easier to follow Sienna's advice if she was allowed to wear her glasses, without which she wasn't going to be able to focus on anything more than half a metre away from her face, and if she wasn't dressed in an upmarket plastic bag. She seemed to have drawn the short straw in the clothes lottery, and had been allocated one of Lazaro's more bizarre creations from his *avant-garde* phase in the 1960s. Strategically positioned fluorescent flowers stopped the dress being absolutely X-rated, but she still felt horribly exposed.

All around her some of the most beautiful women in the world were sipping mineral water from miniature bottles and dropping the kind of names that would have sent a real journalist into a frenzy of excitement. Among them Eve felt lonely, disorientated, and about as glamorous as a transit van in a garage full of sportscars.

She didn't belong here.

She closed her eyes against the sudden wave of homesickness that threatened to knock her for six as she thought of her messy desk by the window in Professor Swanson's office. At this time of year her view of the college quadrangle was almost entirely obliterated by the wisteria rampaging across the window, casting a murky underwater light over the clutter of teacups and student essays and piles of scribbled notes in the dusty book-lined room.

That was her world, and she had been crazy to think for a second that she could cut it in Lou's. Fashion journalists—especially those who were successful enough to shadow supermodels for exclusive behind-the-scenes articles on the A-list events of the year—were generally not shy, shortsighted academics. There was just no way she could pull it off.

'I think I'd better go and get changed,' she muttered, trying to squeeze through the crush at the steps to the catwalk.

The plan had failed before it had even begun, and it was better that she face that fact now. Lou had taken a huge risk in faking illness at the last minute and putting Eve forward for this article, and if either of them had stopped to think about it they would have realised how outrageous the whole scheme was. She was going to let Lou down, but that wasn't the worst part.

The worst part was letting her twin sister Ellie down. And letting Raphael Di Lazaro slip through her fingers again.

Without looking up from the horoscope page, Sienna grabbed her arm and pulled her back. 'No time,' she said cheerfully. 'We're on in a second. Look, it says here that Scorpios should exercise caution in financial matters. Do you think that means I shouldn't buy that Prada clutch bag, then?'

Eve's teeth were chattering violently as she replied, 'I shouldn't think so. Look, it doesn't by any chance say that on Thursday Aquarians should avoid public displays of nudity and stay at home eating chocolate instead, does it?'

Sienna laughed. 'Let's see. Aquarius. "Due to Mercury moving into the pinnacle of your chart, Thursday will see a spectacular reawakening of your love-life. Your destiny awaits you in a most unexpected place." Excellent! You'd better stick around after all!'

Eve grimaced. Even if she could persuade herself to believe in astrology—or destiny, for that matter—she'd have to draw the line at reincarnation. Her love-life wasn't just sleeping, it was dead and buried.

No. If she was going to stick around it would be nothing to do with love or *destiny*, for pity's sake, and everything to do with revenge.

She gave Sienna a watery smile. 'Just my luck the man of my dreams is going to appear in my life the day I'm dressed as Porn Star Barbie.'

The grand ballroom of the Palazzo Salarino glittered in the light from its famous antique crystal chandeliers as the floor-length windows darkened from the blue of late afternoon to the deep mauve of evening. The body of the room was filled with row upon row of gilded chairs, seating the fashion world's premier figures, and the perfection of the scene was reflected in the numerous Venetian mirrors that lined the walls.

On shaking legs Eve stepped out from the wings.

For a second she couldn't see anything at all as a thousand flashbulbs dazzled her, and it was all she could do not to put her hands in front of her face to shield it. The catwalk stretched ahead of her, looking at least a mile long, and beyond it lay the elegant salon with its sea of upturned faces.

Sienna's words came back to her. *'Find someone to focus on…'*

Desperately she scanned the cavernous room, for once glad that her shortsightedness prevented her from recognising the dauntingly famous faces. Her steps slowed and she felt the smile freeze on her face. Was she supposed to smile? She couldn't remember. The audience was a whispering restless mass. It was impossible to single anyone out, Eve thought in panic, willing herself to keep going while every fibre of her being was telling her to turn on her spike heels and run.

Someone was standing in the shadows, leaning against one of the marble pillars with his head tilted back. He was wearing a dark suit that outlined the powerful breadth of his shoulders against the pale marble, and there was something incredibly arresting about his stillness. In the dimly lit room, through the fog of her shortsightedness, it was impossible to see him clearly, but she could feel his eyes upon her.

I can do this, she thought. *I can do this.*

Achingly beautiful, heartbreakingly poignant, the exquisite notes of *Madame Butterfly* drifted through the room, filling her with their bittersweet sexual yearning. She and Ellie had always loved this opera, sneaking to the top of the stairs in their night-gowns to catch this particular aria when their mother used to play it late at night on an old record player. The words were as familiar to her as a lullaby, and hearing them now gave her strength.

Everything around her receded—the cameras, the audience, the syrupy voice of the pink-suited host. The world shrank to encompass nothing but the music and the dark, narrowed eyes of the stranger. He didn't move, but as she swayed towards him she could feel the laser beam burn of his gaze and sense the sexual energy he gave off, like heat. It melted into her skin, making it tingle, thawing her icy shell of insecurity and shyness.

For the first time in two years she felt properly alive.

Reaching the end of the catwalk, she lifted her head and paused. Their eyes locked over the rows of people separating them in a dizzying moment of absolute sexual recognition. For a brief second Eve seriously considered keeping going: jumping down from the catwalk and walking right up to him, as Sienna had said. Her body was crying out to him with an urgency that took her breath away, and the need to touch him, to inhale his scent and taste the warmth of his lips, was almost overwhelming.

The photographers at her feet surged forward in a volley of flashbulbs. Blinded by white light, she could still see the dark silhouette of her mysterious rescuer imprinted on her mind. Wrenching her dazzled gaze away, she turned to walk back up the catwalk, still feeling his eyes upon her and helplessly aware of the wanton undulation of her hips. In the few seconds that their eyes had held he had insinuated himself under her skin, like some mystical enchanter, infusing every cell in her body with molten longing. She was possessed.

Stepping shakily off the catwalk, she slipped through the crowd of girls waiting to go on and, oblivious to their smiles and congratulations, stumbled back to her corner of the communal dressing area. Throwing herself into a chair, she stared at her reflection in the mirror.

She looked like Sleeping Beauty must have in the moment following Prince Charming's kiss—dazed, bewildered, and unmistakably aroused. Gone was the shy, uncertain girl who had stepped nervously through the curtains five minutes ago, and in her place was a tousled maenad with bee-stung lips and eyes like dark pools of invitation.

The horoscope had been spookily accurate. It was exactly as

if she had been sleeping until the electrifying presence of the unknown man had brought her painfully, pleasurably, back to consciousness.

She dropped her head into her hands. Except that clever, sensible Eve didn't believe in all that nonsense, did she?

She had been the shy twin, always in the shadow of flamboyant, confident Ellie. Ellie had been the one who'd devoured horoscopes and believed in destiny, pursuing your dream. While Eve had still been at Oxford, working hard on her dissertation, Ellie had abandoned her degree in Art History and blown her student grant on a one-way ticket to Florence instead.

She'd wanted to experience art and passion and beauty for herself, not hear about it second-hand in some dingy lecture theatre. At some point, when she'd been in Florence for a couple of months, she'd clearly decided to add heroin to the list of things she wanted to experience.

That was where following your dreams and reading your horoscope got you. To an anonymous, sordid death that the police hadn't even bothered to investigate.

They hadn't, so Eve had vowed she would. In the two years since it had happened Eve's life had shrunk even further, until there was nothing left but her work for Professor Swanson and the cold, aching desire for closure and for justice.

But the face that stared back at her from the mirror now was transformed by desire of a different kind. It was the face of a girl who knew what she wanted—and it had nothing to do with revenge. The expression in her eyes was one of white-hot, naked, take-me-and-damn-the-consequences lust.

And, what was more, it suited her. Now all she had to do was find her man and...

'You were brilliant! A total natural!'

Sienna kicked off killer six-inch stiletto heels and helped herself to a miniature bottle of champagne from one of the ice buckets that were dotted around the dressing room. On the other side of the curtain the audience were still clapping and cheering as she took a long, thirsty swig.

In a daze, Eve looked up. The show couldn't have finished already. That would mean she had just spent the last forty-five minutes lost in an erotic fantasy.

'Right, then,' Sienna went on happily, 'That's the work bit over. Now it's party time!' *Oh, God. She* had *just spent the last forty-five minutes lost in an erotic fantasy.* 'The Lazaro parties are always totally wild.' With an alarming lack of inhibition Sienna stripped off the outrageous white leather and tulle wedding dress she had worn for the finale and tossed it aside. 'Have you seen how many celebs are out there? I can't wait to meet them. And there's even a whisper going around that Rapahel di Lazaro is back from abroad. He's supposed to be, like, *so-ooo* gorgeous. I'm definitely going to introduce myself.'

The mention of *that* name brought Eve back to reality with roughly the same force as a head-on collision at high speed. He was the one she should be spending the evening trying to get close to, not her handsome hero.

'Well, if you find him you can introduce me too. I'd love to meet the mysterious Raphael di Lazaro. So far I haven't even been able to dig out so much as a photograph of him. How come he's so elusive?'

Sienna shrugged. She had changed into a backless, barely-there dress in cherry-pink, and was now slipping her feet into a pair of pink satin wedges that even Eve recognised as being the height of fashion.

'He left before I started modelling for Lazaro, but people here are still talking about him. The rumour goes that his girlfriend ran off with his brother—Luca; you're bound to meet him—and Raphael couldn't handle it. I heard he went to South America somewhere, though I'm not sure if that's right. I mean, he's a fashion photographer, and it's not an area you'd really associate with fashion, is it?'

Eve gave a dry laugh. 'No.' *Drugs, yes. Fashion, no.*

'Anyway, that's why he hasn't been around for a couple of years. And even before he went the paparazzi used to give him a pretty wide berth.' Sienna finished applying shocking pink lipstick and paused for a moment while she pressed her lips together. 'He *hates* them, apparently, but that's not unusual in this business. What's more surprising is that they seem to respect that. He must be quite a guy. Hey, Eve…? Are you all right?

'Oh. Yes. Yes, of course.'

'Well, come on, then. We're missing valuable party time! What are you wearing?'

'Oh, nothing much. I mean, not literally—but I've only got this.' Flustered, Eve got to her feet and rummaged inside a moth-eaten antique carpet-bag—her Mary Poppins bag as Ellie used to call it—fishing out a slither of silk which she tossed absent-mindedly to Sienna.

Sienna held the dress up carefully. 'It's gorgeous. Where's it from?'

Eve flashed her a smile and put on a posh, showbiz accent. 'A frightfully exclusive little label called Charity Shop. Frankly, darling, I never wear anything else.'

The lavender-scented air was still warm, and, stepping out onto the romantically lit terrace, Raphael Di Lazaro felt an enormous sense of relief. The ornate grandeur of the *palazzo*'s ballroom, with its wall-to-wall celebrities and trophy wives, had been suffocating. Everything was so highly polished and symmetrical, just like the perfectly made-up, expressionless faces of the models, but it made the dust and chaos he had so recently left behind in Columbia seem positively refreshing in comparison.

Accepting a glass of champagne from a passing waiter, he discreetly checked his watch. This was the kind of event he usually avoided like a hot day in hell, but he was here on business, not for pleasure. This was exactly the sort of environment in which his slimeball brother was most likely to operate.

Half-brother. Since uncovering evidence of the new depths of evil and corruption concealed behind Luca's shallow charm, Raphael was more determined than ever to remember that they shared only one parent. And Antonio Di Lazaro had played such a distant role in Raphael's upbringing that he hardly qualified for the title of father.

Luca was the golden boy in Antonio's eyes. In everyone's eyes.

Grimly, Raphael lifted his glass to his lips, as if the bubbles would wash away the bitter taste that always accompanied this train of thought. Draining it in one long draft, he was surprised to find that his habitual acrimony was tinged with sympathy. It wasn't going to be easy for Antonio to face the fact that his favourite son was facing charges of international drugs trafficking and money laundering. Especially when the money had most probably come from the Lazaro accounts.

But he was jumping ahead of himself. Luca hadn't been arrested yet, and Raphael was here to make sure that nothing happened to prevent that at this delicate stage of the operation.

Looking around for his father, he stifled a yawn. Even when he'd worked for Lazaro he'd despised this celebrity schmoozing, and his time in Columbia had only served to heighten his loathing of it. In fact today extreme tiredness and crashing boredom had made a pretty lethal combination, so that during the endless procession of identikit clotheshorses he'd almost fallen asleep.

Maybe he had, just for a moment. Maybe that astonishing erotic encounter had been nothing more than a dream...

He felt his tired body stir and stiffen at the memory of the girl in the transparent dress. Surely it was too vivid to have been a dream? He could still picture the terror in her huge eyes as she'd stepped into the lights of the catwalk, still remember the surge of protectiveness he'd felt towards her as she'd faltered, still feel the adrenalin rush that had crashed through him as she'd looked straight into his eyes...

Adrenalin? Who was he kidding? What he'd felt was a rush of pure testosterone. It wasn't just sleep deprivation he was suffering from.

OK, so there hadn't exactly been an endless supply of attractive, intelligent women to choose from in Columbia's underworld, and two years was a hell of a long time for any man without a burning religious conviction to behave like a monk, but he wasn't desperate enough to pick up some air-headed model. Bitter experience had taught him that models required the same kind of intensive, round the clock attention and affection as small children. And they were just as likely to get themselves into trouble if left unsupervised. It was a responsibility he wouldn't be stupid enough to take on a second time.

Suddenly his eyes narrowed as he caught sight of Antonio. Emerging onto the terrace, he was making his way slowly in Raphael's direction, surrounded by a small crowd of devotees. He was dressed as immaculately as ever, in a perfectly cut silvery-grey suit with his trademark white rose in the buttonhole, but Raphael was alarmed to see how much his father had aged in the time he had been away. As Antonio approached Raphael could see the unhealthy pallor of his lips, and the lines of exhaustion etched into his elegant, haughty face.

'Father.'

Caught off-guard, Antonio was unable to disguise his shock. Swiftly recovering his composure, he managed a chilly smile.

'Raphael. What a surprise. What are you doing here?'

'I had to come back for the Press Photography Awards in Venice on Saturday, but I have some business to attend to in Florence as well. Lazaro business, actually.'

Antonio's eyebrows rose a fraction. '*Si?* After all this time? You walked out on Lazaro two years ago, Raphael. I cannot imagine what business you would have here now.'

'I need to have a look at the company accounts.'

Antonio's eyes narrowed. 'You are short of money? Is that it? Maybe you should have thought of that before you left your job here to go off and photograph peasants in the back of beyond. Awards don't pay the bills, Raphael.'

A muscle flickered in Raphael's cheek. When he spoke, his voice was dangerously quiet. 'As far as I know I'm still listed as one of the company directors, so I am perfectly within my rights to have access to the accounts. Tomorrow, if that suits you. I'll need to see you once I've finished going through them.'

'Tomorrow is impossible. I have an interview about the retrospective with Italian *Vogue* in the morning, and the perfume launch in the afternoon.' Antonio looked suddenly exhausted, and seemed anxious to get away. 'Anyway, Raphael, you know how I loathe having anything to do with money. Luca is Financial Director, I leave everything to him. He's here somewhere—why don't you speak to him about it?'

'I'd rather not.'

'Don't be ridiculous. Luca is your brother. All that nonsense with Catalina is in the past—you can't still hate him for something that happened—what?—two years ago?'

Raphael felt his mouth twist into a sneer of contempt. 'Believe me, Father, I've discovered plenty more things to hate him for since then.'

But Antonio wasn't listening. With a dismissive wave of his hand in the direction of the *palazzo* he said, 'There he is. Sort something out with him.'

Luca Di Lazaro was leaning nonchalantly against the open French door, his broad frame filling the doorway and effectively blocking the escape of whichever unfortunate girl he had ensnared. Raphael's heart gave a lurch of pure loathing as he watched Luca lean down to say something to the girl. Something meaningless and flattering, no doubt. Something guaranteed to put her at her ease and charm her into a false sense of security.

It was a routine he had perfected on countless naïve young models over the years, as Raphael knew to his cost. His own girl-friend had been one of them, after all.

At that moment Luca shifted slightly to one side, coming to rest with deceptive ease, his back against the door frame. The movement gave Raphael a clear view of the girl he had trapped.

She had changed the transparent dress for a silk slip that, in hiding her delicious body, only seemed to emphasise its voluptuousness. The soft light from the room beyond cast a halo around the contours of her curves.

Adrenalin pulsed through him, hot and powerful. Without hesitating, or giving his father so much as a backward glance, Raphael found himself shouldering his way through the crowd towards them. Company accounts were the last thing on his mind as he wrestled with the primitive urge to push everyone out of the way, grab the girl from Luca and take her as far away as possible.

Luca straightened up as he approached.

'Well, well. The prodigal son returns.' His voice was slippery with sarcasm, and Raphael raked a hand through his hair in an attempt to stop himself punching that bland, handsome face. 'I would introduce you, but we've only just met and I haven't found out this beauty's name yet...'

Raphael's reaction was instant. Giving Luca a smile that would have frozen the Mediterranean, he turned to the woman with a light inclination of his head, praying she wouldn't give him away.

'*Cara?* Is there anyone else you'd like to meet, or are you ready to go?'

He allowed himself a small moment of triumph as he watched the look of surprise and something that resembled anxiety spread across Luca's face before turning his attention back to the girl.

Her eyes were the clear turquoise-green of old glass, and they glinted, catlike, in the light of the crystal chandeliers. Lust sliced through Raphael with the painless precision of a razor-blade as he registered the spreading darkness at their centre.

There was the smallest hesitation before she replied. Her accent was English, her voice low and breathless.

'I'm all yours…darling.'

OK, for one night only Eve Middlemiss—BA hons and general clever clogs—was prepared to admit she'd been wrong.

There was such a thing as destiny. And he was standing right beside her.

They crossed the main reception area of the *palazzo*, his hand resting lightly in the small of her back, his thumb gently caressing the hollow at the base of her spine. Away from the main buzz of the party a few guests stood talking quietly in small groups, and uniformed staff hovered discreetly. Eve was dimly aware of their curious glances as she passed, but was almost beyond caring.

Almost. And then she remembered Ellie.

'I have to get back… I really shouldn't…'

As the words left her lips she knew they were completely unconvincing. She'd tried to adopt a firm, businesslike tone, but failed spectacularly. Something odd had happened to her voice, so that she sounded as if she was auditioning as a sex-line operator, and above the storm of hormone-fuelled emotions inside her a demonic alter-ego whispered, *Forget Ellie just for one night. Do something for your own sake for a change.*

He looked down at her. His face was completely expressionless.

'You don't, and you should. Believe me.'

His grip tightened on her waist, sending another shower of shooting stars down her spine and turning her stomach to water. She tried to laugh, but it came out as a gasp.

'I don't understand… I don't make a habit of this sort of thing…'

His beautiful mouth twitched into the ghost of a smile. 'Do you think that isn't obvious? That's exactly why I had to get you out of the clutches of that…low-life.'

'He seemed very charming.'

'Appearances can be deceptive.'

He pulled her into a quiet gallery off the main hallway, dimly lit by lamps placed on tables along the length of its walls. Just inside the door he stopped and turned to her, his face shadowed. God, her stomach wasn't the only thing he turned to water, she thought, feeling liquid heat seeping into the silk and lace of her tiny thong.

'Shouldn't I be allowed to decide that for myself?' she whispered.

His hair was raven-dark, falling over his forehead and accentuating the hollows beneath cheekbones that looked as if they had been chiselled in marble. Despite the perfection of his features, he carried with him an aura of exhaustion and despair, and she had to curl her hands into fists to stop herself reaching out and touching him, trying to soothe away the tension in his jaw and the haunted look in his dark eyes.

'I couldn't risk you making the wrong decision.'

'What makes you think I'd do that?'

He gave a hollow laugh. 'It's happened before.' Reaching out, he slipped a finger under the slender silk strap of her dress, which had slipped down her arm, and with infinite gentleness slid it back into place. In the silence Eve heard her own small whimper of longing as his fingers brushed her quivering skin.

Wrenching his hand away, he half turned, his haughty, aristocratic face a mask of reserve. Only the dark, glittering pools of his eyes betrayed his desire as he swung back to face her.

The moan that escaped him as his mouth found hers was the sound of a man surrendering control. His hands entwined themselves in the thick silk of her hair, pulling her to him, imprisoning her lips with his, so that her cries of naked desire were consumed in the furnace of his kiss. With savage urgency his tongue explored the velvet depths of her mouth, then, leaving her gasping her pleasure and desperation into the stillness of the empty room, moved downwards to her jaw, her neck, the perfumed, pulsing hollow at the base of her throat. Helplessly she felt her fingers sliding into his hair, willing him onward, downward, to where her nipples strained against the silk of her dress, yearning for the exquisite warmth of his mouth...

A discreet cough from the doorway stopped him in his tracks.

'Signor di Lazaro? Signor Raphael di Lazaro? *Scusi*, but it's your father. I'm afraid it's urgent.'

And then he was gone, leaving her dazed, disorientated, and struck dumb with horror.

This man wasn't her destiny. He was her nemesis.

CHAPTER TWO

IT WAS just a small scrap of paper, torn from the back of a pocket diary or notebook.

Lying in the darkness beneath crisp hotel sheets, Eve held it close to her body, absentmindedly sliding it through her finger and thumb so that she could feel the difference in texture along the torn edge and the slight stiffness where at some point coffee been spilled on it.

She didn't need to switch the light on and look at it to know that the coffee stain was in the shape of a rather fat rabbit, or to read the numbers 592, which were the only remainders of the phone number that had once been written there. She had studied that scrap of paper in such minute detail so often over the last two years that she even knew that the smooth bit underneath her thumb right now was where the words *Raphael di Lazaro* were written. And just below and to the left of that, just by the rabbit's ear, was where it said *drugs*.

The girl Ellie had shared a flat with in Florence—Catalina someone or other—had sent her things back to England following her death, and when Eve had finally been able to face going through them she had found this tucked into one of the pockets of Ellie's jeans. The rest of the writing might have been consigned to eternal oblivion by the coffee, but Eve hardly needed to have it spelled out to her. These had to be the contact details of the person who had supplied Ellie with heroin. And that person was Raphael Di Lazaro.

By the time Eve had found the paper di Lazaro had already disappeared into darkest Columbia, and the Italian authorities had recorded a verdict of accidental death on Ellie and closed the case. But as far as Eve was concerned it wasn't over. She had vowed to expose Raphael di Lazaro for what he was, no matter how long it took her to do it. Which was why, when Lou had called her at work two days ago, to report that a paparazzi contact had spotted him arriving back at Florence's airport, she hadn't hesitated in going along with Lou's ridiculous plan. After all, strutting down a catwalk and pretending to be a fashion journalist were pretty insignificant hoops to jump through in order finally to come face to face with the man who was responsible for Ellie's death.

Her fingers tightened around the piece of paper until it was scrunched up in the palm of her hand. She had certainly succeeded in doing that.

Big style.

Face to face, lip to lip, body to body…

Oh, sweet heaven…

She started violently as her mobile phone burst into noisy life on the bedside table, letting out a shrill explosion of sound whilst simultaneously vibrating madly and glowing fluorescent green in the darkness. Eve made a clumsy grab for it, knocking over a glass of water in the process, and accidentally switching it on just as she swore graphically.

'Eve?'

Oh, God. It was Marissa Fox, editor of *Glitterati*, sounding terrifyingly brisk and efficient.

'Sorry. I mean—yes. Sorry'

Mercifully, Marissa cut her off mid-stutter. 'Look, Eve, I know the whole idea is that you're shadowing Sienna, but can I be an awful bore and ask you to tear yourself away from her for an hour or so and pop down to cover the press conference this morning?'

Eve sat bolt upright in the hope it would make her sound more awake. 'Press conference?' she echoed faintly.

'Yes, darling.' There was a steely edge to Marissa's voice that was more effective than any alarm clock. 'Di Lazaro's doctors are giving a press conference this morning on his prognosis. Not good, according to my sources.'

Squeezing her eyes tightly shut, Eve felt the blood drain from her head.

Was Raphael hurt?

'Eve? Are you still there?'

'Yes.'

'You *do* know that Antonio di Lazaro suffered a heart attack as he was leaving the party last night, don't you?'

'Antonio?' Relief flooded through her, followed by a wave of self-disgust. Why should she care whether Raphael was hurt or not? If someone else had got there first it would save her the bother of doing it herself. But deny her the satisfaction.

'Right. Yes, sorry—of course I knew that he'd been taken ill,' she lied hastily. 'Everyone I spoke to sort of played it down. Is it serious?'

'Well, you'll find that out at the press conference, darling,' Marissa replied acidly. 'Ten o'clock at the Santa Maria Nuova hospital. I'd go myself, but *miraculously* I've managed to get an appointment in the hotel spa for a Seaweed Body Wrap and Triple Oxygen Facial. I'll be cutting it fine for the perfume launch as it is.' She sighed heavily. 'Such a shame that Lou's got this hideous shellfish allergy—she's always rather good at the whole press conference circus. But I'm sure you can manage just as well—can't you, darling?'

Eve groped for her glasses and pushed them on, almost swearing out loud again as she squinted at her watch in the gloom. Nine-twenty.

'Press conference? Absolutely. No problem. I'll be there.' Stumbling out of bed, she made a huge effort to sound like the professional journalist that Lou had told Marissa she was. 'So…is it a…big press conference?' She pulled open the lavishly swagged curtains, wincing as bright sunlight highlighted the chaos in the room, and the fact that Sienna's bed was the only thing that was still neat and unused. 'Are we expecting… er…statements from just the medical team, or will the family be present as well?'

'Family? Good heavens, darling, I shouldn't think so. Antonio's heart attack didn't stop Luca partying till the early hours, so I doubt he'll be in any state to face the press—which just leaves Raphael, and he's utterly allergic to publicity in any form. He's quite pathologically anti-journalists and paparazzi. Ah! Here's breakfast. Do you know, darling, this is supposed to be Florence's *top hotel*, and they don't do wheatgrass juice! Can you believe it? Anyway, darling, must dash. Give my love to Sienna, won't you? Hope you're getting lots of juicy gossip for the interview—can't wait to see the copy. I'll catch up with you both at the launch. *Ciao*, darling!'

Head reeling, Eve exhaled slowly into the sudden silence, and for a moment considered throwing herself onto the bed and screaming very loudly into a pillow. It was tempting, but ultimately not very constructive. And right now she needed help.

Picking her way through the ankle-deep mulch of discarded designer clothing that was the only sign of Sienna's occupancy in the room, Eve speed-dialled Lou.

Waiting for her to pick up, Eve felt her panic start to subside. Lou would know what to do—about the press conference and the case of the disappearing supermodel and yesterday's embarrassing incident, where the guy she'd thought was the man of her dreams had actually turned out to be—oops, sorry—the dark figure who stalked her nightmares.

No. *No. Noooo! Please, please don't be…*

Voicemail.

With a wail of anguish Eve threw her phone down and stood motionless for a moment in the middle of the room, as the panic returned and threatened to overwhelm her. Lou always said that when things went wrong all you had to do was imagine a way in which they could be worse. At that particular moment Eve couldn't think of one.

But a minute later, examining her reflection in the enormous Hollywood-style bathroom mirror, she was spared the bother of trying.

Her face, above a skimpy T-shirt with a picture of Shakespeare on the front, was deathly pale, with last night's mascara still smudged beneath her eyes. Her hair, cut yesterday for the fashion show into what the stylist had called 'sexy tousled layers' was now so sexily tousled that she looked as if she'd enjoyed a non-stop, all-night love-fest. All things considered, out of the two of them it was Shakespeare who looked the livelier. And the more attractive. And he'd been dead for nearly four hundred years.

She had just fifteen minutes to turn the day around and transform herself into a sleek, professional fashion journalist.

Fifteen minutes…and the entire cosmetic collection of one of the world's hottest supermodels.

How hard could it be?

She might have left the hotel without her glasses, but it wasn't hard to find the conference room at the Santa Mariá Nuova hospital. All she had to do was follow the click-clack of kitten heels and the wafts of expensive fragrance of a hundred fashionistas.

Finding a space beside a tarty-looking blonde from one of the less salubrious celebrity gossip magazines, Eve rummaged in her bag for the little tape recorder Lou had lent her and, unable to see properly without her glasses, took three attempts to insert a new tape.

The blonde girl threw her a sympathetic glance. 'Tough night last night?'

'You could say that.'

'Me too. My hangover's so bad I could do with joining di Lazaro in Intensive Care.'

Eve smiled. Thankfully she was spared the necessity of explaining that she was suffering the after-effects of intoxication of a different kind by the appearance of a woman, and two men in doctor's coats on the platform at the front of the room. A searing flare of disappointment tore through her like a physical pain at the realisation that Raphael was not amongst them.

She *had* to see him again, she rationalised silently, gritting her teeth. What had happened last night had raised more questions than it had answered, and whichever way you looked at it she had a whole lot of unfinished business regarding Raphael di Lazaro.

Taking their places at a starched white table, the trio on the platform looked as if they were about to ask for the wine list. Eve recognised the woman from the retrospective as Alessandra Ferretti, Lazaro's formidable and deeply attractive press officer. She took the centre seat, with a doctor on either side of her, and for a moment the three of them spoke quietly between themselves, before Ferretti checked her watch and leaned forward to speak into the microphone in a ridiculously husky voice.

'Buongiorno.'

The army of reporters shifted expectantly, pens, cameras, tape recorders poised. But then a door at the back of the room opened, and everyone swung round to look at the latecomer.

Eve's gasp was lost in an explosion of flashbulbs and a deafening machine-gun rattle of shutters as every photographer in the room instantly went for a shot of Raphael di Lazaro.

His dark hair fell forward over his face. Shadows of fatigue and twenty-four hours of stubble emphasised the high, slanting cheekbones and the sulky, sensual mouth. Even unshaven, and in last night's rumpled dark suit and white shirt, he was still savagely, effortlessly attractive. His face, as he pulled out a chair and slumped into it, was perfectly expressionless, but, watching him rake back his hair with long, suntanned fingers, Eve thought that he looked infinitely weary.

Her insides turned liquid with a potent mixture of loathing and lust.

Alessandra Ferretti was introducing everyone, her sexy drawl making it sound as if she was matchmaking at a cocktail party. 'Dr Christiano is Signor di Lazaro's consultant, and Dr Cavalletti is head of the cardiac team who will be responsible for his care.' She gestured to the white-coated men, then turned to Raphael and laid a slim brown hand on his arm. 'Raphael di Lazaro returned from Columbia only yesterday, but he has been with his father throughout the night.'

A tiny shock pulsed through Eve that Alessandra should mention Columbia so casually, but it was quickly submerged by a wave of irritation at the proprietary way her hand still rested on Raphael's arm.

'What's Antonio's condition now?' asked a reporter from one of the Italian broadsheets.

'*Agiato,*' replied the doctor on the right—Eve was ashamed to realise that she hadn't been paying enough attention to remember which one it was. 'He is in the best possible hands.'

'What treatment will he be undergoing?'

The other doctor cleared his throat self-importantly and launched into an in-depth medical lecture that had all the English-speaking journalists utterly bewildered. At the end of the table Raphael was leaning back in his chair, distractedly drawing on a notepad, totally oblivious to the intense attention of the media and of every woman in the room.

He had the face of a tortured saint in some religious tableau, Eve decided miserably, unable to stop herself from staring at him, or responding to that same aura of desolation she had noticed last night. She had spent the last two years inventing slow and painful deaths for this man, and suddenly she found herself wanting to walk right up to him, hold his face in her hands and kiss away all the anger and pain that she saw there.

She shook her head irritably. *Maybe she'd been right yesterday. Maybe she really was possessed.*

'What about the perfume launch? Is it still going ahead?' a journalist from one of the British glossies was asking.

'We feel that Antonio would want it to,' Alessandra Ferretti said smoothly. 'He has lavished much attention on its planning, and some of the biggest celebrities across the globe are coming to celebrate the launch of *Golden*, Lazaro's most exciting perfume ever, in what promises to be a glittering event in every sense of the word.' Product plug over, she arranged her face into a compassionate smile and resumed a hushed, respectful tone. 'Antonio always puts Lazaro first. It is his life, and to do anything other than carry on with business as usual would be utterly disrespectful of all he has worked so hard to create.'

Her answer was followed by another cacophony of questions, most of them directed at Raphael. How long was it since he had seen his father? Had he come back from South America because he knew Antonio was ill? How had Antonio seemed earlier in the evening?

He answered briefly, his voice harsh with tiredness. Eve kept her head down and her tape recorder raised to catch his answers, fearing that all it would be picking up was the frantic beating of her heart. Beside her, the tarty blonde was desperately trying to get noticed to ask a question.

'Signor di Lazaro! Raphael!'

Suddenly he looked in her direction. Eve froze.

'Where were you last night when Antonio was taken ill?'

'At the retrospective.'

Eve didn't dare breathe. If she kept her head down and stayed completely still perhaps he wouldn't notice her. If only the damned girl beside her would shut up and let him move on to someone else. But she was still talking. A vaguely insinuating note had crept into her voice.

'According to staff at the Palazzo Salarino, it took some considerable time to locate you. What were you doing?'

The silence that followed seemed to go on for ever. Slowly, and with a paralysing sense of dread, Eve dragged her eyes upwards from their intense study of the pattern on the carpet. And found herself looking straight into his.

It was like running at full speed into a wall of ice.

His expression was utterly blank as he held her in his dark gaze. Excruciating, yet indescribably erotic, like being intimately caressed while lying on a bed of nails. His voice, when he eventually replied, was very soft.

'That, it suddenly appears, is a very good question.'

For a second Raphael thought that tiredness had got the better of him and he was hallucinating. But there was no mistaking those eyes, or the softly rounded lips that had filled his head with pleasure during the long hours he'd spent, halfway between sleeping and waking, in a chair at his father's hospital bedside.

So she wasn't a model. It was even worse than that.

She was a journalist.

His grip tightened on the pen in his hand as a wave of self-recrimination swept through him. Going too long without sleep had made him irrational and careless, but that was no excuse for his stupid behaviour last night. Thank goodness that the *maître d'* had found him before things had gone any further, otherwise he might have been waking up to his name all over the front pages in headlines featuring the words 'passion', 'playboy', and probably 'love-rat'.

He looked across to where she stood, head bent, her face partly hidden by a curtain of hair, the tip of her pen held between her softly parted lips, and felt his heart—along with other more basic parts of his anatomy—harden.

In his eyes journalists came a little below single-cell organisms in the evolutionary scale. Just because this girl had the wide-eyed innocence of a blonde Virgin Mary, it would be unwise to rule out the possibility that she might still attempt to concoct some kind of kiss-and-tell story. He would just have to track her down and make sure she didn't.

She'd have her price. They all did. That was what was so disappointing.

'Taxi! Taxi!'

Eve let out a shriek of outrage as yet another of Florence's distinctive white cabs sped past her. That made five. She was beginning to wonder if she might just be invisible.

But of course she wasn't. If she were she would have been spared public humiliation at the hands—or eyes—of Raphael Di Lazaro.

How dared he? she spluttered inwardly. How *dared* he *look* at her like that? As if she was some kind of inferior life-form from the Planet Vulgar, and way beneath his contempt?

'Taxiii!'

If the street had not been crowded with intimidatingly glamorous Italian women, looking cool and inscrutable behind their designer sunglasses, Eve would almost certainly have sat down on the pavement and given in to tears. As it was, there was only one thing left to do.

Find chocolate.

The café nearby was small—just a handful of tables spilling out onto the pavement—but the enticing aroma of fresh coffee and hot pastries was irresistible. Taking her place in the queue of beautiful people at the counter, Eve wondered why everyone in Florence was so annoyingly good-looking. She had just arrived at the conclusion that Calvin Klein must be doing a casting session nearby, when, from the depths of her bag, she heard the tinny trill of her mobile.

Clamping her purse beneath one arm, she dug beneath the layers of old bus tickets, leaky Biros and odd gloves, triumphantly managing to unearth it before it stopped ringing.

'Lou…!'

'Hi, babe. You tried to call me. Everything OK?'

'Where were you? I needed you!'

'I was here. I'm just not answering my phone in case it's Marissa. I'm supposed to be at death's door, remember? The trouble is I got quite carried away with the story when I rang her to tell her, and now I can't remember all the details. Anyway, never mind that. How's it going?'

At the comfortingly familiar sound of Lou's voice Eve felt the sting of tears at the back of her eyes again. The need to offload was overwhelming.

'It's awful. I've completely messed everything up!'

'God, Eve, you'd better not have. Marissa will strangle me with one of her garish designer scarves if she finds out I made up all that stuff about your past modelling success and your dazzling journalistic career. Tell me it's not that bad.'

Eve swallowed nervously.

'Remember the time you interviewed that Hollywood movie star and spent the whole time giving him your come-get-me smile—then found out afterwards that you had lettuce stuck to your teeth? Well, it's about a thousand times worse than that.'

There was a painful pause. 'I don't believe you. But I'm listening.'

Miserably waiting in the queue, Eve watched the sultry girl behind the counter sprinkle chocolate on the top of a cappuccino. Even the waitresses round here looked like supermodels. She held the phone closer to her mouth and dropped her voice to a whisper.

'I kissed Raphael di Lazaro.'

'Sorry? I can't hear you. For a moment I thought you said you *kissed* Raphael di Lazaro!' Lou laughed heartily, and then stopped abruptly. 'Eve? Oh, God—that *is* what you said, isn't it?'

'Yes.'

'OK. Well, in that case I suppose just one question springs to mind—'

'Fantastic,' Eve whispered, staring straight ahead as the tears gathered in her eyes again. 'He's totally not how you'd expect.'

'*No*, Eve! The question was not, What was it like? The question was, In the name of Aunt Fanny, *why*?'

'Oh. I didn't know who he was at the time.'

'Now, wait a minute. I've known you since we both started university, and in all that time, Eve Middlemiss—four years of prime mating opportunities—I have never once known you to snog a guy without first meeting his mother and practising your new signature for after you're married.'

'That's not fair! I—' Eve hissed vehemently into the phone, but was unable to protest further as she'd reached the front of the queue at the counter. Hastily she ordered a chocolate croissant and a double mochaccino latte, adding sulkily, 'With extra cream.'

'Let's be honest, Eve.' Lou spoke more kindly now. 'You're not the kind of girl who kisses strangers. What's going on?'

'I don't know, Lou. It was bizarre—like fate, or destiny, or something. I saw him… No, we saw *each other*, and it was like something just clicked. It felt right. Inevitable, somehow. Like I didn't have to *do* anything because we both knew it was going to happen. It *had* to happen. And it did. After the show I was talking to this guy and, well, I know it sounds stupid, but *he* arrived and just sort of swept me away…'

'And you went with him? Just like that? Jeez, Eve!'

'I know, I know. It was stupid,' snapped Eve, wedging the phone against her ear as she handed money to the supermodel waitress. 'But at the time I was—I don't know—powerless to resist. You don't know what he's like, Lou… There's a sort of strength about him…'

'There was a "sort of strength" about Adolf Hitler too, but it hardly made him the ideal partner. Look, Eve, I don't like the sound of this. What happened last night was nothing to do with destiny, or love at first sight, or whatever fluffy notions you've got. It's far more likely that he remembers Ellie and recognised you, and intends to keep you quiet. It's not safe. I think you should come home.'

'No.' It came out more forcefully than she had intended, and the waitress gave Eve an odd look as she handed her the paper bag containing the croissant. Tucking it under her chin while she waited for her change, Eve continued in an urgent whisper, 'I'm not giving up now. For two miserable years I've waited to find out something, *anything*, that would bring me closer to understanding what happened to Ellie, and now I'm here and I've finally managed to put a face to the name on that bloody scrap of paper. And suddenly none of it seems to fit, and I don't know what I believe any more, but one thing is certain…' Her voice was rising as her resolve increased and, snatching up her hot chocolate, she swept away from the counter. 'I'm not coming home until I find some answers, whatever that takes. Either I'm going to expose di Lazaro as a sleazy drug pusher, or—'

She paused for a second to take a tentative sip of the froth on the top of her chocolate, closing her eyes in pleasure at the rich, sweet aroma. The next moment she had collided with something hard and unyielding.

A tidal wave of hot chocolate spilled over her hand, and made five small splashes on the front of the white shirt three inches from her nose.

The creased, obviously expensive, instantly recognisable white shirt three inches from her nose.

She gave a tiny whimper of distress.

'What? Eve? *Eve?*'

In one swift movement Raphael Di Lazaro had relieved her of the dripping paper cup and extracted her mobile phone from between her ear and her shoulder. His face was dangerously calm as he spoke into it, but his eyes glittered with anger.

'I'm afraid your friend seems to be momentarily lost for words, but let me reassure you that she's perfectly all right.'

Eve's cheek burned where his fingertips had brushed it, and she felt dizzy as she caught a brief hint of the scent of his skin. Vaguely, from the depths of her despair, she could make out the alarm in Lou's voice at the other end of the phone.

'Thank goodness for that. What happened?'

'It's nothing. Just a little accident with some hot chocolate. Tell me, is she always this clumsy?'

Eve heard Lou laugh, relaxing in the warmth of that low, impossibly sexy voice. Traitor. She wouldn't be so amused if she knew who she was talking to.

'Is she wearing her glasses?'

Raphael's chilly gaze flickered over Eve's face. 'No.'

'Oh, she's hopeless. Really, she shouldn't be allowed out on her own.'

'I couldn't agree more, *signorina*.'

Furious, Eve snatched the phone back. 'OK, Lou—lovely to talk to you. But you'd better go and sleep it off now. And remember—no more vodka at breakfast time.'

Snapping the phone shut with grim satisfaction before Lou could protest, Eve steeled herself to look up at Raphael. Even though he still wore that careful, guarded, blank expression, there was no mistaking the hostility it masked.

'So, Signorina Middlemiss…' He paused, enunciating each word very carefully, as if trying not to lose control of his temper. 'Perhaps you'd like to tell me exactly what you think you're doing?'

Her chin shot up in defiance. 'It was an accident—hardly anything to make a fuss about. I'm sure it'll wash out—'

His voice cut through her like the lash of a whip. 'Don't be childish. You know perfectly well what I'm talking about. What were the words you used? Sleazy drug pusher? I hardly think that's the sort of thing the readers of *Glitterati* want to hear about.'

The searing contempt in his tone was like acid on an open

wound. But even more painful was the realisation that Lou's theory might be right.

'So you do know who I am? Surprise, surprise. I might have known that men like you have spies everywhere.'

He raised a hand. For a crazy, delicious, dizzying split second she thought he was going to pull her into his arms and kiss her, as he had done last night. She was horrified at the disappointment that sliced into her as his fingers merely brushed the press ID badge clipped to the front of her scoop-necked T-shirt.

'"Eve Middlemiss. Fashion Assistant. Glitterati",' he read softly, his beautiful mouth curving into a cruel half-smile. 'One hardly has to have a sophisticated intelligence network to find these things out. Five minutes ago I knew almost nothing about you, *signorina*, but a picture is rapidly emerging.'

'Oh, yes? What picture?'

Damn. Only a complete simpleton would walk into that one. She could smell the sandalwood maleness of him, and it was having a catastrophic effect on her ability to think rationally.

'That of a silly, inexperienced journalist on a low-rent publication who is getting involved in things that are completely over her pretty blonde head.'

Well, she had asked.

He took a step back, making Eve suddenly aware of how close together they had been standing, and how the sheer nearness of him had held her spellbound. With space to breathe, the impact of his words suddenly hit her with all the force of a prizefighter's punch.

'You patronising male chauvinist *pig*! How dare you pass judgement on me?'

He had taken something out of his pocket and was leaning on one of the pavement tables, writing.

'Do you really want me to answer that?' he drawled, without looking up. 'Even your friend is of the opinion that you shouldn't be out on your own.'

'My *friend* was *joking*,' Eve hissed though gritted teeth. 'To understand that you need something called a sense of humour.'

Straightening up, Raphael leaned his elegant slim-hipped frame against the table and looked at her for a moment through narrowed eyes. Then, folding his arms in an attitude of complete ease, he began to talk in a swift stream of Italian. His voice was husky and low, almost caressing in its intimacy, and the words flowed over her like warm rain, making her skin tingle and the hairs stand up on the nape of her neck. For a blissful moment she felt an echo of the drenching pleasure that she'd experienced last night in his arms.

And then she realised he'd stopped speaking and was looking at her questioningly. 'So?'

Bewildered, mesmerised, she faltered and shook her head confusedly. 'I… Sorry, I…'

He had the same unruffled stillness about him as a panther reclining in the savannah: a dangerous watchfulness that, even though he was relaxed, made him look as if he could pounce at any moment.

'So. You don't speak the language. You don't know what you're getting into. You're out of your depth. Go home.'

'Are you threatening me?'

He sighed, and suddenly looked very tired. Noticing it, Eve felt again that irrational, treacherous pull inside, and her fingertips burned with the need to touch him.

'No, I'm warning you to be sensible.' He shook his head wearily. 'Please take this. I don't know how much you were hoping to earn from your little "scoop", but I think twenty thousand should more than cover it—don't you?'

'What?' she gasped, her momentary weakness evaporating in a fresh blast of fury. 'You're offering me twenty thousand euros to shut up and go home like a good girl?'

He gave her a sardonic smile. 'You underestimate my generosity. I'm offering you twenty thousand pounds.'

Speechless with shock, she glared at him for a long moment as tears pricked behind her eyes and her breath caught in her throat, choking the words that swirled around her head. *My sister's life was worth more than that!*

A taxi was speeding towards them, and she ran forward to hail it. But her tears and the forgotten glasses, combined with her desperate need to get away from him, made her clumsy. There was a screech of brakes and a blaring of horns as the taxi swerved to avoid her. In a split second Raphael was beside her, grasping her arms and pulling her back onto the pavement.

'*Voi ragazza piccola stupid,*' he spat. 'You stupid little child! You could have been killed!' He was still gripping her arm, and the icy cool of a few moments ago had been replaced with blistering fury. 'Do you not even know that in Florence you don't flag down taxis as you do in London? *Dio*, Eve!'

Ashen-faced, and with tears of humiliation and defeat coursing down her face, she looked up at him. 'Let me go. Please.'

She was still trembling. From shock, and maybe a little from the way he'd said her name, which on his lips sounded like Eva. But also from the realisation that he'd just jumped out into the road to save her life.

He did as she asked, stepping abruptly back as if she were the carrier of a contagious disease. With deliberate calm she turned back towards the road and held out her arm as a taxi came towards her. *Please, God, let this one stop. Please show Raphael di Lazaro, who clearly thinks he's your second-in-command, that he doesn't have to get everything right all of the time…*

She could have kissed the driver as he pulled up alongside her. She turned to Raphael, bravely trying to muster a smile through her tears.

'You see! I'm perfectly capable of—'

She gasped as he reached towards her and brushed his thumb across her lips in a gesture of perfect sensual intimacy. Her eyelids fluttered closed in blissful submission as, for a fraction of a second, she let her lips press against his firm flesh, feeling his warmth, tasting the salt-sweetness of him, unable to stop the cascade of heat that tumbled through her.

Her eyes flew to his, but found them cold and mocking.

'Froth. You were saying?'

His mouth curled into that cruel half-smile as he opened the door for her, then leaned over to speak to the driver. He took a fat wad of notes from his pocket and handed them over.

Furiously, she slammed the door and wiped her hand over her mouth, as much to dispel the feel of his thumb upon her lips as to remove any lingering traces of froth.

'What did he say to you?' she asked the driver as he pulled out into the stream of traffic.

'He ask me how much to airport. Is that where we go?'

'No! Take me to my hotel, please.'

'You sure, *signorina*? The *signore*, he pay me much money to go to airport.'

'I'm sure.'

It was a lie. Right now she would have done anything to skip the perfume launch, get on a plane home and never hear the word Lazaro again.

CHAPTER THREE

EVE wouldn't have thought it possible to be sitting in a gold limousine *en route* to a fearsomely exclusive A-list fashion event and have that horrible sick-in-the-stomach feeling she got on the way to the dentist.

On the seat opposite, Sienna stretched out her phenomenally long legs and sighed theatrically into her mobile. She'd spent the entire journey on her phone to either her agent or her film star boyfriend, and although Eve knew she should have been listening carefully for material to use in the article, her mind kept drifting back to her own problems.

Which was hardly surprising. Given the scale of them.

On paper all the evidence was falling neatly into place, and the fact that three hours ago Raphael di Lazaro had offered her more money to do nothing than Professor Swanson paid her for a year of hard work and long hours was another reason to believe in his guilt. And yet…

And yet the man she had glimpsed beneath that chilly, reserved veneer was neither evil nor corrupt. He had integrity. And he had it in spades.

Eve rested her forehead against the limousine window and shut her eyes, delicately probing the painful possibility that she was mistaking Raphael di Lazaro's undoubted good-looks and dazzling sex appeal for something more meaningful. A year or so ago, before she'd landed the job on the *Glitterati* fashion desk, Lou had done an article on women who fell in love with prisoners on Death Row. Over a bottle or two of cheap red in a wine bar in Oxford, Eve and Lou had discussed this phenomenon, snorting in contemptuous pity at the idea that anyone could let their heart rule their head in such a spectacularly foolish way.

Was she similarly deluded?

But she hadn't imagined the sheer strength that had held her and guided her as she'd walked down the catwalk just as surely as if his arms had been around her. Or the haunted need that lay just behind the expressionless public mask. Or the bone-deep, instinctive courage that would make him step out and grab her from the path of an oncoming car...

No! She banged her head softly but emphatically against the glass, as if to knock the sense back into it once and for all. The facts spoke for themselves. His name was on that paper, right above where it said *drugs*. He had followed her after the press conference and tried to buy her off.

Rational, intellectual Eve pressed her fingers to her temples and took a steadying breath. No matter what her heart was saying, her head knew perfectly well that he was still the most likely suspect. She had come to find answers, and she was still determined to do that. She just hadn't anticipated how painful it was going to be.

Sighing, she dragged her attention back to Sienna, who was thoughtfully examining a glossy acrylic nail. 'Will it involve taking my clothes off?' she was saying, still on her mobile— though whether it was to the agent or the boyfriend, Eve couldn't be sure. The glamorous model looked sensational, in spray-on white trousers and a diaphanous gold chiffon top that fell in soft, semi-transparent folds from a gold beaded choker at the neck. Only Eve would know that it had taken half an hour to construct her perfect cleavage with tape, and that much of the luxuriant black hair was, in fact, nylon extensions.

Nothing is as it seems on the surface, Eve thought bitterly.

They were close enough now to be able to see celebrities emerging from cars like gilded butterflies from their chrysalises. Everyone was faithfully sticking to the theme, and from the women's barely-there dresses to the men's over-the-top tailoring and salon tans the red carpet was transformed into a sea of gold.

Eve's own wardrobe was a little light on glitz, so Sienna had offered to lend her something from her own seemingly endless supply of clothes. It had been a kind offer but, coming as it had from a six-foot supermodel with a chest as flat as an ironing board, not remotely helpful. In the end Eve had been forced to resort to her faithful old jeans and jewelled Indian flip-flops, teamed with the only vaguely metallic-coloured thing she owned—a little vintage lace-trimmed camisole top from the 1930s, its cream silk darkened with age to a deep biscuit gold. In spite of the heat she'd fully intended to throw a jacket over the top, but Sienna had absolutely forbidden it, frogmarching her from the room without listening to her cries of protest.

'Of course you don't look like a hooker! This, in case you hadn't noticed, is *the look* of this summer. Honestly, Eve, I thought you were supposed to be a fashion journalist!'

Good point. She'd allowed herself to get so preoccupied with Raphael Di Lazaro she'd almost forgotten.

The car glided to a halt and Sienna gracefully unfolded her long limbs and stepped out. Waiting nervously for the paparazzi storm that heralded Sienna's arrival to subside before she stepped out of the safety of the limousine herself, Eve tried to arrange her face into a confident smile, but found her efforts considerably hampered by the sticky gold lipgloss Sienna had persuaded her to wear.

Drifts of sand specially imported from Egypt edged the red carpet and rose in mini-dunes at the entrance to the store, which was flanked with two enormous statues of the sphinx. But even

this display of extravagant kitsch didn't prepare Eve for the
spectacle that awaited them inside.

'What do you think?' yelled Sienna above the din, gesturing
around them. 'Didn't I tell you the Lazaro parties are always wild?'

'It's unreal!' said Eve, looking round. Against a backdrop of
gilded palm trees and faux-pyramids, A-list celebrities were
being sprayed with *Golden* by scantily clad 'Egyptian' slave-
girls, in Cleopatra-style wigs and scarlet lipstick. The air was
heavy with the perfume, which smelt like a mixture of fruit salad
and ozone.

In the centre of the floor a vast three-tiered fountain, topped
by Tutankhamen's head, gushed champagne. A youth in a loin-
cloth appeared beside them, proffering a plate of canapés.
Forbidden by Sienna from wearing her glasses, Eve peered short-
sightedly at them.

'What on earth are they?'

'South Sea tiger prawns in a vodka marinade, finished with
eighteen-carat-gold leaf,' said the youth.

'Gold leaf?' echoed Eve faintly.

Sienna giggled. 'No, thanks. I'm catching a plane this
evening. Don't want to set off the metal detectors. Come and get
a drink,' she shouted to Eve, disappearing into the seething mass
of exotically dressed celebrities.

It was impossible to squeeze through the crowd around the
champagne fountain. Eve found herself alone on the fringes,
craning above a hundred glossy, seriously high-maintenance
heads to see where Sienna had gone.

Suddenly an arm snaked round her waist from behind. She
whirled round to look into the laughing bloodshot eyes of the
man from the retrospective. The man Raphael had been so keen
to steal her away from.

'We meet again, *angel*. I see you standing here all alone, and
I wonder how my brother could be so careless as to leave you
unattended in the midst of such...' he looked around with a

wolfish grin '...debauchery. You are like a beautiful rose
blooming in a vase of artificial flowers.' His eyes moved lazily
up and down her body for a moment, while a slow smile spread
across his face.

'You're Raphael's brother?'

'*Si*. Half-brother. Though twice as charming. Luca di Lazaro.'

She took the hand he extended towards her. 'Eve Middlemiss.'

'Beautiful,' he murmured, looking very pleased about something and holding onto her hand for far longer than was necessary. 'And where is Raphael?'

'I'm not sure.' Eve managed a sort of grim smile, in spite of
the lipgloss. 'But I'd like to find him.'

'Don't rush off, *bella*. Let me get you a drink. Is very hot in
here, no? We need a passionfruit daiquiri!'

'I don't really…'

'Don't worry, *bambino*,' he soothed, laying a hot hand on her
bare shoulder. 'It has hardly any alcohol. You'll love it. Trust me.'

In his father's private office on the top floor, Raphael held out
the remote control, flicking from one CCTV image to another.
Antonio had invested in the very best technology available to
ensure that the Lazaro security system was state-of-the-art.
Cameras were placed in strategic positions on each of the store's
three floors, and also covered a large area of the street outside,
and the information they generated was closely monitored by a
highly trained team.

Raphael had considered briefing them on the necessity of
keeping close tabs on Luca, but decided against it. The fewer
people who knew about the investigation into his brother's drug
dealing the better. This was one job he could not entrust to
anyone else, and if Luca made one suspicious move, or got too
close to anyone, Raphael would be watching.

His eyes were gritty and his whole body ached with fatigue.
After the ordeal of the press conference he had planned to return

to his apartment for a few hours of much-needed sleep, but the encounter with Eve Middlemiss had put paid to that.

How much did she know?

His first thought when he'd seen her at the press conference was that she was a scheming, unscrupulous journalist who'd got the little-girl-lost act down to award-winning standard. Now he wasn't so sure. Her naïvety…her total bloody cluelessness…was way too realistic to be put on. And yet somehow she knew enough to blow an international drugs investigation sky-high.

He sighed and passed his hands briefly over his face. The situation with Luca was volatile enough without having an airhead blonde journalist set on writing some half-witted exposé charging around like a bull in a china shop.

No, that was all wrong. Not a bull… Something far more dangerously delicate than that. A fawn, perhaps. She was like a fawn careering through a minefield. The memory of her wide, frightened eyes as she'd stepped in front of the taxi came back to him, followed swiftly by the feel of the soft swell of her breast beneath her T-shirt as he'd pulled her back.

He shifted uncomfortably in his chair as a flicker of desire licked though him, and turned his attention abruptly back to the CCTV monitor. It didn't really matter what metaphor you chose. The fact remained that Eve Middlemiss was a problem. A complication he could well do without.

His mouth set in a grim line of contempt as he studied the screen. The scene it showed was like a nightmarish cross between a third-rate porn movie and a big-budget blockbuster. A very high-profile footballer's wife and an Oscar-tipped Hollywood starlet were cavorting in the champagne fountain as a crowd of onlookers clapped and cheered. Raphael's gaze skimmed dismissively over them, coming to rest instead on the knot of people around the fountain.

Only the tension in his broad shoulders betrayed the strength of his ruthlessly controlled emotion as he located Luca.

Raphael didn't flinch, but the light from the screen showed the sudden shuttered stillness of his face as he watched his brother pick a strand of hair from the slickly glossed lips of Eve Middlemiss. She was looking up at Luca trustingly, her lips pouting and slightly parted, and once he had moved the stray hair, with much careful concern, she tentatively pressed them together. It was a movement that was curiously childlike, but at the same time piercingly erotic.

Gripping the remote control, Raphael saw his knuckles show bone-white through the suntanned skin of his hands. Dimly, as if from a great distance, he was aware of the pounding blood in his ears. He was a man who lived on his instincts, whose survival in the volatile Columbian underworld of drugs gangs and hired killers had depended on his ability to make split-second decisions. Every nerve and fibre of his being was telling him to go down and drag Eve Middlemiss away from Luca.

Now.

But of course it was out of the question. He pulled a hand across his stinging eyes, concentrating on thinking rationally. He'd tried to warn her. She wouldn't listen. She was, contrary to appearances, a grown-up, for goodness' sake. If she chose to play Russian Roulette with the devil all he could do was try to anticipate when the gun was going to go off.

He checked his watch. The party would last maybe two hours—that was about the maximum length of a celebrity's attention span. Leaning back in his chair, he resigned himself to his vigil.

All sense of time was suspended as he switched into professional mode and operated on automatic pilot. With ice-cold detachment he followed Eve and Luca's progress though the party, watching every gesture, tracking every drink, noting every movement. Throughout he remained motionless, unblinking and completely impassive.

Until the moment Luca put his jacket around Eve's bare shoulders and drew her, swaying slightly, towards the exit.

And then, letting out a stream of Italian expletives, Raphael was across the room and out of the door in seconds.

CHAPTER FOUR

IT WAS rush hour.

Sitting in the stream of slow-moving traffic, Raphael swore quietly under his breath. His hunch was that Luca would be taking Eve to the exclusive nightclub where the Lazaro party would continue into the small hours—one of Luca's favourite haunts. Raphael wondered how many girls had taken the first steps on the road to addiction hell in its opulent darkness.

He glanced at his watch. The traffic ahead was barely moving, and it had been just over ten minutes since he'd watched them leave.

Taking an abrupt right turn into a narrow sidestreet marked Senso Vietato—No Entry—he accelerated through the dustbins and empty cardboard boxes.

The backstreets ran parallel to the wide open space of a *piazza*, and Raphael weighed up the possibility of cutting right across it. On one hand it would get him to where he needed to be in half the time, on the other he was much more likely to attract the attention of the *polizia* and be pulled over. And what would happen to Eve then?

She would just be one more in the countless number of girls whose lives Luca had wrecked. Only this time Raphael would alert his contacts in the drug squad and make sure that they were onto him. Once they had caught Luca in the act, as it were, they would have the evidence they needed to make an arrest, and, since Luca was certainly not the kind of honourable person who would keep the names of his associates to himself, he would bring the whole morally bankrupt lot of them down with him.

It was an appealing thought.

One more girl. Surely it was a price worth paying? He should just pick up his mobile and dial the contact number he'd been given. They could have a team of undercover officers at the nightclub in no time.

In his head it was all so obvious.

But somewhere deep inside him something was telling him that Eve Middlemiss wasn't just one more girl. Raphael Di Lazaro was far too accustomed to burying his emotions to consider the possibility that it might be his heart.

As she walked arm-in-arm with Luca along the edge of the *piazza*, Eve peered into the little gold rope-handled carrier she had been given as they left the party and gave a little skip of delight. It wasn't just the absence of her glasses that was making the whole business of focusing the teeniest bit difficult, but she could have sworn that the writing on the little box which nestled beside the miniature bottle of *Golden* said 'Tiffany'.

'Ooh, Luca—look!' She beamed, extracting it from layers of tissue. 'Grown-up jewellery!'

The next moment there was a screech of tyres as a dark blue sports car appeared from one of the narrow side-streets and skidded to a halt inches away from them. Slamming a fist down on the bonnet, Luca hurled a stream of abuse at the driver.

'*Idiota!* Are you blind? Can you not read? It's a pedestrian zone, you—'

He stopped and gave a snarl of fury as the car door opened and Raphael got out. His face was deathly pale but his eyes blazed.

'Don't you ever give up, Luca?'

The malice in Luca's voice made Eve shudder. 'Lighten up,

for once in your miserable life, Raphael. When are you going to see that you can't just treat women like inconvenient items of luggage, and abandon them whenever it suits you? This little beauty was all alone so I looked after her, kept her amused. You should be grateful!'

'Looked after her? *Benedetta Maria.*' Raphael shook his head helplessly and turned to Eve, addressing her with icy calm. 'Can you not find a way to amuse yourself that doesn't involve a near death experience?'

'Excuse *me*?'

'Get in the car. I'm taking you home.'

Eve's heart, having skipped a beat somewhere, was now crashing about at twice its normal speed. Shocked into speech-lessness, she shook her head in disbelief.

'I… You…' she spluttered. 'You are *unbelievable*! All of a sudden it's *my fault* for being in the way when *you* were driving like a complete madman in a pedestrian zone!'

Fists clenched into balls of frustration, Raphael cursed quietly and swung away while he regained his composure. When he turned back to address her his tone was grave, and without her glasses she completely missed the small, rueful smile that ac-companied his words.

'Actually, it *was* your fault—yes.'

Eve saw red. '*Of course*! No—you're absolutely right! Naturally it was up to me to make sure I was not in the way of your testosterone-fuelled display of macho prowess. My fault entirely. But then I'm just a silly, inexperienced journalist on a low-rent publication,' she yelled, sarcastically echoing his words of that morning. 'It's completely over my little blonde head to walk safely along the street. I'm not fit—'

She didn't get any further. Without warning he reached out and slipped a hand beneath the silky fall of hair at the back of her neck and drew her mouth to his. The gentle pressure of his lips sent a surge of hot, liquid need crashing through her, driving out every logical thought and rational argument and replacing it with one thought, one desire.

Instinctively her body curved into his, and Luca's jacket slipped from her shoulders and fell to the ground. Raphael's tongue teased the sensitive softness of her mouth, and a small whimper of longing escaped her as his lips moved from hers to kiss the secret place beneath her ear.

She was lost, drowning in fathomless depths of ecstasy from which she had no wish ever to be rescued. Behind her closed eyelids the darkness swirled and formed itself into a thousand erotic images as the potent cocktail of four passionfruit daiquiris, one shot of adrenaline and a kick of one-hundred-percent pure longing went straight to her head. And her knees. And her…

His breath was warm against her neck as he murmured, 'Sorry. *I'm sorry*—OK? Come with me. Now.'

She heard him open the car door and her eyelids fluttered open, the daylight intruding starkly on her own dark world of fantasy. Raphael wasn't staring seductively into her eyes, but looking over her shoulder to where Luca still stood, watching them as he spoke quietly into his mobile phone.

'Come on. Into the car.'

Dumbly she slid into the low passenger seat and watched him stride grimly round to the other side of the car. The tenderness of a few moments before had evaporated, replaced by cold efficiency. A shiver ran through her as she realised the kiss had been nothing more than a tactic to get her into the car.

As he slipped sinuously into the driver's seat she swallowed nervously and shrank away from him, stunned by the change in him. God, what was she doing? How had she let herself be manipulated so easily? Her hand crept towards the door, but stopped before it reached the handle.

No. This was what she wanted.

She'd decided that she wasn't going back to England until she'd got the evidence she needed to convict him or clear him.

And she wasn't going to find that alone in a hotel room. She might not have exactly planned this little turn of events, but rum-fuelled logic and Dutch courage told her it was actually quite a stroke of luck.

Of course that was the reason she felt compelled to stay. It was nothing whatsoever to do with the fact that her fingers itched with the insane compulsion to touch the long, muscular thigh next to hers, to entwine themselves in his ruffled black hair, smoothing back the lock that fell over his face before…

Get over it! Biting her lip to prevent it trembling, she shrank further away from him, ashamed and afraid of the blatant longing that thrummed painfully inside her.

As he started the ignition with a deafening roar Raphael glanced sideways at her, taking in the quivering lip and huge, frightened eyes. A flash of irritation swept through him.

He was used to issuing orders and having them obeyed, but something had warned him that Eve Middlemiss would go out of her way to do the opposite of what she was told. Kissing her had been the only way of getting her into the car and away from Luca. He'd had no choice, he reassured himself.

So why did he feel like some kind of monster all of a sudden? Because he'd enjoyed kissing her? This was the twenty-first century—surely he could kiss someone without feeling as if he was guilty of some kind of violation? Especially when his motivation was purely her own good.

Purely? a little voice in his head taunted, forcing him to confront the reason for his guilt. Perhaps not. He had kissed her because he didn't have time to argue with her, and because standing there, with her green eyes flashing fire and brimstone, she had been almost impossible to resist. And that was the thing that irked him. He wanted her, and for a whole host of very good reasons he didn't *want* to want her.

Beside him, Eve surreptitiously checked in her bag. At least she had her phone. And her pink penknife.

It had been a birthday present from Lou: a joke, because it contained all the necessary tools for survival—a nail file, a miniature mirror, and most importantly a corkscrew. There was a blade on there too, but it remained stiff from lack of use—unlike the corkscrew—and Eve doubted whether she could get it out quickly enough in a moment of crisis. Oh, well, in that case she would just have to *screw* his brains out...

She let out a gurgle of laughter.

Raphael threw her a sharp glance.

'Something amusing?'

'Yes, I...' But the mental image, conjured by accident or Freudian design, wouldn't leave her. The laughter died on her lips as another wave of lust swept through her with the ruthless inevitability of a tidal-bore. She turned her face to look out of the window.

'Where are you staying?'

'Well, as of this afternoon, nowhere,' she muttered, trying to redirect her thoughts. 'I checked out of the hotel this morning.'

Raphael gritted his teeth. 'So what were you going to do?'

'Luca very kindly offered me a bed—no strings—and if it hadn't been for this stupid pretence that we're in—' She had been about to say *in love* but stumbled on the words and changed it at the last minute. 'Involved, I would be taking him up on it.'

No strings? Knowing Luca, it would be chains and handcuffs instead. How could she be so trusting? Exasperated, Raphael pushed his hair back from his forehead and shot her a sideways glance. Sitting with the glossy Lazaro goody bag clasped in her hands, twisting its silken rope handle around one slender finger, she looked incredibly young and frighteningly vulnerable. The thought of her on the streets or, much worse, in Luca's lair made him feel dizzy. He sucked in a breath and tried to keep his voice even.

'Stay with me.' It came out as a harsh rasp. What was the matter with him? He wouldn't blame her for refusing.

For a second she was very still, then she turned and gave him a small, brave smile.

'Really? Thanks.'

It was easy to see which of the narrow Florentine townhouses was Raphael's. It was the one with the crowd of paparazzi outside.

'Damn,' growled Raphael, accelerating past them. 'Quick. Get down.'

A shout went up from the pavement as one of the journalists spotted the car and gave chase. Eve caught a fleeting glimpse of the blonde from the press conference before Raphael's hand clasped the back of her neck and pulled her head down.

Her cheek was pressed against the hardness of his thigh, and she could feel his muscles flexing as he changed up a gear. His arm covered her, the scent of him filled her head, and the world outside the window was upside down.

'Wh-what are you doing?'

'Unless you want your picture all over the gossip columns, stay there,' he hissed. 'We have some bloody fool on a motor-bike following us.'

She closed her eyes and breathed him in, feeling oddly safe and protected, like when she was a child and she and Ellie would curl up together on the back seat on the way back from some concert or gala performance in which their mother had been singing. The denim beneath her cheek had been washed to faded softness, and it smelled clean and comforting, and the rocking motion of the car as Raphael wove expertly through the back-streets soothed her. Really, that passionfruit whatever had been very nice, but it had made her feel quite sleepy…

Negotiating a labyrinthine path through the ancient narrow streets around the Piazza della Signoria, Raphael tried to keep his mind on the paparazzo motorcyclist and off the tousled golden head in his lap.

Impossible.

He could feel the warmth of her breath against his thigh, in a place where the caress of a woman's breath should mean one thing and one thing only…

Don't go there! Gripping the steering wheel, he cast around desperately for something deeply boring and unerotic to think about, to counter the inevitable effect she was having on him. Railway timetables. Exchange rates. International time zones.

Just when he feared his self-control might snap, he realised the motorcyclist was no longer on his tail. Glancing round to make sure he was nowhere to be seen, Raphael let out an exhalation of relief.

'It's OK—you can get up now.'

She shifted slightly, bringing her hand up to her face and letting it come to rest on his knee, the fingers curling delicately upwards. Hardly daring to breathe, Raphael gently brushed the hair off her face, knowing already what he would find.

Dark lashes swept down over flushed cheeks, mouth pressed into a perfect cupid's bow—she was asleep.

A sharp kick of desire knocked the air from his lungs and an involuntary moan from his lips. The traffic in front of him slowed to a near standstill and, waiting in the queue, he took both hands off the steering wheel and thrust them savagely through his hair, as if in an effort to prevent himself from touching her.

She looked like a child, she behaved like a rebellious teenager, she exasperated him beyond measure and she was causing him an inordinate amount of trouble. But at that moment he wanted Eve Middlemiss so much he couldn't think straight.

She awoke as he turned the engine off. Struggling to sit up, she widened her eyes with horror as she realised where she was.

'Oh…oh, no…What did I…?'

Raphael's face was completely expressionless. 'You fell asleep.'

She gave a little moan of distress. 'Sorry. I can't think what came over me.'

'I can,' he said sardonically. 'At least four disgusting rum-based cocktails, courtesy of my dear half-brother.'

'Rum?' she whimpered. 'But he said they were almost non-alcoholic!'

'That figures,' said Raphael bitterly, getting out of the car.

Eve followed. 'Where are we?' she asked, looking up at the imposing façade of the building with a mixture of anxiety and awe. Four storeys of mellow golden stone towered above her, graced by delicate wrought-iron balconies at the long first- and second-floor windows. A double flight of stone steps led to the front door.

'My father's house,' he replied curtly.

'Won't he mind?' Eve followed him, trying not to gaze too hungrily on the broad shoulders beneath the cornflower-blue linen shirt. She still felt slow with sleep, and dazed by conflicting emotions. If he was a potential drug-pushing sadist, why did she just want to curl up on his knee again?

Over his shoulder, he shot her a stony look. 'I realise that the finer points of this morning's press conference may have gone over your head, Eve, but I thought that even you had managed to follow the general gist. Antonio is in hospital. But,' he continued, opening the door into a beautifully proportioned domed hallway, 'he has a housekeeper who will be only too glad to have someone to fuss over while he is away.'

Eve stopped in the middle of the shining marble floor and looked around her. It was like stepping onto the set of one of the glamorous 1950s movies her mother had loved so much. In front of her a staircase with an ornately embellished wrought-iron balustrade rose to a gallery above, and on the ceiling cherubs cavorted around ample-figured goddesses holding strategically-placed garlands.

She was so busy taking it all in that at first she didn't notice a stout woman with greying hair scraped into a bun appear in the doorway at the end of the hall.

'Raphael!'

'*Ciao*, Fiora. *Come stai?*'

He stepped forward to embrace her, and they talked in rapid Italian for a minute or two before Eve became aware that they had both turned to look at her. Raphael switched back into English for her benefit.

'Eve, this is Fiora—my father's invaluable, irreplaceable housekeeper.'

Eve smiled shyly under the older woman's curious scrutiny, and wondered what Raphael had said about her.

'Fiora doesn't speak much English, I'm afraid, but I'm sure the two of you will manage to get along.' Picking up his keys from a marble-topped console table, he began to walk back towards the door.

Eve was assailed by sudden panic. He couldn't mean to just leave her here—could he?

'Raphael…'

He turned, one dark eyebrow raised in silent question as his eyes met hers. She wanted to run to him and feel the reassuring strength of his arms around her, to beg him not to leave her, to take her with him, but she was rooted to the spot and the words wouldn't come.

'Don't go,' she managed huskily, feeling a deep blush suffuse her cheeks.

For a second she thought she saw the ghost of a smile at the corner of his mouth before he turned away and strode towards the door.

'I'm just going to collect your things from the hotel,' he said. 'I'm sure you'll be OK with Fiora for half an hour.'

Scarlet with humiliation, Eve followed Fiora up the wide staircase.

CHAPTER FIVE

Where on earth had that come from?

Trailing despondently behind Fiora, Eve gritted her teeth and kept her eyes fixed on the floor. *Don't go…*she heard herself saying, the words sounding pathetically girly and weak as they echoed around her head. What the hell had come over her? The man had just virtually kidnapped her, and she was practically falling over herself to thank him. It would be funny if it wasn't quite so appalling.

Well, one thing was certain. She wouldn't be caught off guard again.

Make that two things. She wouldn't be touching another passionfruit daiquiri any time soon either.

Fiora came to a halt outside one of the doors along the impossibly grand corridor and pushed it open, standing aside to let Eve go through.

Entering hesitantly, she had to stop herself from gasping out loud.

The room was like something out of a fairy tale. In its centre stood a huge bed, dressed in beautiful vintage linen and topped with an antique gilded corona from which acres of white muslin were romantically draped. A small sofa and two dainty chairs upholstered in soft duck-egg blue linen were arranged around a low table on which a tray with a coffee pot and two elegant china espresso cups were laid.

It made the plush hotel she'd been staying in look like a youth hostel.

Resisting the urge to throw herself onto the bed and nestle into the pile of silk cushions Eve walked over to one of the floor-length windows and found herself looking out over a walled garden at the back of the villa. The windows opened onto a small terrace, from which one could enjoy the delicate fragrance of lilies and orange blossom that drifted up from the terraced garden below.

Behind her, humming quietly, Fiora bustled about, plumping up pillows and carefully moving some of the silk cushions. Then she disappeared into an adjoining room, which Eve guessed was an *en-suite* bathroom. A moment later she heard the sound of running water.

Returning to collect an armful of thick, snowy towels from the armoire, Fiora caught sight of Eve's bewildered expression. The humming stopped and her face creased into lines of kindness.

'*Bagno*… Bath?'

'Thank you, but…'

'Signor Raphael—he say you…*molto stanco*…?'

Eve gave a little cry of fury. 'How dare he? Anyway,' she muttered sulkily, 'it's not my fault. It's that horrible perfume from the launch.'

Fiora looked shocked, then upset. 'Sorry, *signorina…molto stanco*…how you say?' She put her head to one side and closed her eyes.

'Asleep?' suggested Eve doubtfully.

'*Si!* He say you very sleepy! He say you rest, but I think maybe after *bagno* you feel better?'

Feeling suddenly foolish and ungrateful, Eve managed a smile. 'Yes. Thank you, Fiora. You are very kind.'

Fiora dismissed her words with a wave of her hand. '*Per niente. A dopo, signorina.*'

When the door had closed quietly behind her, Eve pressed her burning cheek against the cool windowpane. The temptation to climb down the balcony and escape over the garden wall was suddenly pretty strong.

OK, so—as any one of her friends would testify—she was hardly a winner in the ice-cool grace and sophistication stakes, but she wasn't usually so totally inept. What was it about Raphael Di Lazaro that had turned her into a dizzy blonde with an IQ lower than her bra size and a head full of marshmallow?

She had a degree from a top British university, for crying out loud, a good job and a clean driving licence. And yet in the twenty-four hours since she'd laid eyes on Raphael di Lazaro she had been behaving like a gawky schoolgirl on her first foreign exchange visit.

If she couldn't snap out of it and take control of the situation she might as well go home now.

The fact that he was horribly attractive was inconvenient, but she was an intelligent and mature woman, and it wasn't as if she'd never seen a good-looking male before. Admittedly the Department of Renaissance Poetry wasn't exactly heaving with them, but that was no excuse for dissolving into a puddle of hormones every time Raphael Di Lazaro glanced at her.

No. The problem wasn't what he looked like, it was the man himself.

Last night when he had kissed her she had had a tantalising insight into what she believed was the real man beneath that iron self-control and breathtaking arrogance. And the real Raphael wasn't anything like the monster she had come here expecting to find.

Suddenly the spark of an idea flickered into life in her head, momentarily illuminating her gloomy thoughts. Reflected in the glass of the windowpane her eyes were wide and dark as her mind raced over the plan that was forming there.

If she was going to find out whether he was capable of the crime she suspected him of, she needed to see that side of him again. More closely. Flirt with him. Seduce him. Peel away the layers until the man she had glimpsed last night was naked before her. Then she'd see who he really was.

She wandered thoughtfully over to her bag and slipped a little photograph of herself and Ellie out of her purse. In it she was sitting down, a small smile on her face. Ellie stood behind her, her arms wrapped around Eve's shoulders, her head thrown back in laughter. Looking at it now, what struck Eve more forcefully than ever before was not how similar they looked, but how different had been their whole approach to life. She had always prided herself on her sense and steadiness, disapproving of Ellie's total abandonment and limitless capacity for fun. Suddenly she saw how blinkered she'd been, and deep inside her she felt the stirrings of anticipation. It was time to live a little more dangerously.

Operation Seduction started here. Make or break.

A shiver rippled through her and she realised that for the first time since she had left England she was properly frightened.

Partly because of what she might find.

But mainly because of what she might lose in the process.

Raphael put down the bag and hesitated before knocking quietly on the door to Eve's room.

He had intended to ask Fiora to bring Eve's things up to her, but had found her up to her elbows in flour in the kitchen. Had he imagined the twinkle in her dark eyes as she had given him a tall glass of iced elderflower cordial to take up to Eve, along with instructions to tell her that dinner was almost ready?

It would have been petty and ungracious to refuse. He had brought Eve here, after all.

He pressed his ear to the heavy wood and knocked again. This time, very faintly, he heard Eve call out—something which he couldn't be sure was 'come in', but definitely wasn't angry enough to be 'go away'—or worse.

Entering her room, he was immediately hit by the delicate, dizzying floral scent of Lazaro perfume. The concealed sound system was playing the bit from *Madame Butterfly* to which Eve had walked down the runway at the retrospective, but the room was empty.

From through the open door of the bathroom came the un-mistakable trickle of water.

She was in the bath.

Closing her eyes, Eve sank back beneath the bubbles and felt all the stress of the day evaporate.

The first stars were beginning to appear in the hazy violet sky thorough the open French doors, but not a breath of wind disturbed the steadily burning candles in the deliciously over-the-top gothic-style candelabras that flanked them.

With a deep roll-top bath in the centre of the floor, it was easily the most stunning bathroom she had ever seen, and discovering the remote controlled stereo system built into one of the cup-boards in the bedroom—complete with extensive CD collec-tion—had been the double-chocolate-fudge icing on the cake.

From where she lay, chin-deep in scented bubbles, she had the whole of Florence laid out before her. She could see the dome of the Duomo, the closely packed terracotta-tiled rooftops of the narrow streets, the twinkling lights of the *piazzas*. Swinging a dripping foot over the side of the bath, she let the beauty of the music and the perfection of the setting work their magic.

Her limbs felt warm and languid from the heat of the water, and a pulse beat insistently at the top of her thighs at the prospect of what she was planning to do. Letting the exquisite notes pour over her, she added her voice to that of Butterfly, remembering as she did so the feeling of Raphael's eyes upon her as she swayed down the catwalk towards him. Her whole body throbbed. Closing her eyes, she let her head fall back against the rim of the bathtub, abandoning herself completely to the music. Arching her dripping arms above her head, she sang with all her heart.

Raphael hesitated. He should leave.

Obviously.

But…

He found himself drawn forward. The hairs on the back of his neck rose as her voice drifted out across the scented air. Unselfconsciously sweet and true, it soared effortlessly up to the highest notes, the acoustics of the bathroom giving it an even more flattering resonance.

And she knew the words, he realised with surprise.

He stopped when he reached the doorway. Through the half-open door, in the candlelit dusk, he could see one glistening brown leg draped enticingly over the side of the bath. He swallowed, somehow managing to stop himself from going further into the room, but unable to prevent his imagination from generating the images of what he would see if he did.

He cleared his throat, both to draw attention to his presence and to clear the sudden constriction there that seemed to be making it difficult to breathe.

A tidal wave of foam cascaded over the sides of the bath as Eve let out a squeal of alarm and slipped down until her chin was level with the surface of the water.

'How long have you been there?' she gasped.

'Long enough to be impressed. You have a beautiful voice. And it seems I was wrong—you do speak Italian after all.'

'Not really,' Eve replied shakily. 'I just know some of the words from *Butterfly*, which somehow never seem to come up in general conversation. Anyway,' she continued, her outrage increasing as her fear subsided, 'was there a good reason for you to sneak into my room uninvited? Or did you just want to frighten the living daylights out of me?'

'I knocked. I thought I heard you say come in. Fiora sent a drink up for you.' He rattled the ice cubes in the glass. 'And she asked me to tell you that dinner will be in half an hour, if you'd care to get dressed.'

'Dressing for dinner?' Eve had a sudden vision of herself and Raphael in evening wear, sitting at opposite ends of a long, polished mahogany table while Fiora waited on them. 'Are you always so formal?'

'I didn't mean it like that. I simply meant as opposed to eating naked.'

His tone was light and mocking. The music had finished, and for a moment the silence spread around them like a dark pool. She was glad the open door stood between them, so he couldn't see the deep blush that was rising from her cleavage to her cheeks at the thought of sharing a meal with him…naked.

She took a steadying breath. 'Not a good idea,' she said as lightly as possible. 'Especially if soup is on the menu.'

'It so happens that it isn't tonight…' He paused for a heart-beat. 'But even so… I'll expect you in half an hour.'

Knickers. So much for Operation Seduction. Not only had he caught her completely off guard, and rather scuppered her intention to appear mysterious and sophisticated, he'd also totally shattered the atmosphere of tranquil relaxation. Hauling herself up crossly, Eve let the water cascade off her body before stepping out of the bath and looking round for a towel.

'Damn, damn, *damn!*'

Still dripping wet, and starting to shiver slightly in the breeze from the open windows, she headed for the bedroom, where the pile of towels still lay on the bed as Fiora had left them. Dusk had fallen properly now, and the only light in the bathroom came from the candles. The rest of the room was filled with shadow. Eve was halfway across the polished floor when she caught sight of herself in the huge and ornately carved mirror.

She stopped, suddenly overtaken by insecurity. The plan was ridiculous anyway. There was no way an inhibited, pitifully inexperienced girl like her would ever be able to seduce a man like Raphael Di Lazaro. Was there?

Slowly she faced the mirror, experimentally pulling in her stomach and thrusting out her breasts, then lasciviously sweeping her hair up off her neck and holding it loosely on top of her head. Her cheeks were flushed from the heat of the bath, and the candlelight cast a glow onto her skin, lending a golden voluptuousness to her generous breasts and softly rounded hips, and throwing flattering shadows beneath her cheekbones and ribs. Crystal droplets of water still glittered on her arms and throat, and ran in slow, caressing rivulets between her breasts and down her thighs.

'You'll be needing this.'

Raphael's voice from the doorway made her start. Holding out one of the sumptuous towels, he moved towards her, his expression unsmiling, his eyes hooded and unreadable.

'Thank you. I can…'

In a trance, she watched in the mirror as deftly he wrapped the towel around her. In the candlelight and against the snowy whiteness of the towel his forearms were dark, dark brown. His movements were firm and capable as he rubbed her upper arms through the thick fabric, and her protestations died on her lips as she meekly submitted to his ministrations. Half in a dream she noticed that her eyes glittered with desire and her lips were plump and parted. She ran her tongue over them.

She stumbled slightly as he abruptly let her go.

'There. Now, do you think you can manage to get dressed by yourself, or shall I send Fiora up?'

His voice was cool and faintly sardonic. Eve's chin rose a fraction in shock and defiance as she registered his indifference. Pulling the towel more tightly around herself, she swept out of the bathroom with as much dignity as she could muster, resisting the urge to slam the door behind her.

* * *

As he impatiently began to extinguish the candles Raphael was painfully aware of the ironic symbolism of the gesture.

If only the burn of his own desire could be so easily snuffed out.

It was a mistake to have brought Eve here. He should have paid for her to stay at the hotel for another night, having persuaded her to book onto a London flight tomorrow morning. Not that it would be easy to persuade Eve to do anything, but her friend to whom he had spoken on the phone that morning could be a possible ally—

At exactly that moment, almost as if he had made it happen himself, he heard the faint ring of a mobile phone above the sound of water draining noisily from the bath. In the semi-darkness it wasn't difficult to spot the greenish glow of its screen on the marble-topped washstand, and he picked it up, wondering if it might be the same girl.

A quiet curse escaped his lips as he recognised the number on the screen.

Luca.

No. He had had no choice but to keep Eve with him, he realised grimly as he slipped the phone into his pocket. Whatever it was that she knew, Luca was onto her, and he would go to any lengths to shut her up. Two years ago he had let his pride prevent him from protecting Catalina. He would not make the same mistake again.

Besides which, she wasn't to be trusted! Irritation prickled through him at the thought that she had almost succeeded in making him forget the small detail of her profession and her purpose for being here. *She was a journalist.*

From now until Luca was safely in police custody he was not letting Eve Middlemiss leave his side. No matter how miserable that was for both of them.

For the briefest moment he caught a glimpse of his reflection in the mirror as he bent to blow out the last candle. His habitual blank sardonic mask had slipped, and he was jolted by the raw emotion that burned in the dark hollows of his eyes.

Swiftly, ruthlessly, he blew out the delicate flame and the image was gone.

But the unwelcome memory remained.

CHAPTER SIX

THE hallway was shadowed and silent as Eve came slowly down the stairs twenty minutes later. Beneath the thin silk of her dress she could feel her heart hammering wildly at the terrifying, exciting prospect of what she was about to do.

Never before had she deliberately, wantonly, set out to seduce someone, and thinking about it like that the idea horrified her.

But she was shamefully aware that it aroused her a whole lot more.

Crossing the marble-tiled hallway towards the lighted doorway of the salon, she pressed her glossed lips together nervously and smoothed the slippery silk of her dress over her hips. It was the same dress she'd worn for the retrospective party, and the only remotely sexy thing she'd brought with her. Despite the stifling heat of the evening she'd added a sumptuously wide pashmina in soft olive-green, which brought out the colour of her eyes. And, more importantly, concealed the tell-tale outline of her nipples which, after her encounter with Raphael in the bathroom, had refused to play along with her brain in pretending that she was entirely in control of the situation.

If she was going to try to seduce him she would do it with a degree of dignity. Not offer herself up on a plate.

The salon was softly lit by lamps, and the scent of gardenia and roses flooded through the open doors beyond which Eve could see the glint of candlelight on crystal. She was trembling as she crossed the room, and her little jeweled sandals made no sound on the polished parquet.

In the doorway, she hesitated. On the terrace a table was beautifully laid with white linen and heavy silver cutlery, and a huge bowl of pink and apricot roses were shedding their velvet petals onto the snowy damask. A large and ornate silver candelabra provided the centrepiece and cast its soft light into the violet dusk.

Raphael's head was bent over a newspaper, a slight frown of concentration furrowing his forehead beneath the lock of wayward hair that habitually fell across it. As Eve watched he swept it back impatiently with lean, tanned fingers. The gesture was utterly unselfconscious, but powerfully, exquisitely sexy.

She wasn't aware of making any sound, but she must have because he looked up sharply. His expression didn't change at all, but neither did his eyes leave her as he slowly rose and pulled out her chair.

'I see you did dress, after all.'

Gratefully she sat down, suddenly afraid that her knees might give way beneath her. There was something very intimate about the beautiful candlelit terrace in the warm evening, and it seemed to change the atmosphere, charging it with some invisible electric force that crackled between them like late-summer thunder on the distant hills.

'Yes.'

He took a bottle of prosecco from the ice bucket and poured it into two slender flutes. 'As you can see, Fiora doesn't do low-key catering.' His mouth twisted into a sardonic smile. 'In this case she seems to have slightly misread the situation.'

She took the glass he offered, trying not to jump as her fingers brushed against his.

'It's beautiful.'

He looked around, as if noticing for the first time. 'It is.

Beautiful, but oppressive.' He gave a short, humourless laugh. 'Welcome to the world of Lazaro. Appearances are everything.'

'Did you grow up here?'

'Yes.'

Her eyes met his over the rim of her glass. She took a slow sip of wine, intrigued by the image of Raphael as a little boy in these vast, formal rooms. Suddenly his emotional inscrutability and hauteur seemed more understandable.

'What was it like? I can't imagine it was a house where children would feel very comfortable. Did you and Luca have a wild time, sliding down the banisters and getting told off for driving your toy cars over the antique furniture?'

She spoke lightly, trying not to notice the way the candlelight emphasised the hollows beneath his cheekbones and the deep shadows of fatigue around his eyes. By contrast, his voice was like gravel.

'Not exactly. Luca and I may be brothers—half-brothers, to be more precise—but we barely know each other.'

'And can barely stand each other, either?'

He grimaced. 'How did you guess?'

She paused, running her fingers slowly up and down the stem of her champagne flute and trying to focus on what he was saying, rather than the electric current coursing around her pelvis. 'Oh, let me see… Could it have been the less than affectionate way you greeted him at the retrospective party, and then again today? On both occasions I got the distinct impression that you were more likely to smash his face in than shake his hand.'

He gave her a wry smile. 'Was it that obvious?'

'I'm afraid so. Even to someone as "silly and inexperienced" as me.' She looked up at him through lowered lashes and smiled teasingly. 'Even to someone as *blind* and silly and inexperienced as me. What I still haven't worked out is why.'

Given that she had to be the world's least experienced flirt, she was taking to it with worrying ease. But flirting with Raphael was as easy as breathing. It was something about the way he moved his long-fingered hands as he spoke, and the triangle of sun-bronzed skin at the open collar of his blue shirt, and his mouth...

What wasn't so easy was remembering that this was just a manoeuvre in a game. She was playing a part, that was all. Cynically acting out a role as a means to an end. The thought made her feel as uncomfortable as the throbbing ache between her thighs.

'Why what?'

With a fingertip, Eve chased a bead of condensation down the side of her glass. She found herself unable to look at him, but was aware of his eyes following every movement.

'Why you hate him so much that you had to lie to him about us being together. Was it just to make sure he didn't get something that you hadn't got, regardless of whether you really wanted it?'

'Who said I didn't want it?' he said softly.

She was spared the need to answer because at that moment Fiora arrived, carrying a tray laden with food. Which was just as well because Eve couldn't have spoken anyway. The charge in the air between her and Raphael could have lit an entire city.

Fiora placed a bowl of salad and a basket of warm, fragrant bread on the table, then laid a plate of delicately scented risotto topped with asparagus spears drizzled with olive oil before each of them. Picking up on the taut lines of tension, she beamed knowingly and hurried away.

Eve picked up one of the slender spears and captured its tip between her lips. It was delicious—the essence of hot Italian summer concentrated into one distinctive taste—and she closed her eyes to savour it, realising how hungry she was. When she opened them again it was to find Raphael leaning back in his chair and watching her intently, his face shadowed and unreadable.

Colour flooded her cheeks as she sucked the fragrant oil off her fingers. She felt dizzy. Her pashmina had slipped off her shoulders, and she was painfully aware that her nipples were jutting against the silk of her dress.

She looked down, picking up one of the fallen rose petals and smoothing its bruised surface with her fingers. It felt like damp flesh. Memories of his hands on her body in the bathroom only an hour ago came back to her in a rush of heat.

It was as if he had read her mind.

'So it seems, Signorina Middlemiss, that you're something of a dark horse. Where did that exceptional singing voice come from?'

'My mother was a singer. A soprano. My sister and I spent our childhoods traipsing around from one concert to the next, sleeping in dressing rooms and doing our homework in the orchestra pit during rehearsals.'

Raphael raised an eyebrow. 'Your father?'

'First violin.' She paused. 'Apparently.'

'You never knew him?'

His voice was gentle, and she found herself not wanting to meet his eyes. It was impossible to hate him when he spoke to her like that.

'No.'

Her answer hung in the air for a moment before the silence swallowed it.

'Lucky you,' he said drily. 'I often find myself wishing I could say the same.'

She gave him a brief smile, grateful in spite of herself that he had been sensitive enough to realise she didn't want to talk about it. 'How is your father? Have you had any news from the hospital?'

'No change. It seems his heart is in pretty bad shape. Though I must say I'm surprised that he has one at all. I never saw much evidence of it when I was growing up.'

'What about your mother? Were you close to her?'

He was suddenly very still. 'Yes. She died when I was seven...'

'Oh, Raphael…' The small intimacy escaped her lips in a whispered caress before she could stop it. If he noticed he didn't show it.

Laying down his fork, he leaned back in his chair and continued. 'My father remarried almost straight away. I was something of a thorn in the side of his new wife, so by the time Luca came along I was safely incarcerated in an English boarding school. Hence our lack of brotherly devotion.'

His voice was low and faintly sardonic, but the pain behind his words wasn't difficult to detect. Her foolish, traitorous heart went out to him.

'And your impeccable English.'

'I had to learn pretty quickly. Not that most of the first words I picked up are suitable for repetition over the dinner table. Pretty Italian boys were something of a novelty.'

'I bet you were pretty, too.' She spoke almost without thinking, then blushed. 'I don't mean… It's just, with your bone structure and colouring…' She looked down at her plate, continuing in a breathless rush. 'My sister and I always longed to go to boarding school. It sounded like heaven to us. Were you happy there?'

'No. It was hell.' Picking up a roll, he tore into it with long, savage fingers. 'After being used to all this, I hated the greyness and the cold. My father wasn't the best correspondent—too absorbed with his new family.' He said the words as if they tasted bitter in his mouth. 'And I suppose I hadn't got over my mother's death.'

'Of course you hadn't! You were just a little boy. Even with the love and understanding of your father it would have been impossible to get over something like that.'

Pouring more prosecco into her glass, he gave a dry laugh. 'You're quite right. Unfortunately, in the absence of love and understanding from my father, I grew up into a bitter, twisted and emotionally bankrupt—'

'Don't say that.'

The words came from her in something halfway between a whisper and a moan. It was as though she couldn't bear to hear him say the things her head suspected to be true and which her heart was so fervently trying to deny. He stopped abruptly and passed a hand over his face. In the velvety quiet of the twilight Eve heard the slight rasp of his unshaven skin.

He was very still, but his eyes burned into hers through the darkness. For a moment neither of them moved. This was her moment—the perfect chance to put her plan into action—but that wasn't what she was thinking as she got up and moved slowly round the table towards him.

She wasn't thinking at all, but acting on pure, primitive instinct.

Her bare arm brushed against the bowl of roses, sending a ripple of anticipation over her exquisitely sensitised skin and a cascade of petals onto the table. Their scent filled the warm air as she reached him: heavy, sensual, intoxicating. As if in a trance she reached out and pressed her palm against his cheek. His gaze didn't flicker, but remained locked onto hers, intense and unfathomable. And then his fingers closed over her hand, pulling her down towards him until her mouth met his.

It was like dying and being reborn. Adrenalin, desire, and ten thousand volts of sexual electricity crashed through her as her parted lips were crushed against his in the savagery of their need. She was dimly aware of moving, so that she was standing over him, straddling him where he sat, but it was as if she was under the control of a higher being, unconsciously obeying an imperative that she neither questioned nor understood. All she knew was that the sensation of his hands—in her hair, caressing her back, moving downwards to the firm curve of her buttocks—was the most unimaginably erotic thing she had ever experienced.

She shifted her position so that she was sitting on his knee, astride him, the thin silk of her narrow slip dress riding up over her parted thighs. His hands found the warm skin, his thumbs making caressing circles on her quivering flesh as their mouths continued their urgent, savage quest.

He made a low sound deep in his throat, a guttural growl of longing, and then tore his lips from hers.

She was aware of his fingers closing like bracelets of steel around her wrists, pulling her hands away from his face. Bewildered, bereft, she got to her feet, pressing the back of her hand against her swollen lips.

'Wh—what..?

Raphael barely glanced at her. His face was like granite.

'Fiora.'

Eve whirled around as Fiora bustled out onto the terrace. The older woman's small eyes were wide and knowing, and she set about clearing the table with great focus, trying to conceal the broad smile that she couldn't quite suppress.

'Here—let me help.'

Eve sprang forward, needing to do something to prevent herself from having to see the look of dark despair on Raphael's face. As she helped Fiora gather the remains of their meal and carry it through to the kitchen her mind was racing, along with her pulse.

It was what she had planned. So why did it feel as if she'd been run over by an express train?

And why did she want to lie right back down on the track and be run over again?

After they'd gone Raphael drew a deep, ragged breath and buried his face in his hands.

He should go and help. He knew that. But first he had to wait for the hard, throbbing evidence of his desire to subside.

Picking up his wine glass, he drained it in one long mouthful and slumped back in his chair. Fiora's appearance had been entirely coincidental. He had been trying to break off the kiss anyway, trying to exercise some form of restraint from where he would make an attempt to find the right words to tell her what they were doing was impossible.

For a few moments there he had been totally out of control, and that was something he found very hard to accept. What in hell's name had possessed him? Never before had he spoken to anyone about those things. What on earth had made him spill out all the tawdry details of his miserable childhood like some spineless, self-pitying wimp?

Being back in this house. Too many memories. Too much unhappiness and resentment. That was all it was.

And yet he'd brought other women here over the years, and none of them had ever seen the pain that lurked in the corner of each beautiful room, nor smelt the loneliness that hung like a mist over the lavish furnishings. Not a single one of those clever, ambitious, sophisticated women had ever suspected that to Raphael this villa was anything other than a comfortable family home. Catalina, the woman he had almost married, certainly hadn't.

Eve had.

But he shouldn't confuse her listening skills with anything else, for pity's sake. She had a knack, it was true, of putting her head slightly to one side when you were speaking, as if she was hanging on your every word, and her turquoise eyes seemed to shine with compassion. But she was a journalist, *per l'amore di Dio*. Using Feminine Wiles to Extract Information was probably one of the training modules she'd completed at college. With distinction.

Maybe she was smarter than she looked. Maybe that blonde softness and the sleepy, seductive look in those clear greenish eyes was carefully cultivated. Maybe that kiss was all part of the act and had nothing to do with love...

He made a sharp noise of self-disgust. Of course it was an act. *Love?* What the hell had make him think of that? It was a word he had banished from his vocabulary and his emotional repertoire years ago—probably about the time that Catalina had accused him of being incapable of it.

He hadn't bothered to argue with her. She'd been right. He'd never really loved her. Wanted her, yes, and enjoyed her athletic model's body and the textbook sex that had made up their relationship, but she'd never really got beneath his skin in that visceral, all-consuming, irrational way that to him meant love.

He frowned as the knife of guilt twisted in that old wound. It hadn't occurred to him that she hadn't felt like that too until she'd left with Luca, and he had to live with the knowledge of what had happened to her as a result every day. But he'd learned from it, and he had vowed never to risk causing such pain to anyone again.

And that included Eve Middlemiss.

She was just a kid—twenty-one or twenty-two at the most. He had brought her here to protect her, not take advantage of her. One destroyed life on his conscience was bad enough. No matter what she did for a living, he would not risk screwing Eve up too.

Cursing quietly, he dropped his head into his hands. It hardly mattered what the truth was.

Either way, from now on she was strictly off limits.

After the muggy heat of the kitchen the warm evening air was like a caress on her skin, and Eve took a deep steadying breath of it as she stepped back onto the terrace. The two tiny cups of espresso she carried rattled slightly in her trembling hands.

The kitchen was immaculate, and Fiora had made sure all the lights downstairs, except the lamps in the salon, were put out before she had agreed to retire to her room. Assuring her that they would take care of everything else, Eve had said goodnight and watched her stiffly climb the back stairs.

Her mind was in turmoil. This was it.

She stopped, feeling the sweat break out on her forehead. The pulse between her legs was like a raw, primitive drumbeat, echoing the pounding blood in her ears. She was bewitched by its insistent rhythm, like the girl with the red shoes in the fairy tale, unable to stop her body from responding, increasingly terrified by the strength of that response. Maybe it was some primeval instinct for self-preservation that at that moment wouldn't allow her to make the connection between Ellie's death and the man she was about to approach...

Maybe it was just pure, old-fashioned, selfish lust.

Trembling violently, she bit down on her lip, assailed by doubt. What if he rejected her? She steeled herself, remembering the chilling moment at the press conference, when she had met his eyes and found only distaste.

But she couldn't turn back now. Not for Ellie. Not for herself.

She walked tentatively towards the table. He was leaning back in his chair, his long legs outstretched. As she came closer and saw his face she realised that he was asleep.

One arm was thrown across his body while the other supported his head, and in spite of the obvious discomfort of his position he looked peaceful. Sleep had softened his features and smoothed away the harsh lines of bitterness and cynicism.

God, he was perfect.

Crushing disappointment fought with an acute sense of frustration as she kneeled beside him and gently she took hold of his hand.

'Raphael?'

He didn't stir. Holding his hand, she gave it a little shake, and he turned his head a fraction so that the light from the salon fell onto the high arc of one cheekbone and gilded the dark crescent of his eyelashes. Then he was perfectly still again.

Hardly daring to breathe, she turned his hand over.

The sleeve of his shirt was rolled back, and gingerly she eased it up a little further. Heart hammering, her eyes swept over the underside of his arm. It was a smooth, uniform butterscotch-brown.

There was no sign of the cruel black scars of drug abuse that had marred Ellie's arms when Eve had seen her in the hospital morgue.

She closed her eyes for a second and exhaled slowly, shutting the lid on the image that haunted her nightmares. Gently replacing his hand, she felt almost light-headed with relief, and had to check herself firmly. Just because he showed no signs of addiction himself, it didn't mean he couldn't be a supplier.

But that was unlikely, wasn't it?

The heat was gradually ebbing out of the evening, and Eve suddenly realised that she was shivering. She hesitated, unsure whether to wake him. Bending down, she put her lips to his ear and whispered.

'Raphael.'

The faint lemon and sandalwood scent of his skin knocked the air from her lungs and sent a surge of honeyed heat rushing through her. She could just discern the beat of his pulse beneath the skin of his neck, and it took every ounce of self-control she possessed to stop herself reaching forward and brushing her lips against it.

She stood up quickly, stealing an anxious glance at his face. He was still far away in the darkest depths of an exhausted sleep, but a faint smile lifted the corners of his mouth. Taking off her pashmina, she draped it over him, then stepped back hastily, suddenly too tired and confused to ask herself why she should want to look after this man.

Picking up the cups of cooling coffee, she had turned to go back into the house when the ring of a mobile phone stopped her in her tracks.

Her first thought was that it was *her* phone, and she should silence it before it woke him.

Her second thought was that she didn't have her phone on her.

The little silk shift had no room for the kind of pocket that would accommodate a mobile phone, and she hadn't brought a bag down with her—so where the hell was it?

Swiftly she replaced the cups on the table and followed the sound. It was coming from Raphael's direction—maybe he had the same phone she did? Leaning over him, she slipped her hands into both front pockets of his jeans.

Nothing.

The ringing continued. To get her hands in his back pockets she had to adopt pretty much the same position as she had done just half an hour earlier. Steeling herself to ignore the butterfly kiss of his breath against her breasts, she managed to reach round him without waking him. Just when she thought her self-control might snap she felt her fingers close around the phone. Gently she extracted it.

It was her phone.

Typically, at that moment the ringing stopped, and Eve was left in the sudden silence feeling more alone than she ever had in her life.

In the safety of her room she threw herself down onto the bed without even bothering to switch on a light, and called Lou back.

'Eve! I was about to file you as a missing person! What's going on?'

'It was my phone that was missing, not me. Although I am beginning to feel completely and utterly lost.'

That summed the situation up pretty well. Lost as in alone in a strange house in a foreign country. Lost as in uncertain of what was going on. Lost as in unrecognisable to herself. The Eve Middlemiss she knew didn't leave her seat at the dinner table to climb on top of the man opposite and eat his face rather than dessert.

'Let's start with the basics, then. Where are you?'

Eve sighed. 'Paradise. Antonio Di Lazaro's villa, just outside Florence.'

'With?'

'Raphael.'

There was a long silence on the other end of the line. When Lou eventually spoke her voice was sharp with anguish.

'Do you want me to call the police now, or would you rather wait until he actually has his hands around your throat and a gun to your head?'

Eve squeezed her eyes shut and massaged her forehead. '*Don't*, Lou. It's not like that. Honestly, I'm not in any danger.' *Except from my own rampaging emotions.*

'How do you know that?'

Eve sighed. 'I just do. I feel safe.'

Lou let out a shriek of disbelief. 'Oh, I see! Well, that's OK then, is it? *You feel safe!* That's the most ridiculous thing I've heard since…well, since this morning, when you came out with that line about Raphael Di Lazaro "having a strength about him". Honestly, what's the matter with you? Has he brainwashed you, or something? Is he there now, with a gun trained on you?'

'No,' she said in a small, cold voice. 'Look, Lou, I know it sounds crazy and I'm not sure what's going on myself. It's just that despite all the evidence I thought I had before I left, my instincts are telling me that Raphael di Lazaro isn't a drug dealer.'

'And the evidence for that interesting hypothesis is…?' The sarcasm in Lou's tone was blistering.

'Nothing yet. But I'm not coming back until I've proved it.'

'Or disproved it. In which case you may not be coming back at all. Alive, anyway.'

After she'd put the phone down, Eve wandered over to the dressing table. Her head ached from the effort of too much thinking, and from not wearing her glasses for two days, and her face was pale and drawn in the ghostly light.

She had never lied to Lou before, and never kept a secret from her—so why was she starting now? Lou only had her best interests at heart, so maybe it would have been a good idea to admit that Raphael hadn't exactly offered her a lift so much as deliberately used his stratospheric powers of seduction to get her into the car. Shortly after he'd offered her twenty thousand pounds to go home and shut up.

And while she was about it she might also have mentioned the bit about him stealing her phone, effectively cutting her off entirely from the outside world.

Why hadn't she said that?

Because, she admitted despairingly, all that added up to one thing. Against which her instinct wasn't worth a damn.

CHAPTER SEVEN

RAPHAEL woke up slowly, swimming groggily up through the fathomless depths of sleep inch by inch, so that he wasn't sure what was real and what he had dreamed.

Eve.

He heard the whisper of her voice in his ear, felt the caress of her breath on his neck, the cool pressure of her fingers on his skin. The scent of her filled his head, seeming to envelop him in warmth and comfort, until he opened his eyes expecting to find her beside him.

He was alone on the dark terrace. The candles had burned themselves out, and the coffee on the table was icy cold. But the subtle floral fragrance persisted. It took him a moment to realise it was coming from the soft wrap she had been wearing that evening, which was now spread over him.

Resisting the temptation to bury his face in it and breathe in her lingering perfume, he groaned quietly as the events of the evening slotted into place in his memory.

That kiss. The stupid, selfish, reckless pleasure of that kiss.

He'd intended to talk to her seriously when she came back, and make it perfectly clear that it had been a complete mistake. But like an idiot he must have fallen asleep. And she had come back and wrapped her shawl around him to stop him getting cold.

Not that there had been much chance of that, given the dream he'd been having...

The thoughtfulness of her gesture exasperated him as much as it touched him. Roughly he pulled the shawl off and stood up, stiffly stretching his cramped limbs, instinctively feeling in his pockets. Almost at the same moment that he remembered he still had her phone he realized it was missing and swore softly.

So the bit where she'd stood over him, her warm breasts rising and falling just centimetres from his face, while her hands moved over his body... That hadn't been a dream, then.

Making his way slowly upstairs, he yawned. At least a few hours' sleep would assuage the tiredness that numbed every muscle, every joint, every nerve in his entire body. If only it would be so easy to satisfy the deep ache of longing in his groin.

He paused outside the door to her room, torn apart by conflicting feelings he was too weary to analyse. But a second later all that was driven from his mind as a scream split the silence.

The man was so close behind her she could almost feel the heat of his breath on her neck. But it was always the same: the closer he got, the harder it was to keep running, until she felt as if she was wading through quicksand, and she knew that he would get her too, just as he'd got Ellie. She felt his hot hands grasping at her and let out a scream of pure terror.

'Shh... It's all right. Shh.... You're safe...'

A pair of strong arms seized her and she screamed again, writhing and clawing in terror.

'Eve! *Eve!* It's all right. It's just a dream. Shh...You're quite safe.'

It was Raphael's voice, close to her ear. It was his arms wrapped tightly around her, and his hands gentle on her sweat-soaked hair as they soothed away the nightmare. Overwhelmed with relief, she collapsed against his chest, desperately grateful for his warmth and strength.

Gradually her breathing steadied, and the trembling that racked her body grew less violent under the steady strokes of his hand. But she didn't want him to stop. The only sound in the still room came from the soft, rhythmic hissing sound of his hand against her hair and the steady thud of his heart beneath her ear. Sleep blurred the edges of her mind, drawing a veil of shadow over everything except his reassuring nearness.

Gently he laid her back on the pillows. She was dimly aware that her brief T-shirt had ridden up, but her embarrassment at the realisation was outweighed by the sudden desolation she felt at losing contact with his body. He pulled the covers back over her, then stood up.

Through half-closed eyes she watched him flex his tired shoulders, then bend to pick up her laptop and several scattered pages of notes for the article, which must have slid off her knee when she'd fallen asleep. As he reached over to turn out the light he paused for a moment and looked down at her. His face was lined with exhaustion, his expression guarded and remote.

'Thank you,' she murmured.

He shook his head wearily. Then switched the light off and was gone.

The sun was climbing higher into a sky the colour of delphiniums by the time Eve made her way hesitantly downstairs, stiff with shame and embarrassment at the prospect of seeing Raphael again.

So she'd managed to make an almighty fool of herself not once but twice in one evening. That was quite an achievement even by her standards.

And on both occasions Raphaël had behaved with dignity and chivalry.

Damn him.

She'd woken early and tried to make some headway on the article, but no matter how hard she tried the words wouldn't come. Sienna and the retrospective seemed like light-years ago—part of another lifetime when she had known what she believed and had been charge of her own actions. Since then her heart seemed to have told her head its services were no longer required and staged something of a takeover, as last night's argument with Lou demonstrated.

She couldn't blame Lou for being worried. If she'd been a thousand miles away in England she probably would have been, too. It was just that here, in close proximity with Raphael di Lazaro, she had never felt safer in all her life.

She found Fiora in the salon, dusting the many photograph frames that crowded the surface of the grand piano. Golden motes danced in honeyed shafts of sunlight falling in through the three sets of French windows, suffusing the room with warmth.

'*Buongiorno, signorina.* You sleep good?'

Eve was just about to reply truthfully that, no, she'd had a dreadful night when she stopped herself. Judging from the meaningful look on Fiora's face, she would assume that meant one thing…

If only.

'Brilliantly, thank you, Fiora.' She beamed. 'It's so peaceful here.'

'*Si, signorina.* Signor di Lazaro, he always say that too. Here is the only place he sleep good.'

'Raphael?'

'Ne, Signor Antonio.' She sighed. 'He so tired *recentemente.* Now we know why…'

Tears filled her small dark eyes and, biting her lip, she reverently dabbed the duster over the photograph frame in her hand.

'Don't get upset, Fiora. I'm sure Signor Antonio will be out of hospital and back here where you can look after him in no time.'

'*Si, si…spero…*' Fiora sniffed, looking fondly down at the photograph. It showed a dinner-suited Antonio, arm in arm with someone who looked suspiciously like an Italian film star. 'Those *infermiera*—they not know him. He like things done just so. He not easy man. But underneath...he is good man.'

Not according to Raphael, thought Eve, who rather suspected that in his current state Antonio would neither know nor care how things were done. Out loud, she said, 'Have you worked for him for long?'

'*Trentacinque anni.* Thirty-five years. I start when he bring Isabella here as a young bride.'

'Raphael's mother?'

'*Si.*' Fiora replaced the photograph amongst the others. Most of them were of Antonio, formally dressed, with a variety of diamond-festooned beauties on his arm. Eve wondered which of them was Isabella.

'What was she like?'

Fiora reached over, picked up a small photograph from right at the back and handed it to her. It was of an astonishingly beautiful girl holding a little boy on her knee, and Eve's heart lurched as she recognised the child's huge dark eyes with their fringe of long lashes, his perfectly shaped mouth. Isabella was dressed to go out, wearing a simple dress of pale green silk-satin, with a tiny cluster of pink satin roses between her creamy breasts. She was looking straight into the camera, smiling radiantly, while Raphael, unsmiling, looked up into his mother's face with an intensity that made Eve's heart ache for him.

'Raphael is very like her.'

'*Si, l'aspetto,* perhaps. In personality he is like Signor Antonio.'

Eve looked up in surprise. 'Really? I thought—'

'Oh, they fight, *certo,* but is because they are just the same. *Ostinato, orgoglioso, difficile...*' She laughed. 'Always they think they are right! That is why they cannot get along.'

'She looks very beautiful. *Molto bella.* And very young.'

'*Ventuno* when they marry.'

Twenty-one. The same age as me, thought Eve in wonder. But found her gaze being drawn away from Isabella's luminous beauty back to the face of the little boy. Without thinking she stroked the pad of her thumb over his face, as if trying to soothe away the anguish that she saw in the dark pools of his eyes.

'You can see how much he loves her. Her death must have been devastating for him.'

She spoke out loud, but almost to herself, assuming that Fiora wouldn't understand. To her surprise, Fiora replied.

'*Si*. For a child to see such a thing…' Her voice trailed off and she shook her head sorrowfully.

In the short silence that followed, Eve's stomach gave a dramatic rumble.

'*Signorina, mia dispiace… Colazione! Poverino!* Come, come with me.'

Thoughtfully Eve replaced the photograph, this time positioning it right at the front, so it obscured Antonio and the filmstar. A thousand questions rose to the surface of her mind, like fish in a pool, but Fiora had already gone, hurrying off to the kitchen with an efficient rustling of skirts.

With a last glance into the sad eyes of the little boy, Eve followed.

Eve took her coffee out onto the terrace. In the shimmering morning light no evidence remained of what had taken place there last night, apart from a scattering of bruised rose petals on the flagstones beside Raphael's chair.

She bent to pick one up, crushing its soft flesh between her fingers and releasing its outrageously sensual fragrance. Instantly she was transported back to the moment when she had put her hand to his face and he had pulled her down to kiss him. A tide of bittersweet remembered ecstasy washed through her.

At that moment she'd been so sure of herself, so confident with her silly plan. Now it seemed nothing more than laughable. She'd thought that by getting closer to Raphael she would be able to see things more clearly, but, like Icarus flying towards the sun, she had been foolish and over-ambitious. The closer she got, the more he dazzled her.

Looking down, she saw that she was still holding the rose petal, but it was crushed and battered beyond recognition.

It seemed like an omen. She had been mad to think she could play games with a man like Raphael Di Lazaro and escape with her heart intact.

Beyond the terrace a broad sweep of lawn sloped downwards to a line of cypress trees in the distance, set along a stone wall. Suddenly the urge to get away from the house was overwhelming. Throwing down the tattered petal, she set off briskly in the direction of the trees.

As she got nearer she could see that the wall formed the back of a low, single-storey building with a sloping tiled roof. After hesitating, in case it was the home of one of the members of the villa's staff, Eve walked cautiously on. As she rounded the last corner she let out a gasp of pleasure.

Before her lay a swimming pool. A perfect, glittering oval of pure turquoise.

The building that she'd just walked around was built in the style of an ancient Roman bathhouse, with marble benches standing in the shade under the wide portico. Wistfully her gaze darted back to the water. The need to feel its soothing chill on her overheated skin was suddenly irresistible.

She opened one of the doors into the poolhouse and found herself in a stunning room decorated in pale, creamy tones. One wall was dominated by a huge mirror hanging over a marble topped counter on which an array of Lazaro cosmetics was arranged. Behind a screen of sandblasted glass in one corner there was a vast walk-in shower, and a pair of huge, squashy sofas covered in biscuit-coloured coarse linen stood either side of a low table on which piles of magazines were neatly stacked.

Feeling like Goldilocks in the Three Bears' house, Eve padded around, lifting the stoppers from jars and peering into cupboards.

She was hoping that someone would have conveniently left something for her to swim in, but, while the room contained every imaginable luxury, there was nothing so practical as a bikini.

Which left her with a choice. Bra and knickers, or nothing?

She didn't need to look at the verdigris clock set into the stone of the poolhouse wall to know it was almost lunchtime—the high, hot sun and her own gnawing hunger were evidence enough. But she felt better. There was something soothing about swimming, and length after length of rhythmic strokes had calmed her thoughts. It was a refreshed, restored and ravenous Eve who hauled herself reluctantly out of the pool.

In the end she had decided that skinny-dipping was a little too risqué; the thought of one of the servants—or, worse, Raphael—finding her, and standing over her as she got out of the water completely naked, had been enough to convince her that bra and knickers was the only option.

It wasn't a choice she had made lightly. The underwear she was wearing was a set Lou had made her buy on a last-minute shopping trip the day before she left, and had cost about as much as she would usually want to pay for a whole outfit. Including shoes and the bus fare home.

Although she'd been vociferous in her objections to the price, she secretly loved the semi-sheer organza bra and matching shorts. They were a delicate creamy cappuccino shade, and a butterfly nestled between the bra cups, its wings made of crisp lace in sugared almond pink. Swimming in things of extreme beauty had felt a little bit like wearing the crown jewels to dig the garden but, all things considered, it certainly beat the alternative.

And now she just had to get them dry again. She stretched out on one of the steamer chairs at the poolside and lifted her face to the sun, but realised within minutes that sitting in the heat for that long would be unbearable. She sat up, biting her lip. It seemed there was only one thing for it, after all.

She unfastened the bra and slipped it off, then wriggled quickly out of the damp shorts and draped them both over the chair at the side of the pool. Going back into the poolhouse, she picked up one of the glossy magazines from the pile on the table and began to flick through it. The next moment she gave an exclamation of delight as she came across a feature-length interview with Sienna.

It was a godsend—just the inspiration she needed to get her into the mood for returning to her own article. In fact, you could almost call it research. Throwing herself down onto one of the oversized sofas, Eve put on her glasses and began to read.

The surface of the water was smooth and still, and Raphael barely hesitated before plunging in with an impressively graceful dive. It felt delicious on his skin, and he swam a couple of lengths beneath its surface, grateful for the cool and quiet.

When he'd finally fallen into bed in the small hours he'd slept only fitfully, tormented by the memory of Eve's sweating, writhing body as he'd held her in his arms while the nightmare faded. A pale slice of blue sky had been visible through the gap in the curtains before sleep had come to him, and even then it had been plagued with more disturbing, sensual dreams that, on waking, had left him feeling raw and edgy with unfulfilled desire.

It was getting beyond a joke. For all his determination last night to make it clear to her that nothing more would happen between them, he could no longer pretend to himself that he wasn't seriously disturbed by her presence. It was an extremely unwelcome feeling, and one he was beginning to bitterly resent. Perhaps it was just as well he was going to Venice this afternoon.

Pushing through the water, he felt the life seep back into his heavy limbs. Yes, getting away from Eve for a couple of days would give him time to clear his head and maybe even run a few checks on her—find out exactly what sort of a threat she posed. In the meantime she'd be quite safe here with Fiora.

Considerably safer than she was with him.

The thought was an unsettling one. He swam faster, cutting through the water with long, savage strokes.

'Lazaro is my favourite label!' Sienna enthused in the interview. 'I love the fluid lines and feminine details. He has an amazing, instinctive understanding of women's bodies…'

Just like his son, thought Eve wistfully. She really ought to be getting back to her own article—her underwear would surely be dry by now. Reluctantly she replaced the magazine and, stretching indolently, padded out into the sunshine at the poolside.

She was just reaching for her things when a movement beneath the surface of the water caught her eye. Giving a tiny whimper of distress, she made a grab for her underwear, but in her haste the bra flew out of her shaking hands, making a graceful arc through the air before landing in the water.

Transfixed with horror, she watched it slowly float down towards the bottom of the pool.

Swimming under the water, Raphael saw something pale and gauzy drifting down from the surface. He glanced upwards through the turquoise depths and saw a figure, slender and golden as a sunflower, standing beside the pool. Her face was indistinct through the water, but there was no mistaking those long legs and generous curves. Grabbing the diaphanous piece of underwear, he kicked up to the surface and shook the water from his eyes as he placed it on the side.

Eve felt the blood rise to the surface of her skin as Raphael's gaze flickered dispassionately over her naked body. Frantically she looked around for something to cover herself up with.

Of course there was nothing.

Swallowing tears of utter mortification, she crossed her arms defensively over her breasts and wished she had the confidence to carry off the stark naked look successfully.

Failing that, a supermodel body would help.

'I was going to ask if this was yours, but actually I think I can work it out for myself.'

The lack of interest in his eyes was like a slap in the face after the passion of last night's kiss and the intimacy of waking up in his arms. Meeting his gaze as coolly as possible under the circumstances, Eve raised her chin a little.

'Top marks, Einstein. Now, if you've quite finished enjoying my humiliation, could I have it back, please?'

He sighed and lifted himself out of the pool in one lithe movement that made the muscles ripple beneath his glistening skin. Getting to his feet, he pushed the wet hair back from his forehead and came towards her, holding out the bra. In his masculine hand it looked absurdly girly and frivolous. And intimate—almost as if he wasn't touching an inanimate scrap of organza and lace but her own flesh...

Eve shrank back, despising herself for the shameful rush of sweet wetness that thought aroused in her.

'Are you going to come and get it, or do you want me to come over there and put it on for you?'

'No!' It came out as an embarrassing squeak.

'No, what?' he asked levelly. 'No, you're not going to come and get it? Or no, you don't want me to come and put it on for you? I hope it's the latter, because I have to admit my expertise lies more in the removal of these things.'

'Just give it to me,' she snapped. Darting forward, she shot out a hand and snatched the bra from where it swung, incriminatingly sexy, from his outstretched finger.

But, having got hold of it, she felt even more at a loss. What should she do now? If she were to turn and go back into the poolhouse she would give him a perfect view of her naked behind, and creeping backwards without turning round was just too ridiculously gauche and embarrassing to consider. Maybe she should just put her underwear on right here, in front of him? Another crimson tide of shame washed through her at the idea. Maybe not.

The realisation dawned that she was stuck there until he chose to leave. And he didn't seem to be in any hurry.

'I'm sorry. I had no idea you were down here.'

Miserably she faced him, aware that whichever way she crossed her arms there was no way she could cover her breasts up entirely. 'You don't have to apologise. It's your house.'

'Even so...' He stopped, seemingly struggling with what to say for a second. 'I wanted to apologise anyway. For what happened last night—'

'Look—please,' she interrupted desperately. 'There's really no need. I don't know what came over me. I don't usually—' She faltered, not wanting to put into words what had happened between them. Not wanting to be having this conversation. Particularly not wanting to be having this conversation while she was naked and clutching her underwear. 'Anyway,' she continued, looking down, 'it's over. Forgotten.'

From behind the damp tendrils of her hair she watched him nod and lift a hand to sweep the water from his face. 'I have to go away on business for a couple of days. I'm leaving this afternoon. Will you be all right here with Fiora?'

His casual words came out of the blue and hit her like darts, causing her head to jerk upwards with shock. And pain. Unexpected pain.

'Of course. I'm not a child. I don't need you to look after me.'

His eyebrows arched upwards sardonically. 'No?'

'No!'

'That wasn't how it felt last night.'

She heard the hiss of her own sharply indrawn breath. Humiliation instantly turned to rage, and blotted out everything else in its enveloping red mist. Planting her hands firmly on her hips, Eve lifted her head and glared at him with open hostility. *'That's not fair!'* It was just some stupid dream... I didn't ask you to—'

She stopped, suddenly realising as he came towards her that in her anger she'd forgotten to cover herself, and was now standing in front of him with not a stitch on, hands on hips, in the manner of a cartoon stripper. All she needed was a pair of high heels and a string of fake pearls to complete the picture.

Brushing past her, he opened a door in the poolhouse and re-appeared a moment later with two towels. Draping one round his neck, he held the other one out to her.

But pride was a terrible thing. Naked, hurt, humiliated, at that moment Eve would have rather accepted help from Satan himself than Raphael di Lazaro. Sucking in her stomach, trying desperately to look as if her lack of clothes was a matter of supreme indifference to her, she pushed her shoulders back and eyed him coldly.

'You can tell Fiora that I won't be staying, so she's relieved of babysitting duty in your absence.'

There. That had wiped the mocking, self-satisfied smile off his face.

It also blew all her plans to tiny smithereens.

'Where are you planning to go?'

She shrugged. 'I'll find somewhere in Florence.'

Suddenly his face went very still. 'It's August. All the hotels will be full of tourists.'

Her chin shot up another inch. 'I'll just have to look at other options, then.'

Throwing him one last haughty glance, she turned round and sauntered slowly back into the poolhouse. It was maybe seven or eight paces, but it felt like miles. And every step was like walking on knives.

* * *

All the way back up to the house he cursed himself. He'd screwed up. Big-time. *He just couldn't stop himself from taking out on her the fact that she'd got under his skin, could he?* And now he'd blown it all.

The villa was cool and dim after the fierce midday glare outside, and it took a moment for his eyes to adjust. In the hallway he could hear Fiora's voice, the particular formal tone she adopted for the telephone. The next minute she came hurrying through to find him.

'Oh, Signor Raphael, *meno male…*!'

She looked stricken. Putting a reassuring hand on her shoulder, Raphael spoke calmly.

'What is it, Fiora? Is it the hospital?'

'Ne, signor. Polizia.'

Not a flicker of emotion showed on his face as he picked up the phone, but all the colour had drained from it.

'Marco? *Ciao.*'

'Ciao, Raphael. Look, I'll get straight to the point. It's not good news. Our chief witness in the case against Luca has met with a nasty accident.'

Raphael sucked in a breath, but his face remained stony as the detective elaborated on the girl's untimely end.

'There must be other witnesses?' Raphael pressed.

'Sure—but we can't exactly hold open interviews for every girl on the modeling scene. The fewer people who know about this the better. Especially if Luca's guys are going round picking off girls they're suspicious about.'

A chill spread down Raphael's spine as Eve's careless words came back to him *'I'm going to expose di Lazaro as a sleazy drug pusher…'*

'So, what now?' he asked the detective.

At the other end of the phone, Marco sighed. 'We watch him. It's all we can do until we find someone else who will testify against him—and keep our fingers crossed that it doesn't take too long.' Raphael could hear the frustration in his voice. 'He's getting more and more unpredictable. My feeling is that he's going to do something very stupid pretty soon. We just have to wait.'

Bloody, *bloody* hell.

Why had he taunted Eve like that? Now she was leaving— heading, in all probability, for Luca's flat—and it was entirely his fault. There was no way he could go to Venice now. He'd have to make his apologies to the award ceremony organizers and try to get Eve to stay at the villa, or get her on a flight back to London.

Unless he could persuade her to come with him to Venice…

'*Va bene,* Marco. Thanks for letting me know.'

As he replaced the receiver Eve appeared in the doorway. She had put on a long white shirt, but Raphael noticed with a painful clenching of his stomach that the fabric was too sheer to hide the swell of her bare breasts beneath it. In her hand she carried the wet bra.

She too must have been dazzled by the glare from outside, because she didn't notice him as she crossed the hallway. As he moved out of the shadow of the staircase she started violently, and let out a small scream of terror.

'You scared me!'

'Sorry.' He shook his head and laughed.

'It's not bloody funny!' she screamed. 'I know you think I'm completely stupid and naïve and *ridiculous*, but just give me an hour and I'll be out of your hair for ever. Then you can get back to your glamorous life and your clever, *sophisticated* friends, un-encumbered with such an embarrassing social liability! I didn't ask you to bring me here!'

Sobbing, she made a run for the stairs, but Raphael caught her before she reached them. For a moment she fought him off, but then found herself cradled in his arms, her cheek pressed against his bare chest while he rocked her and waited for the sobbing to subside.

As soon as she was calmer he disentangled himself as gently

as he could and stepped back. Another minute and no amount of railway timetables and international exchange rates would be able to contain the hard evidence of his desire.

'I'm sorry.' He gave her a bleak smile. 'And, before you say anything else, that's what I was laughing about. It occurred to me that I don't think I've ever apologised to anyone so much in my life before.' He sighed. 'Let's get one thing straight—I'm the one who's at fault here. Not you. And now I've got to go to Venice, so it looks like I won't have a chance to make it up to you…'

'It's fine,' she mumbled, clumsily scrubbing away the tears with the back of her hand. 'You don't owe me anything.'

'It's not fine.' He rubbed his hands over his eyes wearily, and Eve noticed there was a muscle twitching in his cheek. 'Look, why don't you come with me? I've got to go to the Press Photography Awards tonight, which will be extremely dull, but the dinner and champagne will make up for that a little. After that, I don't have to be back for a couple of days… I could show you round, maybe make you amend your appalling opinion of me. Have you ever been to Venice before?'

As she shook her head he could see conflicting emotions sweep across her face and he felt a flicker of optimism.

'Then it's simple—you have to come. We stay at the *palazzo* that belonged to my mother's family. It's pretty old and run down, but right in the centre of the city…' With heroic effort he softened his tone. 'Please… I'd like you to come.'

Slowly, mistrustfully, she looked up at him, as if searching to see whether he was joking or not. Her face was blotchy and red from crying, her lips swollen, but his heart gave a sudden lurch as she nodded.

'OK.'

Relief surged through him.

'Great. Go and pack. We need to leave in about an hour.'

Watching her run up the stairs, he felt the tension in the

knotted muscles of his shoulders and made an effort to relax. At least now he wouldn't have to worry about Luca getting his hands on her for the next couple of days.

He smiled ruefully to himself.

Which left him conveniently free to worry about keeping his own hands off her.

CHAPTER EIGHT

'YOU travel very light,' Raphael remarked drily, taking Eve's single tattered bag as they walked across the tarmac towards the Lazaro jet.

'I know. I'm sorry. I'm hopelessly scruffy,' Eve muttered, miserably aware of the pitiful figure she must cut in comparison with the designer-clad, high-maintenance women Raphael was used to.

Ever since they'd left the villa she'd been unable to meet his eye, frozen by sudden shyness in his presence. She'd accepted his invitation to go to Venice because, as she'd told Lou last night, she had no intention of returning to England without proof of his guilt or otherwise. But she was not yet so deluded that she couldn't see that it was also because leaving him now would be unbearable.

Walking beside him, she felt every cell of her body respond to his nearness. It was going to be an uncomfortable trip, she thought in anguish.

'I thought we made a deal? No more apologies—it's getting quite ridiculous. Anyway, you have nothing to be sorry about. You may not be at the cutting edge of fashion, but you certainly have style.' His tone was offhand—slightly bored, even—and he glanced down at her with a faint smile tinged with irony. 'Perhaps it's what your magazine would call "minimalist chic"?'

Eve looked down at her beloved but distinctly worn jewelled

sandals. 'I think it's what any magazine would call "in need of a makeover".'

'Well, I'm sure Nico will approve,' Raphael said, gesturing to the steward, who was coming towards them to relieve them of their small amount of luggage.

Last time Raphael had used Antonio's jet Catalina had been with him. Catalina and four cases, plus one large trunk containing all her cosmetics. A weekend away with her had always felt a little like embarking on an Edwardian Grand Tour.

'I haven't brought anything smart, I'm afraid. To be perfectly honest, I haven't actually *got* anything smart.'

'In that case we'll just have to go shopping.'

'No! I couldn't. I—'

Raphael cut through her objections. 'After you.'

Eve hesitated for a fraction of a second, then swallowed hard and went up the steps of the plane. In her head she repeated her usual pre-flight mantra. *Flying is statistically safer than crossing the road.* Adding hastily at the last minute, *Therefore I will not give Raphael di Lazaro the satisfaction of seeing me burst into tears on take-off.*

As he stood back to allow Eve to climb the steps to the plane ahead of him, Raphael found himself staring at her, drinking in her fresh simplicity. She was wearing yesterday's faded khaki combat trousers, rolled back to reveal slim, brown ankles, and had changed the damp shirt for a delicately embroidered and pin-tucked Victorian chemise with a low, lace-trimmed neckline that was simultaneously demure and sexy as hell.

Moodily he pushed a hand through his hair. Gone was the overt seductiveness of last night, but the shy self-effacement that had replaced it was having just as powerful an effect on his testosterone levels. Sticking to his resolution wasn't going to be easy, he realised grimly, barely managing a smile at the pilot who awaited them at the top of the steps.

'Welcome aboard, *signore, signorina.*'

'Thank you for getting everything ready for us at such short notice, Roberto,' Raphael said in his native tongue.

'*No problemo*, Signor Raphael. I am sorry to hear about the ill health of Signor di Lazaro…' Roberto drew Raphael slightly aside and said quietly, 'Signor Luca has requested the plane too, but I thought you and the *signorina* would prefer to fly alone. I hope that is all right?'

Raphael gave him a curt nod of acknowledgment, and the two men exchanged a swift glance of mutual understanding. Roberto had been instructed to monitor Luca's use of the jet very carefully indeed.

Eve was oblivious to this exchange, her fear temporarily forgotten as she took in her surroundings. She had expected a miniature plane, with rows of seats perhaps upholstered in a particularly plush fabric. In a daze, she found herself laughing at her own naïveté

This was laid out like a sitting room, with a sofa and armchairs at the front of the plane, facing each other around a low coffee table. Where the villa was decorated in perfect country-house style, the jet had obviously allowed Antonio the opportunity to play with contemporary design: the sofa was upholstered in scarlet leather, while the chairs were an assortment of suedes and velvets in various shades of charcoal and biscuit. The floor was covered in a thick cream faux fur rug, and one curved wall was painted with an enormous art-deco style mural depicting a whippet-thin woman reclining on a chaise-longue and sipping a cocktail through scarlet lips.

'I know,' Raphael said sardonically, coming to stand beside her. 'Hideous, isn't it? I think Luca had a hand in the design, which would explain why it looks like the waiting room in a brothel.'

Eve would have liked to ask him how he knew what a waiting room in a brothel looked like, but she was too shy. The flirtatiousness which had come so naturally last night, when she had still been under the illusion that it was all part of a calculated plan, had utterly deserted her today, leaving an awful stilted awkwardness in its wake.

'I'm not complaining,' she said taking the glass of prosecco he was holding out to her. 'It certainly compares quite favourably with the airborne cattle trucks that are my usual mode of transport.'

'Do you like flying?'

'Love it,' she said determinedly. Raphael thought she was immature enough already. There was absolutely no way she was about to admit to being as frightened as a rabbit on a motorway.

'Have you ever been on a private jet before?'

She attempted a mock-haughty look. 'Me? With my glamorous lifestyle? What do you think?'

He gave a sudden smile, which lit up his face and made her feel as if he had reached out and caressed her. 'I think no. It's completely against my principles, of course, but it's a great way to travel once in a while.' He held out his glass. 'Here's to the first time.'

She could feel the colour rush to her cheeks, just as the liquid heat was rushing into her pelvis. Glancing up in confusion, she met his gaze, and was unable to interpret the look in his hooded dark eyes. Was he testing her? Quickly she looked away.

'Here's to travelling in style,' she amended shakily.

'Or not,' he said, glancing disparagingly round at their opulent surroundings.

One thing that was no different on a luxury private jet from any less impressive aircraft, Eve discovered, was that the whole business of take-off was just as alarming. Try as she might as the plane began to accelerate along the runway, she could never quite get over the embarrassing, irrational fear that disaster was only seconds away, or shake off the suspicion that as the wheels left the tarmac it would probably be her last contact ever with solid ground.

Clutching her wine glass, she shut her eyes. The small plane sped forward, then plunged upwards into nothingness. There was a roaring in her ears as she felt the ground fall away beneath them, and the blackness behind her closed lids swirled and deepened.

The next thing she knew, Raphael was very gently prising her fingers off the glass. Taking it from her, he clasped her hands between his and kept them there, reassuring her with his quiet strength, until the plane had reached altitude and the fog of blind panic had cleared from her head.

Tentatively she opened her eyes, and found herself looking into his. For a second she saw there something dark and unreadable that sent shivers down her spine, but then the shutters came down again. He let go of her hands and leaned back on the scarlet leather upholstery with a look of amusement on his face.

'So take-off is one of the things you love most about flying, is it, Eve?'

She looked down into her lap and fiddled with a button on one of the many pockets of her trousers. 'I'm always worried it won't work.'

'I see,' he said gravely. 'You think that someone might have changed the laws of physics without telling you? Making it impossible under the new regulations for planes to stay up in the air?'

His voice was absolutely serious, but looking up at him from under lowered lids she saw the familiar mocking smile. The colour rose to her cheeks.

If she hadn't turned away she would have seen his face soften. 'Why didn't you tell me?'

'What? And shatter your image of me as a super-cool top international fashion journalist?' she muttered. 'It wouldn't have been fair to disillusion you.'

His lips twitched into a smile.

'Plus,' she went on, 'it's so stupid and embarrassing.'

'Don't be silly. It's neither stupid nor embarrassing—nor, in your case, particularly surprising.'

'Of course,' she said sulkily. 'It's completely predictable that I should be the kind of person who would cry on aeroplanes.'

'You didn't cry.'

'Not this time.'

'Anyway, that wasn't what I meant. I just meant that it's a basic human instinct to feel that the ground is a safe place and the sky isn't. And if there's anyone who lets themselves be governed by their instincts, it's you.'

She hesitated as the impact of his casual words sank in. Just a week ago, if anyone had said that to her, she would have protested hotly, arguing that she was governed by logic and intellect and good old-fashioned common sense. But she'd discovered things about herself in the last two days that had turned her world upside down.

And the strength of her instincts was one of them.

She looked up at him with troubled turquoise eyes. 'I just don't see how it can work.'

He sighed, pushing the hair back from his forehead. 'Think about it like this. It's all about forces. The plane's propellers create a thrust…'

He stood up and walked to the other end of the plane. It was only a small space, but he needed to put some distance between himself and her before every shred of reason or responsibility deserted him. There was no use in trying to kid himself that he was spouting A-level physics to reassure her, when he was all too aware it was just another tactic to divert his own mind from the much more interesting path it seemed hell-bent on taking.

'…which overcomes the drag of the air against the plane. The difference in air pressure on the upper and lower surfaces of the wing creates enough lift to support the weight of the plane in the sky. It all comes down to the friction between the opposing forces.'

She gave him a tiny, wicked smile. 'Ah, why didn't you say that at the start? Friction between opposing forces is something I understand perfectly. Thank you, Professor. Your mission has been successful.'

* * *

Below them the Appennine landscape looked calm and tranquil. Raphael wished he could say the same for his own emotions.

No, he corrected himself. *Not emotions. Hormones. Pheromones. Whatever else it was that made a man want to grab a woman and lose himself in her scent, her kisses, the pleasures of her body.*

Her perfume, the same one that had shrouded him in warmth last night while he had been sleeping, was tantalising him now, affecting his ability to think clearly.

And there was a lot he needed to think about. Since his conversation with Marco he'd been desperately trying to come up with some way of moving the investigation into Luca's drug dealing forward, and an idea had been growing at the back of his mind.

Deliberately he turned his face away from Eve, and with enormous self-control marshalled his thoughts.

Catalina was still living in Venice. She had returned to her home-town, where her parents still lived, after her break-up with Luca, to get over her drug addiction with their support and make a clean break from her old life. Raphael still had their number, and had made occasional contact with them over the past two years to enquire after Catalina's progress.

Maybe it was time to get in touch again.

He wasn't sure that Signora Di Souza would allow it, but if he could just meet up with Catalina maybe he could persuade her to give evidence against Luca and step into the breach left by the dead girl. But could he be sure he wouldn't be putting her in danger?

Raphael's relationship with Catalina had lasted just over two years, and, in spite of the fact that it had been Catalina who had walked out on him, he had always taken responsibility for the break-up himself. He had been too cold, too unwilling to commit. 'Emotionally frozen,' she had called him as she had hurled her bags into Luca's waiting car.

She was right, of course. No wonder she had fallen for the

laughing, charming Luca, whose extravagant romantic gestures were no doubt matched by effusive romantic words.

It must have been like travelling from Siberia to the Seychelles. But it had turned out to be a very poisoned paradise. Within six months Catalina had lost her contract with Lazaro as evidence of her drug habit became impossible to hide. She was lucky to have escaped Luca's clutches before she lost her life.

The rolling fields and verdant hillsides of Emilia Romagna were now giving way to the flatter land around the Venetian lagoon. Raphael glanced up at Eve to tell her that they were nearly there, but the words dried in his mouth. She had kicked off her sandals and was curled up in the corner of the sofa, her laptop balanced on her knee, her glasses perched on the end of her nose. In between bursts of typing she absent-mindedly twisted a lock of hair around one finger. She looked unbearably young.

His insides gave a painful twist of longing, and he had to clench his hands into fists just to stop himself from reaching out and stroking the delicately pale arch of her instep, which was just inches from his thigh on the scarlet leather.

At that moment she moved, putting the laptop to one side and stretching like a contented cat. Leaning over to the fruit bowl on the table, she picked out an apple, then, glancing up, saw him watching her and held it out to him.

'Do you want it?'

Her voice was husky from not speaking for a while, her expression artlessly, unconsciously inviting.

He gritted his teeth and forced a smile, hiding his discomfort behind a mask of irony.

'No, thanks. I may not be the kind of devout Catholic Fiora would like me to be, but even I know better than to accept an apple from a woman called Eve.'

Venice was a city for lovers, Eve thought wistfully, gazing out from the *vaporetto* at the couples walking over bridges and in and out of narrow alleyways, their arms wrapped around each other in sensual intimacy.

Since getting off the jet, Raphael had hardly spoken a word to her. His mind was clearly somewhere else. Or maybe it was just on some*one* else. He was probably remembering all the other times he'd visited Venice, with various glamorous, interesting women who wouldn't blush under the flirtatious banter of the *vaporetto* man, or jump so much they nearly fell into the canal when he took their hand to help them into the boat.

Out of the air-conditioned interior of the plane the air was as thick and sticky as warm honey, so it was a relief to feel the breeze in her hair as the boat moved through the water. At least she was here, she thought, in an attempt to be positive. She had wanted to visit Venice for as long as she could remember, though she had always imagined it would be with someone very significant.

Which, she realised with an agonising stab of despair, in a way it was.

Raphael dragged his gaze away from her and sighed inwardly. Venice was as grimy and glorious as ever, but he kept finding his eyes returning to Eve, enjoying her reaction to the sights more than the sights themselves. The emotions were so easy to read on her face—excitement, alarm, sadness, wistfulness—that he found himself constantly wondering what she was thinking.

And that was a dangerous path to go down.

She was probably eyeing up the local talent, he thought darkly. There were plenty of examples of Venice's beautiful youth to admire, and she was barely more than a teenager, *per l'amore di Dio*. That was what girls her age did.

He gritted his teeth and looked around, suddenly impatient to be off the boat and out of such close proximity with her. Tonight they would attend the awards ceremony, which would at least provide the relative safety of a crowd, and tomorrow he would make his excuses and go and meet Catalina. That done, they could return to Florence—hopefully with some good news for Marco.

'We get off here,' he said suddenly.

The *vaporetto* came to a rocky halt beside a small jetty. Bewildered, Eve followed Raphael, reluctantly taking the hand he held out to her as she stepped onto the wooden boards. He didn't meet her eye, dropping her hand again as soon as he decently could.

'Where are we going?' she asked, having to run a little to catch up with him as he walked off.

'Shopping.'

'Oh… What for?'

'I thought you said you had nothing to wear tonight?'

'Yes, but…'

She was almost running to keep up with him, and in the sultry afternoon heat it was unbearable. She lost her temper.

'Would you just please stop for a minute? I've had enough! We are *not* going shopping! For one thing I can't aff—'

'Here we are.' He stopped abruptly in front of a shop displaying the kind of clothes Eve had only seen on Hollywood's darlings on Oscars night. A stunning gown of midnight-blue taffeta studded with starry clusters of diamonds fell with effortless glamour from the flawless plastic shoulders of a disdainful-looking mannequin. The next thing Eve knew he had opened the door and swept her inside.

'Raphael,' she said, anger and embarrassment fighting within her. 'I said I—'

But the glamorous shop assistant was already beside them. Her face was almost as chillingly perfect as the model's in the window, but it broke into a seductive feline smile at the sight of Raphael.

'Signor di Lazaro, *bentornato*. It has been such a long time since we have seen you.'

'*Grazie*, Claudia. I know it's short notice, but I wonder if you can find something for my friend here, for tonight?'

'The photography awards? You are very naughty to leave it

so late, but I'm sure we can find something.' She turned to Eve, looking her over with dark, appraising eyes. 'This way, please.'

At the back of the shop Raphael deliberately turned his back on the row of changing cubicles and, sinking into one of the vast cream sofas, picked up a newspaper from the coffee table. Claudia understood her wealthy clients as perfectly as she understood fashion, and she had gone to considerable trouble to create an oasis where weary husbands would be only too happy to wait while their wives tried on clothes. The espresso machine was state-of-the-art, a plasma screen TV dominated one wall, and every imaginable publication—from the finance papers to tasteful top-shelf magazines—was represented in the pile of reading material.

It was an area designed exclusively for relaxation. So why did he feel as wound up as a racehorse under starter's orders?

In Columbia he'd found himself in situations that had been volatile and dangerous, but he'd never once felt at a loss as to how to react. He knew what he had to do, and he had no difficulty whatsoever in doing it, whatever the danger. How stupidly ironic that he should come home and find himself in a situation where he knew very well the right thing to do, but found himself ridiculously incapable of controlling his impulses to do the opposite.

In the changing cubicle Eve was still protesting, her soft, musical voice slightly breathless as Claudia ushered her out of her clothes. 'Raphael—listen. I can't afford to buy—'

'I'm not asking you to buy anything,' he said irritably. 'I'm dragging you to this event, so the least I can do is buy you something to wear.'

There was a little pause. When she spoke again her voice was slightly muffled, and he realised she must be taking her top off over her head.

'And what if I won't let you?'

He felt himself smile. 'You could always go in what you had on this morning.'

He heard her small gasp. The smile died on his face as lust kicked him in the ribs.

'*Bellisima, signorina.*' Claudia's voice reached him, the approval in her tone clearly audible. 'It looks beautiful on you. It certainly is a dress that makes a statement.'

'It's the statement it makes that worries me,' he heard Eve murmur. 'Something along the lines of Take me, I'm yours.'

Raphael thrust a hand through his hair. 'It sounds perfect,' he called out drily, trying to make light of the uncomfortable tension that was growing inside him. 'Am I going to be allowed to see it?'

'Uh-uh. No way. It's coming off right this second.'

Gritting his teeth against the vivid images *that* conjured up in his overwrought mind, he steeled himself not to turn round and stared stonily ahead.

But he hadn't noticed that the vast mirror in front of him reflected the row of changing cubicles. Beneath the door of the central one he could see a pair of smooth brown calves and slim ankles, and before his tortured gaze there was a slither of red as a dress slipped to the floor.

Hypnotised, he watched her step out of it on delicate feet.

It was the most perfectly erotic thing he'd ever seen.

He swallowed painfully, unable to tear his eyes away from the mirror. Each one of his senses was on hyper-alert, so that the rustle of silk as Eve slipped into another dress was almost unbearably tantalising, and the sound of the zip was like a physical caress. He found himself gazing helplessly at her small, highly-arched feet, watching her lift her toes, then rise up onto tiptoe for a moment before she stood still again.

There was a moment of silence, which was broken by Claudia's voice.

'Good. But you need to take your bra off to get the proper effect.'

Raphael shut his eyes and leaned his head back on the soft cream upholstery, crucified by desire. In his head he could picture the soft fullness of her breasts as she had stood by the pool that morning, naked, and furious as a kitten. Even when she was angry she had a fierce sweetness that just made him want to gather her up and kiss her quiet, as he had done in the street, when he'd seen her with Luca. He adored the way her clear turquoise eyes darkened almost to aquamarine, intensified by the prim librarian glasses she wore...

'*Signore?* Ready?'

Claudia stood back and held open the door.

The dress was made of gunmetal-grey silk, strapless and unadorned. As Raphael's eyes travelled slowly over Eve's body he felt as if the air was being slowly squeezed out of his lungs and replaced with lead. Her lovely feet had been encased into high-heeled grey satin shoes that made her long legs seem endless. Her hips swelled sensuously beneath the dull sheen of the silk, her slender waist was nipped in, and her glorious, voluptuous breasts spilled out of the top of the boned bodice in hour-glass perfection. Claudia had pinned up her hair and added a dark stain of lipstick to her mouth, giving it a sensuality that was almost indecent.

She looked beautiful. And sophisticated. And glamorous.

And he hated it.

Eve's heart was in her mouth as she stood in front of him. Maybe now he would take her seriously. Maybe now she would be the kind of woman who could seduce a man properly.

He stood up slowly and took a step towards her, his face as cold and hard as granite. Time seemed to stand still as his eyes moved over her and she waited for him to speak.

He said nothing. But then he didn't have to. His face said it all.

'You like it, *signore?*' asked Claudia nervously.

'It's fine,' he said tonelessly and, turning on his heel, strode off to wait at the cash desk.

White-faced and trembling, Eve fled back into the changing room.

CHAPTER NINE

As SHE walked out of the boutique Eve's glance was a blast of winter in the sweltering afternoon. Angrily she handed him the large, stiff-sided carrier containing the dress.

'As you insisted on buying the damn thing, you can carry it,' she said icily.

Without speaking Raphael took the bag and walked away. Eve had no choice but to follow.

The sky was the colour of a bruise as they made their way through *calles* and *campos* still busy with summer tourists and couples walking slowly, hand in hand. The melancholy beauty of the place added to Eve's utter despair as she hurried through the crowd in Raphael's wake. They seemed to be the only people who were rushing—everyone else moved at the leisurely pace of holidaymakers or with the languor of lovers. The anger that had pulsed through her in the shop as she'd torn the dress off and savagely scrubbed away every trace of the lipstick began to ebb away, but she tried desperately to hang onto it, knowing that underneath it there was nothing but a deep well of hurt and confusion.

They had reached a vast, wide-open square, surrounded by colonnaded buildings. As they made their way across it Eve suddenly realised why it seemed familiar. Familiar, and yet powerfully, breathtakingly unexpected in its scale and beauty. She stopped.

'Saint Mark's Square,' she breathed in awe.

Raphael turned round and saw her standing still, lost in wonder in the middle of the square. She was herself again: sweet, fresh-faced, all traces of the sophisticated beauty that had so unnerved him scrubbed away. His heart twisted painfully inside him.

'Something wrong?'

'No. I hadn't realised where we were, that's all.'

'Piazza San Marco. Home of the most expensive cappuccino in the world,' he said scornfully.

'It's amazing.'

'It certainly is. Amazing that tourists continue to fall for it.'

The sky had darkened slightly, lending a strange yellowish quality to the afternoon light. The heat was stifling now, and from out in the lagoon there was a distant rumble of thunder that made the crowds of people scattered around the square begin to disperse in search of shelter. Only Eve and Raphael did not move.

It was as if all the energy of the building storm was concentrated in the air that crackled between them. Eve's eyes flashed with fury.

'Of course I wouldn't expect *you* to find it in the slightest bit impressive or beautiful. You're completely above all that, aren't you, Raphael?

'Beauty?' he said softly. 'No. When it comes to real beauty I'm as much a fool as anyone else.' He took a step towards her, his face dangerously still apart from a muscle twitching in his jaw. 'What I can't stand is when it's cheapened and flaunted for the masses.'

She gave a little gasp as the viciousness of his words stung her.

'You *bastard*. You throw the Lazaro millions around like some sadistic fairy godmother, trying to turn me into Cinderella just so I won't show you up at this bloody ceremony, and then you complain when you don't like the results! Well, I'm afraid you just made a really bad investment. I'm *not* one of your glossy, glamorous, gorgeous women, and I never will be!'

The first fat drops of rain were beginning to fall from the livid sky. His face was pale in the unearthly light, but he gave a short, humourless laugh and dragged his hands through his hair.

'You just don't get it, do you? I don't *want* you to be one of my "glossy, glamorous women", for God's sake!'

She looked at him as if he'd just hit her, then with an agonised sob turned to run away. He grabbed her wrist and pulled her back, just as a monumental flash of lightning cracked the sky.

'You don't want me? Then stop playing games with me and leave me alone!' she screamed. 'If you don't want me, just bloody let me go!'

'No!' The word came from him in a jagged cry. 'I don't want you to be turned into one of those women because you're perfect the way you are! Eve, you're—'

But he didn't finish, because somehow his lips had found hers and he was kissing her as if his life depended on it. The warm rain mingled with the tears on her face, and she tasted of salt and earth and something pure and indefinable that was the essence of Eve, and he drank it in like a man who had been without water for days.

A crash of thunder echoed around the ancient walls of the square, and suddenly the rain was falling harder. Breaking off the kiss, he cupped her face in his hands and gazed at her in agony. Standing there in the pouring rain, with her thin chemise clinging wetly to her body, she was like an orphan of the storm. With a thick groan of anguish he realised that after she had tried on the dress she hadn't bothered to put her bra back on, and the glorious fullness of her breasts was as clearly visible through the transparent cotton as if she had been wearing nothing at all.

Suddenly he knew that he wanted her more than he'd ever wanted anything in his entire life.

She had heard the sound he made, and understood its meaning. Biting down on her swollen lip, she looked into his eyes and saw the torment he was suffering. Slowly, wonderingly, she reached up and, with a fingertip, swept aside the dripping lock of hair that was falling over his forehead, then brushed her lips against his in a gesture of acceptance and invitation.

His breathing was shallow and fast, his eyes almost black with the urgency of his need, and he gave another strangled groan. As a fork of lightning zig-zagged above them he took her hand and they began to run across the square, splashing through the puddles.

When they reached the other side Eve glanced back and gasped. 'The dress!'

The shiny crimson carrier bag was still standing where he had dropped it in the middle of the square.

'Leave it,' he growled, pulling her on.

He stopped at a huge wooden door. Dazed and disorientated with desire, Eve had no idea how they had got there, knew only that as Raphael pulled her up the steps and fitted a huge key into the lock she felt almost dizzy with the intensity of her craving for him.

They stumbled inside, her lips already seeking his before the door had even closed behind them. As it slammed shut they fell against it, mouths hungrily devouring what they had waited so long to taste. In the sudden quiet after the noise of the storm outside, Eve surrendered completely to the torrent of her own voracious longing. Spreading her arms out wide against the door, she arched her back in ecstatic submission, thrusting her breasts against the muscular wall of his chest, loving the exquisite agony as her peaked nipples rubbed against the layers of thin wet fabric that separated their flesh.

As their clothes began to dry a little on their heated bodies, another kind of wetness was flooding her from within. She ground her pelvis against him, feeling the unbearably enticing hardness of his arousal. Her fingers ached to reach for the belt of his trousers, but some sadistic instinct for prolonging the pleasure made her keep her hands pressed against the wall, until she felt she might scream with anticipation.

In the dim, underwater light of the hallway he tore his mouth from hers just as a spectacular flash of lightning illuminated his face. His expression was tortured, haunted, lost, and he pressed the heels of his hands into his eyes.

'Eve, I—'

She didn't wait to hear any more. While thunder shook the ancient casement windows some primitive animal instinct overtook her, making her reach out for him and grab the collar of his shirt. Pulling him roughly to her, she only had time to murmur three words before his mouth crashed down onto hers again.

'I want you.'

This time she was in control. She pushed herself away from the door and felt her legs part, her body curve towards his. His hands cupped her buttocks, caressing her, holding her against him, so that the throbbing of his desire merged with her own hot, pulsing need.

Blindly she felt for his belt, feeling the honeyed surge within her as her fingers found it and began to work on reaching their goal. Swiftly, deftly, she flicked the end of the belt out from its restraining loop, and was just about to undo it completely when his hand closed over hers.

'Not here.'

His voice was harsh and ragged. Placing a hand beneath each thigh, he scooped her up so that she was still facing him, straddling him, her eyes level with his. As he carried her effortlessly up the wide, sweeping staircase her gaze didn't flicker from his for an instant. And all the time her hands were very slowly undoing the buttons of his shirt. Freeing each one, she trailed a feather-light fingertip down his bare skin to the next, until they had reached the top of the stairs and only the button of his jeans remained.

His steps faltered as he felt her fingers work it open. Her turquoise eyes were hooded and opaque, and for a second her eyelids fluttered closed as her fingertips met the silken tip of his erection.

She felt the shudder ripple through his body, and he sucked in a shivering breath. Roughly applying his shoulder to the nearest door, he pushed it open, and in a couple of strides had crossed the room and laid her down on a bed.

There was something goddess-like in the way she rose up on her knees in front of him to finish what she had started. The storm continued to rage around them, but her face was perfectly composed, only the spreading darkness in her eyes and the swollen, rosy moistness of her parted lips betraying her hunger. With her eyes still fixed on his, her fingers moved downwards, and her lush mouth curved slowly into a sensual smile.

Button fly. The game could continue. Inch by devastating… ravishing…exquisite…inch, her caressing fingers moved down his throbbing hardness.

Clenching his fists against the unbearable pleasure, Raphael's groan was lost in an ear-splitting crash of thunder as he pushed her back onto the bed. Shrugging off his unbuttoned shirt, he closed his mouth over hers as his hands found the zip of her trousers and tugged them down over her knees, then turned their attention to her top.

The buttons were tiny. There were hundreds of them. And he didn't have her patience.

'Take it off!' he rasped.

She did as she was told, lifting her arms and wantonly wrenching the thin cotton top over her head in sudden desperation to be free of everything that restrained and separated them. As she did so Raphael drank in the sight of her slender body arching upwards, the delicate ridges of her ribs beneath the pale caramel of her skin, the gorgeous heaviness of her exceptional breasts. Unable to resist her any longer, he bent to brush his lips against one hard, thrusting nipple, then parted his lips to take the deep pink bud into his mouth.

A sharp shock of ecstasy quivered through her. She cried out—a high, keening sound of longing which echoed through the murky rooms of the silent *palazzo*.

Raphael raised his head to look into her eyes. In the purple storm-light his face was mask-like, inscrutable, the intensity of his response concentrated in his dark, glittering eyes. With swift, savage movements he stripped off the remainder of his own clothes and reached out to grasp her hips.

She was so wet. Almost deranged with the strength of his need for her, he ran his thumbs softly along her swollen, secret folds, marvelling at the liquid silkiness, loving her eager sweetness. He was hanging onto his self-control by the finest gossamer filament, and he knew that in a few more seconds he would be lost.

As he entered her he felt her tense suddenly. Looking into her eyes, he saw that her wanton confidence of a moment ago had gone, leaving a naked vulnerability that made the adrenalin surge within him.

'*Eve*,' he breathed. '*Oh, Eva...*'

'Don't stop,' she sobbed. 'Please, Raphael—*please*, just keep—'

She gasped, unable to finish, as he gathered her into his arms and lifted her up. He positioned himself on the edge of the bed and she found herself sitting astride him, in exactly the same way as she had last night on the terrace. But this time she could feel him deep inside her, filling her in every possible sense.

With infinite tenderness he cradled her in his arms and began to rock her. Gently at first and then, as the shadows cleared from the deep pools of her eyes, she picked up the rhythm herself, added to it an urgency of her own. Instinctively she found herself putting her hands on his shoulders, moving to take some of her weight onto her knees, giving her more freedom to tilt her pelvis towards him, taking him deeper and deeper into her with each blissful thrust.

Their eyes met and locked. His were filled with an emotion that she couldn't read but wanted desperately to understand. She let herself fall into their dark, troubled depths and he wrenched his gaze from hers, buried his face in her neck, breathing her in, tasting the delicious dampness of her flesh. The sensation of his lips on the sensitised skin of her shoulder and the taut column of her throat seemed to travel like quicksilver straight down into the molten core of her, adding a spark to the smouldering heat between her thighs.

Just when he thought he could hold off the moment of sweet release no longer, he felt her stiffen and grow still in his arms, then cry out in joy and surprise.

The pleasure he got from hearing that sound was inde-scribable. Even his own blissful, earth-shattering climax a second later couldn't beat it.

In the aftermath of the storm the air was cooler. As the sweat dried on their exhausted bodies Raphael felt Eve shiver, so without letting her go he tugged back the layers of crisp sheets and slid between them.

They lay in silence, their limbs entangled, his head resting lightly against the silken pillow of her breasts while one hand softly caressed the hollow of her waist. The sense of deep peace that had overtaken him as their lovemaking had reached its climax was already beginning to ebb away as the implications of what had happened hit home.

He'd written her off as an unscrupulous journalist, out to do a kiss-and-tell exposé. He'd kept her with him because he didn't trust her. *Because he was supposed to be protecting her.*

And now he knew that her innocence was for real. And he had failed her. He was supposed to be protecting her, but he'd been so carried away by his own lust that he hadn't even managed to use a condom.

A tide of guilt and self-loathing swept through him.

'You should have told me.'

His voice was just harsh whisper, and her hand, which had been running through his hair, suddenly stopped its rhythmic stroking.

'Told you what?'

'That you were a virgin.'

'Would it have made any difference?'

He sighed heavily. 'Of course. Of course it would.'

His words cut into her like sharpened blades, until the ornate plaster cornicing she had been staring at on the ceiling above the bed disappeared in a blur of tears.

That was what she had been afraid of. To him what had just taken place between them was obviously just a casual encounter. Had he known she was a virgin he would have felt under too much pressure to make it into something more. She blinked hard. It was bad enough that he had found out she was pathetically inexperienced without her burdening him with childish emotional outbursts as well.

'I didn't tell you because it isn't important.'

'I would have been more…gentle. And gentlemanly. I'm sorry.'

'I thought you said no more apologies?' She gave a laugh that sounded almost like a sob. 'Or were you fishing for compliments? You were perfect. It was…' She hesitated, lost for words, unconsciously caressing him again as they were both overwhelmed by remembered sensation.

Languidly she ran her fingers through the silky length of his hair, watching it fall back onto her skin, starkly black against the creamy white of her breasts. Every now and again she caught a glimpse of silver glinting in the dark mass. This tiny, unexpected sign of vulnerability touched her unbearably.

'You're going grey,' she said softly, singling out one pure silvery strand.

Sitting up, he gave a bleak laugh. 'Of course I am. I'm old. Too old for you.'

'Says who?' Behind him her voice was achingly tender. 'Your mother was the same age as me when she married your father, and he was a lot older than her. Fiora told me.'

She felt him stiffen. 'Come on,' he said abruptly throwing back the sheets. 'We have a ceremony to attend.'

'Well, I hope the designer gene has been passed down. Because since we left the dress in Saint Mark's Square, all I have to wear is this sheet.'

Buttoning up his jeans, trying not to think about the delicious circumstances of their unbuttoning, he looked at her and was caught off guard for a moment by her astonishing beauty. Her golden hair was tousled, her skin a warm honeyed apricot against the white of the sheets, and her aquamarine eyes shimmered with the afterglow of passion, and what looked like tears.

'I don't doubt you'd carry it off beautifully,' he commented sardonically, walking towards the long wall of built-in cupboards. 'But fortunately you shouldn't have to.' Throwing open one pair of doors, he revealed a row of dresses in a kaleidoscope of colours.

From the bed, Eve gasped.

'Whose are they?'

'My mother's. I don't think she'll be needing any of them tonight, though,' he added with a twisted smile.

While Raphael went back downstairs to find their luggage Eve wound the sheet around herself and moved over to the wardrobe. The luxurious fabric of the countless dresses caressed her fingers, and the faint, unmistakable fragrance of gardenia drifted up from their silky folds. An image of the beautiful, laughing woman in the photograph came back to her, and she felt the sting of tears behind her eyes again. How could Raphael bear to look in here?

She started as he came back with the bags.

'Have you found anything?'

'No. I mean—yes. But there's so much… I wouldn't know where to begin.'

Her heart ached for him as he began to rifle through the rails. Not a flicker of emotion showed on his face.

'Nothing black or red. Or grey. I don't want you looking so-phisticated. I'd much rather you looked like yourself.'

He pulled out a selection of dresses in beautiful shades of

dusky pink, duck-egg blue, pistachio-green and ivory, and threw them down onto the bed.

'Try these to start with.'

'They're gorgeous.' She picked up the pink one from the top of the pile, touching its lacy hem with awe. Behind her, Raphael was busy unzipping his battered leather flight bag and shaking out his dinner jacket, so she took advantage of his preoccupation to drop the sheet and slip into the dress.

'There are probably shoes in there somewhere as well,' he said, without turning round.

With the dress still unfastened at the back, she bent to look in the bottom of the cupboard. Sure enough there were rows of shoes arranged neatly on racks—some of them in boxes, some in soft drawstring bags, some just swathed in tissues.

'How come everything's still here, just as she left it, after all this time?' she asked, taking out a perfect pair of fifties-style slingbacks in palest pink satin.

Raphael shrugged. 'My father didn't want to get rid of them. I guess it was easier to store them here than move them.'

'He must have loved her very much.'

'Not at all. It was the dresses he loved. Most of them are his own designs.'

The bitterness in his voice made her wince. 'Oh, Raphael, no! Surely that's not true? He must have loved her!'

Raphael had put the large, square black case he had brought with him from Florence on the bed, and now he snapped it open. Eve couldn't see what it contained, but it looked sinister-like a gun case. She realised she didn't feel remotely concerned.

I trust him with my life, she thought matter-of-factly. *It doesn't make sense, but I can't help it.*

'He never showed any signs of it. I don't think he ever stopped trying to change her into something she wasn't.'

'What was she like?'

'Sweet. Funny.' His fingers faltered for a second as he realised

who else that description fitted, but he didn't stop what he was
doing or look up. 'She couldn't help but laugh at the absurdities
of the fashion world, which my father always says drove him
mad. To him, fashion is an extremely serious matter.'

'Why did he marry her, then?' Eve asked as, holding the pink
dress up at the front, she slipped her feet into the slingbacks.
Reaching backwards to slip the straps over her heels, she heard
the mechanical whirr of a camera shutter. So that was what the
case contained. Startled, she looked up—straight into the lens.

'Wh-what are you—?'

'When I see something beautiful I want to photograph it.' His
eyes were narrow and unsmiling as he looked at her, then he
raised the camera again and continued. 'She was the daughter of
a *duce*—Italian aristocracy—and she was very lovely. She was
his *muse*—' he said the word scornfully '—before she was his
wife.'

He was lying on the bed, propped up against the pillows, his
face obscured by the bulk of the camera. Breaking off for a
moment, to adjust something on the long zoom lens, he glanced
up at her suddenly. 'Put the blue one on now.'

She did as she was told, stepping quickly out of the pink dress,
still in the delicate satin shoes. The camera whirred on.

'Go on,' she prompted gently.

'From the start she was a target for the paparazzi. Beautiful
young heiress married to celebrated designer—paparazzi
heaven. But she hated it. She was young, shy, insecure—completely unsuited to the role he thrust her into.'

Totally absorbed in what he was saying, Eve slipped her arms
into the blue dress. Without attempting to fasten it, she turned
to look in the mirror, giving Raphael a perfect view of her bare
brown back. He fired off a quick succession of shots, hoping to
capture the way the late-afternoon light was casting a soft halo
around her hair and turning her skin to gold.

She looked at him over her shoulder as she took the dress off again, picked up the green one from the pile and unzipped it. 'So what happened?'

'He couldn't see how much she hated it. Publicity is everything to him. He couldn't see how bloody awful it was for her—how hounded she felt. It got steadily worse after I was born, because she tried even harder to avoid it then—for my sake—which just made her an even more tempting target. Then one day she took me to the dentist. As we came out there were a couple of paparazzi who started hassling her, calling out, taunting her to get a shot. It really got to her. She stepped out into the road to get away from them.'

Eve was aware of the absolute stillness in the room and found herself hardly daring to breathe, the pale green dress draped loosely around her. Fiora's words came back to her. *A terrible thing for a child to see...*

'The car had no chance of avoiding her. Afterwards the driver blamed himself, but it wasn't his fault.'

All that was audible in the sudden silence was the rustle of silk as she crossed the room and slipped onto the bed beside him. She spoke quietly, firmly, but with incredible gentleness, taking his frozen hands within her own and holding them tightly.

'No, it wasn't his fault. Or your fault. And it wasn't your father's either.'

Crucified by the pain of things he had never spoken of to anyone before, Raphael pulled away and strode over to the window.

'It was. He should have...'

He faltered, then cleared his throat before continuing in a low, even tone. 'He should have done more to protect her. From all of that. If he had loved her he would have protected her.'

For a long moment neither of them moved. Then, straightening abruptly, he turned back to where Eve sat in the rumpled wreckage of the bed.

'Anyway—enough of all that. We're going to be late.'

Savagely doing up the buttons on his shirt, he realised she'd done it again. Drawn things out of him that he hadn't even wanted to admit to himself. If it was a journalistic tactic she was bloody well wasted on that silly celebrity gossip rag. She ought to be on the political desk of a top broadsheet.

'Could you do the zip for me?'

She stood beside him, offering him her bare brown back. The bones of her spine were like a tapering string of pearls beneath her gleaming skin, but infinitely more delicate and precious. Feeling the breath catch in his throat, he swept her hair aside and, with massive self-control, averted his gaze from the secret, sensual hollow at the nape of her neck. After tugging the zip upwards, he stepped away.

She turned to face him, and he noticed how the dress—*that* dress—brought out the green of her eyes, how they shone with compassion and understanding.

'Do I look all right?'

For a moment he didn't trust himself to speak—which, he reflected bleakly, was somewhat ironic.

She was supposed to be the one he didn't trust.

CHAPTER TEN

THE world looked completely different as they emerged from the *palazzo* after the storm.

The city's crumbling, softly coloured buildings were blotchy from the deluge, but the sky had shaken off its heavy purple clouds and was now a clear, sparkling blue. The evening light falling on the rain-soaked streets turned them into an enchanted city of pearl and gold.

But it wasn't just Venice that had changed, Eve acknowledged, shivering slightly in the warm evening. She had too.

Raphael's lovemaking had transformed her—invisibly, indefinably, irreversibly. It was as if someone had whispered to her the secrets of the universe, or taken her hand and given her a glimpse of paradise.

Walking along the narrow *fondamenta* beside her, Raphael seemed tall and distant, and though she desperately yearned to touch him she didn't dare breach the small distance between them. Since his revelations about his mother's death he'd been withdrawn to the point of distraction. Only when she'd finally finished getting ready and had stood in front of him had his face shown any flicker of emotion.

And then she'd realised that she was wearing the pistachio-green dress his mother had on in that picture.

She had stammered horrified apologies, but he had laid a finger on her lips to silence her.

'No apologies—remember? It's fine.' But his voice had been oddly flat.

Now, as he stood to one side to let her cross a narrow bridge, she stole a surreptitious glance up at him. No wonder she was completely incapable of taking adequate notice of her incredible surroundings. Even Venice paled into significance compared with his exceptional good looks.

He was born to wear evening dress—his dark, brooding beauty was set off to perfection by the impeccably cut black suit, his long dark hair for once slicked back from his face, showing off its aristocratic hauteur. He had never looked more gorgeous, or more out of reach.

They reached the other side of the bridge and he suddenly looked down at her, his face softening slightly.

'Nearly there. I'm not being a very good tour guide, am I? I keep forgetting you haven't been here before. I should be pointing out all the sights.'

She shook her head, looking down at the pale pink satin shoes so that he wouldn't see her blush as she lied blatantly, 'That's OK. I'm just drinking in its incredible beauty. I don't need to know any more than that.'

'Oh, I don't know,' he said softly. 'To really fall in love with the place you need to get to know it, not just admire what it looks like from the outside.'

'Yes, well, maybe you're right. But perhaps I don't want to get to know it.' Eve looked up at him with a painful smile. 'If I fall in love with it I'll never want to leave.'

Eve hadn't been sure what to expect the awards ceremony to be like, but she had been prepared for a similar media circus to the perfume launch.

She couldn't have been more wrong. The event was being

held in one of the old *settoecento palazzos* just off the Grand Canal, but whereas the watchword at the perfume launch had been glitz, here it was restraint. No red carpet covered the narrow stone *fondamenta* at the top of the steps from the water, and the only cameras in the immediate area were held by curious tourists, delighted at the spectacle of such smartly dressed partygoers.

They entered a vast reception hall filled with chattering women in rainbow-coloured silks and chiffons, and distinguished-looking dinner-suited men. Letting go of her arm, Raphael turned to her and murmured, 'Wait here,' before disappearing into the crowd.

Without the silent strength of his presence Eve felt suddenly bereft. She sighed, looking up at the high, vaulted ceiling. It was a feeling she was going to have to get used to. In a couple of days they would return to Florence, and then she would go back to England.

Alone.

Some time this afternoon, somewhere in the bliss of Raphael's arms and the paradise of his bed, she'd reached the point of no return.

She had fallen hopelessly in love with him.

Literally.

Finding out that he had been involved in Ellie's death would be intolerably agonising now. She just couldn't risk it. The only thing to do was leave while her illusions and her memories were intact.

Of course, she thought, with a momentary flash of desperate hope, there was always the chance that she would discover something that categorically ruled out Raphael's involvement in Ellie's death, and then…

She gasped as someone slipped behind her, covering her eyes with a big, strong hand.

'Guess who?'

'I…I don't…'

'Come on, *bambino*, surely you haven't forgotten me already? I am destroyed.'

The hand was removed, and she turned round.

'Luca! What on earth are you doing here?'

'Now I ask myself the same question,' he said tragically. 'I come all this way to rescue you from the extreme dullness of my big, grown-up brother, and you not even recognise me. My life is ended…'

'Don't be so silly,' she laughed, hitting him playfully on the arm. 'It's lovely to see you again.'

'And you, *cara*… And you.' A big smile spread across his face. 'You look *sensazionale*,' he said warmly, walking around her. 'Delicious, in fact. I could eat you with a spoon.'

'Stop it,' Eve retorted, but she was smiling. There was something very charming about Luca's flirting, especially after Raphael's distance since they had arrived at the ceremony.

'I called you,' Luca said reproachfully. 'I was going to take you out to lunch and give you all the gossip from the retrospective party for your article. But—' he raised his hands in a gesture of helplessness '—you don't answer my calls.'

'Calls? I didn't—' She broke off abruptly. That must have been when Raphael had taken her phone.

Suddenly an idea occurred to her. The smile faded and a worried frown creased her forehead. 'Luca? Could I ask you something?'

'Of course, *bella*, and I can absolutely guarantee that the answer will be yes.'

'No, I mean it. Something serious. About Raphael.'

He sighed theatrically and rolled his eyes. 'If you must. I, however, am much more interesting. Are you quite sure there's nothing you'd like to ask about me? Like which hotel I am staying at? The room number, perhaps?'

But she was not to be diverted. There might not be any love between the two brothers, but Luca must know Raphael better than most. He more than anyone would know of any involvement with drugs in Raphael's past, and because of the animosity between them would no doubt be only too pleased to share the information.

She hesitated, unsure how to phrase the many questions that were crowding into her mind.

Luca had bent a little, and was looking questioningly, speculatively, into her face. His eyes were dark, and seemed to glitter with something slightly malevolent. She shook her head and looked away, confused.

'*Cara?*' Luca prompted.

The moment had passed, and with it her opportunity to find out that her suspicions were correct, or to lay her worst fears to rest once and for all. It was like some sadistic gambling game, with her future happiness as the stakes.

'Doesn't matter,' she muttered in anguish.

Through the crowd she could see Raphael coming back towards her, two glasses of champagne in his hands. There was something hypnotically charismatic about him. Eve found it impossible to tear her eyes away from him, and she experienced an exquisite flashback to the events of the afternoon. Breathlessly she relived the feeling of his mouth on hers, the naked longing on his face as he'd carried her up the stairs.

She felt her stomach flip as he looked up and met her eye, and she had the most delicious sensation that he was remembering exactly the same thing. But the next moment his expression had changed to one of open hostility.

'*Che diavolo…?*'

'Now, now, big brother. Watch your language. We are not in the backstreets of Columbia now.'

'Why the hell are *you* here?'

'Funnily enough I nearly wasn't, as the Lazaro jet that was supposed to be bringing me was suddenly unavailable.' Luca's tone was light, and his smile didn't fade, but there was no mistaking the malice behind his words. 'You obviously don't take enough interest in the Lazaro business, Raphael. If you did, you'd know that we are one of the major sponsors of these awards.'

Raphael glanced around, wondering if any of the smartly dressed guests were actually Marco's men undercover. He hoped so.

'I'm surprised,' he said sardonically. 'It's unlike Lazaro to be involved in anything so worthwhile.'

'Not my idea of good PR, I have to confess. You're absolutely right—usually we prefer to go for sponsorship of slightly more—' Luca glanced around disdainfully '—fashionable events. Alessandra Ferretti always did have a soft spot for you, though, big brother. She obviously managed to twist Father's arm.'

'How is he?' Eve interrupted, noticing the murderous hatred in Raphael's eyes.

Luca shrugged. 'He has not woken up yet.' He rolled his eyes. 'Though why he is so tired I have no idea. I am the one who does all the work.'

'It's the sedation,' Raphael snarled through gritted teeth. 'I spoke to the hospital a little while ago. They're keeping him sedated.'

'Hadn't we better find our table, Raphael?' Eve asked, gently touching his arm and willing him to look at her. Anything to break the terrifying tension that froze the air between the two men.

'Of course.' Luca was suddenly the picture of solicitousness. 'You must go—we can finish our conversation later, *mia cara*. You had something you wanted to ask me, remember?'

Eve felt Raphael tense at the endearment, and, hooking her arm through his, pulled him away from Luca.

'No, no—forget it. It really doesn't make any difference now.'

Eve's initial disappointment that she wasn't sitting next to Raphael at dinner gave way to relief as the man who was to be seated on her right introduced himself. Paul was young, enthusiastic, and, much to her delight, from London. Suddenly the evening didn't look as if it would be such a struggle, and her worries about letting Raphael down with her poor Italian, her sketchy knowledge of photography and her ignorance of the grim realities of global conflict evaporated, as they immediately started swapping notes about their favourite places. Once they'd established a shared passion for a particular deli in Notting Hill there was no stopping them.

However, it didn't stop her from feeling a breathtaking pang of jealousy when the seat next to Raphael was taken by the *über*-sexy Alessandra Ferretti. Dressed in a clinging, tan-enhancing dress of flame orange, she had obviously waited until everyone else was seated before coming to the table to ensure maximum attention. Eve had to admire her faultless instinct for a PR opportunity.

Everyone else seemed to be admiring her cleavage in the low-cut dress.

Immediately Alessandra drew her chair closer to Raphael's and began talking to him. Eve was too far away to hear any of their conversation, but although she wasn't great at understanding Italian, she was a lot better at interpreting body language.

Alessandra's was saying *private party* in loud, clear tones.

'Have you tried their buffalo milk mozzarella?' Paul asked, as waiters brought out plates of antipasti. 'They get them flown in every Thursday from a little producer in Southern Italy.'

Eve shook her head, trying to concentrate on what he was saying, but his passion for this particular Italian cheese faded into the background as she studied Alessandra's greater passion for a particular Italian photographer. Her movements were so confident and lazily seductive as she leaned back in her chair, sipping wine and laughing, or tossing back her long mane of dark hair, that to a casual observer she looked completely at ease. But Eve had noticed the intense, rapacious look on her face in the candlelight as she spoke to Raphael and Raphael only.

He seemed a million light-years away, the events of the afternoon as insubstantial as the mist that was falling over the darkening canal outside. But then suddenly he looked up and gave her the ghost of an ironic smile, and she felt better.

Once the main course had been cleared away the main purpose of the evening could get underway. A distinguished-looking man in his sixties took the podium at the front of the room, and silence fell as the lights were dimmed and he began to speak. Eve couldn't catch much of what he was saying, but was content to sit back in her chair, sleepy and replete, and let it all wash over her.

A huge screen behind the podium had been displaying a constant slide show of images, but now the compère stood aside as the photographs competing for awards in each category were shown. One by one the winners wove their way through the tables to collect their awards. Eve's hands grew tired of clapping as the evening wore on, and the pictures all blurred together as her mind produced images of its own in glorious Technicolor. The wet tendrils of hair dripping down Raphael's sun-tanned neck as he'd wrestled to open the door of the *palazzo*. The ravaged, tortured look on his face as she had pulled him towards her in the dark hallway. His hands, brown against the pale skin of her hips, as he had raised them up to enter her…

She bit back the soft moan of desire that threatened to escape her and looked over at those hands now. Strong, artistic and long-fingered, they were playing idly with a knife, but the rest of him was completely still, his expression absolutely blank. Gradually emerging from her fantasy world, and inching back into the present, Eve noticed that all eyes around the table and in the rest of the room were upon him—and suddenly there was a deafening explosion of applause.

'Bloody talented bloke,' said Paul admiringly, clapping furiously.

Raphael rose from his seat and walked towards the podium and the huge image on the screen behind it. Eve gasped as she took it in. Even without her glasses, its power was undeniable.

It showed a woman holding a chubby, laughing baby. Immediately the viewer's eye was drawn to the child's face, with its clear blue long-lashed eyes and dimpled rosy cheeks. It was a universal image of innocence and sweetness, and only after seeing all that did one take in the rest of the scene. The mother was barely more than a child herself—thin, hollow-cheeked, dead-eyed. The arms that held the baby were skin and bone, the blackened veins clearly visible beneath her papery skin. On the grimy bed beside them lay a child's teddy bear—and a used syringe.

Raphael reached the front, where Luca waited to present him with his award. There was an awful moment when Luca held out his hand and Raphael hesitated, his face darker than the storm-clouds that had gathered over the city that afternoon.

Ignoring Luca's outstretched hand, he turned to the clapping audience. The room fell silent as he began to speak.

'I am honoured to accept the award for Photographer of the Year and, as is only appropriate, will be sharing the prize money between a couple of charities—the Orphans of Heroin in Columbia, and the Drug Recovery and Rehabilitation Centre we set up in Florence two and a half years ago.'

There was a burst of applause, which he swiftly quelled. 'I'm humbly aware that it is the subjects of my pictures who are exceptional, not the person taking them. I'm hugely grateful to anyone who trusts me enough to photograph them...' His eyes flickered over Eve, sending an explosion of sparks through her central nervous system. 'But I hope that, in time, the people of Columbia may have cause to be grateful to me too. For exposing their situation to the world, and continuing to work towards improving it.' He paused, and the silence in the room was almost tangible. 'The work will continue until the menace of drugs and those who produce and profit from them is removed.'

Only as his words were drowned out in another sea of applause and the scraping of chairs as everyone stood up did Raphael turn to face Luca and shake his hand. It looked more like the sealing of a solemn vow than a salutation of thanks or congratulation.

Alessandra Ferretti wasted no time in offering her congratulations as Raphael came back to the table. Wrapping herself around him, she kissed him lingeringly on both cheeks, then drew him swiftly aside before Eve had a chance to even leave her place.

'I've organised a few publicity shots for all the major glossies that should bring in lots of cash for the charity,' she was saying as she led him away.

He turned and met Eve's eye, holding it for the briefest moment before he was swallowed up by the crowd.

'He's a genius. A bloody genius.' Paul sighed wistfully as they stood in front of Raphael's photographs in the gallery.

He had brought Eve up to the *palazzo*'s long gallery, where all the photographs of the nominees were on display. She had dutifully admired the two he had entered—of angular bluish landscapes which, he informed her, were soon-to-be-melted polar ice caps—but found herself drifting on a cloud of cautious euphoria to Raphael's work.

'Look at the composition there,' Paul was saying enviously, pointing to a shot of some little boys with grubby faces, playing football in a dusty road. The arid monochrome of the road contrasted vividly with the lush fields that surrounded them on both sides. Eve peered more closely, wishing she hadn't been too vain to wear her glasses.

'The emotion in some of these shots is just incredible,' Paul continued. 'These people were regarded as villains, the scum who produce the stuff our A-listers are busily shoving up their nostrils, but Di Lazaro's given us the chance to see them differently. Given them—I don't know—a sort of…'

'Dignity,' Eve finished for him. She found that a film of tears had blurred the grimy, smiling faces of the little boys.

'Ah, there you are, Eve.' Alessandra Ferretti appeared from nowhere, on a cloud of extremely heavy perfume. 'Raphael was asking for you. He's going to take you home now.'

She spoke as if Eve was some overtired child who was spoiling the party for all the grown-ups. Determinedly Eve kept her gaze fixed on the children enjoying their game of football on a dusty road in Columbia. She was trying to imagine Raphael there, just a few feet away from them. Like the baby in the winning picture, two of the boys were smiling straight into the camera, and Eve wondered what Raphael had been saying to them.

'He's waiting.'

There was a sharp edge to Alessandra's voice, but it couldn't burst the bubble of joy inside her.

She said an affectionate goodbye to Paul and followed Alessandra along the gallery. 'Tell me about the charities Raphael mentioned. The Orphans of Heroin in Columbia and—what was the other one? In Florence?'

'The Drugs Recovery and Rehabilitation Service. He set that one up as a helpline initially. In our industry—' she said it patronisingly, as though she and Raphael shared a glamorous existence that would be entirely alien to the likes of Eve '—we see lots of people go down that route. Drugs are an inevitable part of the fashion scene. But he wanted to provide a point of contact for young models who needed help to get out of the cycle. He did it pretty much single-handedly at the start—funded it all himself, took all the calls on his own mobile, twenty-four hours a day,' she said with proprietary pride. 'But typically he never talks about it.'

They were going down the stairs now and, suddenly lightheaded, Eve had to grasp the banister for support.

So that was it. Ellie had had Raphael's number scribbled on the scrap of paper in her pocket not because he was a source of drugs, but of help.

Exhilaration flooded through her, as if her blood had been replaced with champagne. Stopping in the middle of the staircase, Eve turned to a bewildered Alessandra and, grinning broadly, said, *'Thank you.'*

Raphael was standing at the foot of the stairs, the light from the chandelier falling onto his broad, straight shoulders and glossy black hair. She wanted to jump down the last four stairs into his arms and kiss the life out of him. She wanted so, *so* much, and suddenly it all seemed possible.

He looked up as they approached, frowning slightly.

'I've neglected you all evening. I'm sorry.'

'I thought we weren't going to say sorry to each other any more?' she said, trying to suppress an absurdly big smile.

Alessandra hovered, looking stony beneath heavily applied lipstick. Placing a hand on Raphael's arm, she darted an accusing look at Eve and said something to him in very rapid Italian.

Raphael's face gave nothing away. 'Well, you'll just have to manage without me I'm afraid, Alessandra,' he replied in English, then looked down at Eve with the faintest hint of a smile. 'Let's go.'

He made no move to touch her, but, walking across the wide hallway, Eve could feel the white-heat of his nearness like a caress.

Alessandra watched them go, and as they reached the door she spoke again in the same quick, incomprehensible Italian, her voice stiff with malice.

Raphael hesitated, then turned.

'Thanks for the advice, Alessandra. But for future reference I'd just like you to remember that if I want your opinion I'll ask for it.'

His quietly controlled tone sent shivers down Eve's spine. But that was nothing to the fireworks that exploded in her pelvis as he slid a protective arm around her shoulders.

Looking meditatively back at Alessandra, he added with quiet bitterness, 'And, though it's none of your business, I hadn't forgotten. I wish I could.'

CHAPTER ELEVEN

AN APRICOT moon was reflected in the canal as they came out into the night air. The ageless tranquillity of the scene was in sharp contrast to the frenzied pulse of excitement that beat inside Eve's veins at the prospect of being alone with Raphael. She was trembling.

'You're cold,' he said, and before she could protest he had slipped off his dinner jacket and draped it over her bare shoulders.

It still bore the warm imprint of his body and a faint trace of the lemony tang of his cologne, underlaid by a deeper sandalwood scent that was all his own.

She looked up at him. He had pulled his silk bow tie undone and opened the top two buttons of his shirt, and her eye was automatically drawn to the hollow of bronzed skin at the base of his throat.

'What did Alessandra say?'

'Alessandra has a talent for stating the blatantly obvious and dressing it up as a profound insight,' he commented drily. 'Which apparently in the world of PR makes her something of a genius. When it relates to my personal life it just makes her annoying.'

'Your personal life?'

'Yes. She thought it would be helpful to point out that you're considerably younger than me.' He wasn't going to mention that she had also spitefully reminded him of Eve's profession. 'She's jealous.'

'Of me? Why?'

As she spoke she stumbled slightly on a cracked paving stone. With lightning swiftness Raphael had reached out and caught her. For a second he held her, looking down into her upturned face. The light from the streetlamp above them turned her blonde hair to silver.

'Now who's fishing for compliments?' he said with a small half-smile.

He let her go and she bent to take off the pink satin shoes with their unfamiliar high heels. As she stood up his jacket slipped off one creamy shoulder, and the harsh streetlight illuminated a crescent-shaped bruise on the side of her neck. Frowning, he brushed his thumb over it.

'How did you do this?'

She bit her lip and glanced down at her bare feet, then back up at him. Just like the first time he had spoken to her, at the retrospective party, her expression was sweet and gentle, but spiked with a hint of amusement.

'*I* didn't, exactly…'

He gave a soft moan and raked his fingers through his hair, remembering how he had buried his face in her neck as their lovemaking had reached its climax.

'*Dio*, Eve I'm s—'

She silenced him with a butterfly-light kiss. 'No apologies, remember?'

'If you do that again,' he growled, 'I'll be apologising to the magistrate in the morning for committing an act of public indecency.'

Pulling away, she took his hand and drew him forward. Enveloped by his jacket, she looked delicate, elfin and very mischievous.

'In that case we'd better hurry. I'd much rather commit an act of private indecency. Preferably more than one, in fact.'

He raised an eyebrow. 'It seems I have corrupted you.'

She turned, giving him a look of such scalding sexuality that he felt his body stiffen in instant response. Sparks of white heat glinted in the depths of her aquamarine eyes as she stood on the tiptoes of her bare brown feet and brushed her lips against his ear.

'Corrupted? No. You have *awakened* me.' Her mouth found his and gently, teasingly, her pink tongue darted between his parted lips. 'And for that I am truly grateful,' she finished in a breathy whisper that sent the blood rushing to his loins.

'So am I,' he murmured, sliding a hand into the front of her dress. 'So am I.'

The match flared in the darkness, illuminating the angular planes of Raphael's face as he held it to the candles in the Murano glass candelabra on the dressing table.

A flickering light spread its gentle fingers into the dark corners of the room, each of the six bright pillars reflected in the dull, silvered glass of the old mirror.

'Come back to bed.'

Eve's voice was sleepy and muffled by pillows as she lay face down in the tangle of bedclothes. The candlelight fell on the golden strands in her dark blonde hair and made her skin look almost luminescent against the stark white linen of the rumpled sheets.

'Don't move.'

'Hmm?'

'Don't move. I have to photograph you like that... You look like something from a religious painting in this light. The original Eve before the Fall—'

'Raphael?' she interrupted gently.

'What?'

'Shut up and get over here, *right now*.'

He laughed softly. 'You can't be wanting more already?' Propping himself up on one elbow beside her, he dropped a kiss into the little hollow at the base of her spine. Her seemingly insatiable passion both surprised and amused him.

'Can't I?'

He fell back onto the pillows, giving a theatrical moan. 'I told you I was too old...'

She flipped over onto her back so she could see him properly. 'Don't you dare start all that again!'

'No? What will you do?'

In a flash she was on top of him, her eyes glinting in the gentle candleglow.

'I'll just have to prove to you that you're not....' She gave a low, wicked laugh. 'Which shouldn't be too difficult as I have some *very* hard evidence right in front of me. Or should that be right underneath me?'

Sliding down the length of his thighs, she heard his fierce gasp as she took the smooth head of his erection into her mouth and moved her tongue languidly across its silken tip. She didn't stop to worry about whether she was doing it right, finding herself absolutely in the thrall of an irresistible, primitive instinct, guided by her own sensual pleasure.

She had never dreamed that bringing pleasure to a man would have this utterly explosive effect on her own desire. Closing her eyes in delirious ecstasy, she felt his hands grasping at her hair and found herself drenched with hot, urgent excitement.

'Now you, *cara*,' he rasped. 'Or, so help me, I won't be able to stop...'

Lifting her easily, he laid her down on the pillows. For a second she glimpsed the barely concealed need glittering in his dark eyes before he bent his head to kiss her collarbone, her breast, her belly button. She could feel the faint rasp of stubble on her quivering, sensitised skin as his mouth moved down the flat plane of her stomach, his tongue tip tracing a meandering path of ecstasy and anticipation. A deep moan of pleasure escaped him as he found the hot, wet triangle at the top of her thighs and he breathed in her hopelessly intoxicating natural perfume.

Her orgasm was swift and savage, and for a moment he wondered if he had hurt her. Gathering her into his arms, he held her until the waves that rippled through her tense body receded, leaving her languid and heavy.

'Raphael... Oh...'

She could feel the pressure of his arousal against her belly, and as she kissed him she tasted herself upon his lips.

Hardly moving her mouth from his, she murmured, *'More.'*

And this time he made sure it was slow and gentle and everything he had been too carried away to make it before. They didn't take their eyes off each other as, with every deep, deliberate thrust, they moved closer to their shared heaven. At the last moment he threw his head back and let go.

When he looked down at her again, tears were streaming down her cheeks. In the candlelight they looked like rivers of gold.

'You're up.'

Opening one azure eye and peeking out from underneath a tousled mass of silky hair, Eve gave a little mew of disappointment.

'And dressed. Very dressed.'

'I brought you some coffee.'

Eve wrinkled her nose.

'Bleugh... Tea?' she croaked pleadingly.

'Sorry. You won't find tea in many Italian kitchens—and here we run on the bare essentials. Coffee will have to do.'

He set it down on the little Victorian bedside table and walked over to the window, thrusting a hand through his hair to prevent himself from touching her. She had slept tucked into his body, but had now turned over onto her front again, and the honeyed length of her back was enticingly exposed. She looked utterly bloody irresistible, and it was going to take every ounce of self-control he possessed to get out of the *palazzo* and keep his appointment with Catalina.

Sleepily she rolled over and sat up, pulling the sheet over her breasts. Which was just as well, he thought grimly. The brief glimpse he'd just had of them was having an extremely profound effect on him.

'Where are you going?'

Her clear blue eyes regarded him steadily over the rim of her coffee cup and he had to turn away as he said, 'Out to meet someone. I told you last night, remember? It's business, but I'm afraid it's pretty important—or I wouldn't go.'

'I remember lots about last night, but that part had slipped my mind. I can't think why. Will you be long?'

He sighed heavily. 'Look, Eve, I have no idea. It could be over very quickly, it might take most of the day. I wish I could say—'

'Perhaps I should stay in bed, then,' she murmured with a mischievous smile. 'Just in case it is over very quickly. It would be silly to waste precious time getting dressed…'

She wasn't making this any easier. The look she was giving him was enough to bring him to his knees with longing, and he could feel the insistent pulse in his groin growing stronger by the second. Another five minutes and he wouldn't be leaving the *palazzo* for hours.

'Finish your article, there's a good girl. You can show it to me when I get back. There's bread and fruit down in the kitchen. Help yourself if you're hungry.'

All too aware of the delights concealed by the thin linen sheet, he didn't dare risk a kiss, and strode towards the door without a backward glance.

In the words of the song, what a difference a day made, Eve thought later, as she typed the final sentence of her article with a flourish. This time yesterday she'd been so miserable she hadn't been able to string a decent sentence together, and yet this morning the words flowed out of her fingertips in long, unbroken ribbons.

There was nothing to this journalism lark, she thought airily as she clicked 'word count'. Hurrah. Just a sliver under two thousand, spell-checked, and waiting to be e-mailed to Marissa Fox.

Humming quietly to herself, she set her laptop aside and got out of bed, stretching her cramped legs. She'd been a little cold after Raphael had left, so she'd slipped on the shirt he had worn last night, happily breathing in the scent of him on the crisp cotton as she'd worked, letting the images it evoked float sensually around in her mind. He was so…sexy, she thought with a little shiver, marvelling at her reflection in the dressing table mirror. She looked wickedly, *glowingly* exhausted.

She giggled. Perhaps *Glitterati* would be interested in an article entitled 'Sex: the new Botox'.

Picking up her mobile, she sent Lou a hasty text message.

In Venice with R. Article finished…

She hesitated, smiling to herself as she considered adding *virginity also*. Lou had been on at her for what seemed like for ever about getting rid of it on anyone—almost as if it were some sort of unwanted Christmas gift. How glad she was now that she hadn't. No one else could have introduced her to the pleasures of the bedroom with a millionth of the passion and tender expertise of Raphael. She felt her heart skip a beat at the memory.

Everything OK, she finished lamely. It seemed a totally inadequate way to sum up the utter euphoria she was feeling, but Lou would see that for herself when Eve returned to London.

Joyfully she clasped the phone to her chest and twirled around. *If* she returned to London. Being separated from Raphael for a few hours today was bad enough, and the thought of being apart from him for any longer was appalling.

Suddenly deflated, she collapsed onto the bed and expelled a long breath.

That attitude was neither healthy nor attractive, and she had always had a strong disdain for clingy women. Come to think of it, this morning he'd seemed a little cold and distant, so she must be careful not to irritate him with suffocating adoration.

Outside the ancient windows of the *palazzo* Venice glittered in the summer sunshine—while she waited in the bedroom like some drippy girlfriend.

Purposefully she got up. No more lovesick mooning. She would go and explore.

Within minutes of leaving the *palazzo* Eve was lost.

She'd thought she knew the way to Piazza San Marco, but after wandering through two narrow and unfamiliar *calles* she had to admit that she was wrong. Each time she had been with Raphael, she acknowledged with a shiver of remembrance, her mind had been on other things.

She could still see the distinctive bell tower of Saint Mark's ahead of her, above the jumbled rooftops, but instead of getting closer to it she seemed to be getting further away.

She'd intended to make her way back to Saint Mark's Square and maybe take a photo of the basilica on her phone to send to Lou, and prove that she really was in Venice. Instead she found herself wandering further and further off the beaten track. The little passageways were filled with the smell of frying garlic from the kitchens of tiny *trattoria* frequented only by locals. Eve's stomach rumbled, reminding her that she hadn't done as Raphael had instructed and made herself some breakfast at the *palazzo*. She had discovered the dingy, old-fashioned kitchen and retreated hastily, preferring to find a café.

Although for the first time in her life she wasn't craving chocolate.

This really must be love.

She crossed a little bridge, nodded politely at an old woman coming the other way, and paused before entering a narrow passageway between two tall, crumbling buildings. It smelt suffocatingly of damp and decay, and she found her heart was beating so hard that she feared the sound must be echoing off the high walls above her. She hesitated, wondering whether to retrace her steps and ask the old woman for directions, but pride and her inadequate Italian prevented her. Quickening her pace, she walked on.

The passageway opened out into a small, sunlit square with a café at the far end. The *campanile* was to the right of her now, so she must have come almost full circle and now be heading back in the direction of St Mark's. She breathed a grateful sigh of relief, and was just wondering whether to stop and order some tea or keep going when the blood seemed to freeze in her veins.

For a second she thought she was going to faint. Blackness blocked out the sun, and blindly she stretched a hand out behind her, groping for the support of a wall to lean on. Gradually her vision cleared, and she was able to see for certain that her first glance had been horribly, sickeningly accurate.

Raphael was leaning across a table, clasping the hands of a fragile-looking dark-haired woman. He had his back towards her, but there was no mistaking the deep indigo linen shirt, the sharply slanting sweep of cheekbone that was all she could see of his face beneath the dark hair. And, she realised with another sickening lurch of her stomach, there was no mistaking his intimacy with the woman opposite him. Holding both her hands between both of his, he was leaning towards her, speaking intently to her. There was no way this was a casual encounter with an old acquaintance.

Or a business meeting.

And then, in front of Eve's horrified eyes, he half rose from his seat and took the woman's face in his hands to press a kiss onto her trembling mouth.

Clapping her hand to her mouth, to try and stifle the terrible sobs that threatened to tear her apart, Eve turned on her heel and ran.

* * *

'Don't ask me to do this, Raphael, *please*!'

Raphael tightened his grip on Catalina's hands.

'I wouldn't if I had any other way of getting Luca locked up. You're our only chance, Cat. You said yourself that most of the other girls who've fallen into his clutches are either lost in the drugs underworld and wouldn't be reliable witnesses or are dead. Like your friend—Ellie, was it? You'd be given absolute protection and treated with complete respect. I promise.'

He felt some of the fight go out of her.

'I trust you Raphael. *Va bene*,' she whispered.

'You'll do it?'

'*Si*, I'll try.'

Almost dizzy with relief, Raphael felt like leaping up and doing a victory dance around the square, but he settled instead for stretching across the table and giving her a quick kiss of pure gratitude. As he sat down again he saw the colour drain from her cheeks and an expression of utter terror come over her face. Wide-eyed and ashen-faced she leapt to her feet, almost overturning the table as she stared at a spot just over his shoulder.

Instantly Raphael was beside her, taking her in his arms.

'Cat? Cat! What's wrong? What's the matter?'

She pointed a shaking finger across the square. 'She was there! She was! She looked at me!'

Raphael glanced over his shoulder.

'Who?'

'Ellie!'

'Ellie? Your friend who died?'

Catalina nodded, burying her face in Raphael's shoulder and sobbing brokenly. Automatically Raphael patted her back, making soft sounds of comfort while his mind raced.

He knew all about the hallucinations that were an after-effect of addiction. *Damn*. Talking about the past had probably triggered something off. She clearly wasn't as together as he'd first thought.

'There's no one there, Cat. Shh… There's no one there. Come on, *cara*, let's get you home.'

Grimly he pulled some money from his pocket and left it on the table, then took the arm of a sobbing, incoherent Catalina.

The tantalising image of Eve in bed at the *palazzo* taunted him, and he cursed inwardly. It looked as if this was going to take a while, after all.

CHAPTER TWELVE

BLINDED by her tears, Eve continued to run, without hesitating to think where she was going. Dimly she was aware of going back over the bridge she had crossed only minutes before. But that seemed like a different lifetime. She was almost surprised to see the same old woman, only a short way along the canal-side from the bridge. How could everything else be so absurdly normal when her world had just collapsed about her ears?

Eventually a stabbing pain in her side forced her to stop running, and she sank down in a doorway and wept.

No wonder Raphael had seemed so uptight this morning. And no wonder he had been so vague about when he would be back. With another flood of anguish she remembered his impatience as he'd said—what was it?—*It could be over very quickly; it might take most of the day*. This woman must be an old flame he had been hoping to rekindle, and he hadn't been sure what kind of reception he'd get.

Well, he certainly seemed to have lucked out, Eve thought savagely. From the way he'd leaned over and kissed her it didn't look as if he was going to be heading back to the *palazzo* any time soon.

She'd been so *stupid*. Stupid and naïve. Right from the moment they had first set eyes on each other she had thought that the feelings that existed between herself and Raphael were rare and extraordinary. She had been so overwhelmed by their power that she'd put herself in a position of potential danger to be with him, and her discovery last night that he wasn't what she'd thought had been a moment of pure joy.

Well, he might not be a drug pushing low-life, but he was a two-timing liar. And the way she felt now, that was just about as bad as it got.

'Eve? Eve, *cara*, I thought it was you! *Tesoro*, what is wrong?'

'Luca! Oh, Luca… How did you…?'

'My hotel is over there. Oh, *bambino*, tell me—what has made you cry?'

Next moment she was in his arms, her head buried in his shoulder as she wept. He smelled of cigarettes and booze, and she found herself thinking that it was a far cry from Raphael's clean, lemony tang, but he was familiar, and he was here—and for that she was immensely grateful.

Gently he held her away from him and peered into her face. 'Shh, *cara*, shh. It is Raphael, no?'

She nodded dumbly.

'Is he hurt?'

There was something slightly wild in Luca's eyes, and he shook her by the shoulder a little as he asked the question again. Taking deep, shuddering breaths Eve managed to shake her head again.

'I saw him with…with…another woman. In a café. He was…' For a moment tears choked her again, and she gratefully took the handkerchief that Luca offered her. After blowing her nose she continued, struggling to keep calm. 'They were holding hands. And then he kissed her.'

Luca gave a low whistle. 'What did she look like, this woman?'

Eve shrugged dejectedly. 'Long dark hair, very slim… I don't know. Kind of fragile-looking, I suppose. Like an anorexic version of Alessandra.'

Luca's eyes glittered and he looked oddly pleased. 'Catalina.'

'You know her?' Eve wailed.

'*Si*. She and Raphael had a big thing a few years ago, when she was modelling for Lazaro. But wait, *cara*,' he said soothingly, as Eve started a fresh bout of sobbing, 'it was all over a long time ago. I can't imagine for a minute that Raphael would want her back *now*.'

'Wh-why n-not?' Eve gulped. She didn't like the tone of Luca's voice.

'Because she is damaged goods, *cara*, that is why. Drink, drugs and a whole lot of depravity have taken their toll. Believe me, I speak as one who knows. She has most definitely lost her youthful sparkle.' He smiled nastily and stroked a finger down Eve's cheek. 'Unlike you, *mio carino*. Come—I know where Catalina's apartment is. Let us go there and—'

'No! I couldn't! I don't want to see them!'

'Calm down, *bambino*, calm down. You are jumping to conclusions. We'll go there, and I bet we find Catalina alone. You will meet her and you'll see what I mean about her. Then you will go back to Raphael and give him big kiss and tell him how silly you are. Yes?'

Eve scrubbed at her cheeks with the handkerchief, feeling the tiniest glimmer of optimism. If Luca thought she was being silly, maybe she was.

'OK.'

'*Bene*. Let's go.'

'Nearly there, *cara*. Catalina's *appartemente* is in that building there, on the first floor.'

Eve followed his gaze. Like many of Venice's buildings, the one he pointed out was painted a soft shade of ochre, and in spite of the fact that the paint was peeling and the stonework flaking it had about in an air of faded grandeur. The three storeys above street level were each dominated by tall, elegant windows, some of which opened onto tiny balconies, and the huge door to the building was set into an elaborate stone frame. The whole impression was of a building where important things had happened over the centuries.

Eve just hoped nothing important was going on there now.

Her footsteps slowed as they approached, until Luca was virtually dragging her along. She stopped altogether as they drew level with the building.

And then she saw them.

'No,' she rasped, staring up in disbelief. 'Oh, God… Luca, look. In the window.'

For a moment Luca didn't speak, and in awful fascination they watched Raphael unbutton Catalina's dress, then kiss her forehead.

'I'm sorry, *bambino*, so sorry. It seems you were right,' Luca murmured.

He had to force her to turn away, but by that time she had already seen Raphael lower the bedroom blind. Tears were coursing silently down her cheeks as Luca led her briskly back the way they had come.

After receiving the news of Ellie's death Eve remembered the curious feeling of numbness that had come over her. Everyone around her had treated her with the utmost gentleness, as if she were an intricate and unstable piece of finely tuned machinery that they were afraid of breaking. She hadn't been able to cry.

She wished for a little of that numbness now. All she wanted to do was scream and rage and beat her fists on the floor, like a child having a tantrum in a toyshop. *I want Raphael, I want Raphael! It's not fair!*

Going back to the *palazzo* was a particularly cruel torture. In a daze, Eve climbed the stairs which Raphael had carried her up only twenty-four hours previously.

'Which room?'

'Sorry?'

Luca rolled his eyes. 'Which room are your things in? You forget, *cara*, this is Isabella's palazzo. I have never been allowed inside it before. I do not know my way around.'

'Here.'

It seemed incredible that everything looked just the same as when she had left it just a couple of hours ago. The unmade bed—the scene of such joy and passion—seemed to mock her, and throwing herself down upon it she buried her face in the rumpled sheets, breathing in the lingering scent of sex and Raphael.

'Come on, *bella*, don't cry.'

She knew she was beginning to frustrate Luca, but she didn't care. His initial tenderness was starting to give way to a restlessness that frightened her a little.

'Your bag? Where is it?'

'I'm not sure. Raphael put it…' She bit her lip against another surge of tears. 'There it is—under the bed. I don't have much else.'

The pale green dress was draped carefully over the back of a little chair, and Eve went over and stroked the satiny material. She had been so happy when she'd worn it. Now she felt exactly as the dress looked—empty and forlorn. As far as Raphael was concerned she was yesterday's news, something to be tidied away when she was no longer required.

'Ready?'

Eve nodded, but didn't turn round. Behind her, Luca's voice was sharp with impatience. 'Come, then. We must return to my hotel to collect my bags first, then we go to Marco Polo. I have ordered that the jet be made ready.'

She looked round, wide-eyed with alarm 'Not the Lazaro jet?'

'*Si, cara*. I may not have been allowed in here before, but you forget—I am a di Lazaro too.'

'But I can't—'

She stopped, aware of how ridiculous it would sound. *I can't bear the thought of it without him.*

Luca's voice was smooth and dangerous.

'I think you can, *bambino*. Unless you want to stay here. Perhaps you would enjoy a little *ménage à trois* with Raphael and Catalina?' He laughed unpleasantly at his own joke, then, seeing her stricken face, put an arm around her trembling shoulders.

'Don't worry, *bella*. Luca will look after you. And if you are a very good girl I will give you something nice to help you relax.'

'What do you mean?'

He grinned and tapped the side of his nose mysteriously. 'I show you later. Now, let's get out of this place. It gives me the creeps.'

'I love it,' said Eve fiercely. She shut the bedroom door and leaned her head against it for a second as tears seeped out from beneath her closed eyelids. The image of the unmade bed was firmly imprinted in the darkness in her head, and she suspected it would stay there for a very long time to come: the scene of such brief but perfect happiness.

It was halfway through the afternoon when Raphael finally let himself into the *palazzo*. He carried a large box of English breakfast tea that he'd bought at a vastly inflated price from the owner of a smart café he'd passed on the way back from Catalina's apartment.

He had left Catalina sleeping deeply, having had to undress her as if she were a child and put her to bed. Getting her home from the café had plumbed reserves of patience and strength he hadn't known he possessed, as she had screamed and sobbed, saying the name of the dead girl over and over again. *Ellie*.

Raphael stopped just inside the doorway of the *palazzo*, his brows drawn together in an agonised frown. He'd sunk everything he'd got into setting up the helpline for girls like her— Catalina said she had even had the number—but it still hadn't been enough to compete with the ruthlessness of Luca.

He'd waited until Catalina's mother had arrived before leaving the apartment, and had spoken to Signora Di Souza at some length about the possibility of Catalina giving evidence against Luca. It had been a huge relief to find that she was in favour of the idea. Together, they'd agreed, they would give her the support she needed to brave the witness box if and when the case came to trial. For the first time Raphael had allowed himself to cautiously believe that it really was a case of when. He would ring Marco immediately.

Taking the stairs two at a time, he felt his mouth curve into a smile. Well, maybe not immediately…

Quietly he opened the door, wondering if Eve had been true to her word and stayed in bed. After all, they hadn't had much sleep last night.

'Eve?'

The room was empty, and there was something about the emptiness that sent a shiver right through him. With a casualness he didn't feel he tossed aside the box of tea and sauntered over to look underneath the bed, where he had stowed their bags.

His was there. Roughly he pulled it out of the way, desperate to find hers hidden behind it.

Nothing.

He stood up and looked wildly around. Snatching the mobile phone from his pocket with shaking hands, he scrolled through in search of the number for Marco Polo airport.

Five minutes later, having ascertained there was no one with the name of Eve Middlemiss booked onto any of the outward flights that day, he allowed himself to breathe a little easier, and sank onto the bed with a groan of despair. If she was still on the island she must have checked into a hotel, for some crazy reason. Which meant he had a lot of calls to make.

Just as he was about to begin, the phone in his hand started to ring.

'*Pronto?*'

'Signor di Lazaro? It's Roberto. I thought I should let you know Signor Luca has just boarded the jet back to Florence.' There was a small pause, then Roberto said more quietly, 'He has with him Signorina Middlemiss.'

Raphael let out a vicious expletive. 'Are you in the air yet?'

'No, *signore*, but Signor Luca is in a hurry to leave. We will be taking off in a few minutes.'

'Thanks for letting me know, Roberto.'

'Ne problemo, signore. Would you like us to fly back for you once we've dropped Signor Luca at Amerigo Vespucci?'

'Si, per favore. Let me know when you can get airspace.'

'Of course, *signore*.'

'Oh, and Roberto…?' Raphael pressed a shaking hand to his forehead. 'Could you ask Nico to keep a very close eye on Signorina Middlemiss, please? She…she doesn't enjoy take-off very much. Look after her for me.'

White-lipped, Raphael let the phone fall from his hand onto the unmade bed, then walked over to the window. This was where he had stood yesterday, just after they'd made love. Just twenty-four short hours ago. Closing his eyes, he could picture it exactly. Eve had sat on the bed in that dress, her beautiful face softened with compassion and tenderness, as he'd talked about his mother's death. Her eyes had been alight with love. And he'd been too bloody stupid to see it.

He clenched his fists and pressed them against the glass. *No! Be honest with yourself!*

He'd seen it. He'd just been too bitter and screwed-up and suspicious to admit he felt it too. He'd tried to tell himself Eve was just doing her job.

'Dio!' His voice was a cry of anguish in the ghost-filled room. For how long had he been using his own cynical, emotionally sterile standards to judge everyone else? He remembered how bitterly he'd berated his father, his damning words coming back to haunt him mockingly: *If he'd loved her he would have protected her…*

He'd been wrong about everything.

He loved Eve, and it didn't make him able to protect her. It just gave him greater power to hurt her.

Frantically throwing clothes into his bag, he just hoped it wasn't too late to say sorry.

* * *

The streets of Florence were deserted as Raphael drove through them in the early hours, jumping red lights and screeching round corners far too fast. He didn't care if he was pulled over by the *polizia*. Marco would vouch for him.

As he got nearer to Luca's flat he began to feel almost light-headed with adrenalin and lack of sleep. Every fibre of his body thrummed, and each minute that passed was like a knife-edge on his frayed nerves.

If Luca had laid one finger on Eve...

He had spent the entire crucifyingly slow journey from Venice thinking about exactly what he would do. And it wasn't pleasant.

This was it. Abandoning his car on the double yellow lines outside Luca's building, he pressed the buzzer and waited for the concierge. He had had plenty of time to work out his line on the plane.

'Raphael Di Lazaro. I'm afraid I need to see my brother urgently. Our father...'

Instantly the concierge opened the door, ushering Raphael in with compassionate haste. He had been reading all about Antonio's illness in the newspaper he had hastily folded under his desk, and wasted no time in offering his sympathy.

'*Grazie.* I'm sorry—I'm still a little shocked—which *appartemente* is my brother's?'

'The penthouse, *signore.*'

Raphael concealed a grimace. He should have guessed Luca would occupy the flashiest apartment in the building.

The lift seemed to take an eternity as it climbed to the top floor. In the greenish tinted mirrors Raphael hardly recognised his own face. He seemed to have aged twenty years in the last twenty hours—which was roughly the time since he'd last seen Eve. Stubble darkened his jaw, and his eyes were almost as shadowed and hollow as Catalina's. He was still wearing the blue shirt that she'd soaked with her tears, he thought in distaste, remembering the dry, feverish heat of her thin body as he'd tried to console her. Eve's cool freshness seemed as remote and unreachable as a waterfall in a desert.

Please, God, let her be there.

The lift doors opened. There was only one door in the small, tastefully bland hallway.

When Luca opened it Raphael experienced a small twinge of surprise that he was fully dressed. An unpleasant smile spread slowly across his face when he saw Raphael.

'Raphael—how good of you to drop in and see me! It's rather a strange hour for a social call, though, wouldn't you say?'

Pushing him roughly aside, Raphael strode into the apartment and started opening doors. 'Where is she?'

'I'm sorry—who?'

'Eve.' He said it like a snarl, not knowing how long he could hang on to his last shreds of self-control.

'Ah! The delightful Eve! I'm afraid you've missed her. By now she'll be just about—' he checked his watch '—touching down at Heathrow, I should imagine. We only stopped off here to kill a few hours before her flight.' His greasy laugh sent a fresh surge of adrenalin pumping through Raphael's body. 'But I'm very glad we did! I guess I have to thank you, big brother—you broke her in beautifully!'

White-faced, Raphael turned back to Luca. 'I don't believe you.'

'What? That she's flying back to London right now?' Luca said with exaggerated innocence. 'Would you like to call the British Airways check-in desk? I can't remember the flight number, exactly, but—'

'Oh, I'll check she was on it, believe me. Although I admit there's a chance that you're telling the truth about *that*.'

'Ah, so the bit you don't believe is that Eve was keen to practise her new-found skills on me?' Luca looked suddenly incredibly pleased with himself, like a magician the moment before he pulls a rabbit out of a hat in front of an eager audience. 'Well, since you did so much of the groundwork, perhaps you deserve to see the photographs.'

For a second Raphael seriously thought he was in danger of passing out as Luca held out a fan of five or six Polaroid snaps of a blonde girl. In the top one she was reclining on a bed, naked except for black stockings and stiletto-heeled shoes.

It was Eve.

'They're not up to your standard, I know, but rather nice—'

The next moment there was a sickening thud and the unmistakable snap of bone as Raphael's fist smashed into Luca's face and he fell backwards against the open door of the apartment. Stepping over his crumpled body, Raphael didn't even look down. It was only as the lift carried him back down to the ground floor that he noticed his hand was wet with blood.

CHAPTER THIRTEEN

London. Six months later.

'AND so she was wondering if you'd like to do an article on it. What do you think? Eve? *Eve!*'

Eve dragged her gaze away from the couple in the corner of the sandwich bar and back to Lou, who was looking at her sternly.

'Sorry—what was that?'

'Marissa. She was wondering whether you'd do a couple of thousand words on single pregnancy for the magazine. It struck us that there's been loads written about actually being a single mum, but not much about going through a pregnancy alone.'

'Probably because most people actually manage to stay with their partner for at least nine months,' muttered Eve gloomily.

Lou took no notice. 'You take the starting point of doing the test—you know, mixed feelings and so on—who do you tell first?— right through to how you choose a birth partner.' She beamed. 'Of course, *I* hope to feature in this article pretty heavily…'

Eve took a sip of her tea, hoping it would dislodge the familiar lump in her throat that signalled the onset of tears. Again. Who would have thought she could still have any tears left?

'It would be quite a positive piece, you see. There's really nothing that a partner does that your best friend or a health professional can't. And maybe does better.'

Eve squeezed her eyes shut for a second. *What about telling you how beautiful you are with that particular fierce sincerity? What about holding you and talking to you in the middle of the night when you can't sleep?*

The man at the table in the corner reached across and smoothed a strand of hair back from the girl's face. In the warm fug of the little sandwich bar he had taken off his outdoor coat to reveal a blue shirt, and though his dark hair was neatly cropped, and his face was much less arresting, he still reminded her of Raphael.

But then, somehow or other, most things did.

At that moment the baby gave a little jump, and Eve's hand fluttered to her belly. No doubt Raphael hadn't given her a moment's thought since he'd returned to the *palazzo* that day and found her gone, but, for Eve, forgetting him just wasn't going to be an option. Ever.

'So you'll do it, won't you? The deadline for copy is a week on Wednesday.'

'I can't.'

Lou almost choked on her latte. 'Eve, you must! This is a great opportunity to earn a bit of extra cash before the baby's born and reach out to other women going through the same thing. OK, forget the positive angle and say how difficult it's been—how you worry that your unhappiness during pregnancy might have somehow affected the baby, how you wonder what to tell it about its father as it grows up.'

'Sorry, Lou. I really can't. I had a letter this morning about giving evidence at Luca di Lazaro's trial. I'm flying out on Monday.'

'Oh, God. You should have said.'

'They're still not completely sure that they're going to use me—and if they do when it'll be—but the prosecution want me to be on hand just in case.'

'Will you be giving evidence about Ellie?'

Eve shrugged, making little dark stars out of a splash of

coffee on the table with the end of a spoon. 'I don't know. I've sent the barrister those photographs Ellie sent me from Florence, of her on the steps of the Uffizi, so they can match them up to some pretty lurid photographs they found in Luca's flat. But they might want me to give evidence about what happened on the journey back from Venice—the stuff I told the police about at the time.'

Lou's eyes were round with dismay. 'Oh, no, Eve… You can't go through all that again. Not in your condition! Do they know you're pregnant?'

'No, but it makes no difference. I've got to do this—for Ellie's sake more than mine. I mean, it's not as if he actually harmed me in any way on the jet. After he pulled his little stunt I made sure we weren't alone for a second.'

'No, but you were still an absolute wreck when you got home.'

Eve sighed. 'I know, I know. But that wasn't entirely down to Luca. He only offered me a line of cocaine—'

'Blimey, Eve, you make it sound like a cup of tea!'

'No—I mean, I was shocked and everything, and his aggression when I refused scared me a bit, but Nico—the steward—was there, and I knew he would make sure I was safe. I must admit it was a horrible, horrible moment when he said that he'd known Ellie and I realised that *he* must have been her supplier, but…well, I was a wreck before I even got on the plane with him.'

No change there, then, she added mentally, suspecting Lou was thinking exactly the same thing. She had been enormously supportive throughout the appalling trauma of Eve finding out she was pregnant, but six months down the line her willingness to hand out a constant supply of tissues was starting to wane. Eve couldn't blame her.

'So, will *he* be in court too?'

'Who?'

'Who do you think? *Raphael*, of course.'

'I don't know.' She hadn't dared ask Marco. 'I hope not.'

'Well, I bloody well hope he is, and that his new girlfriend can see exactly what kind of bastard he is! The kind who seduces young girls and gets them pregnant, then buggers off without another word.'

Eve winced and looked down into the dregs of her tea. 'Not quite without another word. He did call the magazine…'

'Yeah—great,' said Lou with blistering sarcasm. 'What was that message again? *Tell her I'm sorry. She'll understand. Make sure she has my number.* Nice one, Romeo. Like she's *really* going to call!'

'Don't,' whispered Eve.

'Well, honestly! *She'll understand.* Understand what? That he just had to distribute his virile Italian charms fairly amongst the female population? It would be petty of any girl to object to that, wouldn't it?'

A fat tear slid out from under Eve's glasses and dripped into her cup. Noticing it, Lou was instantly contrite.

'God, Eve, I'm sorry. I didn't mean to upset you. I just hate the thought of you having to face that bastard again.'

'I'll be fine,' Eve replied unconvincingly, removing her glasses to wipe her eyes with a paper napkin.

'I'll come with you.'

Eve gave her a watery smile, touched by the determination in Lou's voice. Her sympathy might be wearing thin, but her loyalty never failed.

'Don't be silly. I've had enough trouble getting time off from *my* work at such short notice. Marissa would hit the roof. And I don't know how long I'll be there or anything.'

'Well, I'll phone every day. At least three times,' Lou conceded reluctantly. 'Someone's got to remind you to take your iron supplement.'

* * *

Raphael emerged from the court building and stood for a moment breathing in the damp air of the winter evening. Rain was falling steadily on the street-lit pavement, and he threw back his head and let it wet his face. It had been a long, gruelling day.

It was Catalina's first day in the witness box, and she hadn't coped well. Bit by bit the defence barrister was undermining her confidence, making her version of events seem more and more shaky by the hour. It was exactly what she had been afraid of.

It was also exactly what Gianni Orseolo, the prosecution barrister, had feared.

Appearing in the doorway of the building, Gianni shook out a huge purple and green umbrella emblazoned with the gold logo of his polo club and came over to Raphael.

'Are you walking this way? Good. Not a great day, I think you'll agree. They're tearing her to shreds out there. I'm calling a new witness tomorrow. Catalina won't stand up to any further questioning.'

They watched a grey-faced Catalina being led out of court by her parents, a sight that left them both subdued.

'*Bene*,' said Raphael curtly. 'I think I may stay away tomorrow. I'm not sure I can stand another day of looking at Luca's smug face, and I ought to go and see my father.'

'Well, unless it's urgent I recommend you put it off for another day. Tomorrow's witness could make up some ground for us—it might be worth coming in to see Luca squirming in his seat. How is your father, by the way?'

'Until the trial started he was improving every day. Being back at the villa made a big difference. But all this has hit him hard. He adores Luca.'

Gianni Orseolo came from one of Florence's wealthiest families, and he and Raphael had known each other since they were boys. Not well enough to be in the habit of exchanging confidences, but there was something peculiarly intimate about their close proximity under the umbrella in the dark, rain-lashed street.

'The golden boy, eh? While you were the black sheep? And now Antonio has to shift his perspective a little.'

'And me too.' Raphael thrust his hands deep into the pockets of his long coat and looked out into the rain. 'I'd got very used to the idea of hating my father and blaming him for my mother's death. I… Someone…changed my perspective on that…'

At least that was one thing he had to thank Eve for. At least she had left a tiny glimmer of something good in the ruins of his life.

As always, he ruthlessly pushed the thought of her out of his mind.

'Families are complicated things,' Gianni agreed lightly, 'which is why, Raphael old friend, we are very wise in choosing to avoid that path ourselves.'

Raphael said nothing.

Gianni's car was easily recognisable amongst all the small city hatchbacks and family saloons parked along the street. Raphael gave a short bark of laughter as they approached the ridiculously predictable red Ferrari.

'Very nice, Gianni. Very practical.'

'It is for my purposes. As a young bachelor—' he smiled rakishly '—one has to invest in all the right equipment to attract the right ladies.' He pressed the keypad, setting off a volley of flashing lights on the dash, but just as he was about to stoop and open the impossibly streamlined door he turned thoughtfully back to Raphael.

'I know it's none of my business, but you look like you could do with a good night out.' That was a pretty huge understatement. Secretly Gianni was horrified by how gaunt Raphael appeared, almost as if it should be *he* who was in the dock for drugs crimes, not Luca. 'Look, I'm heading out of town at the weekend. Going to stay in the villa of an old mate with a few friends. You'd be more than welcome—it would do you good to get away from all this and have some fun. I've got the perfect girl—'

'No.' Raphael had left the shelter of the umbrella and was already walking away from Gianni along the darkened street.

'Dinner, then. You'd love this girl—'

Raphael shook his head. 'Thanks, Gianni, but no.'

'Can I at least give you a lift anywhere?'

Raphael had almost disappeared into the darkness, but his voice drifted back through the rain.

'*Grazie*, but I prefer to walk.'

Shaking his head in bewilderment, Gianni slid into the driver's seat and fired up the engine with a roar. If he didn't know Raphael better he'd say he looked like a man with a broken heart.

Raphael had got walking without thinking down to a fine art. Head down, oblivious to the rain, he cleared his mind of everything except the calming rhythm of his footsteps.

As soon as Luca's arrest had been secured he had taken his camera and headed back to Columbia. Not, this time, to the places and people with which he had become so familiar on previous trips, but to the mountains. The days he had spent there, just walking and photographing the landscape, had helped him come to terms with Eve's betrayal, even if they hadn't brought him any closer to understanding it.

Before he went he had called the magazine and left a message and a number. Not knowing what to say to the bored-sounding receptionist, he'd simply asked that she tell Eve he was sorry, hoping she would recognise and respond to the private meaning those words held for them both. When she didn't, he'd had to conclude that it and everything else that had happened between them had ultimately meant more to him than it had to her.

He hadn't been able to make sense of it, so, with his habitual ruthless self-control, he'd blanked it out. As a policy it probably wasn't conducive to long-term mental health and happiness, but he was prepared to take his chances.

The rain was falling harder than ever now, and he could feel it seeping under the upturned collar of his coat and trickling down his neck. Suddenly, with all the pain of a physical blow, he was reminded of Venice. Standing in Piazza San Marco as the storm broke...the fury that had burned in Eve's indescribably beautiful eyes which had turned so quickly to passion...

Gritting his teeth, he ground the key into the lock of his front door and threw it open, then slammed it shut behind him

When denial didn't work there was always anger.

Shaking the rain from his hair, he went along the passage-way to the kitchen and filled a jug with water for the coffee machine. It was the only item in the gleaming kitchen that looked even vaguely used. Signora Arrigo, Raphael's cleaner, worried endlessly about him, and lately had even taken to leaving portions of her home-made pasta or soup in the fridge. Today a small loaf of focaccia rested under a linen towel on the worktop.

Smiling wanly at her kindness, he opened the cupboard to get coffee, then paused. At the very back something caught his eye, and he reached in and pulled it out.

English breakfast tea.

How utterly pitiful he had become. Ridiculous enough that he'd brought it back to Florence in the first place—but as for keeping it for the past six desperate months... That was just deluded. What was he thinking? That one day she would turn up on his doorstep out of the blue? Offer to give him another chance over a cup of decent tea?

There was a loud crash as the packet of tea hit the wall and met its target in the sleek metal bin.

Snatching up a bottle of red wine, Raphael left the kitchen, all thoughts of food and coffee forgotten. His sitting room was on the first floor, and without bothering to switch the light on he went to stand at the window.

Outside, the rain looked like shoals of tiny silver fishes in the streetlights. Raphael took a long mouthful of wine, determinedly driving out the memories that crowded around the edges of his mind, insistent and enticing. Eve's head on his knee as they drove on the street down there. The softness of her hair under his hand. The warmth of her breath on his thigh...

It was the details that haunted him.

Giving a groan of despair, he turned away from the window and reached for the television remote control. News. Football. Anything so long as it offered some blissful respite from the endless torment of his own thoughts.

The screen showed a bare stage, with a Japanese-style paper screen as its backdrop. Raphael froze, rigid with disbelief, as the soprano began to sing and the hair-raisingly beautiful, spine-chillingly lonely aria filled the darkened room.

Madame Butterfly.

Pouring the remainder of the wine into his glass, he leaned his head back against the wall and closed his eyes. The pale light from the window showed exquisite agony on his stricken face.

CHAPTER FOURTEEN

FLORENCE in February was an entirely different city from the one Eve had left in August. A slick of rain darkened the elegant streets. Tourists huddled in waterproofed groups as they consulted their guidebooks, oblivious to the majesty of the buildings that towered above them.

Sitting behind the uncommunicative driver sent by Marco to take her from her hotel to the courtroom, Eve stared unseeingly out at the headlamps of the passing cars and tried not to think about Raphael.

She was shaking. Even the remote possibility of seeing him again was making her heart do things that didn't feel healthy, and she could imagine what her midwife would say if she took her blood pressure right now. For the sake of her sanity, and the health of her baby, she tried to keep her mind focused on Luca.

She was here to close the grim chapter that had started three years ago with Ellie's death. Her own small tragedy was incidental.

The car pulled up in front of a forbidding-looking building, and the driver got out and put up an umbrella before opening the door for her. For a moment he stood impassively, waiting for her to get out, but then, seeing the tears sliding down her pale cheeks, and noticing how much she was trembling, he quickly stepped forward and offered her his arm. He was younger than she'd realised, but his voice, when he spoke, was deep and comforting.

'Don't worry. Please don't cry.'

Gently he held her arm as she got out of the car, and helped her up the steps to the building. Eve felt that without his support her legs would simply give way beneath her.

Speaking in abrupt Italian into a small, hand-held radio, he guided her to a long marble-pillared corridor with benches on both sides, and motioned to her to take a seat.

Eve shook her head. Her back ached from sitting so tensely in the car, and she placed both hands at the base of her spine and flexed it slightly.

'*Caffe, signorina?*'

'No, *grazie*. I'm…'

The words died on her lips as she looked up. Footsteps were approaching from the other end of the corridor, brisk and businesslike, and adrenalin crashed through her like water through a burst dam as she found herself looking straight into the eyes that had haunted her dreams for six tortuous months.

Raphael's face was ghostly pale in the gloom, and the hollows beneath his cheekbones were as dark as if they had been painted on. But it was his eyes that held her attention. In the few brief moments before he disappeared ahead of her into the court room they burned into her with a ferocity that felt like hatred.

'Could you confirm your full name, please?'

Gianni Orseolo's voice was gentle, but still Eve could not suppress her violent trembling, nor look up and meet the eyes of the man seated beside the suave lawyer.

'Eve Maria Middlemiss.' Her voice was a cracked whisper in the sudden silence of the courtroom. She was aware of Luca, seated opposite her, with uniformed police on either side of him and stole a quick glance at him. His air of glossy, laughing insouciance had completely disappeared, and he was grey and tense. His face looked different too, though she couldn't work out why.

'Signorina Middlemiss—you are English, yes?' Eve gave a small nod. 'Can you tell the court when was the first time you travelled to Italy?'

'Last summer. In August.'

Gianni risked a gentle smile. 'Not, perhaps, a good time to catch Florence at its quietest,' he said gravely, and a ripple of laughter ran through the court. Then he was serious again. 'What was the purpose of your visit, *signorina?*'

'I was commissioned by a magazine to write an article on the Lazaro fashion retrospective. It was supposed to be a sort of behind-the-scenes kind of thing. I was shadowing one of the models and had a small part in the show myself.'

'I can see why,' said Gianni smoothly. 'And this was where you met Luca Di Lazaro for the first time?'

Eve squeezed her eyes shut for a second, summoning every ounce of self-control she possessed to prevent her gaze straying to Raphael. *It was where I met Raphael di Lazaro for the first time,* she wanted to shout. Slumped beside Gianni, he was unsmiling, but more brutally handsome than ever.

'Yes.'

'Thank you, *signorina.*' Gianni spoke with quiet dignity, then allowed a small pause before continuing in a more upbeat tone. 'You say you were commissioned to write this article for—' He paused, looking down at his notes. '*Glitterati* magazine. You are a journalist, then?'

'Not exactly. A friend put my name forward for the job.'

Gianni Orseolo's perfectly arched eyebrows shot up dramatically. 'I see. And what is your real job, Signorina Middlemiss?'

'I'm a research assistant for a professor in Renaissance Poetry at a British university.'

Her heart plummeted to the pit of her stomach as she saw Raphael put his head in his hands in an attitude of utter disbelief.

'Some might say,' Gianni continued thoughtfully, 'that you were somewhat overqualified—academically—for writing a piece of lightweight fashion journalism. Why did your friend put your name forward?'

'Because she knew I had a particular interest in Lazaro.'

'What was that interest, Signorina Middlemiss?'

The musty air of the courtroom was heavy with a sense of expectation. Glancing nervously across at Luca, Eve suddenly realised what was different about his face. It was his nose. A large bump, evidence of a recent break, distorted its once perfect line.

Eve took a deep breath before answering, aware that this was the moment she had been waiting for all these years, but feeling curiously empty now it was here.

'My sister had been spotted by a modelling scout when she was travelling in Florence...' she began hesitantly. 'Someone from Lazaro picked up on this and showed a lot of interest in using her for their shows. She was always quite sure it was just about to happen, but as far as I know nothing came of the modelling thing. But she certainly became quite involved with the people, and went to a lot of the Lazaro parties.'

'When was this?'

'Three and a half years ago.'

Gianni turned away suddenly, and again a tense silence fell upon the waiting court.

Eve couldn't help herself. Inexorably, irresistibly, her gaze found Raphael and her heart gave an almighty lurch.

It was hopeless trying to hate him, or even trying to forget him. She loved him. And it was a life sentence.

Gianni prowled forward to the witness box and handed her a photograph. His eyes bored into hers, willing her to be strong, and unseen by the jury he gave her a swift smile of encouragement. Behind him, Raphael's gaunt face was a mask of icy self-control.

'Signorina Middlemiss, if I may ask you to look at this photograph. I'm afraid its subject matter is a little…intimate, and for that I apologise most sincerely.'

Eve looked down and felt her world tilt slightly. Gripping the brass rail of the witness box she steadied herself, taking a deep gasp of air.

'Eve. You're doing well.' Gianni spoke quietly, so only she could hear, and she looked at him in mute distress. 'Take a moment or two to collect yourself.'

'I'm OK,' she muttered through frozen lips.

'Could you tell the court who the person in the photograph is.'

Eve closed her eyes for a fraction of a second, and struggled to keep her voice steady.

'It's Ellie,' she whispered.

Gianni's eyes beamed encouragement into hers. 'I'm sorry, *signorina*, could you speak up? Who did you say it was?'

With her head held high and tears streaming down her face Eve spoke clearly.

'Ellie.'

There was a sudden noise as Raphael stumbled to his feet. All eyes focused on him as he and Gianni had a swift whispered consultation, after which Gianni faced the bench again and cleared his throat gravely.

'My client informs me that the defendant, Luca Di Lazaro, claims the lady in the photograph is, in fact, you, Signorina Middlemiss, and that you and he enjoyed—how can I put this delicately?—a sexual liaison at his flat before your return to England.'

'No!'

Eve leapt to her feet, the word ringing out through the courtroom, but she was oblivious to the curiosity on the faces of everyone around her. She was aware only of Raphael, and the taut, invisible wires of tension that stretched between them.

'She bears a striking resemblance to you, *signorina*,' said Gianni thoughtfully.

Eve didn't take her eyes off Raphael. A muscle was flickering in his cheek, and his eyes were dark pools of despair.

'She was my twin.'

'Was?' prompted Gianni smoothly. Perfectly controlled, he was like some demonic conductor bringing his orchestra to its rousing climax.

'She died of a heroin overdose. In Florence. Three years ago.'

There was an almost audible sigh as all eyes turned on Luca, but Gianni hadn't finished hammering home his point.

'Hence your interest in Lazaro, Signorina Middlemiss, and your visit to Italy last August. You intended to find the man who had killed your sister.'

But it was as if she hadn't heard him. Staring straight at Raphael, she said, 'I would never have slept with him. I was in love with someone else.'

'I see,' said Gianni.

Beside him, Raphael furiously scribbled something on a sheet of paper on the table in front of them.

Gianni glanced down. 'In that case, *signorina*, may I ask why you left Venice?'

'I found out he didn't love me.'

Gianni's eyes flickered back to Raphael, who was bent over the paper again.

'Er...and what made you think that?'

Eve looked down at her hands, still gripping the railing. Her knuckles were pearl-white beneath the skin.

'He told me he had a business meeting. But I saw him in a café with another woman. He was holding her hands.'

Raphael tried to rise to his feet, but Gianni very firmly pushed him down into his seat and calmly turned back to Eve.

'The lady in question was Catalina Di Souza. Signorina Di Souza has already testified, under oath, that the meeting you witnessed was indeed on a matter of business. She was the person with whom your twin sister shared a flat, and the meeting was to discuss the possibility of bringing Luca di Lazaro to trial for—amongst other things, her death. Signorina Di Souza is still very much affected by it, and the apparent intimacy you witnessed was simply an act of comfort and support.'

Eve had gone very pale. 'I see,' she whispered, through bloodless lips.

Slumped in his chair, Raphael thrust another sheet of paper in front of Gianni, who hesitated for a moment, as if weighing up how to proceed. As he paced thoughtfully towards the witness box Raphael seemed to hold his breath.

'I see that you are expecting a child, signorina. When is it due?'

'Obiezione!' Luca's solicitor leapt to his feet. 'This has nothing to do with my client!'

Raphael's eyes burned into her like lasers. Above the commotion from the other bench she spoke directly to him.

'April.'

The elderly judge roused himself with a sigh. 'Objection upheld. Keep your questions to the point, Signor Orseolo, *per favore.'*

Gianni gave him a swift nod, then, seeing the agony on Raphael's face, turned back to Eve. His tone was extremely gentle. 'Who is the father?'

'Obiezione! I must protest…!'

'Signor Orseolo! You have been warned to keep your questions relevant to the purpose of the court. This is utterly irrelevant…'

'No, it's not!' Raphael's voice was like the crack of a whip. 'You are.'

A ripple of excitement ran through the court as people craned to catch a glimpse of Raphael's face. Dramatic to the last, Gianni turned his back on the furiously protesting defence team and faced the judge.

'May I ask for a short adjournment? I will continue questioning the witness afterwards.'

The judge eyed him over his small glasses. 'Your witness is

distressed. *Si,* we will adjourn for an hour. But please, Signor Orseolo, rethink your line of questioning.'

The room erupted into noise and chaos as people rose to their feet and filed out. Eve was led from the witness box and taken out into the corridor.

In an instant her kindly police escort was at her side, but Raphael was even quicker. She'd forgotten how tall he was, and how the aura of power and self-control he gave off was both incredibly reassuring and at the same time deeply unsettling. He moved between her and the policeman, his fury thinly disguised behind a veil of courtesy.

'*Scusi, signore.* We have things to discuss.'

Eve lowered her eyes and gave the policeman a small nod. 'Please. We just need a few minutes.'

Raphael leaned back against the wall in a posture that was hauntingly similar to the one in which he'd been standing when she'd first set eyes on him. His eyes had a dangerous, ferocious glitter, and his mouth curled into a sarcastic grimace.

'A few minutes? Is that all it will take, Eve?'

She looked down at her hands. Without thinking she had folded them protectively over her bump. Raphael followed her gaze.

'So. When were you going to tell me?'

Her throat seemed to have constricted so that it was hard to breathe. Or speak.

'I wasn't.'

He let out a sharp hiss and thrust a hand through his hair in that heartbreakingly familiar gesture of exasperation. 'I see. You didn't think that the fact that I am going to be a father was something I might be interested in knowing?'

'By the time I found out I thought you would be happily settled with the girl I saw you kissing! So, no, Raphael, I didn't think it was a piece of news you would greet with un-bridled joy.'

'How could you trust me so little?' he spat, springing forward and gripping both her arms in steely fingers. Then he let out a short, bitter laugh. 'Oh, God, how ironic. I spent all the time we were together refusing to allow myself to trust you because I thought you were some sleazy tabloid journalist...' He let go of her arms abruptly and looked away. 'What a bloody mess.'

Eve's hands moved over her stomach, instinctively stroking it. Quietly, imploringly, she said, 'Not completely.' It sounded more like a question than a statement.

For a long moment their gazes held, before Raphael turned away, disgust and despair flooding his face.

'So what are you going to do?' His voice was hollow.

She gave a small shrug, as if the pain caused by his words didn't matter and the small issue of raising a child entirely alone was of no consequence to her whatsoever.

'Manage. Survive.'

He drew in breath sharply and raised clenched fists to his temples. '*Dio,* Eve! What kind of a life is that to bring a child into? *Survive?* How? As a single parent? Going out to work and abandoning the baby—my baby—in some awful daycare?'

She took a step backwards and eyed him coldly. 'Why not? Plenty of people do it.'

'Not with a child of mine.'

Anger surged through her, as hot and energising as a shot of brandy. 'Oh, no. I forgot. Di Lazaros abandon *their* children in very exclusive daycares called public schools. Is that what you're suggesting, Raphael?'

His head jerked back as if she'd slapped him, but he recovered his composure quickly and spoke with icy calm. 'No.' He took a deep breath, looking at her measuringly through narrowed eyes. 'No. The last thing I want is for this child to have the same miserable, screwed-up childhood that I had.' He paused. 'That's why I'm suggesting you come and live here.'

Eve opened her mouth, but suddenly her tongue was dry and there were no words there. Hope flickered somewhere in the darkness where her heart had used to be, but she kept her tone deliberately neutral.

'With you?'

Raphael gave a dry laugh. 'Of course not—as the idea is clearly so abhorrent to you. I'll buy you a flat in a decent area with good schools. But I think it would be best if we got married, to protect the child from…any awkwardness.'

The brave little flame of hope guttered and died, leaving her feeling more alone than ever. 'You're asking me to marry you?' she said dully.

'If you want to put it like that, yes.'

She'd imagined this moment so often in the last six months that at the very least she had expected a full chamber orchestra and someone jumping in front of them with a card saying 'The End' as Raphael bent his head and kissed the living daylights out of her. Not a single one of those fantasies had included the words she now found herself saying.

'No, Raphael.'

She took a couple of steps backwards without taking her eyes from his face. In the half-light it was like an ivory mask—pale, perfect, and completely emotionless.

She turned away and began to walk down the corridor, slowly at first, then with increasing urgency, as if she couldn't wait to get away from him.

Her footsteps echoed off the chilly stone walls, and Raphael tried to avert his gaze, knowing that if he watched her go he would be lost. It was the same feeling he'd had when, as a seven-year-old boy at his mother's funeral, he had not allowed himself to look at the flower-strewn coffin because if he had he'd known he would cry.

And he hadn't. Either then or since.

She had almost reached the end of the corridor when his will-power gave way. Clenching his jaw and thrusting his hands deep into his pockets he looked at her. The cavernous hallway was murky, but her hair shone like distilled sunshine in the winter gloom.

With one hand on the door she paused and looked back at him.
'Sorry,' she said.
The word was like a nail through his heart.

Head down against the rain, and wrapped up in her own despair,
Eve almost walked straight past the ancient church, slotted as it
was between two much bigger, much grander buildings. Actually,
from the outside there wasn't much to see: just a wide arched
doorway with a circular stained-glass window in the wall above
it. But inside it was beautiful, and dry, and completely deserted.

Numb with cold and misery, she walked slowly down the
narrow nave, breathing in the scent of incense and lilies and age.
At the altar, rows of votive candles burned in silent tribute to the
hopes and prayers of those who had lit them. Hesitantly Eve picked
up a taper and held it to the nearest flame, watching it flower into
vibrant life for a second before lighting a new candle with it.

'For you, Ellie,' she whispered, holding up the brightly
burning taper for a moment before blowing it out with one tender
breath. Then she cupped her hands around the little votive,
watching her flesh blossom into rosy gold by the light of its tiny
flame. 'For you, little baby.'

Resting both hands on her swollen belly, she looked up, then
pressed a hand to her mouth as a small, involuntary cry escaped her.

It was almost a relief to feel the tears start to flow. But as she
sank down to her knees against a pillar beside the altar rail she
wondered if they would ever stop.

She couldn't have said how long she sat like that, but the storm
of weeping had blown itself out, and she was just working up
the courage to face the rest of her life when a thunderous bang
reverberated through the building as the heavy wooden door
was forced violently open.

Eve stumbled to her feet. With her heart pounding sickeningly
in her chest she peered round the pillar in time to see two men

in dark clothes, their faces hidden beneath balaclavas, fling themselves into the church, each brandishing a gun.

Instinct took over. Flattening herself against a pillar, she kept her breathing steady and closed her eyes, feeling the baby lurch inside her as adrenalin pulsed through her veins. She leaned her head back against the cool stone and waited, wondering how much use two masked gunmen would be in an emergency labour situation.

Hysterical laughter built up inside her, but it turned swiftly to terror as she heard the sound of footsteps coming towards her down the nave. She squeezed her eyes more tightly shut, waiting, concentrating every ounce of energy on not making a sound.

The footsteps came closer. Then stopped.

'It's OK! She's here!'

Raphael's voice.

With a whimper of relief Eve opened her eyes to find him standing a few feet away from her. His face was absolutely ashen, his lips white, and he stepped forward and pulled her savagely into his arms, folding her into the safety of his body, cradling her head, then cupping her face in his hands and tilting it upwards towards him. His eyes moved feverishly over her face, as if he wanted to reassure himself she was really there.

'Thank God you're safe.'

'What's happened? Why—?'

He gave a low groan of anguish and pulled her against him again. 'Because you're a witness in a major drugs trial and you're supposed to be under police protection. You've been missing for over two hours. The judge has had to temporarily suspend the trial. We thought you'd been—' He stopped and took in a sharp breath.

Eve's hand flew to her mouth in horror. 'No! I'm so sorry!'

He shook his head. 'It was my fault. I should never have let you go.' He bent his head and pressed his lips to her bright hair, murmuring, 'I thought I'd lost you again before I'd even got the chance to tell you that I love you.'

Eve pulled away and lifted her head to look at him.

'What did you say?'

He stood back, holding her at arm's length. His aristocratic face, with its hard, high cheekbones and beautiful mouth, hadn't quite lost the shadows of anguish and tension, but his dark, narrowed eyes burned with love.

'I love you. I raced off after you walked out like that because I needed to do something to make up for my complete and utter crassness. I went home to get this…' He let go of her for a moment while he pulled something from his pocket. 'And now I want to do it properly, before anything else happens to come between us.'

He held out his hand. In the centre of his palm lay a single solitaire diamond in the shape of a tear.

'Eve—' He pulled her gently back into his arms and kissed her cheekbone, her temple, the corner of her mouth. 'I love you—'

She closed her eyes in bliss and felt the tears spilling out from beneath her lashes. Protesting against the sudden constriction of their bodies pressed together, the baby squirmed inside her.

Raphael gasped. She opened her eyes and saw through a haze of tears the fierce tenderness on his face.

His hands went to her bump—slowly, lovingly moving across it as his eyes stayed fixed on hers.

'I love you both,' he amended softly, smiling that rueful half-smile that seemed to go in at her eyes and move straight down to her pelvis. Taking her hand, speaking in a low voice that only she could hear, he gazed solemnly into her eyes.

'I, Raphael Antonio di Lazaro, take thee, Eve Maria Middlemiss, to be my sweet and incredibly beautiful wedded wife. I will love you, cherish you—' He broke off, raising her hand to his lips and placing a kiss on the tip of her index finger. 'Comfort you, protect you…' He kissed her middle finger. 'Honour you and make endless fantastic love with you for all the days of my life.' Holding up her third finger, he slid the ring onto it. 'If you'll have me?'

Through a shimmering veil of tears Eve looked around her at the altar, and the effigy of Christ above it, and gave a soft laugh. 'I think it's too late. I think you've done it and there's no going back. I now pronounce us husband and wife.'

'Good,' said Raphael firmly. 'But let's do it again formally anyway. In the meantime, may I kiss the—'

He didn't finish the question. But the answer was undoubtedly yes.

EPILOGUE

RAPHAEL tiptoed to the top of the stairs and paused, a slow smile spreading across his face. From through the slightly open door at the end of the hallway he could hear Eve singing very softly.

Madame Butterfly.

Downstairs, the low murmur of conversation was punctuated by the occasional burst of laughter and the clink of champagne glasses. Their 'formal' wedding, as Eve laughingly called it, was in full swing, with Antonio—on sparkling form—holding court at its centre. Raphael felt sure that he wouldn't be missed for a while.

He pushed open the nursery door. Eve, humming languidly now, looked up at him and smiled.

He felt his stomach tighten. With desire, and also with that primitive protective instinct that she teased him about, but which he knew he could never quite extinguish.

She was curled into the armchair next to the cot, one arm cradling the dark head of Eleanor Isabella di Lazaro against her bared breast.

Little Ellie-Bella, as her doting godmother Lou had nick-named her, had inherited her grandmother's delicate, dark-haired beauty and her aunt's sense of naughtiness and fun. Now, after an afternoon spent playing to the wedding crowd, she was unusually placid.

'Is she asleep already?' he murmured.

'Mmm…' Eve moved the baby slightly, so that her small mouth relinquished the nipple with a tiny, contented sigh. Her dark lashes swept down over her rosy, milk-damp cheeks, and for a moment both her parents gazed down at her with rapt adoration.

'I think that's got to be a record,' Eve whispered, smiling. 'I hadn't even got to the end of the aria.'

'Perfect. No one will be expecting us downstairs for a long, long time.'

With infinite tenderness Raphael took the baby from her mother's arms and pressed a kiss on the soft dark hair before laying her into her cot. Then he turned to Eve with a smile that made her heart turn over.

He held out a hand and pulled her gently to her feet, allowing himself a moment to marvel all over again at her beauty in the simple sheath of heavy cream silk. Her clear turquoise-green eyes sparkled wickedly as he brought his lips down to hers.

'You know, Raphael, I'm not sure,' she whispered against his mouth, so that he could hear but not see her smile. 'Married sex might not be as exciting as it was before. Maybe we should just go downstairs?'

'Actually, Signora di Lazaro,' he said softly, sweeping her up into his arms in a rustle of silk, muffling her cries of pleasure and laughter with his lips as he carried her to the door. 'I'm afraid you're wrong. Married sex is *even better*. And if you don't believe me I'll just prove it to you.'

And he did.

Twice.

LATIN LOVERS COLLECTION
Intense romances with gorgeous Mediterranean heroes

Greek Tycoons
1st July 2011

Hot-Blooded Sicilians
5th August 2011

Italian Playboys
2nd September 2011

Passionate Spaniards
7th October 2011

Seductive Frenchmen
4th November 2011

Italian Husbands
2nd December 2011

Special Offers

Every month we put together collections and longer reads written by your favourite authors.

Here are some of next month's highlights—and don't miss our fabulous discount online!

On sale 16th September

On sale 16th September

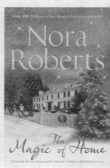

On sale 7th October

Save 20% on all Special Releases

Find out more at
www.millsandboon.co.uk/specialreleases

Visit us
Online

New Voices is back!

New Voices

returns on
13th September 2011!

For sneak previews and exclusives:

 Like us on facebook.com/romancehq

 Follow us on twitter.com/MillsandBoonUK

Last year your votes helped Leah Ashton win New Voices 2010 with her fabulous story *Secrets & Speed Dating*!

Who will you be voting for this year?

Visit us Online   Find out more at
www.romanceisnotdead.com